# PRAISE FOR *THE BARBARIAN NURSERIES*

"*The Barbarian Nurseries* is a book of extraordinary scope and extraordinary power . . . [Tobar] moves nimbly in and out of the minds of a host of characters, viewing even those who seem on the surface the least sympathetic with an awed authorial tenderness. The chief surprise of *The Barbarian Nurseries* is that, despite the social and ethnic schisms it so acutely explores, it turns out to be such a warm novel."
—Richard Rayner, *Los Angeles Times*

"This is a novel about Los Angeles, and maybe the finest we'll see for many years. It is also a novel that triumphantly transcends geography and delivers a stirring look at the borders of our expectations, both great and small." —Tod Goldberg, *Los Angeles Review of Books*

"Brilliantly written . . . [An] L.A.-style Homerian Odyssey."
—Esther Cepeda, *The Sacramento Bee*

"Tobar looks at Los Angeles like Tom Wolfe took on New York in *The Bonfire of the Vanities*. Race, class, crime, immigration, marriage trouble and tabloid-ready news stories—it's all here."
—Billy Heller, *New York Post*

"A ripping novel—and a proper adventure yarn—about power and identity in twenty-first century California."
—Theo Schell-Lambert, *San Francisco Chronicle*

"Tobar plants issues both timely and timeless—race, class, mixed marriage, immigration, servitude, parenting—and raises them up from the fertile narrative soil of Southern California . . . [His] writing continually creates moments of uncommon magic." —*Elle*

"That Tobar is so evenhanded, so compassionate, so downright smart, should place [*The Barbarian Nurseries*] on everyone's must-read list."
—Irene Wanner, *The Seattle Times*

"A panoramic painting . . . [that captures] the textures of its Californian landscape." —Stephen Amidon, *The Guardian*

"Tobar . . . weaves an intricate urban tale animated by a creative, savvy protagonist."
—*The New Yorker*

"Tobar's writing demonstrates faith in the continued power of language to resist superficial visions, to immerse readers in misunderstood places and people labeled 'alien,' to open up the points of view in those people and places and encourage a tolerant ear for their stories."
—Matthew Harrison, *The Common*

"*The Barbarian Nurseries*, in stylistic homage to Charles Dickens, Tom Wolfe and T. C. Boyle, paints a rich Panavision place and time as sprawling and paradoxical as its subject . . . Tobar has crafted an illuminating parable for this historical moment, and an entertaining one, and provided a social mirror within which are faces we need to understand, and face."
—Ed Taylor, *The Buffalo News*

"A real page-turner . . . [Araceli is an] altogether strange and wonderful heroine."
—Craig Seligman, *BusinessWeek*

"*The Barbarian Nurseries* is a huge novel of this century, . . . one that tracks a Mexican immigrant maid not only as static decor in 'real' America's economic rise and fall. Like yard workers and cooks, construction laborers and seamstresses, Tobar's Araceli has flesh, brains, dreams, ambition, history, culture, voice: a rich, generous life."
—Dagoberto Gilb, author of *Before the End,*
*After the Beginning* and *The Flowers*

"*The Barbarian Nurseries* is a grand, amusing read, a mad and sprawling city's less-mad but still sprawling apologia."
—Alan Scherstuhl, *SF Weekly*

"Tobar handles all three characters with cold-eyed sympathy, creating a fascinating novel about the different socioeconomic layers of contemporary Los Angeles."
—Marcela Valdes, *Washington Examiner*

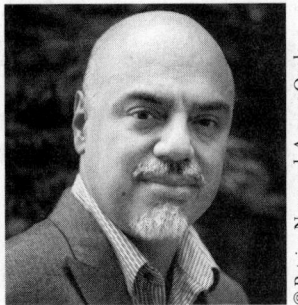

## Héctor Tobar

# THE BARBARIAN NURSERIES

Héctor Tobar is a Pulitzer Prize–winning journalist and novelist. He is the author of the *New York Times* bestseller *Deep Down Dark*, as well as *The Last Great Road Bum*, *Translation Nation*, and *The Tattooed Soldier*. Tobar is also a contributing writer for the *New York Times* opinion pages and an associate professor at the University of California, Irvine. He has written for *The New Yorker*, the *Los Angeles Times*, and other publications. His short fiction has appeared in *The Best American Short Stories*, *Los Angeles Noir*, *ZYZZYVA*, and *Slate*. The son of Guatemalan immigrants, he is a native of Los Angeles, where he lives with his family.

# Also by Héctor Tobar

# THE
# BARBARIAN
# NURSERIES

## Héctor Tobar

MCD PICADOR

FARRAR, STRAUS AND GIROUX NEW YORK

Picador
120 Broadway, New York 10271

Printed in the United States of America
Originally published in 2011 by Farrar, Straus and Giroux
First Picador paperback edition, 2012
10th Anniversary paperback edition, 2021

Grateful acknowledgment is made for permission to reprint lines from
"Concerning the UFO Sighting Near Highland, Illinois,"
by Sufjan Stevens, courtesy of New Jerusalem Music.

The Library of Congress has cataloged
the Farrar, Straus and Giroux hardcover edition as follows:
Tobar, Héctor, 1963–
    The barbarian nurseries / Héctor Tobar.—1st ed
    p. cm.
    ISBN 978-0-374-10899-1
    1. California, Southern—Fiction. I. Title.

PS3570.O22B37 2011
813'.54—dc22

                    2011010703

Picador Paperback ISBN: 978-1-250-82401-1

Designed by Jonathan D. Lippincott

Our books may be purchased in bulk for promotional, educational, or business
use. Please contact your local bookseller or the Macmillan Corporate and Premium
Sales Department at 1-800-221-7945, extension 5442, or by email at
MacmillanSpecialMarkets@macmillan.com.

Picador® is a U.S. registered trademark and is used by Macmillan Publishing Group,
LLC, under license from Pan Books Limited.

For book club information, please visit facebook.com/picadorbookclub or email
marketing@picadorusa.com.

picadorusa.com • instagram.com/picador
twitter.com/picadorusa • facebook.com/picadorusa

10  9  8  7  6  5  4  3  2  1

For Dante, Diego, and Luna

# Foreword
## to the 10th Anniversary Edition

How can it be that ten years have passed since Héctor Tobar's *The Barbarian Nurseries* was first published? My son was nine years old at the time, and I hoped that once he was old enough for me to share this book with him, the United States would be a different place, one more welcoming to immigrants and people of color, and I could tell my son, "Look, this is how it *used* to be for us, but not anymore." Unfortunately, that change hasn't happened. It is heartbreaking to realize that the United States needs *The Barbarian Nurseries* as much as it needed it ten years ago. The book is as timely now as it was then, and its cultural importance remains; indeed, the story within these pages is one that North Americans need to hear and keep hearing.

In 2011, when *The Barbarian Nurseries* was published, Obama was in his first term as president, and we were still reeling from the effects of the Great Recession. The DREAM Act, first introduced in 2001, was reintroduced that year and had failed to pass once again. The country was in the midst of a heated debate over what to do with its undocumented-immigrant population. Tobar's novel deftly navigated the racial discord, the fears and misconceptions about the immigrants among us, and our simultaneous reliance on and rejection of these human beings, thus offering us a complex examination of an issue in American society that is still—to this day—our most polarizing one.

In 2015, we had a presidential candidate who launched his campaign by calling Mexicans rapists and drug dealers and promising to build a wall, igniting anti-immigrant hysteria that would win him the election. The tenth anniversary edition of *The Barbarian Nurseries* is being released at a time when the country is just coming out of the traumatic four years of Donald Trump's presidency, when anti-immigrant rhetoric was at an all-time high, and travel bans, visa restrictions, detention centers, separated families, mass deportations, and asylum restrictions came to define who we were as a country. As we emerge from one of the worst periods of anti-immigrant sentiment in modern history, and we embark on a journey of national healing and reckoning, Tobar's novel resonates with us now more than ever.

The very existence of *The Barbarian Nurseries* is cause for rejoicing. This is a book by a Latinx writer, a writer from a community whose voice is all too often silenced or ignored by the publishing industry and beyond. In a country that is home to nearly sixty million Latinxs, the publishing industry is only six percent Latinx. So it is especially empowering to see the success of *The Barbarian Nurseries*, and I'm honored to champion a book that celebrates the resiliency and tenacity of a Mexican immigrant woman. It is more important than ever for writers of color to have all the opportunities we deserve to tell our own stories, and I am grateful to Héctor Tobar for continuing to widen the literary path for Latinx writers.

A Pulitzer Prize–winning journalist and a child of immigrant parents from Guatemala, Tobar has become an important voice in the Latinx community and beyond for his clear-eyed perspective and his literary activism. Through his books, articles, and essays, Tobar has shed light on the complex issue of immigration and the harsh realities of underrepresented and marginalized communities. His contribution to the national conversation on immigration offers readers a critical exploration of the social, cultural, legal, political, and language barriers Latinxs in the United States must overcome to make a life here. His sharp criticism of our ineffective legal system and his compassionate portrayal of low-wage immigrant workers humanize an issue that is often too politically abstract and devoid of empathy.

I've had the pleasure of personally interacting with Héctor Tobar on several occasions, but one interaction that stands out for me is a panel he moderated at the Los Angeles Times Festival of Books around the time my memoir *The Distance Between Us* came out in 2012. During the panel, I remember Tobar asking me if I worried about being accused of writing Latinx stereotypes. I thought of my father—an alcoholic Mexican man with a violent temper who physically abused his children. I responded that I didn't worry about stereotyping my father because I was very sure that when my father beat me, he wasn't worried about being stereotyped. Only later did I understand that what Tobar was referring to was something else. My father was a maintenance worker with a third-grade education. My mother was a garment-factory worker who only finished sixth grade. These are the immigrant stereotypes that Trump, and others like him, use to instill fear in Americans—of unskilled, uneducated masses invading the country. Yes, there are immigrants like my parents, but there are also immigrants who are like Tobar's heroine, an intelligent, ambitious woman who was forced to give up her college education and artistic aspirations to help her family. If it weren't for the choices my own parents made, I would have been just like her and would have never fulfilled my artistic potential. In reading *The Barbarian Nurseries*, I appreciated that Tobar took a different approach in his portrayal of immigrants, thereby pushing for more diversity and representation of the many layers of Latinx identity and cultural heritage.

With compassion and insight, Tobar has brought to life a Mexican protagonist who will surprise you at every turn, whose voice is vivid, moving, and authentic. With elegant prose and a keen ear for irony, Tobar takes us into the life of a complex character, Araceli Ramírez, an undocumented Mexican immigrant working as a live-in housekeeper for an upper-middle-class family that has fallen on hard times after the economic recession. Tobar deftly renders Araceli's interiority—her longing for what couldn't be, her bitterness for the life she is stuck in, her strong sense of self, and her acute awareness of her surroundings and the people she works for. To her employers, Scott Torres and Maureen Thompson, a couple on the brink of financial and marital disaster,

Araceli is an enigma. Though she is hardworking and responsible, she is taken for granted, and the couple never makes an effort to get to know their employee. They tolerate her presence because they need her, in the same way the country tolerates its immigrant workers, without ever really making her feel welcome.

Tobar also explores the lives of Araceli's status-seeking employers. Scott, a Mexican-American man who's lost touch with his cultural heritage, and Maureen, a white supermom who micromanages the lives of her children. The depiction of Scott Torres offers smart observations and interesting commentary on the dangers of assimilation. What does it mean for a Latinx family to lose touch with their roots? What is lost and what is gained through the process of assimilation and acculturation? As I got to know Scott Torres, I couldn't help but think about my own family. Torres could easily be the adult version of my own children. My U.S.-born son and daughter are growing up with a Mexican mother and a gringo father, living cushy middle-class American lives. They refuse to speak Spanish to me, complain when I cook Mexican food too often, and roll their eyes whenever I tell them stories of my immigrant childhood. In the novel, the severed cultural ties are even more pronounced. The Torres-Thompson children have no connection to their Mexican heritage, and if not for the Mexican maid, would have no exposure to it.

Though his roots are Guatemalan, not Mexican, Tobar understands the complexities of the immigrant experience. He based the Torres-Thompson family on his own immediate and extended family. By doing so, he authentically captured an experience common with many Americans, not just Latinxs—the loss of connection to your past, your origins, to your ancestors. The pressure to succeed in this country can easily lead to the rejection of one's cultural identity in order to blend in to the dominant culture. The obsession with wealth and accumulating material things is a double-edged sword when the more you gain the more you lose. What defines success? And what price do we ultimately pay? The Torres-Thompsons paid for their success with isolation. Scott Torres has no relationship with his parents, especially his Mexican father, whom Maureen Thompson has banished from their lives. As a result, their children haven't seen their grandfather in years. After a domestic dispute that Araceli witnesses, both of her employers leave the house separately, unaware of each other's absence, and Araceli finds herself alone with the couple's two boys. When no word comes from either Scott or Maureen, she is forced to set off on an ill-fated journey across Los Angeles. When Araceli embarks on this journey with the boys to find their absent grandfather, to me, the journey becomes about finding and rediscovering that lost part of the Torres-Thompson family's Mexican identity. Something that I hope for my own children, though maybe not quite in those circumstances.

The setting of the novel moves from an Orange County gated community by the sea to the sprawling Los Angeles metropolis to the Latinx barrios of South-Central L.A. A native Angeleno and a former reporter for the *Los Angeles Times*, Tobar knows the city well, and through Araceli's journey, he takes his readers through an exploration of the varied communities that make up Southern California. The Los Angeles in *The Barbarian Nurseries* is one I know firsthand. Having lived in Highland Park (before it was gentrified), East L.A., Whittier, and South-Central L.A., and repeatedly visited my mother who lives in Pico-Union with a homeless encampment right across the street and a four-star hotel less than a mile away, I admired Tobar's skills in portraying the setting so vividly and accurately: the tastes, the sounds, the textures of these places where marginalized people try to make a home, to survive, to find their way in an unwelcoming world. The Latinx lens through which Tobar invites readers to view California is crucial to us expanding our understanding of the state itself and ultimately the country.

It is disappointing that when lists come out of the "best books about California," Latinx writers seldom make it on them. Latinxs are the largest ethnic group in the Golden State, yet our version of it is often overlooked. Such lists that leave out books by Latinx writers not only are incomplete, they also lack an authentic representation of the state's Latinx identity, including its Mexican ancestry. In *The Barbarian Nurseries*, with his journalist's eye for detail, Tobar gives us his own version of the Golden State, a rich and vivid portrait of the urban and suburban Southern California landscape. He vividly exposes its textures and layers, its idiosyncrasies and contradictions, its social and racial dynamics, its poverty and wealth. This is a novel that must certainly be included in those California booklists.

As I read *The Barbarian Nurseries* and Araceli's experiences in affluent Orange County communities, her isolation and feeling of being out of place, I saw myself reflected in her experiences. Growing up in a gang-infested neighborhood in Northeast L.A., I was never exposed to its wealthy side, nor to its affluent neighbor, Orange County. It wasn't until I went north to study that I began to develop a critical eye for my surroundings, and I wonder if, to some extent, this was also true for Tobar. He and I both attended the University of California, Santa Cruz, although at different times. I experienced great culture shock when I arrived in Santa Cruz, and I imagine that Tobar did as well, both of us Latinxs coming to study in a place where we were the minority. When I moved to Santa Cruz from L.A., I thought I had moved to another state! This version of California was unlike any I had known. It was there in Santa Cruz that I met my first vegetarian and vegan friends, when I first heard the words "compost" and "hippie." It was my first time seeing true affluence, living among Silicon Valley workers and wealthy retirees. (But it was also my first time seeing white homeless people.) I used to walk along West Cliff Drive with the ocean on one side and beautiful homes on the other. I would peek into those houses through their tall windows, imagining myself living in one of them. I would watch the surfers, see the white mothers pushing strollers while power walking. After graduation I had to leave Santa Cruz because I couldn't afford that version of California. So I headed back south and lived in Boyle Heights, then moved to South-Central L.A. with its trash-lined streets and graffitied walls. Living there was even worse after I had seen with my own eyes that there was another, more beautiful version of California, one that might never be mine. And I worried I would always be on the outside looking in. All of these feelings I sensed in Araceli Ramírez, and this is why, when Tobar throws her into a media and political firestorm in the last part of the book, it is even more heartbreaking.

Well, my son is nineteen years old now and when I give him the tenth anniversary edition of *The Barbarian Nurseries*, I won't be able to tell him that this is "how it used to be," but I will be able to say that this is how it is and how crucial it is that we work hard to change things. Coincidentally, just as the DREAM Act was reintroduced in 2011 when the book was first published, it has been reintroduced yet again in 2021 just as this new edition of *The Barbarian Nurseries* is being published. The national conversation about the immigrants living among us and those knocking on our door is a difficult one to have but an important one. If there was ever a time when our society needs to strive for more inclusion, compassion, and goodwill, it is now.

*Reyna Grande*

# BOOK ONE

# The Succulent Garden

The American mystery deepens.
—Don DeLillo, *White Noise*

I

Scott Torres was upset because the lawn mower wouldn't start, because no matter how hard he pulled at the cord, it didn't begin to roar. His exertions produced only a brief flutter of the engine, like the cough of a sick child, and then an extended silence filled by the buzzing of two dragonflies doing figure eights over the uncut St. Augustine grass. The lawn was precocious, ambitious, eight inches tall, and for the moment it could entertain jungle dreams of one day shading the house from the sun. The blades would rise as long as he pulled at the cord and the lawn mower coughed. He gripped the cord's plastic handle, paused and leaned forward to gather breath and momentum, and tried again. The lawn mower roared for an instant, spit a clump of grass from its jutting black mouth, and stopped. Scott stepped back from the machine and gave it the angry everyman stare of fatherliness frustrated, of a handyman being unhandy.

Araceli, his Mexican maid, watched him from the kitchen window, her hands covered with a white bubble-skin of dishwater. She wondered if she should tell *el señor* Scott the secret that made the lawn mower roar. When you turned a knob on the side of the engine, it made starting the machine as easy as pulling a loose thread from a sweater. She had seen Pepe play with this knob several times. But no, she decided to let *el señor* Scott figure it out himself. Scott Torres had let Pepe and his chunky gardener's muscles go: she would allow this struggle with the machine to be her boss's punishment.

*El señor* Scott opened the little cap on the mower where the gas goes in, just to check. *Yes, it has gas.* Araceli had seen Pepe fill it up that last time he was here, on that Thursday two weeks ago when she almost wanted to cry because she knew she would never see him again.

Pepe never had any problems getting the lawn mower started. When he reached down to pull the cord it caused his bicep to escape his sleeve, revealing a mass of taut copper skin that hinted at other patches of skin and muscle beneath the old cotton shirts he wore. Araceli thought there was art in the stains on Pepe's shirts; they were an abstract expressionist whirlwind of greens, clayish ocher, and blacks made by grass, soil, and sweat. A handful of times she had rather boldly brought her lonely fingertips to these canvases. When Pepe arrived on Thursdays, Araceli would open the curtains in the living room and spray and wipe the squeaky clean windows just so she could watch him sweat over the lawn and imagine herself nestled in the protective cinnamon cradle of his skin: and then she would laugh at herself for doing so. *I am still a girl with silly daydreams.* Pepe's disorderly masculinity broke the spell of working and living in the house and when she saw him in the frame of the kitchen window she could imagine living in the world outside, in a home with dishes of her own to wash, a desk of her own to polish and fret over, in a room that wasn't borrowed from someone else.

Araceli enjoyed her solitude, her apartness from the world, and she liked to think of working for the Torres-Thompson family as a kind of self-imposed exile from her previous, directionless life in Mexico City. But every now and then she wanted to share the pleasures of this solitude with someone and step outside her silent California existence, into one of her alternate daydream lives: she might be a midlevel Mexican government functionary, one of those tough, big women with a mean sense of humor and a leonine, rust-tinted coiffure, ruling a little fiefdom in a Mexico City neighborhood; or she might be a successful artist—or maybe an art critic. Pepe figured in many of her fantasies as the quiet and patient father of their children, who had chic Aztec names such as Cuitláhuac and Xóchitl. In these extended daydreams Pepe was a landscape architect, a sculptor, and Araceli herself was ten kilos thinner, about the weight she had been before coming to the United States, because her years in California had not been kind to her waistline.

All of her Pepe reveries were over now. They were preposterous but they were hers, and their sudden absence felt like a kind of theft. Instead of Pepe she had *el señor* Scott to look at, wrestling with the lawn mower and the cord that made it start. At last, Scott discovered the little knob. He began to make adjustments and he pulled at it again. His arms were thin and oatmeal-colored; he was what they called here "half Mexican," and after twenty minutes in the June sun his forearms, forehead, and cheeks were the glowing crimson of McIntosh apples. Once, twice, and a third time *el señor* Scott pulled at the cord, turning the knob a little more each time, until the engine began to kick, sputter, and roar. Soon the air was green with flying grass, and Araceli watched the corner of her boss's lips rise in quiet satisfaction. Then the engine stopped, the sound muffled in an instant, because the blade choked on too much lawn.

Neither of her bosses informed Araceli beforehand of the momentous news that she would be the last Mexican working in this house. Araceli had two bosses, whose surnames were hyphenated into an odd, bilingual concoction: Torres-Thompson. Oddly, *la señora* Maureen never called herself "Mrs. Torres," though she and *el señor* Scott were indeed married, as Araceli had discerned on her first day on the job from the wedding pictures in the living room and the identical gold bands on their fingers. Araceli was not one to ask questions, or to allow herself to be pulled into conversation or small talk, and her dialogues with her *jefes* were often austere affairs dominated by the monosyllabic "Yes," "Sí," and, occasionally, "No." She lived in their home twelve days out of every fourteen, but was often in the dark when new chapters opened in the Torres-Thompson family saga: for example, Maureen's pregnancy with the couple's third child, which Araceli found out about only because of her *jefa*'s repeated vomiting one afternoon.

"*Señora*, you are sick. I think my enchiladas *verdes* are too strong for you. *¿Qué no?*"

"No, Araceli. It's not the green sauce. I'm going to have a baby. Didn't you know?"

Money was supposedly the reason why Pepe and Guadalupe departed. Araceli found out late one Wednesday morning two weeks earlier, following an animated conversation in the backyard between *la señora* Maureen and Guadalupe that Araceli witnessed through the sliding glass doors of the living room. When their conversation ended, Guadalupe walked into the living room to announce to Araceli curtly, "I'm going to look for some *chinos* to work for. They can afford to pay me something decent, not the *centavos* these gringos want to give me." Guadalupe was a fey *mexicana* with long braids and a taste for embroidered Oaxacan blouses and overwrought indigenous jewelry, and also a former university student like Araceli. Now her eyes were reddened from crying, and her small mouth twisted with a sense of betrayal. "After five years, they should be giving me a raise. But instead they want to cut my pay; that's how they reward my loyalty." Araceli looked out the living room windows to see *la señora* Maureen also wiping tears from her eyes. "*La señora* knows I was like a mother to her boys," Guadalupe said, and it was one of the last things Araceli heard from her.

So now there was only Araceli, alone with *el señor* Scott, *la señora* Maureen, and their three children, in this house on a hill high above the ocean, on a cul-de-sac absent of pedestrians or playing children, absent of traffic, absent of the banter of vendors and policemen. It was a street of long silences. When the Torres-Thompsons and their children left on their daily excursions, Araceli would commune alone with the home and its sounds, with the kick and purr of the refrigerator motor, and the faint whistle of the fans hidden in the ceiling. It was a home of steel washbasins and exotic bathroom perfumes, and a kitchen that Araceli had come to think of as her office, her command center, where she prepared several meals each day: breakfast, lunch, dinner, and assorted snacks and baby "feedings." A single row of Talavera tiles ran along the peach-colored walls, daisies with blue petals and bronze centers. After she'd dried the last copper-tinged saucepan and placed it on a hook next to its brothers and sisters, Araceli performed the daily ritual of running her hand over the tiles. Her fingertips transported her, fleetingly, to Mexico City, where these porcelain squares would be weather-beaten and cracked, decorating gazebos and doorways. She remembered her long walks through the old seventeenth-, eighteenth-, and nineteenth-century streets, a city built of ancient lava stone and mirrored glass, a colonial city and an Art Deco city and a Modernist city all at once. In her solitude her thoughts would wander from Mexico City to the various other stops on her life journey, a string of encounters and misfortunes that would eventually and inevitably circle back to the present. Now she lived in an American neighborhood where everything was new, a landscape vacant of the meanings and shadings of time, each home painted eggshell-white by association rule, like featureless architect models plopped down by human hands on a stretch of empty savanna. Araceli could see the yellow clumps of vanquished meadows hiding in the unseen spaces around the Torres-Thompson home, blades sprouting up by the trash cans and the massive air-conditioning plant, and in the rectangles cut into the sidewalk where young, man-sized trees grew.

When Araceli stood before the living room picture window and stared out at the expanse of the ocean a mile or two in the distance, she could imagine herself on that unspoiled hillside of wild grasses. Several times each day, she walked out of the kitchen and into the living room to study the horizon, a hazy line where the gray-blue of the sea seeped into a cloudless sky. Then the shouts and screams of the two Torres-Thompson boys and the intermittent crying of their baby sister returned her to the here and now.

When there were three *mexicanos* working in this house they could fill the workday hours with banter and gossip. They made fun of *el señor* Scott and his very bad *pocho* accent when he tried to speak Spanish and tried to guess how it was that such an awkward and poorly groomed man had found himself paired with an ambitious North American wife. Guadalupe, the nanny, cooed over the baby, Samantha, and played with Keenan and the older boy, Brandon. It was Guadalupe who taught the boys to say things like *buenas tardes* and *muchas gracias*. Araceli, the housekeeper and cook, was in charge of the bathrooms and kitchen, the vacuum cleaners and dishrags, the laundry and the living room. And Pepe, with the hands that kept the huge leaves of the elephant plant erect, that made the cream-colored ears of the calla lilies bloom, and the muscles that kept the lawn respectably short. They filled the house with Spanish repartee, Guadalupe teasing Araceli about how handsome Pepe was, Araceli responding with double entendres that always seemed to go right over Pepe's head.

"Your machine is so powerful, it can cut anything!"

"*Es que tiene mucho* horsepower."

"Yes, I can see how much *power* there is in all those horses of yours."

Pepe was a magician, a da Vinci of gardeners, worth twice what they paid him. How long would the orange beaks of the heliconias in the backyard open to the sky without Pepe's thick, smart fingers to bring them to life? The money situation must be very bad. Why else would *el señor* Scott be outside in this white sun, burning his fair skin? The idea that these people would be short of money made little sense to her. But why else would Maureen be changing the baby's diapers herself, and looking exasperated at the boys because they were playing on their electronic toys too long? Guadalupe, the aspiring schoolteacher, was no longer there to distract them with those games they played, outside on the grass with soap bubbles, or inside the house with Mexican lottery cards, the boys calling out "*El corazón,*" "*El catrín,*" and "*¡Lotería!*" in Spanish. Through the picture window in the living room, Araceli studied *el señor* Scott as he struggled to push the mower over the far edge of the lawn where it dropped off into a steep slope. TORO said the bag on the side of the lawn mower. No wonder *el señor* Scott was having so much trouble: the lawn mower was a bull! Only Pepe, in a gleaming bullfighter's uniform, with golden epaulets, could tease the Toro forward.

Araceli made *el señor* Scott a lemonade and walked out into the searing light to give it to him, as much to inspect his work as anything else.

"*¿Limonada?*" she asked.

"Thanks," he said, taking the wet glass. Beads of water dripped down the glass, like the beads of sweat on *el señor* Scott's face. He looked away from her, inspecting the blades of grass, how they were sprayed across the concrete path that ran through the middle of the lawn.

"The work. It is very hard," Araceli offered. "*El césped*. The grass. It is very thick."

"Yeah," he said, looking at her warily, because this was more conversation than he was used to hearing from his surly but dependable maid. "This mower is too old."

*But it was good enough for Pepe!* Araceli glanced at the grass, saw the brown crescents *el señor* Scott had inadvertently carved into the green carpet, and tried not to look displeased. Pepe used to stop there to adjust the height of the mower, and Araceli would come out and give him lemonade just like she was giving *el señor* Scott now. Pepe would say "*Gracias*" and give her a raffish smile in that instant when his eyes met hers before quickly turning away.

*El señor* Scott swallowed the lemonade and returned the glass to Araceli without another word.

As she walked back to the house, the lingering smell of the cut grass sent her into a depression. Exactly how bad was the money situation? she wondered. How much longer would *el señor* Scott mow the lawn himself and wrestle with the Toro? What was going on in the lives of these people? They had let Guadalupe go, and from Guadalupe's anger she imagined that it was without the two months' severance pay that was standard practice in the good houses of Mexico City, unless they caught you stealing the jewelry or abusing the children. Araceli was beginning to see that it was necessary to take a greater interest in the lives of her employers. She sensed developments that might soon impact the life of an unknowing and otherwise trusting *mexicana*. Back in the kitchen, she looked at *el señor* Scott through the window again. He tugged at the cut grass with a rake and made green mounds, and then embraced each mound with his arms and dumped it into a trash bag, blades sticking to his sweaty arms and hands. She watched him brush the grass off his arms and suddenly there was an unexpected pathos about him: *el señor* Scott, the unlikely lord of this tidy and affluent mansion, reduced to a tiller's role, harvesting the undisciplined product of the soil, when he should be inside, in the shade, away from the sun.

A moment after Araceli stepped away from the picture window, Maureen Thompson took her place, taking a good, long minute to inspect her husband's work. The mistress of the house was a petite, elegant woman of thirty-eight, with creamy skin and a perpetually serious air. This summer morning she was wearing Audrey Hepburn capri pants, and she strode about the house with a confident, relaxed, but purposeful gait. She ran this household like the disciplined midlevel corporate executive she had once been, with an eye on the clock and on the frayed edges of her daily household life, vigilant for scattered toys and half-full trash cans and unfinished homework. The sight of her

husband struggling with the lawn mower caused her to briefly chew at
the ends of her ginger-brown hair. Could *la señora* see the yellow crescents at the beginning of the slope, Araceli wondered, or was she just
put off to see her husband dripping sweat onto the concrete? Araceli examined *la señora* Maureen examining *el señor* Scott and thought it was
interesting that when you worked or lived with someone long enough you
could allow your eyes to linger on that person for a while without being
noticed: Pepe, a stranger, always caught Araceli when she stared at him.

Much like her Mexican maid, Maureen Thompson had also
sensed the disturbing non sequitur playing itself out on the other side of
the glass: her theoretician, her distracted man of big ideas, the man she
had once proclaimed, in a postcoital whisper, "the King of the Twenty-
first Century," frustrated this Saturday afternoon by a technological
relic from the previous millennium. They had been married for twelve
years of professional triumphs and corporate humiliations, of cash windfalls and nights of infant illnesses, but nothing quite like this particular
comedy. *He's having trouble just keeping the thing running. It uses gaso-
line: how complicated can it be?* Her eyes shifted to the drawn curtains
of the neighbors' houses, the blank windows that reflected the blank
California sky, and she wondered who else might be watching. She had
not agreed with the calculus her husband had made, the scratched-out
set of figures whose bottom line was the departure of the more-than-
competent and reliable gardener, a man of silent nobility who, she sensed,
had tended the soil in a distant tropical village. Scott was a software kind
of guy—both in the literal sense of being a writer of computer programs,
and also in the more figurative sense of being someone for whom the
physical world was a confusing array of unpredictable biological and mechanical phenomena, like the miraculous process of photosynthesis and
the arcane varieties of Southern California weed species, or the subtle,
practiced gestures that were required, apparently, to maneuver a lawn
mower over an uneven surface. *Later on he'll look back at this and laugh.*
Her husband was a witty man, with a sharp eye for irony, though that
quality had deserted him now, judging from the sweaty scowl on his face.
*Hard labor will cleanse you of irony*: it was a lesson from her own childhood and young womanhood that returned to her now, unexpectedly.

It was a short walk across the living room to a second picture window, this one looking out to the backyard tropical garden, which was suffering a subtle degradation that was, in its own way, more advanced than the overgrowth of the front lawn had been. They had planted this garden not long after moving in five years earlier, to fill up the empty quarter acre at the rear of their property, and until now it glistened and shimmered like a single dark and moist organism, cooling the air that rushed through it. With the flip of a switch, a foot-wide creek ran through the garden, its waters collecting in a small pond behind the banana tree. Now the leaves of that banana tree were cracking and the nearby ferns were turning golden. Not long after Scott dropped the little bomb about Pepe, Maureen had made a halfhearted attempt at weeding "*la petite* rain forest," as she and Scott called it, making an initial foray into the section of the garage where she had seen Pepe store some chemicals. She had no green thumb but guessed that keeping a tropical garden alive in this dry climate took some sort of petrochemical intervention: pest and weed control, fertilizers. Unfortunately, she had been frightened off by the bottles and their warning labels: Maureen had stopped breast-feeding only a few weeks earlier and was not yet ready to surrender the purity of body and mind that breast-feeding engendered. If she hadn't yet given in to the temptation of a shot of tequila—though she suspected she soon would—why was she going to open a bottle marked with a skull and crossbones and the even more ominous corporate logo of a major oil company?

A downpour of dust and dirt was killing their patch of rain forest; she would have to step in and care for it or it would wither up in the dry air, and as she thought this she felt a pang of anxiousness, a very brief shortness of breath. *It isn't just the garden and the lawn, is it?* Maureen Thompson had spent her teens and her twenties shedding herself of certain memories forged in a very ordinary Missouri street lined with shady sugar maple trees, where the leaves turned in October and it snowed a few days every winter, and the weather aged the things people left on their porches and no one seemed to care. Those days seemed distant now: they fit into two boxes at the bottom of one of her closets, outnumbered by many other boxes filled with the mementos of her arrival in California and life with Scott. Here on their hillside, on this street called Paseo Linda Bonita, one day followed the next with a comfortable and predictable rhythm: meals were cooked, children were dressed in the morning and put to bed at night, and in between the flaming sun set over the Pacific in a daily and almost ridiculously overwrought display of nature's grandeur. All was well in her universe and then suddenly, and often without any discernible reason, she felt this vague but penetrating sense of impending darkness and loss. Most often it happened when her two boys were away at school, when she stood in their bedroom and sensed an absence that could, from one moment to the next, grow permanent; or when she stood naked in the bathroom, her wet hair in a towel, and she caught a glimpse of her body in the mirror, and sensed its vulnerability, her mortality, and wondered if she had asked too much of it by bringing three children into the world.

But no, now it passed. She returned to the living room and the picture window, where the drama on the front lawn had reached a kind of conclusion and the King of the Twenty-first Century was sweeping up the grass on the walkway.

When Scott Torres was a kid living in South Whittier he cut the lawn himself, and as he pushed the machine over the slope of his bloated home in the Laguna Rancho Estates, he tried to draw on those lessons his father had passed down two decades earlier, on a cul-de-sac called Safari Drive, where all the lawns were about a quarter the size of the one he was cutting right now. *Try to get the thing moving smoothly, check the height of the wheels, watch out for any foreign object on the grass because the blades will catch it, send it flying like a bullet.* His father paid him five dollars a week, the first money Scott ever earned. Like the other two adults in this home, Scott had been put in a reflective mood by the unusual events of the past few days, by the departure of two members of their team of hired help, and by the June shift in domestic seasons. Summer vacation was upon them and yesterday had been filled with the summing-up celebration of their two boys' return from the final day of third and fifth grade with large folders filled with a semester's worth of completed homework and oversized art projects that their mother oohed and aahed over. Now he brought the mower over the last patch of uncut grass and gave it a haircut too.

Scott stopped the engine and breathed in the scent of freshly cut grass and lawn mower exhaust, the pungent bouquet a powerful memory-trigger of his days of teenage chores. He remembered the olive tree in front of the Torres family home in South Whittier, and many other things that had nothing to do with lawns or lawn mowers, like working on his Volkswagen—his first car—in the driveway, and the feathered chestnut hair and the Ditto jeans of the somewhat chunky girl who lived across the street. What was her name? *Nadine.* The olive tree dropped black fruit onto the sidewalk and one of Scott's jobs back then was to take a hose and wash away the stains. The neighborhood of his youth was a collection of flimsy boxes held together by wallpaper and epoxy, plopped down on a cow pasture. The Laguna Rancho Estates were something altogether different. When Scott had first come to this house the lawn had not yet been planted, there was a patch of raw dirt with stakes and string pounded into it, and he had watched the Mexican work crews arrive with trays of St. Augustine grass to plant. In five years, the roots created a dense living weave in the soil, and he had struggled to make his haircut of it look even; in fact, he failed. After he raked up the grass he noticed the blades that stuck to his sweaty arms, and as he wiped them off he thought that each was like a penny when you added up how much you saved by cutting the lawn yourself.

Two weeks earlier, he had quickly calculated what he paid the gardener over the course of a year and had come to a surprisingly large four-figure number. The problem with these Mexican gardeners was that you had to pay them in cash; you had to slap actual greenbacks into their callused hands at the end of the day. The only way around it was to go out there in the sun and do it yourself, because bringing these hardworking Mexicans into your home was expensive, and in the end all those hours the Mexicans worked without complaint added up. That was also the problem with Guadalupe: too many hours.

Scott's parents were frugal people, much like Pepe the gardener: Scott could see this in his methodical, cautious count of the bills Scott gave him. Pepe scratched out the amount with a stubby golf course pencil he kept in his wallet along with a piece of invariably soiled paper. Scott's father was Mexican, which in the California of Scott's youth was synonymous with poverty, and his mother was a square-jawed rebel from Maine, a place where good discipline in the use of funds was standard Protestant practice. *Use it up, wear it out, make it do, or do without.*

Scott remembered his late mother standing in the doorway of that South Whittier home under the canopy of the olive tree, watching him earn his five dollars with her frugal eyes, and felt like a man waking up from a long drinking binge as he looked back at the white house with the ocher-tile roof that rose before him. His home had become a sun-drenched vault filled with an astonishing variety of purchased objects: the coffee table handmade by a Pasadena artist from distressed Mexican pine and several thick, bubbling panes of hand-blown glass; the wrought-iron wall grilles shipped in from Provence and the Chesterfield sofa of moss-green leather; a handcrafted crib from the Czech Republic.

*We have behaved and spent very badly.* Scott held on to this idea as he rolled the creaking, cooling mower into the garage, feeling a meek, half-defeated self-satisfaction. *I cut the goddamn grass myself. It wasn't rocket science.* He reentered the house and his Mexican maid gave him an odd smile with some sort of secondary meaning he could not discern. This woman was more likely to ignore you when you said hello in the morning, or to turn down her lips in disapproval if you made a suggestion. Still, they were lucky to have her as their last domestic employee. Araceli was the only person in this house besides Scott who understood frugality: she never failed to save the leftovers in Tupperware; she re-used the plastic bags from the supermarket and spent the day turning off lights Maureen and the children left on. Scott had never been to the deeper reaches of Mexico where Araceli hailed from, and he had only once been to his maternal homeland in the upper reaches of Maine, but he sensed they were both places that produced sober people with tiny abacuses in their heads.

A few moments later Scott had slipped out of the kitchen and looked through the sliding glass doors that led out to the backyard and felt like an idiot. He had forgotten about the garden, the so-called, mis-named "tropical" garden, which was actually a "subtropical" garden, according to the good people at the nursery who had planted the thing. For the first time Scott contemplated its verdant hollows and shadows with the eye of a workingman, a blister or two having formed on his palms thanks to his efforts on the front lawn. He remembered Pepe wading into this semi-jungle with a machete, and the crude noise of his blade striking fleshy plants, emerging with old palm fronds or withering flowers. Scott wasn't ready to enter into that jungle today, although he would soon have to. It seemed to him it would take a village of Mexicans to keep that thing alive, a platoon of men in straw hats, wading with bare feet into the faux stream that ran through the middle of it. Pepe did it all on his own. He was a village unto himself, apparently. Scott wasn't a village and he decided to forget about the tropical garden for the time being because it was in the backyard, after all, and who was going to notice?

# 2

In the Torres-Thompson family, every child's birthday was an elaborately staged celebration built around a unique theme, with *la señora* Maureen purchasing specially ordered napkins and paper plates, and sometimes hiring actors for various fanciful roles. She made HAPPY BIRTHDAY banners with her own art supplies; she scoured the five-and-dime stores for old scarves and suits to make into costumes, and ordered special wigs and props over the Internet. Maureen hung streamers over the doorways, and drafted Guadalupe to create big balloon flowers, while Araceli labored in the kitchen to make cookies in the shapes of witches and dinosaurs. Keenan, the younger boy and middle child, would be turning eight in two weeks, and at the moment the preparations required that Araceli mix the paste for a papier-mâché project. Araceli did not mind doing this, because she appreciated the idea of a birthday as a family event organized by women in kitchens, and celebrated by large groups of people in places open to the sun and air, as they were in the parks of her hometown on the weekends. This birthday, like all the others, would be celebrated in the Torres-Thompson family backyard, in a setting filled with *la señora's* uncomplicated and appropriately child-like decorations, most in the primary colors also favored in Mexican folk art. Araceli believed that if you had transplanted this woman to Oaxaca she would have made very fine pottery, or *papel picado*, or been an excellent stage manager for a theater group wandering through the suburbs of El Distrito Federal.

Araceli took the bowl of completed paste to *la señora* Maureen in the playroom. She found her *jefa* kneeling on the floor over a piece of yellow construction paper with a red pencil grasped between her fingers, wearing an artist's smock over her brown yoga pants.

"*Señora, aquí está su* paste," Araceli said.

"Thanks." After a few seconds passed without Araceli walking away, Maureen looked up and found Araceli examining her work with that neutral expression of hers, a half stare with passive-aggressive overtones. Maureen had seen Araceli's wide, flat face assume this inscrutable look too often to be unsettled by it, and instead she gave her maid a half shrug and quick eye-roll of ironic semi-exasperation, as if to say, *Yes, here I am again, on my knees, scratching away at an art project like some preschooler.* Araceli broke her trance by raising one eyebrow and nodding that she understood: it was the sort of exchange that took place several times each day between these two women, a wordless acknowledgment of shared responsibilities as exacting women in a home dominated by the disorderly exertions of two boys, a baby girl, and one man. Maureen was writing HAPPY BIRTHDAY KEENAN in the classic, serif-heavy font of Roman buildings and monuments. Below these letters, *la señora* was trying to draw what looked like a Roman helmet, a birthday theme inspired by Keenan's recent fixation with a certain European comic strip. Maureen drew one more line with Araceli watching, and then they were both startled by the cry of a baby, seemingly just behind *la señora*'s shoulder. Turning around quickly, Araceli saw a burst of red lights on the baby monitor as Maureen calmly rose to her feet and headed for the nursery.

A few moments later Maureen appeared in the hallway with Samantha, a baby girl of fifteen months with hazel eyes still moist from crying to escape from her crib. She had her mother's milky complexion and fine hair, though the baby's locks were a deeper chestnut. *La señora* held her daughter, bounced and made kissing noises until she stopped her crying, and then did something she had never done before: she handed Samantha to Araceli. In the Torres-Thompson household, this baby girl carried the aura of a sacred and delicate object, like a Japanese vase on two teetering legs. In the last few weeks, she had started to walk, entering a world of possibility and danger, stumbling across the room to her mother's embrace with a precarious Frankenstein step. Guadalupe carried the baby for hours every day, but now that Guadalupe was gone it appeared that some of this responsibility would fall to Araceli, who wasn't sure if she was ready or willing to help take care of a baby. In fifteen months, Araceli had disposed of several hundred soiled diapers, but she had changed Samantha herself not more than three times, and always at the behest of Guadalupe. The truth was Araceli had never been close to children; they were a mystery she had no desire to solve, especially the Torres-Thompson boys, with their screams of battle and the electric sound effects they produced with their lips and cheeks.

But a little girl was different. This one led the life any Mexican mother would want for her baby, with an astonishing variety of pinks and purples in her wardrobe of onesies, bibs, T-shirts, nightshirts, her closet in the nursery overflowing with Tinker Bell Halloween costumes and miniature sundresses, and outfits like this casual track suit of velvety ruby-colored cotton she was wearing today. In El Distrito Federal, these clothes would cost a fortune; if you could find them at all it would be in the marble-floored malls in the affluent satellite fringes where there was valet parking at the front doors and perfume piped into the air ducts. Araceli gently touched one of the lavender barrettes in Samantha's thin strands of hair, and the baby wrapped her small hand around one of Araceli's fingers. In an instant, Araceli found herself cooing, making infantile noises. "*¡Qué linda! ¡Qué bonita la niña!*" Samantha smiled at her, which was so unexpected that it made Araceli lean over and kiss the baby on the cheek. *Maybe that is not something I should do.*

Araceli carried the baby and walked in circles as Maureen built a small collection of papier-mâché helmets, using a bowl as a frame, until she had enough to outfit a platoon of child Romans. Her *jefa* left the helmets to dry and gave a stealthy peek through the playroom's window at the backyard. Pepe was gone and the plants in the tropical garden were mourning his absence even more than Araceli. The translucent stems of the begonia 'Ricinifolia' were performing a deep bow in Pepe's honor, reaching down to kiss the drying soil at their feet, while their asterisk bursts of flowers, each pale pink petal the size of Samantha's thumbnail, were drying and withering and being plucked off by the breeze. Like flakes of ash, the paper-thin petals caught hot drafts and floated magically upward and away from the garden and the window, where two women and a baby girl stood watching.

Later that afternoon Maureen changed out of her smock and yoga pants into jeans and a loose-fitting STANFORD T-shirt of Scott's. She put on a wide-brimmed straw hat and walked purposefully back into the garage, deciding to ignore the bottles of chemicals for the moment as she retrieved a stiff pair of garden gloves and some rusty tools. Then she marched up to *la petite* rain forest and got a good look at the crabgrass weeds that were filling up the dry soil at the base of the calla lilies and the banana tree. These could be removed rather simply, with a hoe, and Maureen began to do so, with a rhythmic and therapeutic hacking. *Hurry, hurry, before the baby starts to cry.* Maureen felt a pang of guilt when she remembered Guadalupe's departure, and she regretted not having told her sons that their babysitter would never be coming back. Samantha would forget about Guadalupe quickly, but the boys would not, because after five years she had truly become "part of the family," a phrase that for all its triteness still meant something. Her boys deserved some sort of explanation, but the thought of giving them one squeezed Maureen's throat into silence: how much longer could she keep up the fiction about Guadalupe's "vacation"?

Moving more quickly, Maureen retrieved a hose from the side of the house and sent streams of water over the ribbed banana leaves: a tree like this was worth having just for the wide sweep and silhouette of the leaves. That had been the impulse of planting *la petite* rain forest in the first place: to hide the adobe-colored wall behind it and create the illusion that these banana trees and tropical flowers were the beginning of a jungle plain where savage tribes lived and vines swallowed the metal shells of downed airplanes. With a quick spray the stand of Mexican weeping bamboo looked healthier, though Maureen didn't have time to rake up the dead leaves clustering at their base. With regular watering and maybe a bag of organic mulch—tropical gardens needed mulch, didn't they?—she might get *la petite* rain forest looking fit and trim again in time for Keenan's birthday.

With Araceli's help they would make it to the day of the party without any major embarrassments. It was to be both a birthday party and the annual, informal reunion of the old crew from MindWare, the company her husband-to-be had cofounded a decade earlier in the living room of Sasha "the Big Man" Avakian, a garrulous charmer and pitchman from Glendale. Maureen had joined them eighteen months later as their first-ever "director of human resources," which in those undisciplined and freethinking early days made her a kind of company den mother. Mind-Ware had since been sold to people who did not wear canvas tennis shoes to work, and the twenty or so pioneers who were its core had been dispersed to the winds of entrepreneurial folly and corporate servitude. Scott came out of his shell when "the Duo of Destiny and Their Devoted Disciples" were reunited and drank too much sangria, which was another reason why Maureen went to the trouble of making each party a small exercise in perfection.

Maureen stepped back inside and found Samantha resting her cheek against Araceli's shoulder in the living room, looking out the big picture window in a somnolent daze while beads of sweat dripped from Araceli's forehead. *She's been holding the baby this entire time.* "Thank you, Araceli," Maureen said as she relieved her maid of Samantha's weight.

Maureen was carrying Samantha to the playroom when a flash of green on the floor caught her eye: her husband had left a trail of cut grass on the Saltillo tiles in the living room. She followed the blades to the hallway that led to the bedrooms and his "gaming" room, and touched them with the tips of her toe-loop leather sandals. Before she could call out to Araceli, the Mexican woman had arrived with broom and dustpan, quickly corralling the stray blades into a palm-sized pile. When it came to the upkeep of the house, Maureen's and Araceli's minds were one. Keeping Araceli and letting Guadalupe go was the better outcome of the we're-going-broke saga Scott had foisted upon them, though she was not entirely convinced they were indeed flirting with bankruptcy. Guadalupe and Pepe were ill-timed and too-sudden losses. But as she watched Araceli sweep up the grass from the floor, Maureen felt less alone before the enormous responsibility of home and family, and somehow stronger. *You pay to have someone in your home, and if it works out, they become an extension of your eyes and your muscles, and sometimes your brain.* This protected feeling stayed with her as she watched Samantha try to take a step in the playroom and listened to the distant and soothing growl of the vacuum cleaner: Araceli was busy erasing the last traces of Scott's footsteps from the carpeted hallways.


Scott entered his sons' bedroom and found his progeny with heads bowed and eyes fixed on tiny screens. Their fingers made muted clicks and summoned zaps and zips and tinny accordion music from the devices in their hands. He considered them for a moment, two boys transported by semiconductors into a series of challenges designed by programmers in a Kyoto high-rise. Keenan, his younger boy, with his black madman wig of uncombed and pillow-pressed hair, was opening his hazel eyes wide with manic intensity; Brandon, his older son, with the long russet rock-star hair, sat slumped with a bored half frown, as if he were waiting for someone to rescue him from his proto-addiction, which was precisely what Scott had come here to do. Maureen had told him to get them out of the house and "run them a bit," because without Guadalupe to get them outdoors and away from their insidious, pixilated gadgets, the first week of summer had failed to add much color to their skin. "Why don't you play football with them?" Maureen had said, and of course Scott resented being told this, because like every other good parent he lived for his children. When he grabbed a book from their library to read or when he watched them swimming in the backyard pool, the money spent on this hilltop palace felt less like money lost. That was the idea behind the home in the first place, to give their boys, and now Samantha too, a place to run and splash, with a big yard and rooms filled with books and toys of undeniably educational value, such as the seldom-used Young Explorers telescope, or the softball-sized planetarium that projected constellations onto the walls and the ceilings.

"Why is your game barking?" Scott asked his older son.

"I'm taking Max for a walk," Brandon said.

After a few perplexed seconds, Scott remembered that his oldest son was raising virtual puppies. He walked, shampooed, and trained his dogs, and the animated animals grew on the screen during the course of an hour or two, soiling the rug and doing other dog things. *We don't own a real dog, because my wife can't stand the mess.*

"Okay, guys, that's enough of that. Games off . . . please."

Brandon quickly folded shut his game, but Keenan kept clicking. "Let me just save this one," he said.

"Go ahead and save it, then." Scott was a programmer and a bit of a gamer himself: he understood that his son was holding a toy that told a story, and that he could lose his place by the flipping of the OFF switch. Scott walked over to see precisely which gaming world his son had entered and saw the familiar figure of a plumber in overalls. "Ah, Mr. Miyamoto," Scott said out loud. The alter ego of the game's Japanese creator jumped from one floating platform to the next, fell to the ground, was electrocuted and then miraculously resurrected, and eventually entered passageways that led to virtual representations of forests and mountain lakes. In this palm-sized version, the game retained an old, arcade simplicity, and to Scott the programmer, the mathematics and algorithms that produced its two-dimensional graphics were palpable and nostalgia-enducing: the movement along the $x$- and $y$-axes, the logical sequences written in C++ code: *insert, rotate, position*.

"You're doing pretty well," he told his son. "But I really think you should get off now."

"Okay," Keenan said, and kept on playing.

Scott looked up and surveyed the books and the toys in the real space around them, the oversized volumes stacked unevenly in pine bookcases purchased in New Mexico, the plastic buckets filled with blocks and miniature cars. Here too he felt the mania of overspending, although in this room much of the excess was of his own doing. How many times had he entered a toy emporium or bookstore with modest intentions, only to leave with a German-designed junior electronics set, or a children's encyclopedia, or an "innovative" and overpriced block game for Samantha meant to kindle her future recognition of letters and numbers? But for the gradual diminishing of their cash on hand, and the upwardly floating interest rates of credit cards and mortgages, he might now be conspiring to take them to their local high-end toy store, the Wizard's Closet, where he had purchased toys that satisfied unfulfilled childhood desires, such as the set of miniature and historically accurate Civil War soldiers that at this moment were besieging two dinosaurs in the space underneath the bunk beds. The bookshelves were stacked with multiplication flash cards, a geography quiz set, a do-it-yourself rock polisher, and a box of classical architecture blocks. Scott's parents had sacrificed to make his life better than theirs; they had saved and done without luxuries: but Scott spent lavishly to ensure the same result for his own children. He remembered the childhood lesson of his father's hands, with their curling scars three decades old, earned in farm and factory work, hands the father urged the son to inspect more than once, to consider and commune with the suffering that was buried in Scott's prehistory, unspoken and forgotten before the clean and sweat-free promise of the present and future.

"Dad, Keenan hasn't quit his game yet," said Brandon, who had gone back up to his bunk to pick up the book he was reading the night before.

"Keenan, turn off the game, please," Scott said, in a faraway voice his boys might have found disturbing if they were a few years older and more attuned to adult emotions like reflection and remorse. He had felt this way, also, the night Samantha entered the world, during those three hours he spent overwhelmed by the fear that he and his wife might be tempting fate by having their third child when they were pushing forty. His God, part penny-pinching Protestant and part vengeful Catholic, would wreak a holy retribution against him and his wife for wanting too much and trying for the girl that would give their family a "perfect" balance. But Samantha had entered the world easier than her brothers, after a frantic but short labor, and was a healthy and alert child. No, the reckoning came from the most likely and obvious place: the private spreadsheet disaster of his bad investments. *I thought I was being prudent. Everyone told me, "Don't let your money get left behind, don't let it sit—that's stupid. Get in the game."* The absurdity that a six-figure investment in a financial instrument called a "security" could shrink so quickly and definitively into pocket change still did not compute. He worried about the two geniuses in this room, if he was about to set them on a tumultuous journey that would begin with the sale of this home and a move to less spacious quarters. Scott considered the precocious reader sitting on the top bunk, and his younger brother, who appeared to have a preternatural gift for logical challenges, judging by his swift advancement through the levels of this game, and wondered if he might soon be forced to subtract something essential from their lives.

# 3

The first guests arrived and rang the doorbell ten minutes early, a terribly rude North American habit, in Araceli's opinion. Rolling her eyes in exasperation, she left a stack of *sopes* waiting to be garnished with Oaxaca cheese in the kitchen and walked toward the finger that had set off the electric chimes, but stopped when two midget centurions with papier-mâché swords ran past her. Brandon and Keenan raced to the door, holding their helmets atop their heads as they ran, and Araceli listened, unamused, as they stumbled over the lines Maureen had told them to recite: "Friends, Romans, countries . . ." Keenan began, and then faltered, until Brandon finished with, "Give us your ears!"

"How cute," the early guests called out. "Little Romans!"

When the second and third guests arrived at precisely the appointed hour, the boys were off playing with the children of the first guests, while Maureen and Scott were busy in the back, which left Araceli to open the door for the *invitados*.

"We're here for Keenan's party?" An American woman with vaguely Asian features and a child and husband in tow tried to look past Araceli into the interior of the house, her expression suggesting she expected to see wondrous and magical things there.

"*Sí, adelante.*" What Araceli really wanted to say was, *Why do you people insist on treating an informal social gathering as if it were the launching of a rocket ship? Why do you arrive with a clock ticking in your head? How am I supposed to finish these* sopes la señora *Maureen wants if you keep ringing the doorbell?* In Mexico it was understood that when you invited people to a party at one o'clock, that meant the host would be *almost* ready at one, and therefore the guests should arrive at their leisure at least an hour later. *Here they do things differently.* The punctual guests walked past her, oohing and aahing at the decorations in the living room, at the Roman-lettered cardboard signs declaring HAPPY BIRTHDAY KEENAN and VIII on either side of the Chesterfield sofa, and the Doric Styrofoam columns topped with plastic replica helmets. Araceli recognized this couple, and the other guests that followed, from parties past. They were people she saw frequently back in the days when she first started with the Torres-Thompsons, when *el señor* Scott had his own company. They arrived dressed in the assertively casual attire Southern Californians wore at their weekend parties: in cotton shorts and leather sandals, in jeans faded to the whitish blue of the Orange County sky in summer, and in T-shirts that had gone through the washer a few times too often. Her *jefa* wanted everything "just right," and now these early arrivers in their unironed natural fabrics were preventing Araceli from finishing her appointed task. The way some of these people dressed was the flip side of their punctuality: they were like children who cling to a favorite blanket or shirt, they valued comfort over presentation, they were unaware or unconcerned about the spectacle they inflicted upon the eyes of the overworked *mexicana* who must greet them. How disappointing to work so hard preparing a home for an elegant event, only to have such unkempt guests.

"Hello, I brought some cookies for the party," the next early arriver said. "Can I leave them with you?"

The woman with the chocolate chip cookies was Carla Wallace-Zuberi, chief publicist of the defunct MindWare Digital Solutions. She was a roundish white woman of Eastern European stock with box-shaped sunglasses and a matriarchal air, and she lingered near the doorway as her husband advanced into the Torres-Thompson home with their daughter, Carla's gaze settling on Araceli as the Mexican woman took a few impertinent moments to assess the cookies. Carla Wallace-Zuberi prided herself on having an eye for strong personalities and here was one that clearly could fill a room, and not just because she was a tad larger than most other Mexican servants. Araceli wore her hair pulled tightly and gathered in two fist-sized nubs just over her ears, an absurd style that suggested a disoriented German peasant. *The only thing this Mexican woman accomplishes by pulling her hair back is to establish a look of severity: maybe that's the point.* A small spray of hair, just a few bangs, jutted forth from Araceli's forehead like the curled plume of a quail, a halfhearted concession to femininity. On this as on all other workdays, Araceli wore the boxy, nurselike uniform called a *filipina* that was standard for domestics in Mexico City. Araceli had five such uniforms and today she wore the pale yellow one because it was the newest. She took the cookies from the publicist with a frown that said: since you insist on giving these to me . . . The publicist suppressed a surprised chuckle. *This is one tough woman, a no-nonsense mom. Look at those hips: this woman has given birth. Of course she is irritated, because she is separated from her child, or children.* Carla Wallace-Zuberi was a self-described "progressive," and a few days before this party she had spent twenty minutes in her neighborhood bookstore perusing the back cover, jacket flap material, and opening paragraphs of a book called *María's Choice*, which related the journey of a Guatemalan woman forced to leave her children behind for years while she worked in California: *How terrible*, Carla Wallace-Zuberi thought, *how disconcerting to know that there are people like this living among us.* This bit of knowledge was disturbing enough to keep her from buying the book, and for the rest of the party, whenever Carla Wallace-Zuberi caught a glance of Araceli, guilt and pity caused her to turn her head and look the other way.

When Sasha "the Big Man" Avakian appeared at the door five minutes later, his eyes caught Araceli's directly in a way that was at once irritating to her and familiar. He was a tall, bulky man with curly chestnut-blond hair, and much darker eyebrows that were shaped like railroad boxcars. Now he raised both boxcars spryly as he made eye contact with the Mexican maid. The Big Man was the partner of *el señor* Scott in that business of theirs, and there was a time when he made frequent visits to this home, assaulting Araceli with this same impish look. A self-described "professional bullshitter," the Big Man saw in Araceli an authenticity lacking in ninety-nine percent of the people who crossed his path. He had no line, no clever riposte with which he could amuse and beguile this woman, the way he could with people who came from his own, English-speaking, California software entrepreneur circle. He had seen Araceli out of uniform and with her hair much longer and not tied back like it was today, and had once managed to make her laugh with a bilingual pun. The memory of her laughter, of her round face brightening and the ivory sparkle of her teeth, had stayed with him. She worked with another girl, Guadalupe, who was too petite and too fake-cheerful to hold his attention, and today he barely noticed her absence. The Big Man also knew, because he had made a point of finding out over the years, that Araceli had no children, no boyfriend that Scott or Maureen knew about (on this side of the border, at least), and that Scott considered her something of a sphinx. Scott and his wife had coined nicknames for her such as "Madame Weirdness," "Sergeant Araceli," and the ironic "Little Miss Sunshine," but she was also extremely dependable, trustworthy, and a dazzling cook. The Big Man's stomach rumbled as he contemplated the Mexican hors d'oeuvres that would be on offer at this party, as at all the others the Torres-Thompsons hosted. He entered the home ahead of his long-suffering wife, and son, without saying any other word to Araceli than a mumbled *"Hola."*

The lingering resentment in the chocolate swirl of Araceli's eyes confronted all the other guests too as they passed through the front door and followed the sounds of screaming children and chattering adults to the backyard. None of the mothers invited to the party had a full-time, live-in maid, and to them Araceli's subservient Latin American presence provoked feelings of envy and inadequacy. They knew of Araceli's cooking and her reputation as a tireless worker, and they wondered, briefly, what it would be like to have a stranger living with them, taking away all the unpleasantness from the porcelain surfaces of their homes. *Does she do anything and everything?* Some associated Maureen and her summer fitness and frail beauty with this Mexican woman and the other one, Guadalupe, who for reasons unknown was not present today. *Give me two extra sets of hands to do the housework and carry the baby and I'd look good too.* For most of the husbands, however, Araceli blended into the domestic scenery as if she were a frumpy, bad-humored usher guarding the entrance to a glittering theater. The memory of her faded quickly before the birthday decorations in the living room and the eye-catching colors and textures of the furniture and ornamental touches to be found there—the mud-colored Bolivian tapestry thrown over the sofa, or the shimmering stone skin of the floor, which Araceli had mopped and polished the night before, and the bookcases and armoires of artificially aged pine where two dozen pictures framed in pewter and cherrywood documented a century of the Torres and Thompson family histories. The guests passed through the impeccable prologue of the living room, thence through an open sliding glass door to the backyard, a semicircle of grass the size of a basketball court framed by the restrained jungle of *la petite* rain forest, which was starting to look dry and wilted because the automatic sprinkler system had stopped working a week earlier. A humming engine accompanied a large inflated castle on the lawn, the swimming pool shimmered with ultramarine highlights in the sun, and a small tent covered a table stacked with toy swords and shields and papier-mâché helmets. Another VIII made from cardboard and painted marble-white dangled from the roof of the tent.

The guests found Maureen standing near the center of the lawn, with the baby Samantha on her hip, looking as elegant as ever in a powder-blue camisole and a taupe chiffon skirt printed with orchids. She gave each adult guest a peck on the cheek, taking a bit of pleasure in the gentility of this gesture, which was foreign to people in the river town of her Missouri youth. "Maureen, you look great!" the guests called out. "How did you lose all the weight so quickly?" "Look at Sam: she's so big now!" "Look at all this stuff for the party! How do you do it? Where do you find the time?" She gave an aw-shucks shrug and guided the guests' children toward the table with the faux-Roman outfits. "We've got helmets and swords for you guys to try out. But no hitting, please!"

By 2:00 p.m. there were two dozen adult guests in the backyard, squinting before the sun-drenched grass as if the onset of summer had caught them by surprise, even though some were holding bathing suits for their children, none of whom had yet shown any interest in the pool. They were in their thirties and forties and had programming degrees and MBAs; they were young enough to have started new careers, and old enough to begin to grow nostalgic for the adventure they had shared with one another first on the single floor of an Orange County business park, and then in MindWare's own, commissioned headquarters, an architectural gem in downtown Santa Ana that now belonged to the county's largest real estate brokerage. They had been plucked from staid jobs in accounting and marketing departments, from the IT bowels of corporate towers, for an undertaking the Big Man had likened, repeatedly, to leading a wagon train across the Oregon Trail. The final months of MindWare's meteoric rise and fall had been filled with a series of competitive enmities and clashes over business strategy, and in the company's last days of independent existence, before the responsible investors had arrived to purge all but two of the original employees, several of the people today present in the Torres-Thompson backyard were not speaking to one another. But time had a way of making those bad feelings a mere seasoning floating atop the sweeter narrative of possibility that had once bound them all together.

"Hey, it's the head of research!"

Tyler Smith had arrived, with his three children and his wife, an immigrant from Taiwan who was telling her charges, in Mandarin, to behave themselves and not jump in the pool without their mother.

"Are they reading yet in Sierra Leone?" the Big Man called out, in an oft-repeated ribbing of the head of research, who had once traveled to West Africa to test MindWare software that was supposed to wipe out illiteracy.

"You're not taking those dialysis treatments anymore, are you, Tyler?" Maureen asked, because the project had left the head of research with a life-threatening kidney infection.

"Stopped two years ago."

"Oh, thank God."

MindWare had been held together by Maureen's concern for their daily well-being, and by Scott's technical creativity and grounded common sense. Everyone liked Scott and Maureen, and the MindWare alumni who had moved away from California timed their annual summer vacations so they could be present at Keenan's parties. Now Carla Wallace-Zuberi drew the group's attention to Scott, who was standing by the humming pump that kept the castle filled with air, wearing khaki shorts, sandals, and an oxford shirt with the sleeves rolled up.

"Scott, the house looks great. The kids are so big."

"Yes, they don't seem to stop growing, no matter what we do." *Each birthday finds us a little heavier*, Scott observed, *a bit saggier, our eyes less bright.* The Big Man was the one member of their crew who looked exactly the same: Sasha Avakian, a onetime fund-raiser for Armenian independence, who in his reincarnation as California entrepreneur had sweet-talked a trio of venture capitalists into funding MindWare and its many offshoots, including Virtual Classroom Solutions and Anytime Anywhere Gaming, some of which were still in business, though no longer under the control or guidance of the people gathering this afternoon in the Torres-Thompson backyard.

"So, it's a Roman theme, huh, Scott?" Avakian said. "A kid army of centurions—and their parents, the Huns!"

"There's always a theme. The party cannot be themeless."

"You had the wizard thing going on the last time I was here. And the astronaut thing a while back. My favorite was the safari theme, the explorer bit. That was a couple of years ago, right?"

"Right," Maureen interjected. She said this without looking at her guest—she was holding the baby Samantha over her shoulder, trying to get her to take her afternoon nap, and was at the same time keeping an eye on the still-empty swimming pool and the inflated castle, where two small centurions were trying to hit each other with their swords in between trampoline jumps.

"How do you find the time to do these things, Maureen?" the wife of the Big Man said. "With three kids?"

"Araceli," Maureen said, turning to look back at her guests. "She's a godsend."

Maureen watched Araceli walk toward her guests with a tray of drinks, and not for the first time felt comfort in her employee's dependability. True, Guadalupe would be laughing and chatting up the guests in bad English if she were here, not scowling at them. But Maureen never needed to tell Araceli what to do more than once.

Araceli's tray contained a collection of blue glass tumblers filled with a sangria concoction that Maureen made for summer parties. Each drink was chilled with ice cubes Araceli had pried from a dozen trays, because Maureen wanted moon-crescent ice in her tumblers. Araceli watched each guest take a glass with the soon-to-melt crescents and went back to the kitchen with the empty drink tray to retrieve more hors d'oeuvres. When she returned to serve the guests she refused to acknowledge those few who were courteous enough to say thank you, and gave a sidelong glare to Mrs. Tyler Smith when she dared to say

*"Gracias." I speak English*, Araceli wanted to say. *Not much, but "Thank you" has been in my vocabulary since the fourth grade.* On one of these trips she crossed paths with *la señora* Maureen, who was walking back into the yard with a baby monitor in hand. Araceli began to lose track of the number of trips she had made with drinks and hors d'oeuvres. Finally came the culinary climax, her *sopes*, which were a California variation on a recipe of her aunt's. The *sopes* had begun their existence as balls of corn *masa* in Araceli's palms last night. Each was fried and garnished with Haas avocados, shredded cilantro, vine-ripened tomatoes, and white Oaxaca cheese, so that as she walked into the crowd of partiers she was presenting the colors of the Mexican flag. *I could eat five of these all by myself,* Araceli thought. Maybe if I go through here quickly enough I can keep them from getting all the *sopes*.

The Big Man began to gather an audience around him, regaling the group with tales from his new "mercenary" work as a consultant/lobbyist. He came to Scott and Maureen's parties because he respected them for their work ethic and loyalty, qualities he did not possess in large quantities himself, and once he was in their home his "gift" to them was to keep their guests amused and entertained. "So there I am, all of a sudden, shuffled into the mayor's office. The mayor of Los Angeles. He's saying goodbye to some people in Spanish. That guy, let me tell you, he's got a thankless job. Because there's a whole city filled with Mexicans who elected him to office—they think their day has come. And that's going to be a problem: because he can't keep them all happy. There's too many Mexicans. It's mathematically impossible."

The Big Man lived in Los Angeles, on its Westside, but to the rest of the partygoers that city and its overpopulated unpleasantness were far away, and the reference to the ethnic divisions in Los Angeles led to a moment of awkward silence filled by the laughs and squeals of children inside the inflated castle. In the circle of Maureen and Scott's friends, discussing any topic related to ethnicity was on the fringe of what was considered polite. Many now had interracial children, and all believed themselves to be cultural sophisticates, and had given their progeny names like Anazazi, Coltrane, and Miró that reflected their worldly curiosity. They avoided discussing race, as if the mere mention of the subject might cause their fragile alliances to come apart. "Mexican" was a word that sounded harsh, somehow, and it caused a few of them to look at Araceli.

Maureen's maid was a woman with the light copper skin of a newly minted penny, and cheeks that were populated with a handful of summer freckles. Araceli's Mexican forebears included dark Zapotecs and redheaded Prussians, and in her family she was on the paler side of the spectrum. But in California, and at this party, she stood out unmistakably as an ambassador of the Latino race. Still, she appeared oblivious to the Big Man's comments as she walked past. Others glanced briefly at Scott: he didn't have any of the qualities associated with "Mexicans" by those in the metropolis who were not Mexican, but his surname was Torres, after all. Scott was sipping his sangria and had just closed his eyes and wasn't listening either. He was, instead, trying to discern all the different fruits in this beverage: grapes from the wine, of course, and also orange and apple. *And is that pomegranate? Pomegranate? That takes me back.*

"Still, I guess they really do deserve a share of the pie," the Big Man said, renewing his monologue with a conciliatory tone, as if there might be a closeted Mexican in his audience. "But this mayor guy, he's a real piece of work," the Big Man continued, and he began to pronounce on the swirl of rumors surrounding the personal life of the city leader. Suddenly his son ran through the cluster of his audience: he was a boy of eight with the same curly hair and round belly as his father, and was wearing one of the papier-mâché helmets, along with plastic breast armor and a skirt of cardboard scraps painted to resemble leather. "Hey, it's the Little Big Man!" someone called out, and the ensuing laughter finally brought the Big Man's monologue to an end.

The adults scanned the backyard for their children and saw how their swords and other homemade Roman paraphernalia were starting to fall apart, littering the lawn with scraps of cardboard and paper. They bit into their taquitos and tasted bits of shredded chicken in a red sauce that was boldly spiced with organic *chile de árbol*. Now Araceli was weaving between them with two *sopes* on her tray: they were the last two, she had just realized, and she was going to try to make it back to the kitchen and impertinently devour them. But just as she broke free of the main cluster of guests, she walked into a patch of open grass to discover the Big Man standing alone and suddenly staring straight at her, and then at her tray and the *sopes*. The Big Man raised his boxcar eyebrows jauntily and extended his hands, using one to take the last two *sopes*, and the other to place his empty drink on Araceli's tray. "Thanks, kid."

"*¡Cabrón!*" Araceli muttered under her breath, but the Big Man did not hear her because he was circling back to the conversation, which had taken the lamenting, retrospective tone that eventually came to dominate the reunions of the MindWare alumni, once the alcohol started to set in.

"We should have set up in India," Tyler Smith was saying. "Everyone is doing that now. Bombay."

"Mumbai," Carla Wallace-Zuberi corrected.

"Yeah. Or Bangalore. Everyone was telling us to do that."

"The stockholders," Tyler Smith said, repeating a word whose connotations only further darkened their shared mood. "The guy from that hedge fund. What an asshole!"

"Shahe!" the Big Man's wife shouted toward the inflated castle. "Shahe Avakian! Take your foot off that boy's neck now!"

"Those bouncy houses always bring out the aggressive behavior," Carla Wallace-Zuberi said.

"The stockholders! The sacred stockholders!" interjected the Big Man, as his molars crushed what was left of Araceli's last *sope*. "The first thing we should have done is killed all the stockholders."

"Uh, that would have included all of us too."

"And the board members too. Where did we find those people?" said the Big Man, who knew perfectly well.

"They actually expected us to make money," Scott said.

"Remember that letter from that stockholder in Tennessee?" the head of research said. "The guy who said he was sticking with us even though he'd lost half of his investment."

"And all those stupid suggestions he made," Scott said. "That we should move our headquarters to Nashville."

"Toyota moved there," Carla Wallace-Zuberi said dryly. "At least the guy was loyal."

"I'm sure he sold what he had pretty soon after."

"I'm still living under the dictatorship of the stockholders," Scott said. He was a midlevel executive at a new company, supervising programmers. "The stockholders measure and quantify everything you do. Most of them you never see, but they seem to know everything you do. Like God, I guess. They'll turn their backs on you if your numbers aren't right, and then go off running in the direction of another guy who does have the right numbers. Like a herd."

This observation caused a pause of agreement and knowing nods. "If you think about it," Carla Wallace-Zuberi offered, "the whole system is like mob rule."

"Woe to the land that's ruled by a child!" the Big Man shouted suddenly, and for no discernible reason. They turned to find his flush face staring at the grass, at nothing, and at that point they all shared the same thought: *He's getting drunk again.*

"He's on a Shakespeare kick," the Big Man's wife explained laconically. "He's saying that one a lot. Because with his new work, he's getting to know a lot of politicians."

"That was from one of the Richards," the Big Man said, holding back a burp, but otherwise recovering himself. "Richard the Second. The Third, maybe. No, the Second." He was feeling the wine in the sangria, and what a pleasant sensation it was.

"This is what we do for recreation now," the Big Man's wife said. "We look for Shakespeare festivals. Sasha says he likes the bard for his speeches. Says he's studying how they're put together—so we get to write off all the trips. We saw a *Tempest* in the redwoods in Santa Cruz. That was memorable. We'll do Ashland this month and maybe Stratford next year, right, hon?" The Big Man gave an approximation of a nod and started to drift away. He wanted to find that Araceli kid and see if she had any more of that silver-dollar-sized tortilla dish—and maybe talk to her. His wife stood there for a moment, her question unanswered, and now she abruptly left the group too, to look for their son. The others in the group watched them leave in opposite directions, and for a moment the Big Man's drunken shuffle and his wife's distracted scanning of the backyard was like a snippet of conversation all by itself, a piece of gossip to mull over.

A few moments later the first of the children jumped into the water with a splash and most of the adults drifted over to the fence that circled the pool. Tyler Smith's wife took off her blouse and shorts to reveal a one-piece bathing suit underneath, folded her clothes and left them on the grass, and followed her sons into the water. Having exhausted the conversation topics of business, politics, and property values, the guests watched her silently as she took a few moments to touch the water with her palms before plunging gracefully below the surface. In a few minutes there were a dozen children in the pool, water glistening on their buff and khaki skins. With their mixed Asian, African, and European features, their epicanthic folds and proud Armenian noses, their Chinese cheekbones and Irish foreheads that were turning deep saffron in the sun, they resembled a group of children Marco Polo might have encountered on the steppes of the Silk Road, at a crossroads where spices and incense and brass pots were traded at the edge of a river.

The Big Man stood alone by the garden and picked up one of the helmets that had been tossed on the lawn and tried it on: the papier-mâché shell wrapped itself around his curls but refused to reach his ears, so he pulled it off and let it fall to the grass. Next he took a few steps toward *la petite* rain forest and examined the azaleas, before turning back to study Araceli, who was standing in the middle of the lawn distributing the last plate of finger foods. *That woman looks miserable and lonely, like someone forced to sit in a stranger's room and listen to the silence for days, weeks, years.* He again remembered her laughter, all those years ago, and wondered what he could say to make her smile again. *How do you make a Mexican woman chuckle? What causes her to let go of her worries and show the sparkle of her teeth like a burst of white fireworks?*

Araceli nearly dropped her tray when she caught the Big Man gawking at her again, his lips rising slowly into an idiotic grin of mischievousness and craving. This was a more direct and prolonged stare than he had ever given her and she quickly realized that he was drunk. Yes, drunk, as confirmed by the fact that he was now stumbling into the garden and trying to kiss one of the flowers.

The Big Man found himself embraced by the banana tree, then escaped its grasp to stand over the azaleas and the calla lilies. Every time he came to the house he spent some time admiring the tropical garden, but today something wasn't right. *These birds-of-paradise need work.* The calla lilies were shriveling and a few snakes of crabgrass were starting to climb up their stalks from below. *What are these little things growing down here? Sow thistles, interlopers from the desert, pale green and drought-resistant, with paper-dry flowers. And look at these tiny holes in these otherwise pretty leaves of the banana tree.* The garden was dying, and in its decay the Big Man felt a slow-moving but irresistible force at work; something as simple as the passing of time, perhaps, or some profound and unseen truth about the family that owned it. The Big Man remembered one of his favorite lines from *Hamlet*: ". . . 'tis an unweeded garden that grows to seed, and things rank and gross in nature possess it merely." *What beautiful poetry, those lines.* His voice rose as he repeated the phrase out loud several times, his poor approximation of a British accent growing more affected each time, especially when he said "merely." He turned to face the other partygoers, and addressed them with full thespian voice.

"'Tis an unweeded garden and things rank and gross in nature possess it merely! An unweeded garden that grows to seed! That it should come to this!"

Maureen was a dozen or so paces away, handing a towel to the Little Big Man at the gate to the pool, when she heard the boy's father yelling. "An unweeded garden! Fie on it! Rank nature possesses it! An unweeded garden! Fie! Fie! Fie!" *What is that lunatic saying about my garden?* She had slaved on those azaleas for an hour, to have Sasha Avakian throw his insulting verbiage at them. Reexamining the garden as the party chatter sounded around her, she could see, even from a distance, that the fat drunk had a point. "An unweeded garden!" Her *la petite* rain forest was dry and exhausted, it lacked water and an application of pesticides. In the middle of the week she had asked Scott to fix the broken sprinklers, but he had either forgotten or decided to ignore her. The Big Man was opening his arms wide as if to embrace the decay of her tropical garden, turning to address the partygoers and reaching up to grab one of the drooping banana leaves for dramatic effect. His circular, repetitive soliloquy had drawn the attention of the children, who paused in their water-diving, mock sword battles, and bouncing games to look at the Big Man with the perplexed and furrowed brows of boys and girls working their brains to understand an adult truth just beyond their comprehension. The adults were ready to laugh off his drunken speech, but for the reaction of Maureen, who had left the pool and taken several steps toward the Big Man with full, jaw-tightened fury. Then they turned to the garden and saw what the Big Man and Maureen had seen: a living thing that was aging, suddenly, a green corner of this perfect home that had become stricken with a deadly disease.

"That it should come to this! But two months dead!" the Big Man shouted. "This unweeded garden grows to seed. And things gross and rank in nature possess it. Merely!"

Maureen heard one of her male guests give a chuckle that seemed laced with knowing. She turned to find the party responsible, but instead caught Carla Wallace-Zuberi studying her with a mixture of puzzlement and pity. In an instant the rage left Maureen's face, and she unwittingly presented an image of wan surrender as she folded her bare and sunscreen-protected arms across her camisole and turned away, shaken. All of her cutting, drawing, gluing, weeding, and arranging had been for naught. *What a farce.* Her papier-mâché creations were splitting apart too, and her sons were hitting each other inside that stupid castle, and she had forgotten to clean the pool, and her guests were swimming in filthy water. *It's all tumbling around me, but do I even care?*

Later in the afternoon, long after the Big Man had sobered up and left with his embarrassed wife, Maureen said goodbye to the last guests filing out the front door: Tyler Smith and his wife and sons. Mrs. Tyler Smith stopped on her progress toward their car, startled by the spectacle of the flaming ball of the sun as it raced toward the ocean horizon, the purple wisps in the stratosphere, and the blood-orange pastel glistening in the water. "What an amazing view," the wife of the erstwhile head of research said, trying to convey sympathy and solidarity. "This is an amazing house, Maureen. You're so lucky to live here." Maureen gave a distracted thank you: she was still thinking about the Big Man and *la petite* rain forest and how the weeds and wilting flowers had ruined everything. After two weeks of driving herself to the point of exhaustion in pursuit of a liberating confab with their friends, the Big Man's booming voice had drawn the eyes of all of their friends to the telling flaw in their home. Damn him. Damn that fat jester, and damn Scott for letting Pepe the gardener go.

# 4

Night had fallen and the kitchen window had become a mirror once again, leaving Araceli to catch glimpses of herself as she listened to the dishwasher, to its timed sprays and its rhythmic swishes, and the click-clack of cycles beginning and ending. One more load and she would retire for the evening, out the kitchen's back door, past the trash cans, into the guesthouse. The last three glass bowls, two pots, and assorted serving spoons and spatulas were soaking in the sink, where steaming water and detergent worked to dissolve the final vegetable, olive oil, and fruit-fiber memories of the party concluded hours earlier. If this were her own home, and not the home of *la señora* Maureen, Araceli would simply take a sponge and scrubber to these dishes and be done in ten minutes, but *la señora* insisted on running everything through the searing, sterilizing water of the dishwasher. Still, Araceli could have ignored her *jefa* this evening, because *la señora* Maureen was fighting with *el señor* Scott and thus too busy to wander over to the kitchen and check on Araceli. The argument had been going on intermittently for three hours, with long and toxic silences in between, having started just moments after Maureen's final goodbye, and it had filled several rooms with recriminations and miscellaneous shouting, with descriptions of the flaws in the tropical garden, passing on, through an odd and not entirely logical chain, to events deep in the couple's shared past. Araceli wondered how it was that her *jefa*, clearly simmering with outrage after the departure of the last guest, had been placed so quickly on the defensive. "You said the same thing in Barcelona!" Maureen yelled from the living room. Araceli had missed what it was Scott had said that reminded Maureen of Barcelona, a city that came up in their conversation from time to time, most often in sensuous and nostalgic tones that suggested, to Araceli, the romantic postcard images of embracing middle-aged couples in certain magazine and television advertisements common to both English- and Spanish-language media. Araceli would like to visit Barcelona and the Gaudí towers, and if she had a passport with the stamps and stickers that would allow her to come and go from the United States, she would take the several thousand dollars she had saved and buy an Iberia ticket and be out the door with not more than a week's notice.

"Jesus, I was twenty-five!" Scott insisted from another room, his voice muffled because he was deeper in the house. Araceli could only hear Scott intermittently, when the dishwasher paused, or when he wandered into the living room to parry one of Maureen's assertions with a weepy, prepubescent voice one moment, and a husky old-man's rant the next. "You're so totally pathetic!" he said, following up with uniquely raw English vulgarity, which Maureen shouted back at him with a "you too" added for punctuation's sake. Araceli guessed that if she were to leave the kitchen and burst into the living room and step in the acoustic line of fire, they would stop. She had done this before, entering to the scene of Maureen's reddish eyes and Scott's straining temples, one party or the other halting in midsentence at the sight of their underpaid Mexican employee. Other immigrant servants might be made uncomfortable by being forced to hear their employers baring intimate and apparently irreconcilable grievances, they might even shed a tear at the sense that "their family" was spinning apart—Araceli did not. She felt distant from their dysfunction. But it was annoying, all this shouting, so she quickly and without much hope for success took some basil leaves from the refrigerator and placed them inside a glass jar filled with water. This was an old Mexican folk remedy against angry spouses, one her mother used frequently. Fifteen minutes later, the arguing had stopped and the dishwasher too. She threw in the last of the bowls and serving spoons like the good employee she was, and snuck out the side door of the kitchen, across the lawn, empty and quiet under the yellow bug light, and into her room, her sanctuary.

When the argument finally exhausted itself, Maureen withdrew to her bedroom and slipped inside the cotton and wool cocoon of her quilted comforter, alone. On any other day she wouldn't have been able to go to bed before restoring order in the rooms beyond the closed pine door, without forcing her two sons to help recover the scattered toys around the home and backyard, returning them to storage bins and shelves, but the boys had retreated to their room hours ago. Now she took comfort in the silence and order in this one room, where a vintage clock gave a steady and reassuring click and an incandescent bulb glowed through the maroon fabric of the lampshade, its light suggesting a hearth in a mountain cabin. Once again, she'd take the lamp's companionship over her husband's. He was sleeping on the couch, or in his beloved game room, and in his absence this shared niche of theirs had a feminine pulse, it was an organism of finely spun fibers, wood grain, and old metal. Scott sullied it daily with his discarded clothing, the stacks of memos and the electronic toys masquerading as office tools that she gathered up and placed in the drawer of his nightstand. How many computer chips did a man need to order his life? This gadget man, this collector of ring tones and black plastic slabs with glowing green lights, had wounded her with viciousness and sarcasm for daring to express her hurt and humiliation over the garden fiasco.

All that was left was to surrender before the weight of sleep, a mass made heavier by the torture-memory of many nights of sleep interrupted by Samantha's crying in the predawn darkness. Would the baby have a nightmare as she remembered her father's straining eyes and gritted teeth, like the toothy goblins that populate a child's scary story? *Maybe we would be better off alone, my daughter and boys and I.* She pulled the comforter up to her chin, and was aware how childlike that gesture was, to seek solace in the softness of fabric. *Nothing looks right when you haven't slept.* Sleeplessness made them both slaves to their reptilian brains and brought them to the brink of shouting. *That is why he is less forgiving, why he is less willing to bury what I said on La Rambla.* In the morning, when they were rested, they would see the abundance of blessings in their lives, the sharp and clear voices of their boys, the flower-bud mouth of their daughter, the powerful sense of nurturing purpose she felt when the five of them traveled and ate together, when they assembled before breakfast tables with pancakes, orange juice, and chocolate milk.

There was still so much to do in this house, but it was getting late. Araceli would take care of it all in the morning.

Stepping out of her room the next morning, Araceli noticed bits of trash in the backyard that had escaped her attention in the fading light at the end of the party the day before, shredded pieces of papier-mâché armor that gave a light dusting of newspaper snow to the grass. The vanquished shell of the piñata, a traditional Mexican ball with seven spikes representing the seven deadly sins, had been split into several pieces, with one spike at the base of the banana tree. She moved quickly to pick up what she could and resolved to return later with a rake, then opened the door to the kitchen, where the white-tile sparkle and faint scent of detergent told a story of order and calm. There was nothing left to do here. She was about to walk out to survey the damage in the living room when she noticed a note in Maureen's handwriting on the tile counter of the kitchen's center island: *Araceli: We went to The Strand for breakfast. Be back around noon. Sorry about the house.* Ah, the warring couple made up this morning. *Qué bueno.*

In the living room she found a few tossed red fabric capes Maureen had made, along with toys and dolls the guests' children had looted from the boys' and Samantha's rooms and left scattered on the furniture and floors. She gathered plastic board-game pieces in her palm, a foam ball, and a book entitled *Airplanes*, and proceeded to the boys' room. Harvesting toys and placing them in the appropriate receptacle was another element of Araceli's daily routine and it could be said she knew the children's play and reading habits better than Maureen did. Araceli visited the boys' room at least three times a day and had given it her own, private nickname: *El Cuarto de las Mil Maravillas*, the Room of a Thousand Wonders, because it was filled with objects designed to amaze and delight, from the colored-glass Art Deco mobile of planets and comets hanging from the ceiling, to the Viking ship made of interlocking Danish blocks and the collection of two or three hundred books of widely varying sizes. When she was in this room alone, Araceli sometimes spent several minutes with the books, especially the series of twelve hardcovers designed to introduce young children to Michelangelo, Rembrandt, van Gogh, Picasso, and other great masters of art. There were other books that produced three-dimensional dragons and castles when opened, or that made cricket sounds, jungle hoots, and whistles. Any child anywhere in the world would kill to have such a room, and to have a mother whose chief preoccupation was to "stimulate" her progeny, though of course these boys didn't appreciate it. *If I had grown up with a mother like* la señora *Maureen . . .* The mental comparisons between Araceli's own austere childhood and the abundance that enveloped the Torres-Thompson boys were inevitable when she entered this room—it was the only time in her workday Araceli felt self-pity and resentment at the absences and inequalities that were the core injustice of her existence. *It is a big world, divided between rich and poor, just like those humorless lefties at the university said. What would I have become with a mother like Maureen and a room like this?*

Next Araceli made all the beds in the house, picked up the pillows and blankets from the couch where *el señor* Scott appeared to have slept, and folded them up and put them away. She returned to the living room, to run a duster over the furniture, turning its feathers lightly as she touched the tall, distressed-pine bookcases and the vases, as if applying a touch of invisible rouge on everything. She lingered a bit longer, as she usually did, over the family photographs arranged inside one of the bookcases, including a sepia-toned picture of *el señor* Scott's father: in the photograph, the elder Torres was a boy only slightly larger than Brandon was now, but scrawnier-looking, his eyes an expression of startled confusion as he leaned against an adobe wall in ill-fitting corduroy jeans. Northern Mexico, Araceli guessed, a dry village where nopals offer the rare green touches to a khaki landscape. Araceli never lost the momentary feeling of paradox that came with finding this relic of a Mexican family history in the home of a wealthy California family. Next to it was a second photograph of the same boy as a teenager, in front of a bungalow in a city that Araceli guessed was Los Angeles in

the 1940s or 1950s. A few times the person depicted in these two photographs had come to this house to visit, transformed into a senior citizen with a penchant for irritating remarks. *"El abuelo Torres,"* Araceli
called him, with mordant irony, since the old man never spoke a word
of Spanish, despite the faint accent that flavored his English and suggested a tongue that was secretly hoping to pronounce an *eñe* or an *erre*
or two every time he opened his mouth. He never answered Araceli's
*"Buenas tardes"* with a *"Buenas tardes"* of his own. Araceli had the impression that he had been banned from the home, since it had been
about two years since she had seen him, and what Mexican grandfather
doesn't want to see his grandchildren every chance he gets?

Araceli allowed the feathers to tickle the poor Mexican boy in the
photographs a few times more than necessary, then went to the laundry
to begin sorting through the clothes. The few things to be ironed she
left for last, then stacked the rest in piles according to family member,
from Scott's sweatshirts and pajamas, to the tiniest stack of onesies
and little skirts for Samantha. One o'clock and the Torres-Thompsons
were still away. *¿A dónde habrán ido?* The clothes were destined for the
orderly backstage of the Torres-Thompson home, the walk-in closets in
each bedroom, spaces organized with design-magazine minimalism.
The shelves were thin white wafers of metal that floated in the air, sweaters and towels and blue jeans forming rectangular clouds above Araceli's head. She derived a good deal of satisfaction from the uniformity of
these stacked clothes, from the way the folds rose in neat, multicolored
waves from the shelves, and from the light scent of mothballs that she
had strategically placed here and there after Maureen discovered some
telltale holes in a sweater.

When Araceli finished with the ironing she was done for the
day—and it was only two o'clock. There was still no sign of the Torres-
Thompsons as she closed the kitchen door behind her and stepped into
the backyard for the short walk to the guesthouse, which was a baby
clone of the main home, with the same cream-colored paint scheme,
the same window moldings, the same black wooden door, the same brass
doorknob. Opening this door was the small triumph at the end of Araceli's workday, her principal North American achievement, to have a room
of her own for the first time in her life. It contained the baroque collection of recycled objects that constituted her possessions: posters that

had been salvaged from *la señora* Maureen's "spring cleanings," various art pieces Araceli had assembled (including a mobile hanging from the ceiling), and a spare table with a particleboard top that she used as a work space. One of the room's two windows opened to the backyard, where the adobe-colored wall that defined the Torres-Thompson property was visible through the retreating foliage, and for a moment she imagined Pepe walking through his old garden, shaking his head knowingly. She took off her uniform, purging herself of her servant identity as the big blouse and pants fell into her hamper. Probably she wore the uniform precisely for this moment when she could put on her own clothes, a pair of leggings or jeans that transformed her into the Araceli who once haunted galleries and clubs in Condesa, Roma, and other Mexico City neighborhoods. *Thank you, family, for these uniforms. I send you thousands of dollars earned with my sweat and you send me five* filipinas. Then into the shower, and away with the smell of cleaning agents and fabric softener and into a nimble wakefulness in which she was fully herself.

She went to her worktable and reached inside and pulled out a piece of construction paper on which she was assembling a collage. The half-started project before her was taking form, in this early phase, with pictures cut out from the magazines Maureen discarded every month: *International Artist, Real Simple, American Home, Smithsonian, Elle.* Reaching under the table, she picked up a handful of magazines and then opened the table's small drawer and took out an envelope. A collection of hands fell out. Araceli couldn't draw hands very well, and she had begun gathering them as a kind of study, a communion with the anatomy of fingers, cuticles, and lifelines. There were hands from a Rembrandt, hands from an ad for skin lotion, hands wearing gardening gloves, a hand reaching out to shake another hand. There were just two hands glued to her construction-paper canvas so far, and she had placed them at the center of the composition-to-be. Painted in oil and open in a pleading expression, they were from Caravaggio's painting *Supper at Emmaus*, a favorite of one of her art history instructors at the Instituto Nacional de Bellas Artes; for some reason they had popped up in an insurance advertisement.

After an hour of trying out various hand arrangements, searching for more hands in the magazines, and attaching a few to her collage,

Araceli stopped, rubbed her eyes, and tossed herself onto her bed for a nap. She looked at the framed picture of her four-year-old nephew, the only family picture in a gallery dominated by shots of old friends from Bellas Artes. All had been scattered to the winds of employment and migration, to jobs in restaurants in the Polanco district of Mexico City, and to American cities and towns with exotic names she had collected on a handful of envelopes and postcards: DURHAM, NC; INDIANAPOLIS, IN; GETTYSBURG, PA. At moments like this, when she was alone to encounter the lonely contradictions of her American adventure, the natural thing to do was to turn on the television and forget. Instead, she threw her arm over her face and closed her eyes, embracing the exhausted darkness and the acoustic panoply it contained: a singing bird whose call was three short notes and a fourth long one that sounded like a question mark. The very distant bass of an engine, and then the much sharper and high-pitched vibrations of a car pulling into the cul-de-sac of Paseo Linda Bonita, the motor puttering to a stop, the driver setting the brake. Now the voice of a woman talking in the next home, less than five feet from her second window, which opened to the narrow space between the two properties. She heard a girl responding to the woman, and though the words were indiscernible, it was clearly a mother-and-child dialogue, a series of questions and observations perhaps, moving forward at an unrushed rhythm. Each time Araceli heard these feminine voices she remembered the room in Mexico City she'd shared with her older sister, and their whispered conversations in the post-bedtime darkness. In the dry winters they awoke to the sound of their mother sweeping away the daily film of grainy soot that settled down from the atmosphere and built up in the courtyard her family shared with five others. The broom was made of thin tree branches tied together and made a scratchy, percussive sound as it struck any surface, leading Araceli the girl to think of it as a musical instrument that produced a rhythmic song many hours in length: clean-clean, clean-clean, clean-clean. During the day, her mother, aunt, and cousins gathered on the courtyard's concrete to sort beans, hang clothes, and tend to a bathtub-sized planter filled with herbs and roses. Araceli had run away from that home, but sometimes in a restful moment she returned to the cold skin of its cement walls, to the steel front door that popped like the top of a can when opened, and to the rough, pebble-covered floor of the courtyard outside.

Araceli missed Mexico City's unevenness, its asymmetry and its improvised spaces. She missed those women and those voices, and her mother's
observations about tomatoes and men, and the aroma of sliced onions
and marinated beef in industrial pots floating about the courtyard when
they gathered outside on a good-weather Sunday, a table and conversation squeezed in between parked cars.

When she woke up, some twenty minutes later, Araceli expected
for an instant to see her mother, and for an instant longer she felt the
faint sensation that there was a household chore for her mother she had
left undone.

# 5

Over the years, Maureen had developed the habit of keeping her eyes lowered and focused on the driveway when she pulled her sport-utility vehicle out of the garage, so as to avoid eye contact that might draw her into chitchat with her cul-de-sac neighbors. Exchanging pleasantries would force her to remember certain unpleasant encounters. The family next door was a very even-tempered aeronautical engineer and his wife, slightly younger than Scott and Maureen, with a lone daughter who was about Keenan's age. A single "playdate" in which Keenan accidentally ripped off the arm of one of little Anika's treasured imitation-antique dolls and left her weeping uncontrollably had embarrassed Maureen so thoroughly, she had not knocked on their door since. The boy-girl divide was too wide, you had to keep them in separate worlds, which would be a problem when Samantha got older. Opposite the Torres-Thompsons was the Smith-Marshall family, whose two boys were about the same ages as Brandon and Keenan, but who were so thoroughly medicated for aggressive behavior and general weirdness that Maureen shuddered when she remembered stepping into their home. "Something not good is going on in that family," she had told her husband. "The mom is in a place you get to by taking pills that come in pretty pastel colors." In general, Maureen was put off by the undeniable superficiality of the Laguna Rancho Estates, by the plastic surgery fad that had swept through the place in the same way Astroturf porches had once swept through the small-town Missouri neighborhood where she had grown up. Her encounters with the remade women of the Laguna Rancho Estates made Maureen self-conscious enough about her middle-aged looks that, after having three children by natural methods (excepting the epidurals, of course), she had briefly contemplated a tummy tuck of her own. But in the end the idea of submitting the imperfections of her midriff to a surgeon's blade put her off: she wouldn't become one of those silicone Californians the people back home would sneer at. High-priced real estate in a new subdivision attracted the kind of people who could throw money at their insecurities, a description that Maureen would apply to herself in the occasionally candid moment. The difference was that she didn't mind, too much, looking at the mirror and seeing a slightly older version of herself than the one in her memory, the odd silver strand in the rusty sweep of her hair, and the crow's-feet advancing from the very slight folds in the corners of her eyes, an odd Gaelic mutation that suggested squinting in the face of a powerful Atlantic breeze. She preferred the look of distinction and experience to the scrubbed and washed-out look of one eye and cheek job too many, or the unreal orange hue produced by electric suns. *I'm not any less superficial than they are. I just have a different aesthetic. I'll take a weather-beaten chair or table with character over a brand-new but flavorless piece of furniture.* Maureen wanted to age as gracefully as humanly possible in a climate where each day was a battle to defend her complexion against the dry air; she wanted to raise her children without the aid of prescriptions for psychotropic compounds, and without a game console like the one their father played with. What Maureen wanted, the only thing she could say with certainty she wanted, was to bring goodness and beauty to the life of her family.

For that reason she was headed to her local nursery to research some clever, cheap, and elegant solution to the problem of the dying rain forest in her backyard.

Through the smoky glass of the sport-utility vehicle, Araceli watched freeway destination signs pass overhead. SAN DIEGO. LOS

ANGELES. NEWPORT BEACH. Being the car-trip escort to *la señora* Maureen used to be one of Guadalupe's responsibilities. *Other people go to work in factories. I have to squeeze into this automobile, with this woman and her children. All for that moment at the end of the week when they give me an envelope with two pictures of Benjamin Franklin and one of a man called Grant.*

No one talked, but Araceli could hear Brandon and Keenan tapping away at their electronic toys in the backseat. Brandon's hair was auburn, darker than his mother's, though he had the same smart, wide-apart eyes that to Araceli suggested ancestors in some rough-hewn European village, like those peasants of Daumier and Millet in Araceli's art history textbook, the largest of the handful of books in her personal library: gleaners, sowers, potato eaters. Brandon's fingers moved over the buttons of his little machine with artistic precision and for a moment it occurred to Araceli that he might do well with piano or guitar lessons, but *la señora* Maureen never pushed him. Sometimes you had to push children to do things that were good for them: if she ever found a partner to share her dreams, they would raise their offspring with that piece of Mexican wisdom. Maureen had the air conditioner on high and the cold made Araceli's nose run, and she gave a theatrically loud sniffle and feigned a cough, but her *jefa* didn't seem to notice.

The idea had come to Maureen after her perusal, at a local bookstore, of various gardening guides. She had begun with a handbook or two on tropical gardens, but was quickly intimidated by their instructions for elaborate irrigation systems and complex recipes for organic fertilizers, and tips for keeping alive fragile species. The authors lectured her on keeping the air and soil humidity above seventy percent, and insisted she install various electric sensors, then teased her with shots of couples standing next to their Balinese jungle gardens, and stone paths lined with breadfruit trees and palm fronds dripping water. A tropical garden, she decided, was like a "special needs" child: you could make him bloom if you made him the center of your universe, but she had three children already, thank you very much.

Wandering deeper into the stacks, she came upon a book titled *The Wonders of the Desert Garden.* Its cacti and assorted succulents caught her interest, as did a chapter called "Southern California: the

Sonoran Possibilities" that carried several photographs of the agave, aloe, and the Golden Barrel cacti in the Huntington Gardens in San Marino. In another she found a map that showed the Sonoran Desert reaching to a mountain range in California: on a clear day, you could see these mountains, the Palomars, from the toll road that cut through the hills behind her home. *We're practically on the fringes of the Sonoran and the Mojave.* It made so much more sense to try to re-create an ecosystem that was native to this part of California, rather than one native to Southeast Asia or the Amazon. Desert gardens, by definition, needed very little water. The moisture that came from the occasional ocean breeze or from the fog bank that climbed up from the sea into their hillside cul-de-sac was more than enough.

They arrived at a nursery, Maureen leading the way with Samantha in her arms, Araceli and the boys trailing after, walking through the narrow spaces between the tables with plants.

"Yeah, your tropicals are high-maintenance, no doubt about it," the nursery manager concluded, after hearing Maureen describe her garden's decline. "Probably your succulents are something you wanna look at." The nursery manager was a sun-blanched woman of about thirty in jeans and a wide-brimmed straw hat, and she led Maureen and her retinue through aisles of potted vincas and roses underneath a canopy of translucent fabric, to a section at the back of the nursery where the sun blazed down on a crowd of mini yucca plants and other succulents filling several tables, alongside some potted cacti that were as tall as Samantha. "Over at our Desert Landscaping location in Riverside we've got a spectacular saguaro, five feet tall. A majestic plant, really, a centerpiece to an entire garden. With your succulents, drainage is key. Of course, it's all low-maintenance once you get it in . . . For a small fee, we'll do the landscape design for you." When you first encountered them, Maureen thought, these plants possessed a menacing aura: the armor of their spines, the short hair of barbs. But their architecture was graceful and sturdy, especially the baby saguaros, with their interlocking arches. Pastel-green was the predominant color, but when you spent time looking at them you noticed subtle variations in hue. Maureen examined a plant that looked something like a desert sea urchin, and detected orange-red highlights in the tips of its spiky arms. They soaked up the noonday rays with the same gusto with which the banana trees soaked up water. "You're gonna save a ton on your water bill, no doubt about that," the nursery manager said, as if reading Maureen's thoughts. "And you'll save on labor too, because these things practically take care of themselves."

"Brandon, *cuidado*," Araceli said.

Maureen turned to see her oldest shaking his finger and mouthing the word *Ouch*, and then laughing. "Didn't hurt," he said. Yes, Maureen would have to build some small barrier to discourage the boys and Samantha from wandering into the desert garden—if she decided to go ahead and follow her instinct, which told her that replacing the water-starved tropicals with a succulent garden was the perfect solution to her problem. Their thick, sunproof skins would forever remove from her property the humiliation of the Big Man reciting lines about weeds and "gross nature."

Walking up alongside Maureen, getting a glimpse of her from the side while trying not to stare, Araceli saw her employer's eyes focusing. Clearly her *patrona* was planning some big, dramatic statement with these plants. The nursery manager was explaining things and studying Maureen, examining her reactions. The nursery manager could see *la señora* was a moneyed person: Araceli's Mexican presence trailing behind the children was equivalent to that of a German luxury vehicle, or a piece of gaudy jewelry hanging from Maureen's neck. Add to the picture Maureen's regal bearing, the long languorous crescents of her recently styled hair, and her air of pampered distraction, and it came as no surprise to Araceli that the nursery manager was giving her that special treatment *norteamericanos* reserved for people with serious money to spend. She answered Maureen's questions with "Sure," "Of course," and "We could probably do that." For a moment the unctuous manager added to Araceli's lingering, growing, and not entirely explicable sense of dread. She didn't like walking between these armored plants, every one of which was designed to inflict injury, and she didn't like the anxious and impatient look on the face of her *patrona*. Maureen was pulling at the crescents of her hair again, biting the ends.

"Well, we'll be in touch, then," Maureen said to the nursery manager. After looking absentmindedly at the collection of small succulents arranged haphazardly on the table before her, she turned to Araceli and announced, "Let's go to the mall."

# 6

The park consisted of a rubber mat and the requisite slides and swings, resting at the bottom of a slope of irrigated fescue overlooking the beach and the ocean. Midmorning dew covered the grass and the park was deserted, a fact that Araceli found disappointing somehow. She expected crowds, children running, the smoke of barbecues drifting skyward, but here the only movement was from the empty swings being tapped forward by the invisible hand of the ocean breeze, their plastic seats garnished with mist. In the distance, the roar of the surf, and sometimes the whine or purr of a car gliding down the street that curved around the park. The overcast was a whitish gray roof, as it was most summer mornings before the sun came to burn off everything to blue. The tableau was quiet, oceanic, meditation-inducing, but for the sound of Maureen berating her two sons inside their idling car.

Thirty minutes earlier, alerted by a series of screams and shouts, Maureen had discovered her two sons gripped in a pretzel headlock on the living room floor underneath the bookcases with their picture frames and two glass vases from Andalusia that rattled when, in their wrestling, Keenan had managed to push his brother backward into the furniture. "You're going to break something!" Maureen had shouted, referring simultaneously to their bodies and the objects in her bookcase. They grunted and yelped and Maureen had struggled to separate them as Keenan tried to dig his teeth into his older brother's wrist, while Brandon screamed "Get off me" and tried to free himself with a kick. *I order them off the television an hour ago, and without the pacifying power of that screen, they are trying to draw blood.* There was no play in this, they were like two drunks on the sawdust-covered floor of a bar. Once or twice a week this happened, a testosterone brawl born suddenly from a moment of peaceful brotherly play. Maureen believed a mother had to eradicate the disease of Y-chromosome violence during childhood, lest her family one day be consumed by the gunplay horrors broadcast on the television news. She had decided to whisk them out of the house, into the punishment of open space and an afternoon spent with Araceli as their caretaker.

Inside the car, with Keenan still in tears and Brandon glaring defiantly out the window, Maureen launched into a familiar monologue of threats that revolved around the loss of "privileges." "Boys!" she said by way of conclusion. "Sometimes I wish I could just leave you with your father and take Samantha and just go. Go someplace far away." Then, turning to face the boys directly, she said, "I wish I could just leave you with your father!" It was an unforgivably mean thing to say and Maureen would regret it later, after she had driven off with Samantha and seen the defiant expression of proto-adolescent withdrawal on Brandon's face, a narrowing of the eyes that suggested a future rebellion with sweaty and disheveled male textures. But in her frustration Maureen told herself she didn't care, because there was only so much boy craziness a woman could put up with.

"Listen to Araceli," Maureen told her sons after opening the door and lining them up on the sidewalk next to their housekeeper. "She's in charge. And if I hear from her that you didn't behave, you're going to lose your Game Boy privileges for the rest of the summer." Turning to Araceli, she announced, "I'll be back about one." Araceli was standing with her arms folded across her chest, dressed from head to toe in a pink *filipina*, looking back at her *jefa* with bemused irritation. Maureen thought briefly that perhaps this was not such a good idea, suddenly leaving her boys at a park with this ill-tempered Mexican woman of unproven child-rearing skills. Araceli was allergic to her boys; she would just as well limit her contact with them to making their meals and picking up their scattered toys, but in Araceli's severe disposition there was an air of ample responsibility, the sense that she wouldn't panic in an emergency. Maureen looked around the park and saw a pay phone: she gave her maid a handful of quarters. "You should really get a cell phone," she said, provoking no response from Araceli. "I'll be at home with Samantha. Call me if there's a problem. I can be here in fifteen minutes."

Araceli tugged at her uniform, wishing she'd had a chance to change. She had been plucked by Maureen from the laundry room as she folded a stack of *el señor* Scott's boxer shorts and in the chaotic evacuation of the boys from the home she had carried that underwear into the dining room and left it on the table, and it annoyed her to think it would still be there when she got back.

When the car turned a corner and disappeared, the boys and Araceli shared a few moments of contemplative silence. *She's really gone*, Brandon thought, *our mother left us here on the sidewalk*. Even though it had been announced with that angry speech, his mother's absence felt stark and sudden, and for a moment he imagined that he had been dumped into the plot of a melodramatic novel, like the parentless hero of a multivolume series of books he recently finished reading, the adventures of an adolescent boy unwittingly thrust into an adult world of crime and magic. He was alone out here in public, without even Guadalupe to take care of him. Araceli did not yet register in Brandon's mind as a protective force, and he quickly scanned the park like a young warrior about to enter a dark and threatening forest. He imagined a "strike force" suddenly descending on the park, a hooded army of armed underworld types, the machine-gun-toting villains in one of the books he was reading.

"Do you think the Russian mafia would ever come to Orange County?" he asked his brother.

"What?"

Keenan believed that his big brother read entirely too much and knew him to be an incessant confabulator, prone to confusing and scaring his younger brother with fantastic thoughts. At their very expensive private school, Brandon's big imagination caused him to run afoul of the otherwise laid-back teachers there, primarily because he had freaked out many of the girls with new and ever more elaborate versions of the Bloody Mary myth, causing them to avoid the girls' bathroom, with a handful of peeing-in-the-hallway incidents the result.

"You know," Brandon insisted. "Like in *Artemis Fowl*."

"Nah," Keenan said. "It's too sunny here for the Russian mafia."

Brandon was still only eleven years old, and the morbid and fantastic imagery from his middle-reader novels did not linger in his mind's eye for long; in less than a minute he was running down the grass with his brother chasing after him, the reasons for their living room fight forgotten. Araceli followed them down the slope of the park toward the rubber play mat and swings and took a seat on a bench facing the ocean. Brandon watched her as she looked off in the distance at a lone surfer tossing himself into the waves, the charcoal skin of his wet suit swallowed up by water the color of the backwash in her mop bucket. Araceli was a major planet in Brandon's universe, and he studied her often as she shuffled around the Paseo Linda Bonita house. Sometimes he wondered if she was angry at him, if he had done something to upset her, because why else would someone be so quiet in his presence for so long? But after careful consideration of his actions—he was, in his own estimation, despite a few flaws, a "good boy"—Brandon arrived at the conclusion that Araceli was just lonely. And when he thought about her loneliness, he concluded that she should read more, because anyone who read was never alone. In books there were limitless worlds, there was truth, sometimes brutal and ugly, and sometimes happy and soothing.

Brandon considered giving her the book he had managed to bring with him, but then he thought better of this, and instead left it on a bench and joined his little brother on the plastic body of the play structure and its short hanging bridge, and began to playact with battle sounds formed by trilling tongues and popping cheeks. Araceli listened to them and slunk down on the bench, looking up at the gray sky and wondering why it was that here along the beach the sun seemed to come out less during the summer than it did during any other season. The blankness of the sky reminded her, for some reason, of Scott's underwear left on the table, and of other things left undone at the house up on the hill, where Maureen was probably just now arriving to the quiet of a house without boys. Araceli would give anything to be back in Mexico City on one of those summer days when balls of white drift across the blue canvas of the sky and you can follow them on their march across the valley of the city, and know that they will soon drop a cooling rain shower on your face. She wanted to feel something cold or warm, because in this uniform, in the amphitheater of this park, she felt like a stiff pink box and not like a human being. Looking down at the beach, she saw the surfer climbing out of the water, a brown-haired teenager in a black wet suit, and in an instant she imagined he was Pepe the gardener, dripping water from his bare chest. She imagined herself sitting on the beach on a towel, Pepe walking toward her with beads of water clinging erotically to his pecs, climbing up the sand to reach her, leaning over her, dripping salt water over her dry and lonely skin.

Ten miles away from the Laguna Rancho Estates, on the third floor of an office building in a business park on a wide and sparsely traveled boulevard, in a corner of the city of Irvine, itself sparsely populated by various medium-sized corporations with generic and quickly forgettable names, Scott Torres toiled at work, sitting before a flat-panel computer screen displaying five different images of the perimeter fence at the Cincinnati/Northern Kentucky National Airport. He waited with a dulled sense of anticipation for the knee-high grass at the base of the fence to be whipped back and forth by a gust of wind or the backdraft of a passing airplane, a confirmation that the image was, in fact, "live." Over the course of the morning, Scott had opened windows on his screen that revealed various locales in the United States, noting that it was raining at Minot Air Force Base in North Dakota, and watching the long, Arctic-summer shadows stretch underneath the Alaska Pipeline. The pipeline to the Bering Sea was a favorite summer place to spend time at the Elysian Systems office because there was a chance you might see an elk or deer scurrying across the tundra. All day long the computers on the third floor of the Elysian corporate headquarters were open to windows showing lonely stretches of fencing that seemed static and frozen in time, like the peopleless backdrops to a deep and disturbing dream, with only the effects of the weather and the moving of the shadows to prove they were objects in a real, living world.

Scott and his programmers at Elysian Systems were drawn to the images for their clandestine, remote allure and for the rare pleasure of officially sanctioned voyeurism. They had been given access to this government system to develop software, a contract that happened to be the only source of positive cash flow in the Elysian Systems corporate spreadsheet. When Scott thought about his responsibility to enforce this contract by telling his seven programmers never to discuss their project "with any individual outside our direct work group," or when he was forced to ask them to sign numerous promises of confidentiality and loyalty to the United States of America, he could not help but feel silly, because such admonitions ran counter to the iconoclastic programming ethic of his youth, and even the essential élan of his initial foray into entrepreneurship. This was the central contradiction of Scott's professional life, to be the enforcer and organizer of a project that did not fire his imagination, and to be the oddball in a moneymaking culture that as of yet generated little money. He was a relic, an aging survivor from that clan of "robust" programmers who came of age in the interregnum between the slide-rule epoch and the Ethernet era. There were moments during the workday when he felt this characterization growing among his underlings and Elysian's executives; it was a fleeting sensation, a truth just beyond his grasp, like knowing the meaning of a word but not remembering the word itself, the syllables that described the idea unwilling to gather on your tongue. *No one here admires me, no one looks up to me*, Scott thought, except maybe Charlotte Harris-Hayasaki, a young and as yet unsuccessful game designer who was as misplaced at Elysian Systems as Scott was, and who often stole glances at him through the glass of his office.

The executives running Elysian Systems were serious, middle-aged, and worked on a separate floor, the fourth, as if to immunize themselves from the eccentricities of the programmers: the executives wore suits and ties, and decorated their walls with plaques earned during their days as mid-grade managers at detergent and soft-drink companies. They had charged this government contract to Scott, the "vice president of programming," even though any first-year graduate student in computer science could have managed to write the essential code. The contract was for the "accountability software" of the "Citizen Anti-Terrorist Sentry System," CATSS, by which the Department of Homeland Security, the Department of Defense, the Department of Energy, and other agencies farmed out guard duty at airports, nuclear power plants, and military bases to thousands of Americans sitting at home staring at their computer screens.

Scott's programming mission was to find ways to make sure the "citizen sentries" were actually monitoring the 12,538 cameras in the system, instead of using their computers to play solitaire or shop for shoes. His programs gave these people, like rats in a laboratory experiment, meaningless tasks to do while watching the camera images on their computers, then rated them on those tasks and produced a waterfall of statistics that was especially pleasing to Washington. Scott clicked through fence images from a half dozen more places, including a perimeter fence in a piñon forest in Los Alamos, New Mexico, then went back to the work he was supposed to be doing: analyzing his programmers' progress on a project to design animated fake "intruders" who would "walk" and "dig" and perform other suspicious acts alongside the fences and gates, frightening the citizen sentries into pushing the ALERT! button on their computer screens and causing an Elysian Systems server to register another entry in the VIGILANT column. He tried out "turban man," an image of a swarthy fellow with a towel wrapped around his head running and ducking: the actor was his lead programmer, Jeremy Zaragoza, and the clip had been filmed at a rented studio along with others of "binocular lady" and "shovel man," all played by various programmers in this office. Scott made turban man run along various fences: the challenge was to create animations in correct proportions to the various barriers on the screen as they ran and shoveled alongside them, which was proving to be trickier than anyone had anticipated. After watching turban man pass improbably back and forth through the steel mesh fence at the San Onofre power plant, like some superhero possessed of special powers, Scott absentmindedly clicked open the latest numbers from NASDAQ, which had been especially bad all morning.

No one in Elysian Systems bothered to hide the fact that they were using their computers throughout the workday to watch their stocks and mutual funds and 401(k) accounts, not even the executives up on the fourth floor. *Before, we played Nerf football in the hallways, and practiced tango dancing in the cafeteria. Now we watch our retirement shrink in multicolored graphs. Football and tango were better for the soul.* This morning, as on most mornings in recent months, Scott squinted at his screen in frustration at the dynamic displays, updated at five-minute intervals, that confirmed his poor financial judgment, his bad bets. For several years the market had risen dependably, and people started to think of it as a machine that made money, but that wasn't its true nature.

The market did not behave according to any pattern Scott had been able to discern. Turning the market into the graphs and charts of the type filling Scott's flat-panel display created the illusion that it was a mathematical equation, that it obeyed rules like those hidden inside the core of computer games, where players spent hours exploring and prodding to uncover the underlying logic, the key that opened the jewelry box. The equations that ran the market were, in fact, too vast for any computer to decipher: they were the sum of the desires and fears of millions of people, divided and multiplied by the ostensibly rational but really quite subjective calculations of "analysts." The math was twisted further by the fiscal legerdemain of accountants who could be as creatively fuzzy as impressionist painters. The numbers their spreadsheets spit out, Scott now knew, were inflated by narrative inventions like those Sasha "the Big Man" Avakian used to confabulate at meetings with venture capitalists. Scott had learned these lessons while watching the Big Man run their company, but unfortunately he had no way to apply them to his own investment decisions, and he had spent several frustrating years moving the "go-away" money from MindWare around the market and into various "instruments." Five years ago the charts and graphs pointed, unmistakably, toward exotic new fields being tested in Research Triangle laboratories, and if they had continued to follow that logic Scott would not be working at Elysian Systems today, he would not have a mortgage to worry about, and Pepe the gardener would still be cutting the lawn and tending to the backyard garden and Scott would be liberated of his wife's complaining to him about it.

   As was their custom, the regulars at Laguna Municipal Park South began arriving around noon. They brought packed lunches, strollers stuffed with extra diapers and moist towelets, and carried pay-as-you-go cell phones to talk to the barrio relatives who were watching over their own children as they earned dollars caring for their *patrones'* boys and girls. The weekday routine of the park was broken this morning by the appearance of a new woman, a fellow *latinoamericana* who occupied the bench by the play structure, and who instantly reminded the regulars of locales deep to the south, and not because of her broad face and caramel skin, or the way she slumped on the bench and sneered at the play structures. No, it was the uniform that reminded them of their home countries, the excessive professional formality of matching pink pants and the wide, pocketed blouse that was known back home as a *filipina*. It was the uniform of the high-society domestic back home, though hardly anyone wore one in California, where most employers preferred their domestics in the sporty and practical attire of jeans and tennis shoes, complemented with the odd gift garment from the boss: a quality hoodie from Old Navy, or a sturdy cotton blouse from Target. The new woman in the park was sitting with her arms folded defiantly across her chest, as if she were a prisoner taking some fresh air in the recreation yard, watching over two boys who themselves were very familiar because they used to come here with Guadalupe, a favorite of the group.

"*¡Buenas tardes!*" announced a perky older woman in sweatpants and a loose-fitting blouse as she took a seat next to Araceli. "Those are Guadalupe's kids."

"*Así es,*" Araceli said.

The woman introduced herself as María Isabel and pointed out that she had brought a girl to the park who was about Keenan's age. Araceli watched as the girl and Keenan stood on opposite sides of the elaborate play structure, as if contemplating the gender divide and the walkways of plastic and compressed rubber that stood between them, until Keenan made another mouth explosion and returned to the game with his older brother.

"I heard that Guadalupe might quit," María Isabel announced. "So, you took her place?"

Before Araceli could answer, María Isabel rose to her feet to push the girl, who had run over to the swing, and then turned toward Araceli in anticipation of an answer.

"No, we used to work together."

"That Guadalupe was a funny girl. Always telling jokes. Did she ever tell you the story about the little boy getting lost in the women's section in the mall?"

"Yes."

María Isabel gave the girl another push, the wide fan of her charge's blond hair catching the air and billowing in the moist morning air, her pendulum movement and the creaking of the apparatus keeping a kind of harried time. "Push me higher, María," the girl yelled, and María Isabel obeyed and gave another heave. María Isabel was a woman of oak-bark hue with freshly dyed and aerosol-sprayed short hair, and she was wearing smart matching accessories of gold earrings and a thin gold chain on her wrist that were mismatched with the bleach-burned T-shirt draped over her short frame. *This woman arrives at work dressed as if she were a secretary, and then strips down into janitor clothes.* "You tell a few good stories and the time just flashes by," María Isabel continued. "A lot of us come here every day. Later on we'll probably see Juana. And Modesta and Carmelita. Carmelita is from Peru and the nicest woman you'll ever meet. Maybe we'll see Fanny, though I hope not. Fanny is a mess."

Araceli said nothing and for a moment they watched Brandon chase Keenan over a bridge of plastic slats, until Brandon lost his footing and fell over the edge, headfirst onto the black mat below. Keenan laughed as his brother climbed up and rubbed his head, unhurt.

"*Niños traviesos*," María Isabel said with a tone of mild exasperation that she intended as a gesture of sympathy with Araceli. "But I'd rather take care of children. If you've got a girl, it isn't any work at all. A boy is a little more work, but I'll take even three boys over an old lady. That was my last job, taking care of a *viejita* on her deathbed."

"Really?" Araceli said, unable to mask her complete lack of interest.

María Isabel lauched into a story about *la señora* Bloom "wrestling with death" and "trying to keep him from taking my old lady away." Araceli was going to speak up and say, *I really don't want to hear this story*, but at that instant María Isabel shifted her gaze to an object or person behind Araceli and began to wave.

"Juana! *¡Aquí estoy!* Over here."

Within a few minutes Araceli was sitting in a circle of Spanish chatter, with three more women greeting Araceli with smiles and *holas* and polite kisses on the cheek.

"You're taking care of Guadalupe's kids," said Carmelita, a stubby-legged woman from Peru. "Those are good boys. She loved them."

"This is one of the nicer parks around here," said Juana, who had oily, uneven bangs, and the coffee-colored skin of her ancestors in the mountains of Veracruz. "They clean it every night. And the police patrol past here, so you hardly ever see any vagrants."

As the women gathered in the play area, Araceli had a fleeting sense of nostalgia for the company of colleagues, the banter of coworkers, the space that Guadalupe and Pepe had filled in her life. The women told her about their families and the American homes they worked and lived in, while simultaneously keeping an eye on their charges, who were swarming over the play structure and filling the air around it with the squeals their parents called "outside voices." Carmelita sat on the mat a few feet from Araceli and allowed the boy in her care to stand in his leather shoes and overalls, walk toward her, and then fall into her embrace. Modesta, a freckled and green-eyed *mexicana*, raised a finger at a girl climbing the roof of the structure's plastic cube, and the girl immediately clambered down to safety. They were all parents themselves (and María Isabel a grandparent), and their motherly self-assurance fell over and calmed the children around them like a rain of warm milk. Once they'd finished greeting Araceli, their conversation drifted, as it often did, to the practical problems of child-rearing.

"This is a good place to practice walking. If he falls, he can't hurt himself."

"If you don't let them fall, they don't learn to walk."

"I remember when Kylie was that age. *Es una edad de peligros*: they fall as much as they talk. She still has that scar on her forehead, underneath her hair."

"I finally got Jackson to eat the squash, after I tried that recipe with the food machine. *Un milagro*. But it didn't work with his sister."

"Each one is different. God makes them that way."

Araceli watched and listened, saw the children on the play structure casting glances at their paid caregivers, and the caregivers looking back as if to say, *You are okay, I am here*. They knew that each child was his or her own shifting landscape because the estrogen that ran through their veins, and their own histories as mothers, allowed them to see these things: Araceli sensed that North American employers and Latin American relatives alike revered them for this power. *They all seem to possess it—and to know that I do not.*

After a while their attention returned to Araceli, the quiet, awkward woman in their midst, and the small mystery and break in the park routine she represented. What, they now asked directly, had happened to Guadalupe?

"I guess they didn't have enough money to pay her what she wanted," Araceli told them. "Or to keep her."

"Or she didn't want to stay," María Isabel said knowingly.

"*No sé.*"

"Yes, I remember her saying something about the money," María Isabel said. "First they asked her to work for less. Then her *patrón* said they were going to need just one person to cook and clean and take care of the kids too. To do everything. Guadalupe said she thought it was too much work for one person. And that she wouldn't do it, even if they asked her . . . So I guess they hired you."

Araceli said nothing.

"Do you know where she went?" Carmelita asked.

"No."

Suddenly the newcomer looked perplexed and agitated. Araceli could see now that all the scenery at Paseo Linda Bonita had been shifting around her, even before Guadalupe left: calculations were being made, consultations undertaken. Araceli worked harder than Guadalupe, she was infinitely more reliable, but she didn't chat with her bosses, or make friendly with them, and so they had revealed their crisis to Guadalupe, the flighty and talkative one. But they hadn't even bothered asking Araceli what she thought, and had instead simply foisted more work upon her. Araceli saw her standing in the world with a new and startling clarity. She lived with English-speaking strangers, high on a hill alone with the huge windows and the smell of solvents, and lacked the will to escape what she had become. She quietly accepted the Torres-Thompsons' money and the room they gave her, and they felt free to make her do anything they asked, expecting her to adapt to their habits and idiosyncrasies, holding babies, supervising boys at the park, and probably more things that she could not yet imagine.

"Sometimes, you just have to pack your things and go to the next job," María Isabel said. "That's how it was when *la señora* Bloom died . . ."

"Again with *la viejita*," Carmelita said. Juana and Modesta rolled their eyes.

"I was telling the story to Araceli when you all got here. And I never finished."

"The Day of the Dead isn't until November," Carmelita said with a wry smile. Already Juana and Modesta were starting to drift away, walking closer toward their charges. "Why don't you wait until nighttime to start telling your scary stories?"

"There's nothing scary about it. It's a story about a human being. About two human beings. Me and *la señora* Bloom."

"Araceli doesn't want to hear that story," Carmelita said.

"No, no, it's not a problem," Araceli said. Already, this woman's rambling had revealed one unexpected truth, and if she allowed her to go on, she might reveal another.

"Like I was saying, *la señora* Bloom lived by herself, with only me to keep her company. None of her kids even lived nearby. The one daughter who called to check in every week, she lived in New York. So one day, finally, *la señora* Bloom gave up and let go. I was talking to her, just like I'm talking to you right now, about my ungrateful children in Nicaragua. Then I looked at the bed and I saw her with her eyes open. I waited for them to close, but they never did. So I crossed myself about twenty times, and called the ambulance. Two very nice young men came, and they said, 'She's dead.' And I said, 'I know that.' And then they said, 'There's nothing we can do.' They said I had to wait for the coroner. And they left her with me. So here I am all alone with a body in the house! I call the daughter in New York and there's no answer. Just the machine. I keep trying, all day long, and I'm thinking, I can't say that into the machine, *Your mother is dead.* So finally I tell the machine, 'Please call your mother's house.' But she never did. I was all alone with that body for fifteen hours, until the brown van came and they took my *viejita* away."

María Isabel stopped and saw Araceli looking off at the ocean, but plowed on. "The house smelled like death to me: so I cleaned all night long, until all the disinfectant was gone. Finally the coroner called: they wanted to know what to do with the body. 'I don't know,' I said. 'I can't reach the family.' So they tell me, 'If we don't hear from someone in forty-eight hours, we're going to cremate her.' *Así de frío.* So I started yelling at them, saying, 'Don't you have a mother? Would you burn your own mother?'"

"*Increíble,*" Araceli said flatly.

"By the time I finally heard from the daughter, my *viejita* was just a box of ashes. After I got the box, *then* they all show up at the house. The daughter, the son-in-law, the other daughter, the long-lost brother, who I had never met before. *Todos.* And they start asking me questions as if it were all my fault. One of them wanted to search my things when I moved out, but when I started crying they let me go."

"I've never taken care of an old lady," Araceli said distractedly. "And I've never taken care of children until now."

Araceli stood up, gave a perfunctory *"Con permiso"* to María Isabel, then walked over to the play structure, where Keenan was now running across the bridge with the girl María Isabel had brought. At the other end of the play structure, Brandon was sitting on a step, reading a book. *Where did he get a book? Is he always carrying one, the way other boys hold toy trucks or security blankets?*

"What are you reading?" Araceli asked him. In four years of living with the Torres-Thompsons, it was the first time she had ever asked this boy that question: it felt like a correct, motherly thing to do.

*"El revolución,"* Brandon answered, holding up the book to show her the title, *American Revolution*.

"La *revolución*," Araceli corrected.

She sat next to him, another thing she had not done before, and looked at the pages as he read them. The book contained short snippets of text and pictures of long muskets, reproductions of old paintings of battles, studio shots of museum artifacts like rusting buttons and uniforms. There was something sad about a young boy sitting in a park reading about men in white wigs who were dead. She wanted to tell him that he should put down his book and play, but of course that wasn't her business, to talk to him like his mother.

"What happened to Guadalupe?" Brandon asked suddenly.

"Yeah," Keenan chimed in from the play structure. "Where's Lupita?"

Araceli was momentarily taken aback. Guadalupe had taken care of these boys for five years, she was like a big sister to them, and no one had explained her absence.

*"¿Tu mamá no te dijo nada?"*

"No. Nothing."

"I don't know why, but she is gone," Araceli said, hoping to forestall any further questions.

"She's gone? You mean she's not coming back?"

"Is she working somewhere else?" Brandon asked in a distracted voice that suggested he already had an inkling that Guadalupe had quit. "Is she mad at Mommy? Is she getting married?" Brandon was continuously peppering the adults around him, including Araceli, with questions, and these queries about Guadalupe seemed more like the casually curious questions he posed to Araceli from time to time: "Why can't we have turkey dogs two days in a row? . . . Why do you say '*buenos días*' in Spanish but not '*buenos tardes*'? . . ." In the Torres-Thompson family, doing your best to answer Brandon's questions was a house rule. *La señora* Maureen was proud of her inquisitive oldest boy and liked to brag about the very first "brilliant" question he had asked when he was four years old: "Why do moths always fly around the lightbulbs?" Neither of his parents knew the answer and they scrambled to reference books and the Internet before giving their incipient genius the information his young brain demanded: moths use the moon to navigate at night, and the lights confuse them, so that "they think they're circling the moon."

When a boy got answers as satisfying as that one, they only fed his desire to ask more questions. "An atomic bomb? Why? How does that work? How do bald eagles see fish in the water from way up in the sky? Who is Malcolm X, and why is his last name X?" The boy was destined to be either a brilliant scientist or an irritating attorney.

"Did Lupita go back to Mexico?" Brandon asked his temporary caregiver. "What part of Mexico is she from? Is it the same time there as it is here? Can we call her?"

"*No sé*," Araceli said, giving an annoyed looked to make it clear that this answer applied to all of Brandon's questions. "*No sé nada.*"

Araceli felt a sudden warmness on her face: looking up, she saw a shimmering white disk of phosphorus eating through the clouds. *The sun will come out*, Araceli hoped, and then she said it out loud and Brandon looked up and nodded and returned to his book, lingering over a picture of two armies gathered at opposite sides of a bridge, engaged in a standoff of martial posturing. As he read the accompanying text, running his fingers over it, Araceli gave out a loud sigh.

The nursery manager paid a quick visit to Paseo Linda Bonita and left Maureen three pieces of paper. First there was a schematic drawing on a sheet from her sketchpad in which small symbols represented the various succulents the consultant proposed planting in the Torres-Thompson backyard. Second, there was a form in which the price of creating this desert garden was laid out, with separate quotes for "labor," "flora," and "base material," and the alarmingly high figure of the sum total. The third and final piece of paper was a drawing that depicted the succulent garden as it would look from the perspective of the sliding glass doors of her home. The cylinders of a miniature organ pipe cactus would rise to the right, creating an anchor to the composition that would draw the eye leftward, toward the cluster of barrel cacti, mesquite shrubs, and large yuccas with arms blooming like human-sized flowers. When Maureen looked at the numbers on the smallest piece of paper she winced, and felt the dream of the drawing slipping away, becoming so many grains of pencil graphite dissolving into the white blankness of the paper. Then she remembered the argument that she would present to her husband, the logic that would make the garden real, the words the nursery manager had said in a matter-of-fact tone, because the truth of it was so self-evident: "I know it looks a little high. But in the final analysis you're gonna save a good chunk of money each year off your water bill, and even more off your gardening bill. Because this is the sort of garden you just put in and forget about. Maybe two or three times a year you go in and weed the thing, but otherwise you just stand there and watch it look pretty."

The drawing of the garden looked like a desert diorama, and Maureen imagined the dreamlike effect you got at an old-fashioned natural history museum, the sense of standing in a darkened room before a window that looks into another, brightly lit world. The succulent garden would create the illusion that their house was a portal into the unspoiled landscape of old California. Only Scott and his calculator stood between Maureen and the diorama coming to life. Against this obstacle, there was the accelerating decay of the current garden: in time, it would resemble a dried-out mulch heap, or one of those corners of Brazil ravaged by cattle ranchers. She could make this argument to her husband, or she could simply take control of the situation—as she did with every other problem in this home—and present him with a rather costly fait accompli. He'd be angry, but he'd pay the bill, because he always had before.

# 7

Every other weekend the Torres-Thompson family engaged in a ritual of austerity, a temporary purging of the primary luxury that smoothed over their lives. It had been Maureen's idea, years back when hired help in the home was still a novelty. They would reconnect with their self-reliant past and spend forty-eight hours cooking their own meals, doing their own dishes, making their own beds. This act of self-abnegation required getting their full-time live-in off the property. Maureen had dreamed up the maid-free weekends after realizing that Araceli didn't expect to have days off, that she was content to spend her weekends in the guesthouse in the back, entering the main home to cook meals and wash dishes on Saturday and Sunday with only slightly less energy than on the weekdays. "If you want to, it might be good if you took a couple of days off every couple of weeks," Maureen told Araceli. "Leave the house, you know. But only if you want to." In Mexico bosses did not give their employees choices, and ambiguous statements like Maureen's were a common way around the unpleasantness of a direct command: so Araceli took the suggestion as an order.

Araceli's biweekly excursions took her to the home of a friend in Santa Ana, an hour away by foot and bus. After a while, Araceli had grown to appreciate the routine that got her out of the Torres-Thompson universe and into the Mexican-flavored neighborhoods of Santa Ana's barrio, squeezed in between the railroad tracks and the bargain shopping of the city's Main Street. On this particular Saturday, she swung by the dining room to say goodbye to Maureen and discovered her *patrona* on her hands and knees, with several sheets of newspaper spread over the tile floor of the dining room, trying to interest her two sons in a Saturday morning art project using three fist-sized blocks of sculptor's clay. Keenan was kneading a lump, and the baby Samantha had ocher-colored fingers after sticking them in a bowl of clayish water, while Brandon was on the couch reading a book. Maureen looked up at Araceli with a smile of parental pride—*We are doing something educational, my children and I*—and if Araceli had a slightly more cynical bent she might have concluded the scene had been arranged for her benefit. *Yes, Mexican woman, you are leaving us to fend for ourselves, but as you can see we Americans can manage okay.*

"*Adiós,* I am leaving now," Araceli said, tapping at the small travel bag hanging over her shoulder.

Maureen looked up from the table and said, "Okay. See you Monday," and then added a gentle reminder. "Morning. See you Monday morning."

"*Sí, señora.*"

With that Araceli was through the door and free from work, relishing those first few, very light and liberating steps down to the sidewalk, a happy reencounter with the person she once was, the woman who lived in a true city, with crowds, art, subways, and beggars. The twenty-minute walk to the bus stop took her downhill along the curving streets of the Laguna Rancho Estates, past one block where, for reasons Araceli never understood, all the houses were exactly alike, each a copy of a tile-roofed home from a white Andalusian village, each with the aesthetically misguided and culturally inappropriate addition of garages with tiny arched windows in their tin skins. The garages were as Spanish-phony as the made-up names on the street signs, which still brought a smile to Araceli's lips. Mostly variations on the words "*vía*" and "*paseo,*" the street names had lots of pretty vowels that, when put together, meant absolutely nothing. Paseo Vista Anda. Via Lindo Vita. Her *jefes* lived on Paseo Linda Bonita, which was not only grammatically incorrect, Araceli noted, but also a redundancy.

Paseo Linda Bonita and all the other *paseos* and *vías* in the Laguna Rancho Estates bent and twisted in arbitrary ways, as if the designers had intended to frustrate impatient motorists, unpunctual deliverymen, novice mail carriers. When Araceli first came to work here she too had been disoriented by the anti-linear geography of the place, more than once finding herself turning into an unfamiliar dead end, having to retrace her steps back out of the maze. Now she reached the front gate, a stone portal with a guard shack and two big black iron gates with the letters L, R, and E superimposed in polished steel. A man of chocolate skin and cornrow braids was posted there, and he gave a distracted half wave back as she walked past, headed to the bus stop marked by a fiberglass sign, ORANGE COUNTY TRANSPORTATION AUTHORITY. Only the maids and construction workers used this bus stop, so there was no sidewalk, just the dust and pebbles of the shoulder and a post driven into the undeveloped meadow that ran down to the beach. Araceli turned her back to the road and gate and faced the rolling expanse of yellow grass that mamboed in the breeze, the remnant of the "*rancho*" the Laguna Rancho Estates were named for, the millennial silence interrupted only infrequently by the sound of a vehicle moving behind her with a low purr. Looking past the meadows at the blue ocean beyond, she saw a large vessel many miles offshore, a black box drifting northward across the horizon, like a flat cutout in an arcade game. It was routine to spot ships as she waited at the bus stop, and seeing another evoked a fleeting sense of hopelessness: their slow, industrial drift seemed free of any romantic purpose, and their presence somehow tamed the Pacific and robbed it of openness and adventure.

Araceli waited. She had spent her formative years in Mexico City lines standing before elevator doors and cash registers, in buses stranded before stoplights, and in constipated thoroughfares, but it seemed illogical to find herself waiting in this open, empty stretch of California. Making a Mexican woman stand under this bus sign for thirty minutes was a final subtraction from all that was supposed to be relaxing, leisurely, and languorous about these neighborhoods by the sea. When her time became her own again, when she was a woman with a party outfit stuffed into a travel bag, Araceli reverted to the city dweller she was by birth; she was in more of a hurry, restless. *Ya, vámonos, ándale*, let's get moving. *¡Ya!* In Nezahualcóyotl, you didn't have to walk twenty minutes to get to the bus stop, all you had to do was walk half a block, and there would be two or three buses waiting for you, double-parked, the drivers honking at one another and all the taxis and shuttle vans around them. No one complained: that was life in Mexico City, you waited as the multitudes shuffled around you, jabbing elbows into your chest, pushing grocery bags into your stomach. Araceli never would have imagined herself also waiting in the United States, so pathetically alone on a winding road.

Not long after Araceli walked out the door, Maureen noticed that Samantha had worked bits of clay into the zipper of her yellow pajama jumpsuit, a discovery that caused Maureen to feel the sudden weight of motherly sleeplessness behind her pupils. Looking up at the clock, she noticed her morning sense of being fully awake and alert had not lasted past nine-thirty. As soon as a baby entered the world, you were sentenced to two years of interrupted sleep, unless genetic probability favored you with the rare "easy baby," the ones fated to become grown-ups with the gentle dispositions of Buddhist priests. In three tries Maureen had never been so blessed; each child had sapped a bit of her youth with nights similar to the last one, which had been interrupted by Samantha's cries at 12:04 a.m., 2:35 a.m., and 4:36 a.m. The years of infant and toddler helplessness took a toll on a mother's body too; they were an unexpected extension of those nine months of gestation that a mother endured not in her womb and hips, but rather in the muscles around her eyes, and in her arms and spine. This Saturday would begin with the cleaning of this clay-covered baby and move later to the harried cooking of lunch and dinner, all the while keeping an eye on the boys so that they didn't spend too much time on their electronic toys, and on Samantha to make sure she didn't injure herself, and would end with the washing of the dishes in the evening after she had put her children to bed.

On most days Maureen didn't mind the responsibility; she felt the purpose and nobility of motherhood flowing through her body like warm blood, and saw those exalted notions alive in the healthy, glowing skin of her children and in the nurturing home she had built around them. Today would not be one of those days. Today she would see only the frayed ends of a family project that was subtly coming apart, with two boys of growing muscle mass and bad attitude, and little time for the arranging, sorting, and creating that made up Maureen's notion of what family life should look like. In the back of the closet a year of the boys' schoolwork and art projects were gathering dust because Maureen didn't have the time to catalogue them as was her wont, nor had she filed away the pictures from Samantha's first birthday. If Samantha napped and Scott did the dishes she might get to those things today. He was probably hiding in that carpeted nook of his, with a game, and thinking of this she felt the sense of petty injustice that overcomes a slave upon learning she is carrying the heaviest rocks of all.

All the disciplined orderliness and empty lawns of the Laguna Rancho Estates disappeared in the barrio where Araceli's friend Marisela lived. The Santa Ana neighborhood was cluttered and improvised, and the homes stucco and clapboard, ash-gray and flaky fuchsia. There were palm trees and olive trees and avocado trees and jacarandas, some overgrown and older than any of the homes, with tree roots buckling the sidewalks into waves. Some lawns were green squares of watered perfection, and others were eaten up with patches of dust upon which lawn chairs and frayed couches rested, and clusters of people sat talking with wide sweeping gestures, while women and children stood on the porches behind them and examined the landscape like mariners on the prow of a ship.

The bus stopped on Maple Street and Araceli stepped off and walked a few blocks to the white wood-frame house where Marisela lived with a family from Zacatecas. She climbed onto the porch, which was covered with a worn carpet of plastic grass, opened the screen door, and entered the uniquely Mexican set of cultural contradictions that was the home of Octavio Covarrubias, a longtime friend of Marisela's family and the owner of this house. She found him in a torso-swallowing blue lounge chair: he was reading, in a rather conspicuous display of his lefty bona fides, the Sunday edition of the Mexico City daily newspaper *La Jornada*, which he received by mail every week, devouring its star-studded lineup of radical Mexican literary and political commentators. Covarrubias was a semiretired carpenter and one of the thousands of proletarian, Spanish-speaking autodidact intellectuals scattered across the Southern California metropolis, and he had two large moles above his left eye that he called Io and Europa, after the moons of Jupiter. His wife and adolescent progeny, meanwhile, were sitting semierect on a couch as they absorbed the pings, sizzles, and cheers of a television broadcasting a Mexico City–based variety show hosted by a garrulous man whose vulgar shtick annoyed thoughtful people on both sides of the border. The living room décor further echoed the contrasts between high and low culture, with the velvet painting of tongue-wagging dogs on one wall looking across the space at the bowed, dignified heads of the mother and child in a Siqueiros woodcut on the other. Even on the bookshelf, the gravitas of Elena Poniatowska and José Emilio Pacheco were pushing up against the pulp crime of *Los secretos del cartel del Golfo* and *The True Story of Los Zetas,* announcing to Araceli her arrival at the home of a workingman grappling for ideas, arguments, and facts to understand his world.

Octavio lowered his newspaper to say *"Hola, Araceli, ¿qué tal?"*

Araceli returned the greeting and asked if Marisela was in.

"She's waiting for you."

Araceli zigzagged around the children in the living room and made her way to the last bedroom in the back, where she found Marisela lying on her back on a bed, pushing buttons on her cell phone.

"No one ever calls me," Marisela said without looking at Araceli. She was a short and roundish young woman who always wore jeans that were a size too small. Araceli liked Marisela because she was blunt and often unaware of the fact that she was offending people, and because she was a *chilanga*, a Mexico City native. They had met in a Santa Ana thrift store, two Latinas sorting through the same rack of men's vests, and weeks later it was Marisela who introduced Araceli to the friend who knew a gringa in Laguna Rancho who in turn knew another gringa, named Maureen Thompson, who was looking for a new maid.

"The only call I got today was from *el viejo,*" Marisela said, turning on her side to look at her friend now. "He didn't even ask how I was doing before telling me he needed money."

"Is your brother still sick?"

"No, he got better. Now they need one hundred dollars because there's a hole in the roof."

Once it had been taboo to complain about their families and the demands they made. A Mexican daughter in exile was supposed to place individual ambitions aside and make ample cash transfers in the name of younger siblings and nephews. So their money flowed southward, every month without fail, even as the months and years passed and the voices on the other end of the telephone became older and more distant. Their U.S. wages fertilized a tree of family narratives that had grown many new and gnarly branches that no longer involved them directly. Now Araceli and Marisela complained openly and without guilt, because it had become painfully clear that their families didn't understand the complications of life in the supposedly affluent United States of America, and because their relatives were using their telephones as probes to discover how deep the well of dollars went, as if they sensed, correctly, that the faraway daughters in exile were squirreling away money for their own selfish use.

"I'm going to send them fifty instead of one hundred," Marisela said.

"They need to learn to take care of their own problems," Araceli said, the phrase having become a refrain in their conversations.

"Exactly. I'm going to keep that extra fifty dollars to buy another hat like this one I'm going to wear tonight. I got it at that new place on Main Street. Let me show you."

Marisela went to the closet and emerged with a cowboy hat made of black jute straw, its brim bent up saucily on two sides, like a bird about to thrust its wings downward. "*Qué bonito*," Araceli said through half-gritted teeth, because they had an unspoken agreement not to speak ill of each other's party clothes, what with Marisela's having adopted the rural, denim-centered tastes of the Zacatecas people who dominated this neighborhood, while Araceli stuck stubbornly to the pop-inspired trends of Mexico City.

"And it hardly cost me anything at all."

Several hours later, after watching a bit of television in the living room, and then getting themselves dressed and primped in Marisela's bedroom and bathroom, they were out on the street and walking down Maple Street, headed to a *quinceañera* party. Marisela wore her new hat and a pair of jeans with arabesque-patterned rhinestones swaying on the back pockets. Araceli had let her hair down so that it reached halfway to her waist, brushing it out for a good long while. The effect of this liberated mane on her appearance was striking to anyone who knew Araceli the maid: all the tension of her workday face disappeared, and with her temples freed of the pulling strain of the buns in which she imprisoned her hair, her face took on the relaxed expression of a young woman without children to take care of or meals to prepare. She was wearing her "Saturday night *chilanga* uniform": short black leggings with flamingo-colored trim that reached halfway down her calves, a black miniskirt with a few sequins, and a T-shirt with the word LOVE across the front, a peace symbol filling the o. Three strands of necklaces made of raspberry-colored plastic rocks, and a few matching bracelets, were her chief accessories. It was a bold statement of where she came from. Similar versions of her *uniforme de chilanga* had previously earned Araceli a derisive comment or two from Marisela. "You know that people here think you look ridiculous. This isn't the Condesa district."

"That, my dear, is precisely the point."

But today Marisela also kept to their pact and said nothing as they walked to the party, her teeth gleaming in their ruby lipstick frame, the most expressive part of her face, given the large, wraparound sunglasses she was wearing, another example of *norteño* chic, with encrusted "diamonds" on each side, eyewear that possessed an aeronautical quality, as if Marisela were preparing to be the first Zacatecas astronaut blasted into space.

"I don't really know the people at this party that well," Marisela was saying. "The girl who is having the *quinceañera,* her name is Nicolasa. She's very tall, very pretty. I know her aunt, Lourdes is her name, because I used to work with her at that clothes factory."

"I remember you telling me about Lourdes."

"Actually, I do know some *chisme* about these people." It was more tragedy than gossip, a story with dark, nausea-inducing contours, complete with psychopathic border smugglers and a father who disappeared once the family was safely ensconced in California. Abandoned with two children, Nicolasa's mother had soldiered on until illness struck. "She got too sick to work, and too sick to even take care of the kids. So some people from the government came by and took the kids. They put them in something called Foster Care."

"Foster" was one of those words than never quite found a home in Araceli's mental arrangement of the English language. She'd heard it before and sometimes confused it with "faster"—much in the same way some English speakers themselves confused words like "gorilla" and "guerrilla," or "pretext" and "pretense"—and she'd wondered if the American fix to broken families known as Foster Care somehow involved finding the quickest solution possible: instant guardians for the parentless, quick meals for the unfed.

"In Foster Care they separate siblings," Marisela continued. "So this girl and her brother lived in different places for, like, three or four years."

"What about the mother?"

"She died."

"*Dios mío.*"

"I wish I could remember what she had."

"AIDS?"

"No, it was something more like cancer. But anyways, my friend Lourdes tried for a long time to get them out of Foster Care. They tried looking for the father too. Finally Lourdes's sister and brother-in-law tried to adopt them, but of course it took forever, because they were stuck in Foster Care and once they're in that I guess it's really hard to get them out."

The story stayed with Araceli as she walked with Marisela past old bungalows whose windows and doors were open to catch a breeze in the final hours of a dying summer afternoon. Araceli saw kitchen walls shimmering in stark incandescent light, and heard a radio tuned to a Spanish-language broadcast of a baseball game, and a murmur of voices followed by a chorus of laughter, and she wondered about the voices she could not hear, and the tales of betrayal and loss they might tell. Araceli knew she could knock on any door, ask a question or two, and find herself inside a melodrama about a family forced to endure separation and travel great distances, and to struggle with the authorities and with their own self-destructive foibles.

They arrived at a bungalow decorated with a string of lights gathering in luminance in the twilight, its unseen backyard pulsating with accordions, trumpets, and clarinets. Marisela and Araceli had missed the actual *quinceañera* ceremony, because it had started on schedule, in violation of the Mexican social conventions Marisela and Araceli still followed, although they had arrived in plenty of time for the party that followed. After pushing in a splintery wooden gate, the two women stepped onto a concrete patio thick with more spectacled recruits to the Zacatecas space program who were shuffling about in cowboy boots and swaying inside jeans, while streamers dangled over their heads, brushing against the tops of their ten-gallon hats.

Following Marisela, Araceli cut through the dancers and found her way to a corner, against a wooden fence, where the nondancers held plastic cups and studied the patterns of the shifting feet on the dance floor with serious eyes, as if trying to decipher the meaning of the interlocking circles. Three pairs of women were dancing together, which was not unusual at these parties, the men of northern Mexico being a shy bunch, and when the music stopped and another song started, Marisela turned to Araceli to ask, "*¿Bailamos?*" In an instant they were dancing on the patio, Araceli laughing loudly as she led her friend in a merry-go-round waltz, their legs intertwined and arms around each other's waists. "Just watch," Marisela shouted into Araceli's ear above the music. "We dance like this once, and all these guys will be all over us." Soon enough, several *paisanos* holding beers were trying very hard to look unimpressed by the sight of a tall woman with thick polyester legs protruding from her miniskirt, spinning deftly in her checkerboard flats and dancing cheek-to-cheek with her short friend in the persimmon-colored blouse.

When Araceli and Marisela stopped dancing, a young man in a baseball cap stepped out of the crowd and grinned and squinted into Marisela's sunglasses, as if studying himself in the reflection there. He spoke words Araceli did not hear, and when the music started again he pulled Marisela into the center of the patio, and soon they were swallowed up in the mass of moving bodies like rocks plopping into a lake.

Araceli walked to the fence on the edge of the patio and prepared herself for the possibility that none of the brass-buckled astronauts would step forward and lead her back out onto the concrete floor to spin around. *When Marisela finishes with that little guy she doesn't seem to like so much, maybe we can dance again.* At that instant, Araceli felt a tap on the shoulder and turned to see a lofty mass of flesh and denim standing before her. He was a man of about her own age, but significantly taller, with a head that was sprouting a full fountain of sexy, moist black curls. "*¿Quieres bailar?*" he asked. *Where did you come from?* she wanted to say, and soon found one of her hands rising for the nameless man to guide her onto the patio. Her partner was husky but moved well, clasping her hands with confidence and with the slightly callused, blackish bronze hands of a man who earns his living outdoors. As they spun to the repetitive swirl of the trumpet and clarinets, Araceli took in the motion of his slacks, the churn of his shirt. Little miracles like this happened to people like Marisela all the time, but only very rarely to Araceli: to meet a stranger and, in an instant, to find herself moving in synchronicity with him.

Halfway through that first song, he leaned over as they danced, pressed his cheek against hers, and said, loud enough to be heard against the blaring music, "Hey, you dance well!"

"I know," she shouted back.

The music stopped. People around them wiped perspiration from their foreheads and headed for the edge of the patio dance floor. Before Araceli could prepare herself for the inevitable *Thank you and goodbye*, the music had started again and the curly-headed man was asking, "¿*Otra?*"

"¡*Sí!*"

During the second song he said his name was Felipe and after the third he asked her name. When the music stopped after the fourth song she asked him where he was from, just so he wouldn't go away. "Sonora," he said. "A little town called Imuris. It's near Cananea. ¿*Y tú?*"

"El De Efe."

When it became clear he did not want to run away, she asked Felipe if he knew anyone else at the party. A few people, he said.

"I don't know anyone."

"Look, over there," he said. "It's the girl who is having the *quinceañera*."

Araceli turned to see a tall young woman with mahogany skin who wore a tight white dress covered in constellations of beads. Nicolasa had the confident look of a young woman enjoying her day of neighborhood celebrity, and was listening to an older man and studying him with smart, dark eyes that occasionally darted away from him to the landscape of the backyard party: the crowd, and the strings of lights, and a large white sign attached to the fence that read FELIZ 15 NICA. Her black hair was parted in the middle and long braids ran down over her shoulders: a girl's hairstyle and a woman's face and body. Next to her was a boy with the same complexion but a foot shorter: her brother, apparently. He looked small and vulnerable, and possessed all the tragic aura that his sister lacked: without the black suit he was wearing, he might be one of those boys you see weaving between the cars in Mexico City, raising their palms to catch coins and raindrops from the sky. Now the big, beefy man talking to them raised a bicep to show them a tattoo, a portrait of a cigarette-smoking soldier in a steel helmet, with SGT. RAY, R.I.P. written inside a scroll underneath.

"They've been through a lot," Felipe said.

"So you know that story?"

"You mean about their mother dying and being adopted and all that? Yeah. Everybody does. Everybody in the neighborhood, at least."

"I'm not from the neighborhood."

"Yeah, I know. I think I would have remembered you," he said, naturally and simply, without any secondary meanings.

"You see that guy next to them? He got back a few months ago from the war. His name is José. He's a cousin of the lady who owns this house."

"What about you? What's your story?"

"I paint houses. And some construction. But mostly I paint houses."

"That pays well, *qué no*?"

"It's okay. But I like to paint other things besides walls. *¿Entiendes?* The other day I was painting at this family's house and I heard *la señora* asking my boss if he knew anyone who could paint a design on a table for her. I stepped in and said I could do it, because I like to draw. She wanted a dragon for her son's room, so I made her one. A big red dragon. She liked it and the boy did too. That was fun."

"You're an artist!"

"No, I wouldn't call myself that. But I like to draw. The dragon turned out okay."

"I studied art," Araceli offered, making a conscious effort not to speak breathlessly: a dancing artist had fallen into her lap, and she wanted to tell him everything, all at once. "I was at the Instituto Nacional de Bellas Artes in El De Efe, but only for a year. Then I had to quit." Araceli thought she should explain why, but stopped herself: among *mexicanos* of their status, in this place called California, no explanations were necessary when describing dreams that died.

"I could tell by looking at you that you're really smart. You look like one of those girls from the show *Rebelde*. A student. I could tell. That's why I asked you to dance."

At the end of the evening, the two of them having danced for two hours, Felipe said he had to leave because he had to be up early the next morning. *Tomorrow is a Sunday, why would you have to be up early?* Araceli wanted to ask, but she resisted the temptation. He asked for her phone number, which she wrote on a slip of paper he tucked into the front pocket of his shirt.

"I work in a house," she told him. *Trabajo en una casa.* It meant, *Yes, you can call me, but a gringo will answer, and be polite, please, and don't call me in the middle of the night because my* jefes *won't appreciate that.* He appeared to understand and smiled as he turned away, and Araceli got one last good look at the backside of his slacks as he left: he was husky when you looked at him from the front, but from the back he was much better proportioned, the width of his shoulders stood out, suggesting a certain musculature. He was a sensitive *mexicano* trapped, like her, in a too-big body.

On Sunday afternoon, some thirty-six hours after the departure of her only domestic help, Maureen found herself sitting on the floor of her walk-in closet, listening to the steady static that came from the baby monitor, and to the distant sounds of heads being smashed, flesh being pierced, and stone walls crashing to the ground. Allowing the boys the pleasures of movie-made warfare was the only way she was going to get a little time to herself, to sort through her box of family pictures and to arrange the photographs of Samantha's first birthday in the album she had purchased months ago. Maureen did this to calm herself, and as an affirmation of the nurturing progress of her family. She took a picture of Scott holding Samantha at the party and placed it next to another that showed the baby sitting before her cake, with Brandon and Keenan on either side, helping her blow out a wick that burned atop a wax number one. The blending of features in the faces of their children was plain to see: there was Ireland in the specks of emerald in Keenan's eyes, Maine in her daughter's prominent jaw, and Mexico in the way Brandon's long nose stretched. Her children blended the features of many branches of the human tree. In their faces she saw the hands of an eccentric creator, an artist who surprises his audience with the unexpected.

On the other end of the Paseo Linda Bonita home, Scott was gripping a console control with two hands, playing a football simulation of cutting-edge visual complexity. He had purchased the newest release two days earlier, thinking that he could justify the cost as a professional, tax-deductible expense, because he had designed a game or two in his day and might again. But the unadorned truth was that a bestselling game like this was beyond his talents, which had been honed in the days of "real programming." You had to manage and inspire large groups of people to bring a game like this to market: artists, teams of technicians conducting motion studies, and brain trusts of football mavens to work out the strategy book. This game was a big Hollywood production: the credits were buried deep in the disk for true geeks like Scott to find, and ran on for several pages, as if for a David Lean epic.

A man needed to play, to feel the exhilaration and escape of sports, even if he was sitting down while doing it, so Scott returned to the task at hand: leading his team of animated San Francisco players to victory over a Pittsburgh team. The glossy realism of the animation more than made up for the lack of exertion, and as he completed a third-and-long backed up against his own goal line, Scott thought that a virtual triumph was the most ephemeral source of adrenaline out there, but it did make it easier to do the dishes afterward. Maureen expected Scott to leave the kitchen spotless, to attack the stacks of bowls and oily pans in the sink, wipe the counters, and sweep the floor. It was an absurd rule of Maureen's that the house had to look "presentable" when Araceli walked in the door on Monday morning. Unfortunately, the disarray built rather quickly in Araceli's absence, with dishes filling the sink and loose laundry invading the hallways and bedrooms, while children's shoes walked midstride on the living room floor and plastic warriors massed for battle on the dining room table, surrounded by a toast-crumb snowfall.

Maureen had decided to aggressively ignore this growing disorder, and was still in the closet, retreating deeper into family nostalgia, remembering the gentle, funny, and neglected but handsome man her husband was. Back then, she had thought of his surname, Torres, as a signpost announcing her arrival at a remote, exotic village.

After all these years what had seemed like silent strength had been revealed to be a deeply rooted stoicism, a disconnectedness from people. The promise of a Latin journey seemed closer to fruition after their marriage, when her new mother-in-law had graciously presented her with an album of Torres family pictures, including some bleak photographs of her father-in-law as a boy, and others of him as a cocky young man. She had framed a couple of these sturdy old images and placed them in the living room for guests to see, but they were artifacts in a historical vacuum, since in her few conversations with the old man he refused to talk much about his life in the black-and-white, Spanish-speaking past. "We had a raw deal when we were kids, but we never complained about it. And I sure as hell ain't going to complain about it now." The old man had dedicated his life to the erasure of the language and rituals he associated with short hoes and lettuce fields, with the transience of old Ford trucks and night arrivals at labor camps and menacing urban ghettos. The old man confused amnesia with reinvention, and thus the only trace of Mexican in her husband was that very faint brownish red she saw when he allowed himself to stand under the sun for an hour, and perhaps his Julius Caesar nose, which may or may not be Indian. Everything else about Scott was as pale and severe as the Maine winters her late mother-in-law used to talk about, though Maureen never would have dared to say such a thing out loud, to anyone, because as an American "white" woman it wasn't her place to make such judgments.

Her journey through the albums having failed to transport her away from the messy and complicated present, Maureen put her family memories back in their shoe boxes and decided to start cleaning the house. As she picked up dirty pajamas and towels, she marveled, not for the first time, at how much work Araceli did. This home, even when you thought of it in the most abstract sense, as a place of security, order, and happiness, depended on the Mexican woman as much as it did on Maureen. Allowing Araceli to leave for two days was, Maureen realized, a way of claiming it as her own.

She was in the kitchen, holding Samantha and heating up a bottle of milk, when her oldest son entered the kitchen to ask for something to eat.

"How about a sandwich? Turkey and cheese?"

"Okay."

"Is the movie over? Did you turn off the TV?"

"Yes," Brandon said. "And yes."

She looked at the dishes in the sink, remembered to scan the backyard for toys, and thought about what she would make for dinner and what she could get the boys to do this afternoon: perhaps a game of Scrabble Junior. *It takes concentration to do all these things at once.* Already today she had played Risk with her boys and had set them to work with aprons and paintbrushes and butcher paper. Later she would wade into her boxes of colored scrap paper and fabric strips and assemble another art project. There was an element of performance to being a good mom, but no one gave you executive bonuses for getting through the day, for keeping three kids fed, entertained, and stimulated without doing the easy thing and leaving them in front of the television. It took stamina and a certain optimistic and demanding outlook.

Maureen had the baby on her hip and was walking to the bedroom to retrieve her children and call them to an early dinner when she caught a glimpse of her husband, sitting on that boomerang-shaped chair before the mirage of a high-definition television monitor, a series of color images quick-flashing in response to the movement of his fingers. *Again? What is the fascination? I am carrying the baby and he is playing.* She took in his frantic fingers, and the intense look of excited concentration she could see in profile, and decided the moment presented an opportunity.

"Honey, I wanted to ask you something."

"Uh-huh," he said, giving a quarter turn in her direction without taking his eyes off the screen. "Sorry, I'm in my two-minute offense here."

"Okaaaay. Well, I came up with a plan for the garden. Something that will save us some money in the long run. But it's gonna require a big expense to get started."

"Uh-huh."

"I'm going to have them put in some desert plants."

"Cool."

"I'll go ahead and do that, then."

"What?"

"The desert garden."

"But how much is it going to cost?" he said, giving a half turn in her direction while the screen behind him replayed the last running play.

"Not too much. Honest."

"Really," he said, and then the pull of the game caused him to turn fully to the screen.

"Honest, I promise," she said to the back of his head.

"Cool," he said, and Maureen thought that at any other moment she would have been angered by his failure to pay full attention to her.

"So I'll just charge it, then," she said.

He did not answer, but instead leaned his body forward in his chair. On the screen the animated representation of a football quarterback threw a very long pass, and through a mesmerizing miracle of technology the game's eye followed the ball through the air and into the hands of an animated receiver, though Maureen had already turned away and was in the hallway when that very masculine corner of her home filled with a semiconductor-produced simulation of a multitude, a sizzle of voices and cheers celebrating a touchdown.

# 8

The kitchen window offered only a partial view of the sidewalk at the bottom of the sloping lawn, and when the work crew rolled up to the cul-de-sac at Paseo Linda Bonita, Araceli saw only the top half of their truck. Three men of Mesoamerican heritage stood in the back, peering over a side panel of rough-cut plywood with the startled look of Aztecs about to enter a town filled with conquistadores. They looked around at their alien, affluent surroundings for a few moments, and began talking to a person invisible to Araceli, and she could lip-read them saying "*¿aquí?*" and "*¿bajamos?*" The answer to both questions was yes, apparently, and soon they were jumping off their perch to the street below. Two more men who had been sitting on the floor of the truck rose to their feet, one of whom was holding a long machete, which he proceeded to strike once against the truck's plywood panels, as if to test the blade. Both the eager-to-work peasant expressions of the workers and what Araceli could see of the truck itself seemed like anachronisms, and Araceli half expected them to admit they were lost and turn around and drive away. The presence of these roustabouts in their used clothing inspired in Araceli a familiar and comforting burst of sarcastic thoughts: *I'm sorry, but there is no farm here. There are no cabbages to* *pick, as you can see! Put your machetes away: we have no bananas to harvest!* To her surprise, another man, an older Mexican-American type dressed in a freshly ironed plaid shirt, came walking up the path.

Araceli was headed for the door, preparing the polite words by which she would inform this man that he and his poorly fed day laborers had obviously come to the wrong place, when she saw her *jefa* reach the door first and open it.

"You're late," Maureen said abruptly.

"I'm really, really sorry, lady, but my usual guys didn't show up. So I had to pick up some new guys." The raffish "guys," five in all, were now standing near the bottom of the walkway behind their foreman, hands in their pockets and silent.

"Day laborers?" Maureen asked in a tone that suggested concern.

"Yeah, but these guys are cool. I've hired them all before."

"As long as you finish in time. You need to be done by eleven. You know that, right?"

"We'll be outta here by ten-thirty, I promise. I got another job at eleven anyway over at Newport. I brought a couple more guys than usual to get done in time. Trust me."

*What is going on?* Araceli wondered as she watched Maureen show the contractor the gate where his crew could enter the backyard without tramping through Araceli's freshly cleaned living room. *These men have come to do some serious labor,* Araceli concluded, *something involving plants and soil, and of course I am the last to know, because my patrona doesn't feel the slightest need to inform me.* Araceli felt mildly insulted, an emotion that had become familiar in the days since she had discovered that she was now the do-everything *doméstica,* her workload doubled without a corresponding raise.

She walked across the living room to the glass doors that opened to the backyard and watched as the contractor and Maureen gathered before the withering tropical garden. Half the calla lilies were tan and irrevocably dead, the banana tree would never again produce the tiny fruit that it used to give each spring, and the ferns were as dry as Egyptian parchment. The river boulders inside the little stream had lost their rich black texture and turned a brittle, pale gray because the small pump that fed the stream stopped working days ago, which Araceli could now see in retrospect was a final, unmistakable sign of what was about to happen.

Having finished their conference, the workers and their boss made for the side gate and their truck, while Maureen contemplated *la petite* rain forest for the last time. A few minutes later the contractor was back with his laborers, each of whom was holding a machete and studying the boss as he consulted with Maureen. He gave the workers a set of instructions with wide sweeps of his hands and pointing fingers. Not one of these workers, Araceli guessed, had been in this country for longer than a year. The one with the droopy mustache and the sweatshirt that said LOUDON COUNTY HIGH WRESTLING TEAM was likely a grandfather. The stringy young guy next to him was wearing a Banamex giveaway T-shirt and appeared to be the newest one in this country. The grandfather looked intently at the boss, suggesting he was anxious to prove himself, and they all seemed to have a need to get a good day's work out of their systems, having just won the lottery and wrestling match back at the hiring site.

The boss was addressing the workers, and through the window Araceli could make out his bad, shouted Spanish. "*¡Comienzan con estos! ¡Con puro machete!*" At the sound of the first machete whacks Araceli felt the briefest pang of nostalgia. Adiós *to Pepe's garden, to the green leaves and flowers that carry the memory of his hands.* The hacking machetes reverberated loud enough to be heard even when Araceli retreated to the kitchen and turned on the water in the sink. She heard them too in the laundry room, the messy, sickening sound of blades cutting into fleshly stalks. A whack, whack, whack filled the house, punctuated by the long, rising whistles of the men calling back and forth to one another. "*¿Qué hago con esto?*" "*¿Todo?*" "*¡Está bien duro el bambú!*" Each time she wandered past the sliding glass doors of the living room, she turned to catch glimpses of the day laborers raising their machetes and slashing, stalks and branches falling to the ground starkly and suddenly, as if murdered. These roustabouts were machete experts and each of their blows sent a living thing flying into the air: they worked in a line, advancing into *la petite* rain forest like men assigned to clear a cane field.

"They're chopping down the garden!" Brandon said as he came running into the living room, drawn by the sounds. "Keenan, look! They're chopping it down! The bamboo! Look!"

Brandon watched them work and remembered the British children in *Lord of the Flies*, on a tropical island armed with spears and a knife, behaving like savages—and he thought he'd like to pick up a blade and join them.

"They're taking away our jungle," Keenan said. Once the boys ran through shady caves formed by the healthy branches and jumped over the tiny stream, and arranged toy soldiers between the stalks of bamboo. They hadn't played there in ages, not since Pepe left, as if they too were put off by the garden's slow death in the dry, Pepe-less air.

After forty minutes of chopping, nothing in the garden was left standing and the plants were an organic heap the men walked over like soldiers in a battlefield, checking to see if any of the vanquished were still living. For the first time, Araceli could see the entirety of the curving, adobe-colored cement wall that marked the boundary of the Torres-Thompson property. Like an empty canvas, it assaulted the eyes with its blankness: she could understand why Maureen and Scott had gone to the trouble of planting a big tropical garden to cover it.

Maureen reappeared to examine the work, and tapped at some of the fallen stalks with her sandaled foot. The roustabouts began grabbing armfuls of chopped-up plants and carrying them back to the truck, and two of the workers appeared with rusty pickaxes and shovels, and started hacking away at roots. The men were covered in dust, soil, and a sprinkling of shredded bamboo leaves, ferns, and flower petals. Araceli heard an engine start on the street, and then a series of high-pitched, banshee screams. Following the sound, she stepped away from the glass doors facing the backyard and drifted to the picture window in the living room, but could still not see the source of this deathly wail until she walked out the front door. The roustabouts were tossing the remains of *la petite* rain forest into a machine attached to their truck, which was spitting a verdant cloud into the back. Pepe's garden was being turned into green dust and Araceli watched, entranced, as the machine covered the workers' arms and faces with a dappled chlorophyll skin that affixed itself to the sweat and soil on their faces and arms. Soon they resembled science fiction creatures, or maybe just the poorest of the poor castes of Mexico City, the people who scavenged through the trash all day until they were wearing the gooey black contents of discarded plastic cartons and boxes on their faces and arms.

By 10:30 a.m., the workers and their foreman were smoothing out the empty black soil with heavy iron rakes. They picked up their equipment and were gone, the truck pulling away as Araceli watched from her post in the kitchen. *I should have offered them something to drink. But they were in such a hurry.*

Forty-five minutes later Araceli was mopping one of the bathrooms when she was surprised, again, by the rumble of a truck and the squeal of brakes, followed moments later by a second rumble and squeal, and the opening and closing of doors. Once again she approached the picture window in the living room. An American woman of light complexion with oval-shaped sunglasses emerged from the first truck, followed by two mestizo-skinned men in identical forest-green uniforms. Four more men in green uniforms emerged from the second truck, and soon they were all walking up the path toward Araceli.

The doorbell rang and this time Araceli beat Maureen to the door.

"Hi, good morning!" the American woman said. "We're from the landscape company."

"*¿Cómo?*" Maureen quickly reached the door behind her and Araceli was forced to step aside before she could ask the many questions she wanted answered: *What have you come to do to my backyard? Why didn't anyone tell me you were coming? How long will you be here? Did you bring your own lunch?* Araceli could only watch through the glass as this new crew of workers traipsed around the side of the house, led by Maureen to the backyard and the fallow plot where the tropical garden had once stood. Araceli opened the sliding glass door to hear what the woman was saying to her *patrona* and watched as the stranger opened a scroll to show a large schematic drawing to Maureen, who beamed giddily in the scroll's creative glow. Then the stranger began to talk, in English, to one of her crew members.

"Fernando, did we bring enough base?"

"*Es un espacio grande,*" he answered in Spanish, surveying the space before them. "*Pero sí. Creo que nos alcanza.*"

"I guess we start with the willow, right?"

"*Es lo que nos va a tomar más tiempo,*" Fernando answered. "*Y también el ocotillo. Eso va a ser todo un* project."

"I had forgotten about that one. Let's start with the ocotillo, then."

Fernando wore a white oval patch on his uniform that read FERNANDO, and all the other workers had name patches too. These uniformed men didn't whistle or shout as they walked around the backyard. Instead they examined the turned-up earth of the backyard with considered glances, sometimes kicking at a clump of soil, or picking up a stray leaf or flower stem. They worked with efficient and practiced movements, consulting with one another and their boss in short bilingual conversations like the one Araceli had just overheard. In this strange country that Araceli now called home, the market for labor in the soil was stratified, and these men were jokingly known at Desert Landscaping as "high-end Mexicans." Most of them were natives of Guanajuato and Jalisco who had known one another for half of their adult lives; in many loyal years of work for Desert Landscaping they had developed an artisan familiarity with the root systems of the ocotillo, the saguaro, and the assorted Sonoran and African succulents that made up the Desert Landscaping catalogue. They earned triple the wages of their untrained, subcontracted morning counterparts, had some limited medical benefits, and, though Araceli did not yet know it, they had brought their own lunches, sandwiches, and burritos made by their wives and girlfriends and stored in black metal lunch boxes each had hauled to hundreds of work sites over the years.

As the men carried bags of sand from the truck to the backyard, Maureen sat on the grass, holding on to Samantha while admiring the schematic drawing, thinking that the money involved would be well spent. The nervousness of the last few days lifted away, a hair-chewing anxiety heightened by the anarchic chopping, hacking, and slicing of the first crew of the morning. *What am I doing, allowing these sweaty barbarians into my home?* But no, she was taking charge of her little domestic empire again, and now there was this crew of handsome if somewhat older Mexican men, and this woman nursery manager/landscape designer who was the kind of desert bohemian you encountered in the inner Southwest. When Scott saw the finished product he'd say they should have done this years ago. She watched the uniformed workers bring a few plants that were growing inside wooden crates and plastic pots, including a specimen that resembled a tree in miniature; its thick branches had a taupe skin that looked like bark, and its fleshy petals seemed to be made of emerald clay, and the entire plant had the heaviness and simplicity of a work of sculpture.

"Isn't this the biggest jade plant you've ever seen?" said the nursery manager, who had caught Maureen's perplexed examination of the specimen, which spread out some four feet and stood about three feet tall. "In the late fall, or the early winter, whenever you get the first good rain, it's going to give off hundreds of tiny white flowers. Most of these plants are going to flower at one time or another. Some in the spring, others in the fall."

"It just makes so much more sense, from an ecological point of view," Maureen said. "Down on the beach, it's misty and cloudy right now. But up here, the sun is beating down on us—over time, it kills anything that needs water."

"You've got your own little microclimate here," the nursery manager said. "I could feel the weather changing as I came up the hill. You're getting a hot counter-draft to the ocean breeze from those mountains. That makes this like an African savanna. You can fool the plants in the garden, you can make them think they're really somewhere else, but it takes a lot of work."

"I love this one too," Maureen said. It was some sort of agave, an arrangement of concentric rosettes, one stacked inside the other, painted pale green and crimson, and all the colors in between. "It's like a flower without being a flower."

"It's called Morning Light. I've got a whole bunch more like that for you. We're going to do a little section of Morning Light, surrounded by some nonthreatening succulents, like this one over here, *Cheiridopsis africanus*, which is from South Africa, of course. In general, I'm going to put your more barbed and spiny plants away from the edges and from the path, so it won't be so dangerous for your kids."

"Excellent."

"*¡Con cuidado!*" the nursery manager called out suddenly, and un-expectedly, in Spanish.

A group of men were entering the backyard with a ten-foot-long plant wrapped in white canvas, rolling it on two platforms, but they had gotten the wheels stuck at the spot where the cement of the driveway ended and the lawn of the backyard began. They carried the package sideways into the backyard, straining under its weight, and stood it on its end; then they began to unwrap it slowly and its branches opened up and stretched out like a man waking from a long sleep. "This, to me, is the pièce de résistance," the nursery manager said. "It's the compositional anchor to the whole garden."

"Oh, my God, it's huge. Is that the . . . what is it called?"

"It's an ocotillo. I call it 'the burning bush' because it looks like something from the Ten Commandments. It must be a good twenty years old. This one isn't from the nursery, of course, it's a transplant. We rescued it from the Palm Springs area, from Rancho Mirage, to be exact. It was on some land that was being cleared for a subdivision, a stunning stretch of desert. I got five of these from those developer gangsters, and half a dozen amazing willows too, one of which is over in the truck. They didn't just give them to me, of course. They sold them to me. Really nice of them. They destroy a bunch of native habitat for all kinds of desert animals, they're chasing the roadrunners into the hills, literally, but they make a little extra selling off the flora. But I only paid them a fraction of what they were worth. I got them for a song." The nursery manager gave the quick, sly laugh of a woman claiming winnings at a poker table. "Speaking of money," she added with a congenial, gently pleading smile.

"Yes, I have something for you," Maureen said, reaching into her pocket. "You said credit was okay."

"No problem. Let me just phone this in."

As the nursery manager took a few steps toward the edge of the backyard to use her cellular phone, Maureen worried about the stack of bills that little plastic rectangle would have to produce, and swallowed. She wondered, for the first time in ages, whether the charge would clear. When the nursery manager got off the phone, the transaction apparently complete, Maureen felt a bit like a shoplifter. *This ocotillo now belongs to me.* The exotic arms of the "burning bush" rose above her from a rough-hewn planter box, each decorated with black barbs arranged in a swirling, candy-cane pattern; it was a beautiful creation from a land with a harsh but practical aesthetic. *I would like to think of myself as being pretty and barbed like this plant, a survivor of three-digit temperatures, rescued from greed by muscled Mexicans in freshly starched uniforms.* The workers brought in more succulents, including one with cone-shaped bursts of saffron petals, a desert equivalent to Maureen's departed birds-of-paradise, and a tiny shrub with pastel turquoise branches as delicate as coral. A succulent garden played more to the sunlight than her subtropical garden ever could; *la petite* rain forest was dark and colorless by comparison.

The workers brought in bags of sand, walking in a line from the truck to the backyard with the bags slung over their shoulders, like Egyptians toiling in some pharaonic project. They took pocketknives from their belts—each one of them had a tool belt—and soon they were ripping the bags open and spreading orange sand and rocks through the backyard, and for a moment longer the patch of ground looked as bleak and barren as Mars.

At the offices of Elysian Systems, Scott Torres was moving the mouse of his computer in subconscious circles, making the white arrow on his screen flutter until he finally clicked and dispatched four words that bounced at the speed of light from his desk to the company mainframe in the basement, and back up to the programmers' cubicles he could see through the glass and half-open shades of his office. As expected, Charlotte Harris-Hayasaki broke into a smile at the sight of the box that popped up in the lower right-hand corner of her screen, asking, *Wanna have lunch???—Robustus.* "Robustus" and variations thereof (Robustus65, Scotus Robustus) was his screen name on several email and message systems, a Latin nod to his roots in "robust" programming. Charlotte turned away from her screen and looked straight at him through the glass and gave him a groupie-girl smile and a thumbs-up. He discreetly raised his own thumb, then sent her another IM that read, *Meet you outside at 1 p.m.* This would be his third lunch with Charlotte Harris-Hayasaki in the past month, each beginning with a furtive meeting in the parking lot, because even though programmers were the employees least likely to spend time imagining the secret lives of coworkers, they could not fail to notice the evolving "special friendship" between the boss and his female underling. Scott did not find the round, fashion-challenged Charlotte attractive in any sinful way; he was drawn instead to her callow programmer enthusiasm, her youthful appetite for his old dot-com stories. During her interview she had made it known that she was aware of his small contribution to the early history of the dot-com boom: he was mentioned in the short Wikipedia entry on Sasha "the Big Man" Avakian, and in one or two others. In the last few weeks Scott had taken to plugging his name in several search engines, feeling narcissistic as he did so, and had been somewhat dismayed that the Scott

Torres Ford dealership of Salinas, California, generated twenty search hits for every one about Scott Torres the programmer.

Scott had been raised not to worry about leaving a mark on the world. Both his mother and father limited their ambitions to their private universe, to the steaks whose fat sizzled and crackled over charcoal briquettes, a beagle panting on a concrete patio, and the unassailable moral rewards of family safety and health. Escape from work in the strawberry and cabbage fields of California, or from the horizonless hamlets of Maine to the modest affluence of South Whittier, was accomplishment enough. Scott followed this path and was thus content to dedicate himself to solving the mathematical and logical challenges that make computers do magic, and took his greatest pleasures in the wide-eyed astonishment that greeted his creations when they came to life. Back in the day, the Big Man responded to Scott's programming feats with manic bursts of verbal excess that usually began with "This is going to change everything!" Scott's professional success changed his image of himself, as did a mysterious shift in the culture at large, which had caused Scott to lose his geekiness, though now he seemed to be getting it back again.

Two and a half hours after surreptitiously meeting in the parking lot, Scott was sitting opposite Charlotte at the Islands Restaurant in Irvine, working on his second mango margarita and winding up his long story about the development of MindWare's "virtual university" software, having taken special delight in describing the poor skills of the first group of hackers who tried to defeat Scott's security and cheat on a medieval history test. He looked down at his watch and noticed the time. "Holy shit, it's almost four." They rushed back to the office, with Scott registering only briefly the way Charlotte squeezed his hand for two seconds when they said goodbye in the parking lot, Charlotte taking the elevator while Scott took the stairs. *How incredibly lame of me*, Scott thought as he walked into the office. *Like they're not going to notice we were gone for three hours.*

He stayed late at the office for appearance's sake, and it was nearly sunset as he meandered out of the building. By the time he reached home, the long summer dusk was almost over, the last glowing embers of daylight had dropped below the silver blue Pacific, and in the half light he didn't notice the clods of dirt in the driveway, the scrapes in the cement left by the second gardening crew as they rolled in the willow and a bush of desert lavender. When his field of vision passed the sliding glass doors, he failed to focus on the strange silhouettes in the backyard cast by the new flora. The significance of his wife's announcing "Honey, they put in the new garden today" escaped him as he worked to corral his two boys into the bathroom for their nightly shower, and for a half hour of reading in their bedroom. What a relief to have these familial tasks to throw himself into after an agonizingly slow and pointless day at the office. Here, in these neat and orderly rooms with his sons and his daughter, he was king, provider, and executive rolled into one. Not for the first time Scott thought that the private satisfaction of reading to his sons in this bedroom with the Art Deco solar system floating over his head was a very good exchange for the adulation of the past. When he spotted his daughter walking in the hallway in her pajamas, smiling up at him and raising her arms in a wordless request to be lifted, and when she wrapped her small arms around his neck and tucked her head against his cheek, the sensation that Scott the Geek had miraculously found his place in the world only increased. "I can never be mad at you, Samantha, even if you wake up ten times at night." Fatherhood was a medal and a slap every ten minutes: you could be a persecuted pygmy holding back a scream of surrender at one moment, and then an immortal hero and prince the next. Scott forgot about the snide executives and the money evaporating from his bank account, and tucked his children into bed and kissed them good night.

# 9

*Go away, go away.* In his sleep, Scott flailed at the loose pillow tickling his nose, but in his dream he was pushing Charlotte Harris-Hayasaki away. Her hands were cold and sweaty, they were gripping at his cheeks and eyelids, and he was afraid Maureen would see Charlotte holding him and get the wrong idea, and that a horrible argument would ensue. He was sitting at his desk at work, in a cluttered office lined with stacks of boxes, and Charlotte was standing behind him as he tried to type something on his keyboard, and Maureen was in the next room and might walk in any minute. He felt an apocalyptic dread of his wife's power to banish him from family and home, and could hear Maureen breathing in the next room as Charlotte moved her hands down to his chest and began unbuttoning his shirt. He wanted to break Charlotte's grip, but she wouldn't let him go, and finally he turned to grab his young employee by the shoulders and give her a good strong shove, but when he did this he heard a screaming that brought the fuzzy movie running in his head to an abrupt halt and transported him in an instant to his darkened bedroom and the sound of his daughter's voice crying from the baby monitor.

"Wah! Wah! Wah!"

Maureen, a comforter and a pillow thrown over her head, gave a murmur that sounded like the word "yes" but showed no signs of waking up as Scott stood up from the bed and made his way to the nursery. His wife had built up so much sleep debt that she was immune to Samantha's screams, and Scott felt a strange combination of sympathy for her and annoyance at the general situation as he walked through the darkened hallways. When they went to bed there was always the hope that this night would be different from the others over the past fifteen months, that this might be the night when their youngest progeny released her grip on their biological clocks, bringing forth a morning in which the California sunlight returned to its normal soothing hues, losing the stark whiteness that had assaulted their eyes since Samantha's birth. But no, here Scott was again, awake at 2:06 a.m., according to his watch—*I fell asleep with my watch on, Jesus.* He noticed that he was still wearing his button-down shirt from the workday, though he had managed to get his pajama bottoms on. He reached the nursery and found his daughter, as usual, standing up in her crib with her favorite yellow blanket, looking disoriented and confused, her rust-colored locks in a sweaty disorder. *Come to me, my little girl, while I get you your milk. One day soon you'll be a big girl and this torture will stop.*

While Scott tended to their daughter, waiting in the kitchen for the microwave to warm her milk, Maureen slipped in and out of various episodic dreams, and then into the longest one, whose images would linger in her consciousness after she woke up. Mexican day laborers were tramping about her home, eating her food, sitting on the tables, playing with Samantha. A man with stringy and shiny hair that resembled black hay was trying to take apart her coffee table with the point of his machete, using it like a screwdriver. *What are you doing here? Please leave. Please.* Dirt encrusted their faces and their fingernails, and they bumped into one another and into the furniture as they walked about the house. They were leaving small piles of red sand on the living room floor and she pleaded with them again, but they answered her in Spanish, or rather in a jumble of words that resembled Spanish: *la cosa mosa; la llaga es una plaga; waga, waga, waga.* After she woke up, Maureen would think, *I've never dreamed in Spanish before.* The men were filling their mouths with salad greens and big gulps from plastic milk jugs, and she started to look for Scott because maybe he could get them to leave, but she couldn't find him. She walked into the kitchen, where someone had turned on a garden hose that was spraying water into the air, causing her to run back into another room lined with closet doors, which she opened, looking for her husband in between the brooms and boxes until Samantha's cries sounded in her dream and she opened her eyes.

The baby monitor was flashing red lights as it broadcast Samantha's wailing. The clock on her nightstand said 4:29 a.m. and Scott was snoring almost as loud as Samantha was crying. *Thank you, Scott. It would be nice if my husband could get up at one of these middle-of-the-night feedings and tend to the baby and allow me to get a full night's sleep.* When she reached the nursery and saw the empty bottle on the floor she realized that he must have been up earlier. *I slept through the baby crying again.* It was always a somewhat disturbing realization, that you could sleep through the ambulance-siren blasts of a baby girl.

While Maureen carried Samantha and tried to soothe her back to sleep with a lullaby, "turban man" and "binocular lady" were running inside Scott's final dream. He was trying to force his software creations to take a seat in the back of his car, but they were busy running through the fences and climbing the play structure in his backyard, and now Samantha was running after turban man. In his dream Scott began to laugh at their antics, and the laughter shook him out of the dream and into the light of day. "Whoa, that was wild," Scott said out loud, but there was no one to hear him: Maureen was in the shower and the first light of morning was squeezing through the blinds. As he rose to get dressed, something caught his eye, a series of odd shapes squeezing through the narrow spaces between the blinds: a collection of green tubes and triangles, and some sort of brown cloud. What could it be?

He pulled open the blinds to a strange apparition that, for a few moments, seemed to be a continuation of one of the dreams he had been having. The succulent garden, lit from behind by the first rays of morning light, pulsated in turquoise. The ocotillo stood proud just a few yards from his window, the exotic barbs of its branches leaving Scott with a nagging sense of dislocation, as if he were standing in a place that was not his bedroom, looking through the window into a backyard that belonged to someone else. He searched his bedroom for the familiar visual clues that indicated this was indeed the same room he had gone to sleep in—the bed with its wooden frame, the faux-vintage windup clock, which actually ran on batteries—then looked back at the succulent garden again. He gawked at the plants a few seconds longer until the phrase his wife had uttered the night before suddenly popped into his head and put everything into its proper place: yes, she had said something about the garden, hadn't she?

"Hey," he said to Maureen a minute or so later, as she stepped back into the bedroom, dressed and with a towel wrapped around her head. "We've got a new garden."

"Pretty awesome, isn't it?" Maureen said with a muted cheerfulness that masked her anxiety.

"Uh, yeah. But it's huge."

"I think there's twenty or so different species of plants."

"Really?"

"Uh-huh."

"And how did you get all that stuff in here?"

"The landscapers did it."

"Landscapers?"

"From the nursery."

"Didn't that cost a lot of money?"

"Yeah, it cost a bit, but we talked about that," Maureen said, draping the towel over the doorknob, leaving it for Araceli to pick up later.

"We did?"

"Yes."

Maureen casually walked toward the door. "But we won't have to work on it anymore," she said. "In the long run we'll save money . . . I have to check on the baby."

She left Scott alone in the room with this information, and after a few moments he decided to file it away in the archive of unexpected and unexplainable things that happen to a guy when he gets married: like coming home to discover your new wife has tossed out your old clothes; or suffering her jealousy when, after ten years of marriage, the name of an old girlfriend of yours comes up; or her suddenly insisting one day that you no longer eat red meat, and then a week later coming home to find she has prepared you steak fajitas for dinner. *So now we have a desert in our backyard. First she wanted a jungle, now she wants a desert. "In the long run we'll save money," she says. Maybe we should dig*

*up the front lawn and make that like the Mojave too. It must have taken
a helluva lot of work to get that in here. How much could it cost?* He
should probably ask her, but was certain the question would provoke
another argument. And it did look pretty, in a gnarly and harsh sort of
way, once you got used to it.

The boys were in the pool and Maureen sat in a chair playing
lifeguard, while at the same time making sure Samantha didn't stray
into the desert garden. As she rubbed sunscreen on the back of the
baby's neck, she studied the barrel cactus and told herself not to worry
so much about it, even though the ankle-high fence that surrounded
it wasn't a barrier that could keep Samantha away. Already the boys
had tossed a ball into the garden, though they were sufficiently put off
by the menacing barbs of the plants not to wander inside. Overall, she
was pleased with herself for having removed that dying tropical blight
from her home and bringing this property back in concert with the
desert.

"Araceli, we have a new garden," Maureen said with a smile to her
employee. "*¿Te gusta?*"

Araceli placed a large jug of *agua de limón* on the squat folding tray
next to Maureen and used the glass stirring rod to make the cloud of
lemon pulp inside swirl, and then finally looked up at the garden.

Well, there was certainly something exotic about this patch of desert her *jefa* had purchased. Standing this close to it, Araceli got the
sense of being transported to a place of mystery and timelessness even
as the boys screamed from the pool a few yards away, and as Maureen
sat in her folding chair, sunscreen glistening from her bare legs, a floppy
canvas hat protecting her against the sun. But no, Araceli couldn't say
she liked it. There was a certain minimalism to this new garden with its
red volcanic rocks and expanses of scarlet and mustard-colored sand
filling the space between the plants—Araceli's aesthetic, however, had
always leaned toward the ornate and complex. She remembered her startling first impression of the tropical garden on the day she interviewed
for this job at the Torres-Thompson household: she had emerged from
the house on a hot day like this one to encounter a jungle of defiant wet-
ness fighting back against daylight. Later she had studied the garden for

hundreds of hours while working in the kitchen, laundry, and master bedroom, and from the window of her *casita* in the back. She liked the way the leaves of the elephant plant caught the slightest breeze, the way the calla lilies changed their shape from early morning to noon, and the movement of the false stream. This new desert garden was a static construction, while the tropical garden was a work of performance art, with Pepe as its star, stepping inside its verdant stage to send streams of water that cascaded over the tops of the plants, catching the sun's rays and making rainbows.

"Well, what do you think?" Maureen insisted. "You don't like it. I can sense you don't like it."

What could Araceli say? She really didn't possess the words in English to communicate what the tropical garden and this new desert garden made her feel. How did you say in English that something was too still, that you preferred plants that you could feel breathing around you?

"*Me gustaba más como era antes,*" she said in Spanish, and then in English, "I like it before . . . But this is very pretty too, *señora.* Very pretty, *muy bonito.* Very different." Empty words, Araceli thought, but they seemed to be what Maureen wanted to hear.

"Yes, it is very *bonito,* isn't it?" Maureen said with satisfaction. "And *muy diferente* too."

That morning at the headquarters of Elysian Systems, Scott invited his staff out to lunch to celebrate shipping the final version of the CATSS "accountability" program to the government. The corporate guys on the fourth floor had suggested he do these sorts of things, because even a bunch of loner programmers expected the occasional perk. "You take them to a nice place, you blow off half a day of work, and you pick up the tab," said the executive, as Scott tried not to frown at the paperweight on the executive's teak desk awarded for "outstanding leadership" by a lumber trade group in the Pacific Northwest. "Then you expense it. You go back to the office and everyone works just a little harder the next few days."

They gathered in the nearest chain restaurant that served decent mojitos and margaritas and plodded through two hours talking about

sports, video games, celebrities, and other banalities. His programmers were five men and two women, the oldest about five years younger
than him. They had bounced around various software companies in
search of the place that offered the most pay with the least work expected and they all considered the drudgery of programming at Elysian
Systems to be a necessary compromise with their free-spirited, late-hacker
ethos. *That's why I hired them: because I saw a little bit of myself in each
of them. I wanted to surround myself with me.* You could get them going
if you talked about open sourcing, and the fences big companies were
putting around their code. "There's all kinds of languages out there, but
they're not accessible," said Jeremy Zaragoza, who was a thin twenty-
eight-year-old of indeterminate ethnicity. "So your average kid in suburbia can't just open a machine and start playing with the code." Scott
had grown tired of these conversations—he'd been listening to them, in
one form or another, for two decades—and he said nothing, and eventually their talk exhausted itself, until their silent gathering was overwhelmed by the sounds of a lacrosse game on the cable television in the
bar, as the programmers quietly fingered scattered french fries and rattled glasses of iced tea while the play-by-play man screamed, "Spinning!
Shooting! Score!"

"Hey, my nine-year-old said something really funny the other
day," Mary Dickerson said suddenly, startling everyone to attention.
She was a frumpy, raspy-voiced woman and the underling closest in age
to her boss.

"And what was that?" said Scott, who was the only other person at
the table with children.

"Well, I guess he's been listening to me and his dad talk a lot, because he asked me, 'Mommy, which is worse: a fool, or an idiot?'"

"Good question!"

"I've often wondered that myself!"

"So what did you tell him?"

"'Well, Patrick,' I said, 'a fool is someone who is aware that they're
stupid, sort of, and doesn't care. You know, like a court jester. At least
that's how I understand the word "fool." And an idiot is someone with,
how should I say, a medical condition. They just can't help being stupid.
Which one is worse is, I guess, in the eye of the beholder.'"

"Good answer!"

"We aren't allowed to use the word 'stupid' in my household," Scott said, rolling his eyes.

"So what did your little boy say?"

"He said he thought it was worse to be an idiot. And then he went back to playing his Game Boy."

Moments later, the check arrived, setting off a round of programmer stretches, sighs, and yawns. By the time the waitress returned with Scott's credit card in a leather holder, Mary Dickerson was already on her feet and ready to leave.

"I'm sorry, but the system is rejecting this card," the waitress said with a no-nonsense directness that contrasted markedly with her cheeriness when she first took their order more than two hours earlier. She was a tall black woman in her forties, her safari uniform covered midway through her shift with salsa and coffee stains: her suddenly stern demeanor caused the procession of programmers toward the front door to stop.

"What's going on, Scott?" Mary Dickerson said, more as a rebuke than a question.

"Are you sure?" Scott asked the waitress.

"Yes, honey. I am. Shall we try another one?"

Scott opened his wallet, quickly surveyed the various plastic representations of creditworthiness and family photographs contained therein, and concluded that rather than taking a chance on a second card, the best course of action would be to make a run to the nearest automated teller machine. He looked at his now-standing employees, who were all staring at him as one does a second-rate substitute teacher in junior high school, and remembered that there was a dispenser of cash about three or four hundred yards away, at the other end of the asphalt lake upon which this restaurant, an armada of automobiles, and a dozen commercial establishments floated. Scott would hop into his car and drive to the machine and the round trip would take less than two minutes. "I'll be right back," he said to the waitress.

"What?"

"Just gotta get some cash." He could feel the discomfort of his employees' forced gathering propelling them toward the door. "Sit down. Don't leave. Please." Mary Dickerson glared at him with her mouth agape as he rushed out the door.

When he returned, six minutes and forty-five seconds later according to the timer function on his watch, a Mexican busboy was wiping off the empty table, whistling the melody of a reggaeton song, and all of Scott's employees were gone except for Charlotte Harris-Hayasaki, who greeted him by the cash register with a sympathetic grin.

"We all just paid it, split it eight ways," she said. "Everyone really wanted to go. So I paid your share."

*Which am I now?* Scott wondered. *A fool or an idiot?*

Back at the office, it took sixty seconds at his computer terminal for Scott to uncover his wife's latest credit-card betrayal. At the top of his online statement there was a charge from a company called Desert Landscaping for an astonishing four-figure amount, as much as he would have paid Pepe the gardener for two years of work, if not more. The cactus garden, he could now see, was another obnoxious vanity foisted upon him by his wife, equivalent to three months of their inflated, adjustable-rate mortgage payments, which were the chief obstacle to Scott getting their finances back into the black again, along with the several thousand dollars he spent on private school for his two sons every month. In fact, thanks to his spendthrift wife, they were going to have to struggle to round up the cash to pay for the boys' "facilities and activities" fee at the start of the next semester. He squeezed his face in a half wince as he scrolled through the page in search of the interest rate he would pay on said credit card. *Twenty-six-point-four percent, compounded!* There were formulas taught in finance classes that calculated how quickly the "force of interest" could destroy a family with the slow but powerful engine of exponential calculus. Now he scrambled to grab a memo pad, and scratched out a worst-case scenario.

$$x = \$9,250\left(1 + \frac{.264}{12}\right)^{12 \times 3}$$

The result was a five-figure catastrophe: he would be a servant to that borrowed money for the foreseeable future. Its preposterous largeness made him feel bullied and violated, as if his wife had grabbed him by the shirt collar and tossed him into a locked room whose walls were plastered with receipts, bills of sale, service contracts, and warranties, each a mocking reminder of her relentless and happy assault on their disposable income. His three kids were trapped in that room with him too, prisoners to the debt as much as he was. Scott stood up from his chair and grabbed at the air around his temples, and began pacing in his claustrophobic work space, fighting the desire to kick at his chair, or pick up everything on his desk and hurl it against the glass. Finally he flung a pencil at his computer screen with the violent windup of a rioter throwing a rock at a liquor store; the pencil snapped in two but failed to do any damage to the screen itself. "Fuck!" He looked out through the glass and noticed that Jeremy Zaragoza, Mary Dickerson, Charlotte, and all his other employees were staring at him with expressions that combined various degrees of glee, concern, and puzzlement. *Yes, here I am in my cage, the boss who lives at the mercy of his wife's weaknesses and wants.* Soon he would be wandering away from his post as corporate laughing-stock, to spend a day searching for neighborhoods with affordable homes and half-decent public schools.

**W**hen Araceli cooked and cleaned, she daydreamed, and when she daydreamed, her train of thought often ended at the Instituto Nacional de Bellas Artes, just off the Periférico Highway in the western part of Mexico City. She had opened her eyes in the morning remembering Felipe, and how he painted dragons, and thought that at the National School of Fine Arts painting dragons would have invited contempt and ridicule. Only a narrow strip of park, with jacaranda trees and walkways where dogs sniffed and pulled at leashes, separated Araceli's temple of artistic knowledge from the boorish city that surrounded it, buses and microbuses congregating nearby and nudging against one another like cattle in a slaughterhouse pen. At the Instituto Nacional de Bellas Artes all the first-year students were too somber of disposition to paint or draw anything but abstract representations of their inner demons, or starkly detailed studies of the overcrowded, exhausted city. *That was my problem: I was too serious.* If she had contented herself with painting dragons and fairies for her nieces and nephews, Araceli concluded, she wouldn't be the miserable migrant she was now. Those first, few light days of art school she would walk into the main lobby and study the board announcing various exhibitions and gallery openings, watch the students march back and forth in their creative torment across the patios, holding brushes and portfolios, and feel she was standing at the center of the artistic universe—or considerably closer, at least, than she had been at her home in Nezahualcóyotl.

Araceli felt especially attuned to the visual world then, and as she crossed the sooty metropolis her eye was constantly searching for compositions. On the Metro she studied the tangle of wires between the tracks, the contorted faces of passengers squeezing through doors, and the rivers of scampering feet that flowed up and down the wide stairways linking one Metro line to another, and the improvised geometry of the underground passageways that intersected at odd angles. One of her instructors had looked at these first-year sketches and pronounced, "You will make a first-rate cartoonist," and even Araceli knew that was a slight. Then her classmate Rafaela Bolaño told her she too had been declared a "cartoonist," and it became their running joke. "We are starting a new movement, Rafaela, you and I. We are the Visceral Cartoonists!"

In the end Araceli was done in not by the snobby teachers, but by the long journey across the city from home to school and back again, east to west to east, and by the lists of required materials submitted at the beginning of each term. At the art supply store the clerk gave a satirical grin as he laid the required oils on the counter before her, each an import from England: quinacridone red, raw umber, terra rosa, titanium white, 150 pesos a tube. And then the brushes whose supple bristles suggested the hides of large mammals migrating across the Mongolian steppes; the collection of flesh-toned pastels from Germany, the entire human spectrum in a pine box; and finally the textbook tomes with prices as flashy and exorbitant as their glossy pages of illustrations. "They come from Spain, so it's all in euros, which is really bad for us Indians here in Mexico," the clerk said. Beyond the cost of these accoutrements, there was the simple question of having enough money to buy a *torta* for lunch, and the exhaustion that overcame her after the final, hour-long journey home on the Metro and on the bus as it inched forward the last three miles along the main drag of Nezahualcóyotl with its littered sidewalks, the multitudes of factory workers fighting the gridlock on Ignacio Zaragoza Boulevard, pushing against the domestics and the peddlers of pirated CDs. She would rise up before dawn to finish assignments she'd been too tired to complete the night before. "Araceli, why are you killing yourself like this?" her mother said one morning, her words heavy with a sense of futility and absurdity. "*¿Para qué?*" The decision to go to art school was, for her mother, a superfluous act of filial betrayal, because daughters, unlike shiftless boys, were expected to place family first. A wayward daughter counted as much as six wayward sons on the scale of neighborhood shame. When Araceli gave up art school after a year and started working, handing over half of her earnings to pay for her baby brother's future college education, her parents stopped assaulting her with their prolonged silences.

Probably Felipe had an artist's soul and had also been forced to surrender his ambitions. "You look smart, that's why I asked you to dance," he'd said. Felipe, she sensed, had long ago made the accommodation Araceli still struggled to live with; he could make art without feeling the sense of injustice that ate away at Araceli whenever she thought about her mother and the Escuela Nacional de Bellas Artes.

In the late afternoon, when Araceli was finishing cooking dinner and was getting ready to set the table, she noticed that she had absentmindedly arranged Maureen's silver forks, knives, and spoons into patterns on the kitchen counter while polishing them earlier in the day: an asterisk, a series of overlapping triangles, an arrow. Araceli imagined, for a moment, a sculpture that would make an ironic statement about the fine curlicue designs on their handles: she imagined taking a blowtorch and welding forks, knives, and spoons into tangled sculptures of machetes and plows. *That would be fun, but expensive.* She was rubbing a spot on the last spoon that had somehow escaped her cleaning when she heard the front door slam, hard enough to provoke a faint rattle of the dishes in the cupboard. *What was that? One of the boys again?*

After a minute or so Araceli began to hear raised voices, *el señor* and *la señora* yelling at each other. The usual back-and-forth barking and pleading, their voices pushing through the closed door as an irritating and genderless vibration. She considered the basil remedy again, but then thought better of it: their fighting was part of a natural rhythm, a kind of release; they would fight and a day or two later Araceli would see Scott rubbing his wife's back, or Maureen clasping his hand as they watched their children play in the backyard. After observing the Torres-Thompsons for several years she could begin to see their arguments as a kind of marriage fertilizer: they were ugly, one recoiled before their nasty smell, but they appeared to be necessary. She listened as the shouting continued, rising in volume so that she could begin to make out clear phrases: "Because you have to be more responsible!" "Don't humiliate me," and finally a laughing shout of "Pepe? Pepe?" Well, Araceli's curiosity was piqued now, she had to see what was going on, so she opened the door to the living room but pushed it too hard, bringing forth a moment of unintended theatricality in which the yelling instantly stopped and both Scott and Maureen turned to face her, their foreheads and cheeks burning with an identical angry hue. No, Araceli hadn't intended to do that; she wanted to hear more clearly what they were saying, not to stop the fight altogether. One glance at her *jefe* and *jefa* told her that this argument was significantly more serious than any that had come before, that the words passed between them were dangerously close to finding a physical expression in the exercise of limbs and muscles. Scott was standing in the center of the living room with his arms tensed at his sides, and as he turned to look at Araceli she saw a man with an expression she barely recognized: here was a man who felt his power slipping from him, who strained to open his eyes wide to take in the room and the woman before him, as if he had never really seen her before this moment. A few feet away, Maureen sat on the couch, before the coffee table and its plane of blown glass, legs crossed and arms folded, in that tenuous state of mind that exists between being amused and being afraid. Araceli sensed she was trying very hard to convince herself that her husband's yelling was nothing more dangerous than the grumbling of an eight-year-old.

Araceli raised her eyebrows and prepared to turn away, but then something happened that had never happened before: they resumed their argument, without caring that Araceli was still in the room. Scott raised his finger and declared, "Don't you dare, don't you dare say another fucking thing." *I didn't think he could do that. He screams while I watch.* Maureen rose to her feet and began to walk toward Scott, causing Araceli to immediately turn around and close the door with the same speed and sense of repulsion that one uses to change the television channel upon encountering a gory, tasteless scene from a horror movie.

Inside the kitchen Araceli removed her apron: she would leave the dinner ready, in covered bowls on the marble counter, and then leave the kitchen and seek shelter in her room for the time being. When men raised their voices in imitation of carnivorous mammals, smart women made for the exits; that's how it was in her home, in many other homes, in too many homes to count in the stacked cubes of the Nezahualcóyotl neighborhood where women conspired during the day to undo the tangles men made with their words at night. *Sometimes you just have to run away. You have to close the window, close the door, and seal off your ears from the sounds people make when the dogs inside them decide to come out and snarl.* Araceli made a conscious effort not to listen to the back-and-forth coming from behind the pine door, not to hear what words were being said as she finished putting clear plastic wrap over the bowls filled with pasta and fish sticks.

Araceli was reaching for the back door when she heard a half-grunted "Be quiet!" followed by an unmistakably female scream and a high-pitched crash that sounded like fifty porcelain plates striking the floor and shattering all at once. Instinctively she ran back across the kitchen, pushed open the swinging door, and found Maureen on the floor, half sitting and half prone upon the ruins of the coffee table, raising her arms in an attempt to steady herself without getting cut on the pool of shattered glass around her. She looked to Araceli like a woman who had been dropped from an airplane, or who had fallen from a cloud, landing on a spot of the earth she did not recognize, and who was surprised to see she had survived. Scott stood above her, raising his hands to his temples as he looked down at his wife.

"Oh, my God, I didn't mean it, I didn't mean it," he said, and he reached out to help her.

"Get away from me!" Maureen shouted, and he instantly stepped back. "Araceli, help me. Please."

The Mexican woman froze. *What have they done to each other, these people?* Araceli felt the need to restore order and understood that the violence in this room might spin into something unspeakable were it not for her presence. *Today I am the civilized one and they are the savages. They have taken the living room I have worked so hard to give the sparkle of a museum and they have transformed it into a wrestling ring.* Lucha libre. *If I hadn't come in they would be grabbing the chairs from the dining room and throwing them at each other.* Stepping gingerly around the ruins of the table she had cleaned that morning, and too many other mornings to count, with blue ammonia spray, Araceli reached out and took the hand of her *jefa* and helped her to her feet.

BOOK TWO

# Fourth of July

"You know, Bigger, I've long wanted to go
into these houses . . . and just *see* how your
people live."

— Richard Wright, *Native Son*

# 10

Waaaaaaaaaa!

The alarm startled Araceli awake at the lazy hour of 7:30 a.m., the summer sun already blasting through the curtains. On most mornings she would have been long awake, but the memory of the powerful matriarch of the mansion momentarily helpless on the floor had kept her from sleeping well. During the summer the Torres-Thompson household got a later start to the day and Araceli could often spend some time in the morning with the hosts of the Univision morning show as she got dressed, half listening to their interviews with diet experts, the celebrity gossip, the reports on the latest drug murders in Guerrero and Nuevo Laredo, the videos of the dead being pulled from overturned buses, and the like. Now she had witnessed a kind of news event in this home, too close and too raw to be entertainment. The crash and scream had invaded her dreams, causing her to sleep right up to the deadline announced by her digital clock. By now, *el señor* Scott would have made himself some toast and be out the door—on this morning, perhaps more than any other, he would have wanted to avoid contact with his servant. Araceli took her time getting dressed and put on her white *filipina*, dreading the stony mood that awaited as soon as she entered the main home; a day of silences from Maureen, followed by the tense sharing of the domestic space in the evening when Scott returned from work. When a man tosses his wife to the ground, there can be no easy forgiveness.

With some trepidation Araceli opened the door to the kitchen, and then the door from the kitchen to the living room. No one, nothing, all quiet, as orderly as she had left it the night before, when she swept up the glass and steel ruins of the coffee table and collected them in two boxes she placed next to the plastic trash barrels outside. Only the conspicuously empty space in the living room hinted at what had happened the night before. Perhaps she should examine the floor for any traces of glass, lest the baby Samantha pick one up and place it in her mouth. Leaning down, Araceli examined the ocher surface of the Saltillo tile floors and found two slivers, each smaller than a child's fingernail. She held them in her palm to examine them, meditating not so much on the shards as on the unexpected violence that had produced them. *This house will not return to normal so quickly.* Suddenly Araceli the artist, the Araceli who didn't care, longed for the ordinary. She was the strange one, the *mexicana* they couldn't comprehend, but it would fall to her to bring the Torres-Thompson household back to a calm center by restoring the broken routines: the comfort of served breakfasts, lunches, and dinners, the tonic of a sparkling kitchen and smartly made beds at the end of the day. She tossed the shards into the trash and started breakfast, following the rotation *la señora* had established on a refrigerator calendar. Friday: Cream of Wheat.

Brandon wandered into the kitchen first, at 8:36, followed by his brother a few minutes later. They sat at the kitchen table, eating silently, their spoons hitting the bottom of their bowls with a comforting clank-clank, Brandon reading a thick book with a dragon on the cover as he ate. Araceli wondered how much they knew about their parents' altercation the night before. Probably they heard everything, she thought, and this was almost true: they had retreated to the television room and the comfort of cartoon warfare just as the shouting had reached a peak, but before their father had shoved their mother backward into the coffee table. Brandon had guided his softly weeping younger brother away with a "Hey, Keenan, let's go watch a movie," and the crash and their mother's short scream had been lost behind a closed door of soundswallowing Mexican pine, and in the swirling orchestral theme music that accompanied a boy on his animated martial-arts adventures through a world inhabited by dueling tribes of warriors. When Maureen had shown up sometime later to tell them to get ready for bed, they had assumed everything was normal because they were too young to pick up the muted exhaustion in her voice, too unknowing of the cruelties that adults could inflict upon one another to recognize the meaning in the puffy droop in their mother's eyes.

Maureen awoke atop a cushion of comforters on the floor of the nursery, next to her daughter's crib. With its lavender walls, Samantha's incipient doll collection, and the stuffed purple pony in the corner, the nursery was a safe room, its femininity a shield against the masculine harshness outside. He didn't follow her there; he didn't hit her or yell at her with her baby girl by her side. Having failed to injure Maureen with his words, Scott had infected the household with fear and unpredictability and the silencing power of his muscle. He unleashed a monster, to ravage her body and violate unspoken codes, to inflict the injuries his words could not. At first the argument about Maureen's spending on the desert garden had played out as the mirror image of the argument about Scott's neglect of *la petite* rain forest. In this case it was Scott who was the aggrieved party, having been humiliated before his employees, but somehow Maureen had wrested the upper hand, shifting the discussion to Scott's failings as husband and parent, and their roots in his emotional distance. She had taken the argument back to South Whittier, to that sad little two-story home of thin drywall and crabgrass lawns, with the box rooms that had mirrors along the walls to create the illusion of space. It had been her misfortune to visit this property as their courtship reached its climax, to see the Torres family home in all its faded, lower-middle-class glory, and last night she had allowed herself to blurt out certain truths he refused to see, long-held but never-spoken observations that focused on that brittle woman whose admonitions were the font of her husband's ambition and also much of his self-doubt. It occurred to Maureen now, in the morning, that bringing her late mother-in-law to the conversation was not a good idea: the rage she provoked by doing so was entirely predictable, but not what happened next. He had taken two purposeful and irrational steps toward her, and attacked her with the muscles of his forearms and hands, sending her sprawling backward across the room and into the table. There was the moment of stunned helplessness as she lost her balance and the table collapsed and shattered underneath her, followed, seconds later, by a moment of clarity, the sudden understanding of a long-suppressed fear.

*I always expected him to do this.*

Maybe from the first time they dated she sensed that the nervous, faded-cotton exterior of Scott Torres concealed a roiling core. That was the attraction to him in the first place, wasn't it? Before she had seen the home in South Whittier, before she had lived with the man, she saw the anguished exertions of an artist searching for perfection, though he possessed only some of the language and social gifts that oozed from painters, actors, and writers. He suffered to bring his creations into the world, and when they did not come he could turn sullen and angry in a disturbingly adolescent kind of way. His daydreams and his projects were his best friends and companions, and often they caused his face to brighten with a mischievous sparkle. There was something charming, she decided, about a man whose brilliance lay in solving problems that could not be easily explained in words. *I will make you* my *project, Scott Torres.* She had taken this shy man and, like a wizardess, had given him at least some charm, and a surplus of family riches. And now he had rewarded her with the same common violence that sent women to shelters. Hours later she could still feel his assault just below her collarbone, and see the two bruises that seemed to float on the surface of her skin like jellyfish.

Fatherhood did this to men. They weren't prepared for it. After the boys were born there were days when Scott glared at the clutter of baby paraphernalia in their home, the spit-up stains scattered on the rugs and their clothing, with the resentful eyes of a prison convict. *What? Did you expect it to be easy? This sagging you feel around your eyes, the ache in your arms, that is called parenthood, and it is no longer the exclusive province of women.* Then came the scattered moments of aggression when his toddlers committed minor sins, when Brandon was a two-year-old just learning the power of felt-tip pens to deface freshly painted walls, or when Keenan tossed a wineglass on the floor, and

Scott blared a too-loud "No!" When she was halfway into carrying Samantha, he punched the wall, leaving a crater for a week before fixing it, never bothering to explain what had set him off. *It's true what my mother said. You can think you know someone as intimately as they can be known, you can commune happily with their odors and their idiosyncrasies for years, but then they show you something distasteful, something frightening precisely at the moment when you're too far in to get out.* Maureen's father was old Missouri Irish and the hurtful memory of his living room explosions had led her to adopt her mother's maiden name when she was eighteen. Now the neighbors had likely heard Scott too, they knew that his wife and children were inside cowering. They all knew.

Maureen felt the curtains of an ancient, unerasable shame being drawn across the windows of this bright home. *I have to flee. Again.* When she was eleven Maureen walked out and no one heard the slap of the screen door because her older sister and her mother were in full-throated battle with her father. On that day she ran out in her spring sundress and sandals, jumping down the steps, running to the corner, and then walking when she looked over her shoulder and saw no one was following, past other small houses like hers in that Missouri river town, underneath the impossible pinks of the flowering dogwoods, past the lonely Baptist church and the venerable, abandoned gas station and its gravel bays. Past the fields at the edge of town, with pebbles in her sandals, she walked slowly toward the unfettered horizon that loomed over the stubs of early corn, feeling comfort in the promise of other fields fallow and freshly plowed, and then to the hills where tractors cut plow lines that flowed around the undulating contours of the landscape, until she finally stood alone at the entrance to a solitary farm. Two silos stood guard there, each looking like a man with steel-pipe arms and a tin-roof hat, and she thought how much better it would be to have a father who was as tall and stately and silent. She thought these things until tires rolled on the dirt path behind her, and she turned and saw the police car that would take her home.

Now Maureen would leave and stay gone for a few days, and her absence would teach Scott a lesson. She would leave and decide later whether, and under what conditions, she would come back. But how would she cope on the road with three children, driving on the interstate?

How long could she even control her boys in a claustrophobic hotel room? She envisioned herself with her three children at a nearby hotel suite, the boys pushing each other backward into the fold-out couch, the minibar, in subconscious imitation of their father. Did she really want to be around that boy energy, their unpredictable physicality? A woman alone with two boys and a baby girl would not work. Her mother was in St. Louis, and if Scott was right about the credit cards Maureen wouldn't be able to buy plane tickets to get there. Maureen went over her options during a mostly sleepless night and in the last hour before dawn she knew exactly what she would do: she would raid the emergency cash that the ever-cautious Scott kept in a washroom drawer next to the earthquake kit. And then she would leave with Samantha for a few days, allowing Scott to contemplate her absence and take care of the boys. Araceli would be there to keep the household from falling apart and the boys from going hungry. It was what she had always wanted to do anyway, to take off with Samantha for a few days, for a "girls' vacation."

As she carried a half-asleep Samantha through the house and to the car, she thought, *It's going to be another hot day.* For the moment, however, there would be the chill of early morning, and she tossed a blanket over her daughter. She wanted to be out the door before Scott woke up, to avoid any further, unpleasant confrontations and present him with a fait accompli, but when she entered the garage at 7:45 a.m. she discovered his car was already gone; he was off to work about an hour earlier than usual. This did not surprise her, though it did cause her to pause in her escape plan: if she left now, her two boys would be alone in the house, because Araceli was still in the guesthouse, and not yet at work, separated from Brandon and Keenan by two walls and the five paces or so it took to walk to the kitchen's back door. *Damn it!* To leave now would violate a taboo of motherhood: she would have to carry Samantha back into the house and start her escape all over again. *If I go back in, I might not leave at all, I might lose my nerve.* She opened the garage door to confirm his car was also absent from the driveway, then stepped outside into the morning air. Now the light came on in the kitchen, and from the driveway Maureen could see, through the window, the sleepy rebellion on the face of her Mexican employee as she began the breakfast routine. Araceli was in the house, and the sight of her was enough to set Maureen on her journey again, to surrender to the momentum and sense of emancipatory purpose that had brought her to the driveway in the first place. She opened the car door and gave a faint sigh as she freed herself of her sleeping daughter's weight and strapped her into the car seat. She had a vague idea of where she was headed: to that spa in the high desert mountains above Joshua Tree she had read about in the arts section of the newspaper, the one said to be relatively cool even in the heat of summer, the one with the babysitters who took care of your child while they pampered you in steam and lavender.

Maureen was outside the gates of the Estates, turning onto the road that skirted through the meadows, when she realized she had forgotten her cell phone. It was too late to go back home, if she did so she might cancel her expedition altogether, so she directed her car to the first gas station and a public phone and called directory assistance, and reached a half-awake clerk at the spa-hotel and made a reservation. Minutes later, mother and daughter were on the unencumbered early morning highway, heading out of the city, sprinting eastward in the face of an incoming bumper-to-bumper, heading toward the dry foothills at the edge of the metropolis.

Inside the game room, beneath the flat-screen and the game console, Scott Torres awoke on the floor at 5:35 a.m. after a night of surprisingly uninterrupted sleep, six hours in which the memory of what had happened in the living room disappeared in the inky cube of a lightless room and he lived in blissful nothingness. Within three seconds of opening his eyes, the series of events of the night before replayed itself in his memory with the stark simplicity of those PowerPoint presentations the executives concocted on the fourth floor at Elysian Systems. He remembered the staccato dialogue of exchanged insults, each slightly more crude than the next, and then his attempt to get away while Maureen followed him around the room, yelling at the back of his shoulders. *That's what happens when you call a woman that word you should never use: they either sulk away or come at you with newfound ferocity.* She had counterattacked with a spiteful commentary about Scott's being unable to see a horizon beyond "the stupid stucco coffin" in which his mother, separated from his father, had lived her final days alone; it was a remark so stunningly cold that it had caused the argument to stop while Scott took in the realization that he had married a woman who could insult the dead. His thoughts had turned to the many ways he might impose his will with his hands at precisely the moment Maureen took a step toward him to renew the argument: he pushed her away with the full, furious strength a man in his early forties could muster, a half-defensive shove that had sent her sprawling backward into the coffee table.

For an instant before she lost her balance he felt a strange and childlike gratification. *At last!* When she hit the table—such a fragile construction, that piece of Mexican craftwork—and Araceli entered the room, it all disappeared. Now a hollow numbness occupied the space between his eyes. Maureen had violated a trust by spending that money, she had damaged their family, but of course he had lost the moral high ground when he pushed her. Would she ever forgive him for her fall, see the full picture of events, and apologize for what she had done and said? *There is a less than fifty percent probability.* Or would she believe that her fall and the broken table had absolved her of any need to acknowledge how vicious she had been? *The much more likely outcome.* If she'd managed to get a full night's sleep she might feel something other than the outraged sense of victimhood of the night before, when he feared, for a moment, that she would call the police. By the feminist calculus that followed these events, he was an abuser, a male inflictor of bodily harm, and therefore would be permanently expelled from the garden of family love, into the purgatory inhabited by the alcoholics, the goons, and the serial adulterers. Perhaps, after the erasures a few hours of sleep could bring, Maureen would see the crash and fall for what they really were: an accident, an act of mutual stupidity and clumsiness, like a pratfall in a comedy skit. *This is what happens,* he would tell her, *when two middle-aged people push their sleep-deprived bodies to raise small children, a task we should leave for twentysomething decathletes, ballerinas, and other spry and limber people.*

Scott would tell her these things in due time, but after just a few minutes awake, he had decided that for the moment a full retreat was in order, an escape from his wife's sense of entitlement, from her new fascination with rare desert flora, which appeared to have replaced earlier fascinations with rustic Italian furniture and abstract California art. Let her figure it out on her own: or rather, with Araceli, who did the bulk of the work, who kept the house livable and the children fed and gave Maureen time to dream up schemes that would empty their bank accounts—now, as many times before, he thought of Araceli as a kind of subtraction from his wife. In Maine's "Down East," where his mother was from, and in the unknown Mexican places his father had lived, they understood about respect and responsibility. He was still the son of scrappers and survivors.

*I have to get the hell out of here.* It was what he told himself those last days at MindWare, when he longed to work with adults again. Living with Maureen was looking like the final act at his roller-coaster start-up, when the Big Man spent an extravagance on five-star hotels, dinners at restaurants on the Strip, and a thousand dollars in golf lessons in a quixotic campaign to seduce the venture capitalists, raise cash, and fend off the board. At some point you had to say, *Stop, it's over.* Suddenly, those old sayings of his Mexican father didn't sound so silly and quaint: *Live cheap and smell sweet. Never hang your hat where you can't reach it.* After grabbing a few clothes, he was out the door and in his car, gliding down toward the ocean with only the red eye of Scorpio watching him.

Such was the domestic discipline in the home on Paseo Linda Bonita that several hours passed before either Araceli or the two boys noticed that Maureen and Scott were gone. Having been conditioned by a half summer's worth of their mother's anti-television, anti-computer exhortations, Brandon and Keenan began their day with appropriately mind-nurturing and solitary activities. It was a quiet, sisterless morning, and through the open summer windows and the screens the house filled with the squeaky *chee-deep chee-deep* of the tree swallows that were acquainting themselves with the ocotillo in the backyard. Samantha's usual prespeech utterances and screams were not there to ring in the ears of her brothers, though the boys were not yet conscious of her absence. The boys did not know that their sister was already halfway to the Sonoran Desert with their mother just as they were finishing their Cream of Wheat with Araceli. Keenan drifted over to the Room of a

Thousand Wonders and began assembling a three-level spacecraft with Danish plastic mini-bricks, while Brandon climbed onto the couch in the living room and lost himself in the fourth volume of a detective-fantasy thriller for "middle readers" that involved teams of elves capable of time-bending magic. So gripping was the escape of the boy-detective protagonist from yet another band of machine-gun-toting criminals, that Brandon failed to notice that the coffee table was missing.

After the usual and easy post-breakfast cleanup in the kitchen, Araceli wandered about the house picking up dirty laundry, starting with the pajamas in the boys' room, and then moving to the nursery. She was preoccupied, once again, with Felipe, because after putting away the saucepan she had used to prepare the Cream of Wheat, she had a sudden premonition that he would call her today—perhaps it was some sort of psychic displacement produced by having witnessed the fight between Scott and Maureen the night before. In the presence of violent disagreement, a germ of happiness might take root. *Hoy el gordito me va a llamar.* Araceli was daydream-dancing with her "little fat man" when she entered the nursery and noticed the comforter on the floor and quickly surmised that Maureen had slept there. A few minutes later the conclusion was confirmed when Araceli entered the master bedroom and found the bed exactly as she had left it yesterday afternoon. Clearly, *el señor* Scott had not slept here either; he had probably bedded down with the big television set, and indeed, on her final stop on the laundry search Araceli found a sleeping bag and pillow tossed on the floor there. Well, of course they didn't make up before going to bed, that was no surprise. Araceli made her way to the laundry room, got the first load of Maureen's clothes into the washer after checking for and failing to see any blood: *It appears they did not kill themselves.* Finally, she circled back to the kitchen, unsurprised that in her wanderings through the house her path did not cross with that of *la señora* Maureen. It was a big house and on many days Maureen wandered in and out, unannounced, quite often.

At 12:15 p.m. the boys came back to the kitchen table for lunch, and it was only after they had devoured the last of the chicken tenders Araceli had prepared that Keenan, who was always slightly more attuned to any change in his surroundings than his older brother, finally asked Araceli casually, "Where's my mom?"

Araceli turned from the sink, where she had a saucepan soaking in lightly soaped water, and faced Keenan.

"*¿No está en la casa?*"

"No, she's not here."

"That is strange," Araceli said. It occurred to Araceli, for a second, that she should utter something to *disimular*, one of those verbal misdirections that Mexicans are especially good at, a fiction such as, *Oh, now I remember, she went to the market*, that would lift the look of mild concern that had suddenly affixed itself to Keenan's hazel eyes. Instead she said nothing and thought how on any other day Maureen exiting the house unannounced without the two boys for an hour or two or three wouldn't cause her any concern, but after the events of the night before . . . ? Given the swirling cloud of disorder and emotional collapse gathering around this household, anything was possible. One day a crew of men hacking the garden with machetes, the next her *patrones* wrestling in the living room. What next? *Maybe my crazy jefa left the baby with me too and didn't tell me.* In the time it took to scrub the saucepan the idea morphed from preposterous to credible. *The baby is wandering somewhere alone in the house! I have to find the baby!* Araceli bolted from the kitchen, her hands dripping with dishwater, leaving Keenan's unanswered "What's wrong?" in her wake as she moved in big, loping strides to the living room, and to the nursery and through the hallways, into the walk-in closet, calling out, "Samanta! Samanta!" eating the "th" in much the same way the baby herself would in six months' time when she tried, for the first time, to pronounce her own name. Finally, Araceli sprinted out of the house and into the backyard, across the lawn, and toward the cool, still blue plane of the swimming pool. *No, please, no, not here,* aquí *no, in the name of* Nuestra Señora Purísima, *no.* The baby was not in the pool, nor in the desert garden, nor anywhere else within the confines of 107 Paseo Linda Bonita, because Maureen had taken the baby with her, of course. Araceli could see that the baby was with *la señora* Maureen. There was no need to panic.

Back in the living room, Araceli tried to regain her breath and her sense of composure. She stood at the empty section of tiled floor where the coffee table had once stood and tried to sort out what exactly was happening in this household.

•

After the last of the lunch dishes had been put away, at about the time Araceli had removed the ground turkey from the freezer to begin to defrost for dinner, she began contemplating calling Maureen on her cell phone. This presented a small problem of etiquette. For all her feistiness and independence of spirit, Araceli was still a slave to certain customs and habits, and her undeniably inferior social standing prevented Araceli from immediately picking up the phone and demanding of her *jefa: Where are you and when are you coming back?* That wasn't Araceli's place; she had to come up with a pretext for calling, something related to her professional duties, such as they were. The better part of an hour passed, with Araceli distractedly wiping off counters and tabletops and sweeping floors that were already as spotless and shimmering as they were ever going to be, before she thought of something plausible to say: she would simply ask Maureen if the children would eat Spanish rice for dinner. This would be an exceedingly thin and probably somewhat transparent reason for calling, although *la señora* had mentioned before the onset of summer something about forcing the boys to broaden their palates and working a few vegetables into their diet of processed meats and cheeses. Araceli would now suggest that Latin American staple, asking if she should throw in some peas and carrots. She moved to the refrigerator and the list of "emergency phone numbers" located there, a typed list Maureen had prepared on Scott's computer more than a year earlier, in one of her last acts of domesticity before she went into labor with Samantha. The list had been made for Araceli and for Guadalupe, neither of whom found the need to consult it, and it had not been updated since.

*Maureen, cell* was at the top of the list and Araceli quickly punched the numbers into the kitchen phone, anticipating her boss's voice on the other end and the calming effect it would have not just on Araceli, but also on the children once Araceli could provide information about their mother's whereabouts and expected hour of return. It was 2:29 p.m., according to the oven clock, and the boys were now ensconced in front of the television set, aware that they had done so without permission for the simple reason that their mother wasn't around to be asked. Araceli listened with her ear on the receiver and began to worry after the fourth ring, surprised and a bit angry at the sixth and seventh rings. The ringing stopped and the voice mail message began. "Hi, you've reached Maureen Thompson . . ."

Araceli found herself answering, "*Señora*," until she realized it was a recorded voice. She tried again with the same result. *Something strange is going on*, Araceli decided, looking at the clock again. 2:34 p.m. For the first time, Araceli wondered if Maureen would be home by the time *el señor* Scott arrived home from work at 5:45, and Araceli pessimistically concluded that the answer was no. *She leaves me with her two boys all day without telling me. ¡Qué barbaridad!* Up to now, her boss had been the epitome of responsibility and what Mexicans call *empeño*, the putting of effort and thought into one's actions. Maureen was precisely the kind of person hundreds of thousands of Mexicans came to the United States hoping to work for, a smart and civilized employer who never needed to be reminded it was payday, and who with her daily conduct taught you some of the small secrets of North American success, such as the monthly calendar of events posted on the refrigerator and in the boys' bedroom. June 2: *School is out.* June 22: *Keenan's day!* August 17: *Ob-gyn.* August 24: *Brandon's day!* September 5: *School begins!* ☺ Planning, organization, compartmentalization. Respect and awareness for the advance of the clock, the ritual and efficient squeezing of events and chores into each day and hour. These were the hallmarks of daily life with Maureen Thompson.

These thoughts occupied Araceli as she stood in the living room before the picture window, absentmindedly staring at the lawn, which was returning, again, to a state of unevenness and unkemptness, when she heard a faint electronic tone. After much circular wandering through the house, she traced the sound to the backyard and the ocotillo: at the very top of the tallest arm of the desert plant, a mockingbird was imitating the tone emitted by Maureen's cell phone, a series of four marimba notes. A few seconds later Araceli heard the sound repeated, this time clearly coming from the master bedroom, and she rushed back inside. In the half darkness of the late afternoon a light glowed near one of the lamps on the nightstand. Araceli moved to pick up the device, something she never would have imagined herself doing just that morning, because there were certain personal objects in the home she never touched—wallets, jewelry, and loose bills left lying about.

On this day, however, the unexplained absence of her boss caused such objects to begin to lose their radioactivity, and Araceli picked up the phone with the tips of her fingers, like the detectives in those American television dramas, and read the message on the display: 7 MISSED CALLS.

Araceli had left Mexico City just as the cell phone craze had taken off, and had never owned such a device. She did not know that pressing two or three buttons would reveal the identity of the callers, in this case herself (HOME) and SCOTT, who had just phoned five times in the past hour from his office in an attempt to talk to his wife directly.

Scott usually arrived, punctually, at 5:45 p.m., an hour that Araceli knew well because it marked the beginning of the winding-down phase of her workday: *el señor* Scott would come in through the door that led to the garage, and his sons would bother him about playing in the backyard or starting a game of chess, and Samantha might teeter-run to him with her arms raised. This was the signal for Araceli to leave dinner in a handful of covered Pyrex dishes ready to be served, ask Maureen if she needed anything more, and then retire to her room with her own dinner, to return later for the final cleanup. Such were the work routines carved into Araceli's day during four years of service. Rarely were these rhythms broken: the light and weather in the outside world shifted, with dinner served in darkness in the winter, with white sunshine outside in the summer, and once with a rain of ash visible through the windows. Awaiting the arrival of this hour now became Araceli's quiet obsession. She watched the clock on the oven advance past five, and then walked into the living room to check on the Scandinavian timepiece on the dresser to see if it had the same time. The boys were taking care of themselves. After a motherless lunch, they could feel their mother's authority in the home waning further, and they had switched on their handheld video games.

Her putative hour of emancipation came and went without Scott coming through the door. The pasta and *albóndigas* were ready. She'd finished her work for the day. *Where is this man?* At 6:45 p.m. Araceli impulsively walked out the front door, down the path that led through the lawn, to the sidewalk of Paseo Linda Bonita and its silent and peopleless cul-de-sac. She stood with her arms folded and looked down the street, hoping to see *el señor* Scott's car coming around the corner, but the vista never changed from the blank-page sweep of wide roadway. *He's not coming home either.* No lo puedo creer. *They've abandoned me.* The sun was just beginning its rush toward the daily ocean splashdown and Brandon and Keenan were in the house without a parent in sight. She could hear the air-conditioning turn off suddenly in the home next door, and then in another, leaving a disconcerting silence that soon took on an idiotic, satirical quality, as if she were standing not in a real neighborhood, but rather on a stage set crafted to represent vacant American suburbia. *Why is it that you almost never see anyone out here? What goes on in these luxurious boxes that keeps people inside?* There was no human witness on Paseo Linda Bonita to see Araceli in her moment of distress, no nosy neighbor to take note of the anomaly of a servant in her *filipina* waiting impatiently for her bosses to arrive, gritting her teeth at the darkening street. Araceli began to contemplate various scenarios that might explain this new and strangest turn of events. Perhaps the violent encounter in the living room had been followed by others, with Maureen finally deciding to leave her husband for good. Or maybe she was in the hospital, while Scott had taken flight lest he be arrested. Or he might have killed her and buried her in the backyard. One saw these news reports about American couples bringing the narrative of their relationships to a demented end with kitchen knives and shovels: Araceli had expanded her knowledge of U.S. geography from the maps in Univision stories that showed the places where North American men murdered their pregnant wives and fiancées, places with names like Nebraska, Utah, and New Hampshire.

Araceli would like to leave too, but she could not, thanks to the chain that ran back to the house and those two boys anchoring her to this piece of California real estate. She could not run away, or stray too far, because there were children in the home and to leave them alone would be an abdication of responsibility, even if they had been left in Araceli's care against her will. *¿Qué diría mi querida madre?* Subconsciously, Araceli began to pace the sidewalk, reaching the boundaries of the next property and turning back, because anything might happen to those boys, unsupervised: they might even start a fire. She could not therefore simply continue walking down the hill, and this realization caused her to stamp her foot into the concrete like a child forced back inside for supper.

Araceli was still outside, about twenty-five yards beyond the closed front door, when the phone rang inside the Torres-Thompson home. She did not hear it. Anticipating that the person calling was his mother, Keenan interrupted his game play at the second ring and ran from the living room to the kitchen, stood on his tiptoes, and grabbed the dangling cord of the receiver from its perch five feet off the ground on the kitchen wall on the fourth ring.

"Hello? Mommy?"

"Hi, sweetie."

"Mommy, where are you?"

"I'm just taking a little break."

"A break?"

"Yes, honey. A little vacation."

"Why?"

"Because I'm angry with your father."

"Oh."

The pause that followed lasted long enough for even young Keenan to feel the need to fill it, though he couldn't think of anything to say.

"Mommy loves you," Maureen said finally. She was in a hotel room with musty old Navajo rugs and sage burning on an incense tray, watching her baby girl devour a banana. The squeaky tones of her younger son's voice evoked images of domestic routine: *Araceli must have the situation in hand*, Maureen thought; *she is helping Scott*, and Maureen felt her concerns about the boys and home she had left behind lift quickly. "Mommy's just a little angry with your father."

"When are you coming back?"

"Soon, honey. Soon."

These words comforted Keenan sufficiently that he started thinking about getting back to his game. It had been ages since he'd played it as long as he had today.

"What have you been doing today?"

"We're playing on our Game Boys," he said. "I got to the top of Cookie Mountain. Brandon showed me how to do it. It was really cool."

Maureen winced. *Scott gets home and the first thing he does is let them play those mindless games.*

"Did you eat?"

Keenan looked across the kitchen and noticed the dishes Araceli had left on the counter. "We're having spaghetti and meatballs," he said. Maureen heard the "we" and assumed it included Scott. Satisfied that her boys were being taken care of by Araceli, and that Scott was hovering nearby, she said goodbye to her son and hung up the phone quickly, the better to avoid any awkward conversations with her husband.

Years of being married and raising children had brought Scott's and Maureen's parental clocks into sync. Thus, a minute or so after Keenan had replaced the phone in its cradle, the phone rang again. Keenan had returned to the living room and turned his Game Boy back on, and now he circled back to the kitchen, picking up the phone on the eighth ring.

"Hello?"

"Hi! Keenan?"

"Dad?"

"Yeah, it's me."

"Where are *you*?" Keenan said. Scott was sufficiently distracted by his surroundings and the circumstances under which he was making the call—he was standing in the patch of grass by the street outside Charlotte Harris-Hayasaki's apartment building—that he failed to notice the subtle verbal clue that perhaps not everything was right in his home.

"I'm taking a little break from being home."

"A vacation?" Keenan asked.

"Yeah, like a vacation."

Keenan was less interested in this conversation than the one he had just had with his mother. Hearing their two voices within minutes of each other had returned to him a sense of normality, and he wanted to get back to his game, and also start eating the spaghetti and meatballs on the counter.

"How's Mommy doing?"

"She says she's really angry at you."

His wife had spent the day filling his sons' ears with soliloquies about what a horrible man he was, the completely predictable sequel to the pratfalls and crashes of the night before.

"I know she's angry at me," Scott said, the words coming out with a sad sense of finality. In an instant, his mood changed. *How dare she try to turn the children against me.* "I'm angry at her too," he said. He imagined his wife hovering nearby, and that she might take the phone away from Keenan and start to harass him about where he was, so he said his goodbyes quickly, telling his son to listen to what his mother told him to do.

"Okay, Dad," Keenan said, even though his mother wasn't there, because like his father, he was in a hurry to get off the phone too.

## 11

"I'm scared. Araceli, can you sleep with us?"

Keenan asked this with the comforter pulled up to his chin, in bed after forty-five minutes of crying and confusion Araceli would not soon forget. It seemed to Araceli that getting the boys into their room with their teeth brushed and under the covers, in her best approximation of what their mother would have done, was a Herculean task in itself, and that asking her to throw herself on the floor next to them was asking one thing too many. She needed a moment alone, to step back and think what to do next. The boys had begun to panic an hour or so after dusk, when the windows turned into black planes broadcasting images of parentless rooms. "Where's Mommy?" "Where's Dad?" They had peppered her with these questions and had grown increasingly insistent on receiving some answer other than "I don't know," "Soon," or the Spanish "*Ya mero.*" Araceli told them they had to go to bed, and this had set off a round of silent tears from Brandon, and a strange, high-pitched grunt-growl from Keenan. They were going to bed with neither their mother nor their father in the home, with only the surly Mexican maid in the house, and suddenly they felt as lost as two boys separated from their parents on a busy city street. Brushing their teeth and changing into pajamas had calmed them to the point that they could wipe the tears from their faces; the nightly routines their mother had inculcated in them became, for a moment, a soothing substitute for her presence.

"Will you sleep with us, please?" Keenan repeated.

Araceli desperately wanted to return to her room, but of course that wasn't possible: if she retired to her *casita* in the back she would be leaving the children alone in the house.

*You shouldn't just give in to children. You shouldn't just give them anything they ask for.*

In Araceli's family home in Nezahualcóyotl children were obedient, quiet, and nondemanding: girls, especially, were expected to occupy quiet, scrubbed spaces that adults were free to ignore. Her own childhood equivalent to the bedtime routine in the Room of a Thousand Wonders took place in the spare room of tile floors she shared with her sister, floors both sisters had been required to mop from the age of ten onward. At bedtime the only good night was a quick look-in from their mother, a check of their obedience. They feared their mother's disapproval and the idea that they might delay her from that final reward of her workday: the climb to the roof, where pennants of denim and polyester caught the breeze and, in their cool evening stiffness, announced, *En esta casa, yo mando*: In this house, I am love, a river of order and sustenance that flows steady in all seasons.

"I won't sleep here next to you, no," Araceli said. "But I will sleep close. Over here, in the hallway. Okay?"

"In the hallway?"

"Yes. *Aquí*."

She opened the door to their room and in a few moments she had taken two comforters from one of Maureen's closets and tossed them on the floor, along with a pillow.

*"Aquí voy a dormir. Aquí voy a estar."*

"Okay."

Araceli, for the first time in her life, bedded down in her *filipina*.


Araceli awoke before dawn with the children asleep, the chorus of morning birds yet to begin outside the windows, and walked through the empty house as if in a trance. There seemed to Araceli a slight chance that either Scott or Maureen had returned during the night, but each flick of a light switch revealed only a stark tableau of dust-free furniture: the comforter was still taut on the bed in the master bedroom, there were no blankets on the floor to indicate anyone had slept in Scott's game and television room, and the kitchen showed no signs of anyone having been there since Araceli gave the last wipe to the counters as the boys prepared for bed the night before. She circled back to the master bathroom, the space Araceli most strongly associated with Maureen's physical presence, and surveyed the objects as if one of them might tell her when *la señora* would return. *¿Dónde estás, mi jefa?* A paddle brush resting in a wicker basket on the marble slab of the sink drew Araceli's eye. This inelegant piece of black plastic did the daily hard work of Maureen's morning and bedtime grooming, and a thick weave of Maureen's russet hair had built up between the nylon bristles, and for an instant Araceli imagined the strands rising from the brush and taking form, and then Maureen herself emerging magically underneath, calming her children with her motherly exhortations.

*There's nothing I can do but wait.* It occurred to Araceli, momentarily, that she had been spoiled by life with these people, that she had been conditioned to a crisis-free life, above all by Maureen's relentless attention to daily routines, and the comfort of schedules assiduously kept. Over the last four years the two women had built many wordless understandings between them, so that, among other things, towels and dirty clothes circulated through the house as efficiently as the traffic on the empty streets of the Laguna Rancho Estates, from wet bodies to hampers to washing machines to shelves, touching the hands of both women in their circuit. Disposable diapers moved from plastic packages on store shelves to babies' bottoms to special trash cans with deodorizers, and finally to the master trash cans in the back of the house, only briefly tainting the aroma of a country retreat that emanated from the pine and oak furniture, and from a handful of strategically placed bowls of potpourri and lavender.

Maureen was the center of gravity of this home, and with each hour her unexplained absence became harder to fathom. *Why would she leave, where is she?* If there were an explanation it might be easier to cope, and Araceli decided that she would call Scott and demand one: *What did you do to* la señora? *Did you hurt her?*

It was 8:30 a.m. and the boys were still asleep when Araceli marched to the refrigerator and called the second number on the list: *Scott, cell*. In four years of working for the Torres-Thompson family, Araceli had not once called Scott. This morning she would call him and simply demand to know why she had been left alone with two boys when since the beginning it had been made clear she was not to be a babysitter. After a night of being forced to be a mother and father to two boys, after sleeping on the floor in her clothes, Araceli was beyond politeness or deference. *¿Dónde estás?* she would ask, in the familiar *"tú"* instead of the formal *"usted,"* in violation of ingrained Mexican class conventions, as if she were the boss and he were the employee, though of course the monolingual Scott would never pick up on her sassiness.

The phone rang once and moved to voice mail. She called again, with the same response.

Scott's phone was in Charlotte Harris-Hayasaki's apartment, which was on the second floor and inside one of those signal shadows that bedevil cell-phone engineers. He was sleeping, after staying up late into the night telling Charlotte about his fight with Maureen, and then falling asleep on her couch. By the time he awoke, just before noon, his phone would be dead because in the harried flight from his home he had neglected to pack the charger.

Araceli called a half dozen times in succession, the final attempt coming as Keenan came into the kitchen and demanded, "I'm hungry! I want something to eat!"

The sight of his thin eyebrows squeezed in irritation and the corners of his mouth drooping plaintively set Araceli off. A missing mother, a missing father, children expecting to be fed: it was all too much. *The pots and pans, the salads and the sauces—that is my work. I am the woman who cleans. I am not the mother.*

"I am not your mother!" Araceli shouted, and realized instantly her mistake, because Keenan turned and ran away, screaming, "Mommy! Mommy! Mommy!" His shouts filled the living room and became fainter as he ran deeper into the house. Araceli chased after him, cursing herself and the situation and calling out "Keenan, Keenan" until she found him sitting with his arms wrapped around his knees on the floor of the bathroom, the one he shared with Brandon, with shower curtains depicting a coral reef teeming with tropical fish, and decorative rubber jellyfish affixed to the mirror, a tile-lined annex to the Room of a Thousand Wonders. Tears and mucus cascaded over his cheeks and lips and into his mouth. A very faint, motherly impulse to reach down and wipe his tears and clean his nose gathered in Araceli's chest, but she resisted it. Instead, she picked up a bar of amber-colored soap and said, "Keenan, *mira*."

She held the soap delicately between thumb and forefinger and drew lines on the mirror, making quick, sweeping movements to capture and hold his attention, like those clowns in Chapultepec Park who squeezed and stretched balloons into dogs and swords. In less than a minute she had produced a creature on the glass. It floated in the multidimensional space between Keenan and his reflection, ghostly and amber, and he stopped crying the moment he realized what it was.

"A dragon," he said.

"Yes. A dragon," Araceli said, her mouth bursting open into a rare display of happy teeth. "For you, Keenan."

The boy wiped the tears from his face and considered the fanciful animal, which had been rendered in half flight, seemingly ready to pounce.

"That's really tight," he said.

"I'm going to make you pancakes," Araceli said. "Pancakes with bananas. You like that, no? Nice?"

He nodded. After she had coaxed the boy back to the kitchen and served him chocolate milk, after she had prepared the banana pancakes and served them with generous portions of Grade AA authentic Canadian maple syrup, and after the boys had left the kitchen for the entertainments of Saturday morning television, Araceli was once again alone with the telephone list on the refrigerator.

Below Scott's cell phone on the list of emergency numbers there was *Scott, office*, which she called even though it was Saturday. "We are currently closed. Our office hours are . . ." Next was *Mother*, meaning Maureen's mother, a woman with cascading ash-colored hair who had visited this home three times since Araceli began working here, most recently in the days after Samantha was born. She was a reserved woman whose main form of communication was the lingering, considered stare, and she had rarely spoken more than a few curt words at a time to Araceli. There had been one unguarded moment, though, during the older woman's first visit to this house, when she had encountered Araceli in the kitchen and said, "You're lucky to have this job. You know that, right?" The house on Paseo Linda Bonita was a freshly minted masterpiece then, the virgin furniture was free of child-inflicted scratches, the walls were freshly painted, and *la petite* rain forest still resembled a small, transplanted corner of Brazil. "Working with my daughter and grandchildren, in this amazing house. I hope you appreciate it." The words contained an odd patina of regret and envy: as absurd as it sounded, Maureen's mother resented Araceli for working in this home in daily proximity to her daughter, for the perceived intimacy of their relationship. *I could cook and clean too*, the old woman was saying without saying it, *as good as, if not better than, you, Mexican woman. I could live in the small house in the back and see my grandchildren every day, but of course my daughter won't have me.*

For Araceli to call this *gringa acomplejada* and ask to be rescued was a measure of the desperation of the moment.

Araceli punched in the number. "The area code for this number has changed," said a recorded voice. *¿Cómo?* She tried the number again and heard the same message, then tried it again with the new area code but this time heard three loud tones, ascending in frequency, followed by the message "The number you have reached has been disconnected or is no longer in use . . ."

*¡Caramba!*

Next on this list was *Goldman-Arbegasts*, the family that was the Torres-Thompsons' best friends, although they had missed, for some reason, the most recent birthday party. Yes, these Goldman-Arbegasts were responsible people, the mother was a somewhat taller and more even-tempered version of Maureen, another matriarch of schedules and smartly dressed children.

"Hi, you've reached the Goldman-Arbegast residence," said a woman's voice. "We're not here right now because we're in Italy."

"No, we're in Greece!" said a boy's voice.

"No, we're in Paris!" interrupted the voice of a man.

"No, we're in London!" said a second boy's voice.

And then in chorus all four voices said, "We're in Europe! On our dream vacation!"

Araceli put the phone back in its wall cradle and looked at the remaining two numbers on the list: they were both for the doctors who had treated Maureen during her pregnancy and delivery, and thus useless for the crisis Araceli now faced.

Who could she call now? No one immediately came to mind. She did not know the neighbors, not their names or anything about their relative trustworthiness, and it would be dangerous, she sensed, to share the secret of their isolation with strangers. She had no phone numbers for any uncles or aunts that might exist in the Torres-Thompson universe: Scott was an only child and Maureen had a sister that Araceli had never met. As the hours passed and Scott and Maureen did not return, the strangeness of her predicament only grew. Araceli sensed, for the first time, a larger malaise, the consequences of one or more hidden family traumas at work, as in the convoluted narratives of a *telenovela*. The woman whose hair filled the brush, whose voice kept the boys bright-eyed, eager, and well behaved, could not and should not have abandoned them. Araceli expected to hear the long-gaited slapping of Maureen's sandals on the Saltillo tiles at any moment, but until then there was no place she could walk to where Brandon and Keenan might be welcomed as relatives or friends. Nor was the phone ringing with calls from the outside world, with compadres and acquaintances calling in to chat: in fact, the phone didn't ring very often at all. It seemed impossible to Araceli that a family and a home could become something akin to an island surrounded by vast stretches of salt water, and that its young inhabitants and their innocent housekeeper might become castaways. The peninsulas that linked this island to a continent of annoying relatives and nosy neighbors had been quickly and definitively washed away. Araceli realized now that the daily solitude she felt in this home, the oppression of the droning appliances and the peopleless views from the picture window, was not hers alone. This American family whose home she inhabited had come to this hill above the ocean to live apart from the world. *They are runaways, like me.* It was an obvious truth, but one Araceli had never fully pondered before. Among Mexicans the peculiar coldness of the *norteamericanos* was legendary because it came to infect the many *paisanos* who lived among them. One heard how individualism and the cult of work swallowed up the hours of the American day, their sunsets and their springtimes, causing their family gatherings, their friendships, and their old people to disappear. But it was quite another thing to be thrust directly into an American family's lonely drama, to find your *mexicana* self a player in their game of secrets and silences, their separation from one another by long stretches of freeway, by time zones and airline hubs and long-distance phone rates. And what about the absent family patriarchs? Not once had she heard Maureen speak of her father, there were no pictures of the man anywhere. Was he dead too, like Scott's mother? And if so, why was he not mourned with photographs? Or was he simply banished from the home like the boys' Mexican grandfather? It seemed to Araceli that *el viejo* Torres should have his number on the refrigerator. Why wasn't it there?

Maureen's room at the High Desert Radiance Spa was a two-room suite in which both rooms opened to a strand of Joshua trees, their twisted limbs arranged on a gently sloping hillside in the poses of a modern dance troupe. Just after sunrise, she stepped outside and sat in a plastic chair on the small cement patio, while Samantha slept inside the room, curled up under her favorite blanket in a fold-up crib that housekeeping put away every afternoon. The evening chill would be baked away soon, but for the moment wisps of freezer air whispered to the Joshua trees and nudged the tumbleweeds forward. Yesterday morning she and Samantha had walked the spa's hiking trail ("difficulty: low"), following it to the opening of a scrub canyon, where Samantha climbed up a small sandstone rock shaped like the belly of a very pregnant woman. *Oh, to have brought a camera to capture my little mountaineer!* The hours here passed with few thoughts of shouting men or broken tables. A mother and daughter on their own had a mellow symmetry, and since arriving at this oasis Samantha had not had a single tantrum: obviously this girl needed more time alone with her mother; she relished not having to compete for attention with two older boys. Maureen herself felt replenished. There was an essence of herself that she had neglected, a part of her soul that was attached to this dry, austere, and harsh place. A California equivalent to the Missouri grasslands, to the places where her homesteader ancestors stood on the blank slate of the land. *I am a woman of open spaces.* The only male presence in her get-away was the kneading hands of a man named Philip, who applied oils scented with sage and chamomile to her skin, and who left only the few, forbidden centers of her body untouched. *Now I know all the things I haven't allowed myself to feel for years.*

The plan had been to return home Monday morning, to face Scott again and perhaps to forgive him. Perhaps. But then the good people at the front desk had mentioned their Monday discount. She would have just enough of the emergency cash left to stay one more night and take one more session on that table.

$O$n Saturday night, Araceli put the boys to bed with none of the drama and screaming of the night before. They had spent the after-noon in various illicit pursuits, chief among them an hour-long gun battle with plastic pistols that fired foam bullets, the boys laughing as the projectiles bounced harmlessly off the furniture and their bodies. Araceli had forced the boys to clean up the house, and they had simply acquiesced when she declared, "*Ya es tarde,* time for sleep." Once they were in bed, she pulled back the blankets to cover them, in imitation of the mothers she had seen in movies, because she couldn't remember her own mother doing such a thing. These boys seemed to appreciate and need the gesture, and Araceli even touched Brandon on the fore-head when she noticed the tears welling in his eyes.

"Do you think Mom and Dad will ever come back, Araceli?" he asked.

"*No te preocupes.* Your mommy will be back soon. And Araceli is taking care of you now." Araceli spoke these words more soothingly than any she had ever addressed to these boys, or to any other children, and she felt a sudden and unexpected welling of altruism coursing through her veins, a drug that straightened your back and made you feel taller. *What else can you tell two lost boys but that you will take care of them?* "Araceli will take care of you," she repeated. "I will sleep here, on the floor, again. *¿Está bien?* A little later. After I wash the dishes."

$A$raceli pulled herself from the hallway floor just outside the door of the Room of a Thousand Wonders the next morning with the boys still sleeping. They were sweating inside their brightly colored pajamas, shirts and pants with superheroes imprinted on them, men of rippling muscles in various flying poses whose courage offered protection against such evil threats as temporary parental abandonment. Their wet hair was matted against their foreheads, strands clinging to beads of perspiration. Keenan was curled up in a fetal position, clutching a pillow and a stuffed lion between his arms. *If I am still taking care of them tonight, I will tell them to go to bed in shorts.*

She wandered through the house again, quickly peeking into the garage to see if Maureen's or Scott's car was there, and then to the living room and the gallery of faces inside teak and cherrywood on the bookshelves. These pictures, Araceli realized, were the only clues that could untangle this family mess. The portraits of the grandfather, *el viejo* Torres, called out to her most loudly, smiling wryly from the final decades of black-and-white photography, a teenager standing before a Los Angeles bungalow, his swarthy skin rendered in tones of gray and darker gray, hands on his hips and an irresistible twinkle in his eye. This relic had been here since Araceli had started working for the Torres-Thompsons, when the old man was still coming to the house regularly, before he uttered the words that caused his banishment. *What did you say,* viejo? *And where might I find you?* Araceli remembered the looks of exasperation on the faces of Maureen and Scott when they discussed *el viejo* Torres in the kitchen one Saturday afternoon, and snippets of conversation: "What a jerk." "What a dinosaur."

Probably Maureen had not yet gotten around to removing *el dinosaurio* from this family gallery because he was on the bottom shelf, in a lesser spot in relation to the recent school pictures of the boys with eager smiles and moussed hair, and of Maureen herself holding the newborn and slippery Samantha while sitting up with exhausted ecstasy on a hospital bed. Maureen in the delivery room was on the shelf next to a recent shot of Samantha with a red bow in her thin hair and to the bronze-toned image of a woman with pinned-up hair and a giant curtain of a dress staring back from the Victorian era, the folds in the corners of her eyes suggesting she was Maureen's grandmother or great-grandmother. Next there was a recent shot of Maureen's mother, taken in a pine forest, a gray-haired woman in khaki shorts and hiking books, with a faint and uncharacteristic smile. *This is the woman's shelf: there are four generations of girls from Maureen's family here.* Araceli considered too, on the second shelf from the top, the wedding pictures of Scott and Maureen, including a shot of the couple laughing and bending their bodies in an expression of the kind of uncontainable hilarity that hadn't been seen in the Torres-Thompson household for quite some time.

Of all these people, Araceli concluded, old man Torres was the only adult still alive and likely to live in a place reachable from Paseo Linda Bonita. They hadn't yet purged the old man from the family, not completely—he was a resilient *mexicano*, apparently. *If their parents don't come back, I'll take them to this old man's house.* Araceli would have to prepare herself for the worst contingency. She had been used to thinking this way once, her naturally pessimistic outlook had served her well in her single-woman bus journey to the border, and then through the sprint, hike, and crawl into California, and in the first few harrowing and lonely weeks in the United States. Those were days of important lessons, though the subsequent four years in this household on Paseo Linda Bonita had led her to the false belief that the world might still have sanctuaries where prosperity and predictability reigned. Standing here now in front of pictures of the absent and departed members of the Torres and Thompson clans, she realized she might soon have to start thinking like an immigrant, like a desperate woman on the highway uncertain where the asphalt and the invisible trails of carbon monoxide might take her.

Scott awoke on Charlotte Harris-Hayasaki's couch, following a forty-eight-hour bacchanalia of popcorn, nachos, pizza, diet soft drinks, and power beverages consumed in front of Charlotte's flat-screen TV and game console, fighting Persian armies and completing post routes to sinewy wide receivers. Charlotte listened to his complaints about his wife, she fed him munchies he consumed compulsively and without joy, and she nestled into a spot on her vinyl couch next to him, her leg and sometimes her shoulder touching his. She tried rubbing his neck: "You have to watch out for the carpal tunnel with these game controllers." But she wasn't able to stir those passions that begin below a man's waist and reach, through circuits of nerve and muscle and irrationality, to moist lips and tongue. Instead, she had set free an inner boy.

To steal a few minutes of play here and there was one thing, Scott thought: to fully indulge your inner gamer was another. These games were meant to be played by the hour, the better to appreciate their narrative mazes, the overwrought art of their virtual stages. Now, in his second morning here, Scott continued his playing tour of Charlotte's impressive and diverse collection, chipping onto the green at Pebble Beach to the sound of the roaring surf nearby, negotiating with Don Corleone in his study, forging blades of steel in a medieval foundry, and carrying his new weapons into battle against hordes of bearded Vikings on a Scandinavian beach.

"They'll probably put them in the Foster Care. Until they can find their parents. What else are they going to do?" That was Marisela's considered opinion, rendered by phone, and it matched Araceli's own assessment of what would happen if she called the police. "And of course they'll start asking you questions. The police have to ask you questions."

"That's not good."

"No, not for you."

"And the boys?" Araceli asked.

"They'll probably put them in the police car, take them to the station, and then to Foster Care."

"What else could they do?"

Children who spent their nights under blankets decorated with moons and stars in the Room of a Thousand Wonders should not have to spend a single night in the Foster Care. Araceli imagined communal sleeping arrangements, bullying twelve-year-old proto-psychopaths, and cold macaroni and cheese without salt. Children raised in the recirculated air and steady temperatures of the Paseo Linda Bonita would not last long in the drafty warehouses of Foster Care. She imagined the boys cuddling under unlaundered blankets, and suffering the cruel admonitions of caretakers who did not realize how special and smart they were, how they read books about history, how they had learned to identify Orion and Gemini, quartzite and silica, from the library in the Room of a Thousand Wonders. Children with the sensitive intelligence of these boys—qualities their mother did not sufficiently appreciate, because she saw only their boisterous and disorderly masculinity—should not and could not be exposed to the caprices of Foster Care.

Araceli did not want to be responsible for that loss of innocence. There was a finite amount of innocence in the world and it should be preserved: like Arctic wilderness and elephant tusks, it was a precious creation of nature. And what would the police say or do to her? Probably they would report her to the immigration agents in the blue Windbreakers, the ICE people—it was difficult to imagine that a Mexican woman without a green card could call the police and present them with two unaccompanied and guardianless American children without herself being drawn into a web that would eventually lead to her deportation.

Perhaps she was getting ahead of herself. If by Monday morning neither Scott nor Maureen had returned, she would call Scott's office and demand that her boss return home immediately.

Araceli was in a deep sleep on the floor in the Room of a Thousand Wonders, dreaming that she was walking through the corridors of her art school in Mexico City, which did not resemble her art school at all, but rather a factory in a desolate corner of an American city, when she was awakened by a series of screams.

"Mommy! Mommy! Mommy!"

She sat up, startled, and in the yellow glow of the night-light saw Keenan yelling at the wall next to his bed.

"Keenan, *qué te pasa?*"

"Mommy!"

"Keenan. *¡Despiértate!* You're having a night mirror!"

"Mommy!"

"It's just a night mirror!" Araceli insisted, and with that Keenan stopped, turned, and searched for his Mexican caretaker. To his young eyes his room had become a small submarine in a deep ocean of darkness, a bubble of light and security in a frightening world without his mother and father. The captain of this craft was the Mexican woman with the wide face now looking up at him from the door to the hallway with startled and irritated eyes.

"What?" Keenan asked in a high, perplexed voice suddenly stripped of his fear.

"You said he's having a what?" Brandon said from the perch of his bunk above Keenan.

"A night mirror."

"What?"

"A night mirror," Araceli repeated. "You know, when you see ugly things when you're sleeping."

After a pause to digest her faulty pronunciation, Brandon said in a scholarly voice, "No, in English we say *nightmare.*"

"*Pues, una pesadilla entonces,*" Araceli said angrily. "Nightmare," like many other expressions with Old English origins, was a word she would never be able to wrap her tongue around, especially since it bore no resemblance to the Spanish equivalent.

"Yeah, a *pesadilla* is what you say in Spanish," Brandon said diplomatically. With that he and his brother put their heads back on their pillows, and both boys thought that "night mirror" was in many ways a more apt description than "nightmare": Keenan looked at the wall and thought of it as a reflection of his motherless room and a window into a parallel world, and within a few minutes he was asleep again, as was his brother.

Araceli listened to their boy-sized puffs become rhythmic, the quiet song of children at rest. *This is the third night I am spending alone with these boys. I should be the one crying out in my sleep. I should be the one screaming for my mother.* ¡Mamá, ayúdame!

Unable to fall back asleep, she decided to get up and make herself tea. She took her steaming cup of *manzanilla* to the silent living room, lit one of the lavender-scented candles there, and sat on the couch. Maureen never brought a match to these candles—why buy something and never use it? Araceli sipped her tea and watched the yellow flame flicker and cast long shadows throughout the room, the soft, dancing light falling upon the pictures in the Torres-Thompson gallery, coloring the faces with nostalgia and loss. *Here are people related by blood, but distant from one another.* Pobrecitos. The photograph of the younger version of *el abuelo* Torres was the one most closely related to her own experience: the urban setting was familiar, along with the mestizo smile. Had he run across the desert to reach the United States as Araceli had? Araceli had a photograph like this of her mother in Mexico City, a snapshot taken by one of those men with the big Polaroids in the Zócalo, when her mother was a young woman recently arrived from provincial Hidalgo. *My mother still felt like a tourist in Mexico City then, and so does the young man in this picture—he is a young man in the first days of his Los Angeles adventure.* In this picture too there was a just-arrived feeling, the brow raised in something between astonishment and self-assurance. Now something behind the young man caught her eye. Three numbers could be seen floating above his slicked-back hair, attached to a wall behind him: 232. A street address. She remembered how her mother carefully wrote dates and other information on the back of family photographs. On a hunch, she picked up the frame, turned it around, and moved the tabs that held the photograph in place and pulled it out. She found words and numbers written on the back in the elegant, masculine script of another era, the florid penmanship of a teenager educated according to the standardized rules of Mexican public education, the looping letters teachers of the Secretaría de Educación Pública had tried to force upon Araceli too, until she rebelled.

*West 39th Street, L.A., Julio 1954.*

On Monday morning, Araceli approached the preparation of the oatmeal with a sense of finality. After breakfast was cooked and served she would be free, because *el señor* Scott was sure to be at his office, the desk altar where he never missed a weekday prayer. When they finished eating, the boys went directly to the game room and within a minute or so the sound effects of steel striking steel were wafting toward the kitchen, where Araceli stood before the refrigerator, a tremor of anticipation in her hands as she picked up the telephone and began to punch in the number.

"You've reached Scott Torres, vice president of programming at Elysian Systems. I'm currently on the phone or away from my desk. Please leave a message or press zero to talk to the operator."

Startled to hear another recorded voice, she pressed zero. After a single ring, an actual human voice answered, a woman.

"Elysian Systems."

"*Con* Scott Torres, please. Mr. Scott Torres."

"I'm sorry, he called in sick today."

"*¿Qué?*"

"Excuse me?"

"He called sick?"

"Yes," the operator said, speaking slower now, because the person on the other end of this call was obviously English-challenged. "He called *in* sick."

"*¿Cómo que* sick?"

Now the operator was amused by the incongruity of a woman with a thick accent and poor telephone skills calling a cutting-edge, if somewhat small, software company, and asking for a midrange executive in the same tone of voice these people probably used to order their spicy food.

"Sick, yes. Ill. Unwell. Would you like me to transfer you to his voice mail so you can leave him a message?"

"A message? Yes. Please."

Araceli thought quickly about what she should say while Scott's message unfurled again over the phone, her pulse racing anew.

"*Señor Scott. Estoy sola con los niños.* I am alone with the boys." She stopped and seconds passed as she thought how she should elaborate on that central fact. "*¡Sola! Por tres días ya. Se nos está acabando la comida.* The food is gone almost. *No sé qué hacer. La señora Maureen se fue.* I don't know where she is . . ."

A loud tone sounded on the receiver and the call went dead.

**S**cott Torres was not at his desk because he was recovering Monday morning in a hotel room, alone, having fled Charlotte Harris-Hayasaki's apartment after two nights, his marital fidelity more or less unblemished. Thanks to the hotel minibar, he was hung over and had awakened at 8:45 in a bright, sun-drenched room with open curtains, stumbling over to the phone to report in sick to the office switchboard some ten minutes later, having forgotten, in his unsettled state, that he'd given the entire programming department, including himself, the day off for a four-day weekend. He showered, dressed, and paid the hotel bill in cash. It was time to go home and face Maureen.

**A**fter hanging up the phone, Araceli lingered by it for several minutes, because it seemed within the realm of possibility that Scott could receive her message immediately and call her back. She had already decided that she would not spend another night sleeping on the floor of El Cuarto de las Mil Maravillas. Before the day was out either she would have reached one of her *patrones* with the message of her plight, or she would head out for the Los Angeles address of the Torres family patriarch, the clapboard building depicted in the glossy photograph. During her first few weeks in California, Araceli had lived at a similar address, a 107 East Twenty-third Street, and she believed that if the address corresponded to the logical system one expected from an American city, a 232 West Thirty-ninth Street must not be far away. It was not within Araceli's experience, or that of most people who had been born and raised into adulthood in Mexico, that families picked up and moved themselves and abandoned their old properties every few years, in the same way one might discard a dress that had been worn once or twice too often. Property in Mexico stood as a constant. Once in possession of a deed, and sometimes without a deed at all, a family would plant itself on a patch of topsoil and allow themselves to become as rooted as noble old oak trees, their branches of children and grandchildren a canopy blossoming over the land. Either old man Torres himself or someone related to him would certainly be living at this West Thirty-ninth Street address, just as one could find twenty to thirty people connected by blood, marriage, and poor judgment to Araceli at Monte Líbano 210 in Nezahualcóyotl and the adjoining houses.

This escape plan liberated Araceli's mind of the mocking ticks of the clock, of her dependence on absent bosses. She had taken control of the situation.

At 10:45 a.m. she entered the gaming room and found the two boys sitting on the couch amid the ambient noise of a cheering crowd. There was a football game taking place on the flat screen in front of them, only the players were frozen in their positions, several stopped in midstride, an image that seemed unnatural precisely because the players looked so lifelike. The virtual football teams were waiting for one or both of the boys to set them in motion with controllers that had been tossed on the rug and forgotten. Having grown bored, finally, with the pleasures of computer-generated fantasy, the boys were both reading, Brandon immersed in a Bible-sized tome, Keenan with a book of brightly colored cartoons depicting the adventures of a journalist mouse, the text rendered in a crazy pasticcio of changing fonts.

"When are Mom and Dad coming home?" Brandon asked.

"Get ready," Araceli announced, ignoring the question. "After lunch, we go to your grandfather's house."

"To Grandpa John's?" Brandon asked.

"Yes."

"Excellent!" Keenan said. They had not seen their paternal grandfather in two years, a time at the very limit of young Keenan's pool of memories, though the old man had left a lasting impression on both of them because he was a bit of a libertine, a dispenser of large quantities of hard candy who didn't care if a movie was rated PG-13, and who often handed over meaningful sums of cash that raised the eyebrows of their parents. The boys associated him, most strongly, with visits to a soda fountain in his neighborhood, a place where a certain dish of chocolate in excess was served. They remembered their grandfather sitting in a booth across from them, wringing his hands in delight as they devoured their dessert and turning down their offers of, "Wanna try some, Grandpa?" Brandon and Keenan packed their rolling suitcases and backpacks with extra speed, anticipating another visit to that temple of sugar, and the condominium with the expansive recreation facilities where the elder Torres lived alone in a long-dashed hope that his grandchildren might visit him and use the kidney-shaped swimming pool. They packed their bathing suits and Game Boys too, until Araceli told them to leave all toys behind and to bring more underwear instead.

# 12

Brandon and Keenan led the way, rolling small suitcases that click-clacked along the cement walkway, backpacks filled with books and a few small toys hanging from their shoulders. Araceli locked the door behind them and crossed herself, against her secular inclinations: she would be traveling with two children and one never knew what one might encounter on the road. At the corner and the first turn that led away from the Paseo Linda Bonita cul-de-sac, Brandon stopped to look back at Araceli, his eleven-year-old eyes finding reassurance in the plump image of improvised motherhood she presented. She wore jeans and a billowing cotton blouse, and over her shoulder she carried one of his mother's old backpacks (used, in its day, to transport Keenan's diapers and bottles) and a floppy khaki safari hat Maureen liked to wear on all-day summer excursions to theme parks. Minutes earlier, she'd packed the very minimum for herself—two changes of clothes, the unspent and unbanked cash she had on hand, tucking away her savings passbook in a drawer. In the backpack's front pocket she placed the photograph of their destination, along with a package of the moist wipes Maureen used to clean the baby's bottom, and the only piece of identification in her possession: a Mexican voter registration card. Then she'd announced to the boys the route they would be taking, speaking with a voice of confident authority and in clipped clauses that wedded English nouns with Spanish verbs. "*Primero bajamos al* front gate, *y luego al* bus stop, *y después* al train station *que nos lleva* a downtown Los Angeles, *y finalmente tomamos* the bus *a la* house *de tu* grandfather." The boys were eager to leave, imagining their grandfather's conspiratorial whispers, his aftershave aroma, and his swimming pool at the end of their journey. But before taking his next step forward, Brandon waited until Araceli's eyes caught his one more time, because after less than a minute walking under the July sun, he was struck by the strangeness of what he was doing: undertaking an expedition through streets he knew only from the windows of his parents' automobiles. From the edge of the sidewalk he looked up at Araceli and then once again at the street: heat waves shimmered up from the asphalt in imitation of a lake, as if they were standing at the edge of a pier, in a skiff about to push off into roiling waters.

"*Vámonos,*" Araceli said, and Brandon resumed the march, Keenan and Araceli behind him in single file. Brandon listened to the barking of unseen dogs that marked their advance down the hill, the animals communicating through what Brandon concluded must be a language: *Humans! Alert! Unknown humans! Alert!* Until they reached the front gate the only people they encountered were two Spanish-speaking gardeners trimming the edges of a freshly cut fescue lawn who were too engaged in their work to take notice of a countrywoman leading two North American children down the street on foot. When Araceli and her charges reached the gate of the Estates, they failed to capture the attention of the pregnant young woman on duty at the guard kiosk that morning: she was on the phone and was simultaneously inspecting the credentials of a battered moving van and its Mexican driver. They walked another block down the sidewalk-free public access road, Araceli leading them now, trying to get the boys to walk on the grass shoulder, which required them to grab their suitcases by the handles and carry them. Then, for the first time in their young lives, Brandon and Keenan waited for a city bus. "What color is the bus?" Brandon asked. "Will it have seat belts?"

·

Seat belts on a bus would be a good idea, Araceli thought as the grinding bus climbed and coasted toward the Metro Center transportation hub. The boys sat next to each other in the row in front of Araceli, grabbing on to the rubber safety bar attached to the seat in front of them, leaning forward with the wide eyes of boys taking a ride at the amusement park, and for a moment Araceli was struck by their smallness and fragility, and worried about the bruises and broken bones an accident could bring. These boys never traveled without the protection of seat belts and the crash-tested engineering of American family vehicles. A bus crash could send bodies flying against metal and glass. Araceli had learned this in Mexico City; she knew the dangers first-hand. True, this American bus driver did not bob and weave through traffic like his Mexico City counterparts, who plied their routes with homicidal aggressiveness in rattling and rusty vehicles. Once she had stumbled upon the scene of a bus accident, during her final visit to the art fair in Coyoacán, moments after purchasing a small oil painting rendered on a piece of wood that depicted a suited and masked *lucha libre* wrestler standing stiffly with his bride. The tableau of stupidity and suffering she encountered that day finally convinced her it was time to leave Mexico. The bus passengers had suffered no visible injuries, though a few were sitting on the edge of the sidewalk theatrically rubbing their necks while a taxi driver remonstrated with them. A few paces away a skinny teenager with chocolate skin and oily hair was gasping for breath as he lay on his back in the gutter, his eyes blazing open to the dirty blue sky as two dozen of his fellow citizens gathered around him, studying him with the distant, emotionless stare *chilangos* are famous for. *Look. A young man is dying right here in front of us. This is something we don't normally see. It's all so more real than what's on television, isn't it? This isn't an actor. He is a poor man like us, just trying to make a few more pesos like the ones he is still clutching in his hand. We can't help him; we can only look and thank the Virgin that it isn't us down there.*

"Is he dying, Mommy?" a child's voice asked.

"*¿Y la pinche ambulancia?*" shouted an irritated voice from the back of the cluster.

The young crash victim was a street vendor: a few paces away his bicycle lay bent, while a passerby gathered his scattered load of loofah sponges and stacked them in a small pyramid next to the bicycle. *Yes, the boy is dying, but they might need his loofahs in heaven.* Araceli was standing at the edge of Coyoacán's seventeenth-century plaza, in sight of the domed church and the gazebo, next to a line of trees whose trunks were painted white to discourage drivers from crashing into them. She felt bile rising in her throat as the other bystanders pushed their elbows against hers. A red trickle flowed from the young victim's nostrils, and when he stopped blinking the crowd started to thin, people walking away in a silence as yet unbroken by the wailing of an ambulance. At that moment Araceli fully and finally comprehended the cruelty of her native city, the precariousness of life in the presence of so much un-regulated traffic and unfulfilled need, a city where people born farmers and fishermen sprinted before cars faster than any horse or sailing ship. The crash cured her of any lingering procrastinator's malaise and set in motion her oft-delayed plans to leave for the United States. That night she made a fateful phone call to a friend in downtown Los Angeles, and believed she heard in her friend's upbeat voice a place where cars, bi-cycles, and pedestrians each occupied their own byways, sensibly and safely moving through the city.

**S**cott's route from the Irvine Hampton Inn to his hillside home took him along the five northbound lanes of Interstate 5, a high-way that was considerably thinner and less traveled in Scott's youth, when it had been known as the Golden State Freeway. The highway was an immense channel of metal and heated air, and at forty miles an hour or seventy-five, its straightness and width exercised a hypnotic power over drivers. As he navigated through the thinly populated fringes of Orange County, at a late-morning post-commute hour with only moder-ate traffic, Scott found his thoughts about the coming reencounter with Maureen intermingling with the running dots and dashes of the white lines that demarcated the lanes. The lines were a siren speaking in murmurs of rushing air that bade him to *follow-me, follow-me, follow-me,* to mountain passes, meadows, and interchanges as yet unknown, to places where no one would know he had pushed his wife into a table. When this trance of happy forgetfulness ended, Scott found himself just one hundred yards from his turnoff, but still in the number-one lane, too late to cross the three lanes of traffic to reach the exit for the freeway that led to the coast and the Laguna Rancho Estates. Damn! Scott gritted his teeth and gave a second half curse as his usual exit and overpass grew smaller in the rearview mirror. He was speeding toward the metropolitan center of Orange County and the course correction back home required shifting lanes and taking the next exit, but Scott's hands resisted moving: instead, they allowed the car's momentum to continue carrying him forward and away from Maureen. *Maybe I'm not ready to go home yet.* The car stream was like a data stream and maybe he needed to see where the information took him, so to speak. He passed Disneyland, left Orange County and entered Los Angeles County at La Habra, and a short while later approached the Telegraph Road exit to his old South Whittier neighborhood. Now, at last, he exited, and headed for the inelegant, weed-happy patch of suburban sprawl where Scott the adolescent and teenager had been introduced to the joys of FORTRAN and masturbation.

He entered the late twentieth century industrial parks of an old oil patch called Santa Fe Springs, onto surface streets plied, at this hour, by fleets of tractor-trailers, then past a baseball field and a high school with soccer goalposts, where a single, middle-aged Latino man was sprinting with a ball at his feet. Scott followed the splintering posts that carried telephone voices, antiquated analog signals pushed through copper, toward the horizon and the Whittier hills beyond. He reached the first neighborhoods, where the homes boasted miniature gabled roofs, and jumbo vans and pickup trucks in the driveways of mini–Spanish cottages and mini-ranches, their humble size a kind of camouflage. *South Whittier does not want you to remember it; it wants to pass unnoticed.*

When he reached the intersection of Carmelita Road and Painter Avenue, the vista changed abruptly, shifting Scott's mood along with it, because everything at that familiar crossroads was laden with painful memories from the predigital, pre-Internet era. The homes here were taller, and yet flimsier than those he had just passed, and were more uniform, each having been built by the same developer from the same "Ponderosa ranchette" kit. He hadn't been to his old neighborhood since his mother's death, and for a moment the weathered, fairy-tale pastels of the two-story homes glimmered as strangely as they had on the August day of her funeral. He slowed the car to the speed of a brisk walk as he turned the final corner and saw the old Torres family homestead and its watered-down mustard stucco with a flavoring of avocado trim, hiding behind an overgrown olive tree. He had expected to feel a superior satisfaction returning to this place, because he had become bigger and more worldly in the decades since, conquering the nodes and networks that united the world. Instead, he felt smaller. *We were still fucking poor and I didn't even realize it.* He looked for a place to park his car on the dead-end street, but found all the available spaces taken up with sedans of dated styling, pickup trucks abused by their loads, and a station wagon. Did they even make station wagons anymore? There were never this many cars when he played baseball here.

Scott parked a half block away and stepped out of his car, surveying the workday quiet as he walked toward his old home, but he stopped when something in the backyard of the next-door property caught his eye. The Newberrys had once lived here, with their Ozark cheeks and corduroy jeans. Peering down the end of the driveway, he noticed something that was foreign to his memory: a large glass and metal box with a pitched roof and a small crucifix on top, plastic party streamers flowing out from the roof to the adjacent garage. Stepping closer, he saw a statue of a suntanned Virgin Mary inside the box, her clasped hands and powder-blue mantle rendered in painted plaster, a garland of fresh white roses draped around her neck, votive candles aflame at her feet. *This is so strange, so Mexican.* These people had taken his old neighborhood, once connected to the rest of modern America by AM radio and VHF television signals broadcast from zinc towers, back into history, to a rural age, a time of angels and miracles.

"*Buenas tardes,*" a woman's voice called, startling him. "*¿Le puedo ayudar en algo?*"

Scott looked to his right and saw a woman of about fifty in sweatpants: she held a broom, and judging from her otherworldly smile she believed he was in need of spiritual direction.

"No, nothing, nada," he sputtered. "I used to live in the house next door. I came to see, sorry . . ."

"Isn't she beautiful?" the woman said in accented English, and Scott sensed a religious speech about to begin and backed away. "*No tengas miedo,*" the woman said, trancelike, as Scott scurried away. He *was* afraid: of her statue, her Spanish, her weird religiosity, and the power of all those things to chase away his old neighbors. What had they done to the Newberrys? The Newberrys weren't rich. They were from Little Rock. "She wants to help you," the woman continued in English, and Scott wondered how many years ago the Newberrys had left and if they knew there was a Mexican lady praying to a statue in their old backyard.

The Laguna Niguel train station was a typical example of the soulless functionality of late twentieth century American public architecture, and as such it deeply disappointed Brandon, who expected the "station" to be an actual building, with schedules posted on the wall and long wooden benches inside a high-walled waiting room. When Araceli had told them they would take a train, it had conjured images in Brandon's head of locomotives spitting steam, and passengers and baggage handlers scrambling on covered platforms underneath vaulted glass ceilings. Instead the station consisted of two bare concrete runways, a short metal awning where six or seven people might squeeze together to find shelter from the rain, and four refrigerator-sized ticket machines. Brandon thought of train stations as theatrical stages where people acted out momentous shifts in their lives, an idea shaped by a trilogy of novels he had read in the fifth grade, a series in which each book's final scene unfolded inside the Gare du Nord in Paris. His only previous train ride had come some years back on the Travel Town kiddie train at Griffith Park, and there too the station consisted of a kid-sized replica of an actual building, complete with a ticket booth and a swinging LOS ANGELES sign. The small steel rectangle that announced LAGUNA NIGUEL in the spare, sans-serif font of the Metrolink commuter rail network didn't rise to the occasion, and Brandon frowned at the recognition that actual life did not always match the drama and sweep of literature or film. Nor were there the large crowds of people one associated with trains in the movies. In fact, Brandon, his brother, and Araceli were the only people on either side of the platform.

As the boys projected hopeful eyes at the rusty sinews of the tracks that stretched away from the station, Araceli scanned the space that immediately surrounded them. Until she got them to their grandfather, these were her boys. It was one thing to be in charge of children inside the shelter of a home, protected by locked doors, or in the fenced boundaries of a park—it was quite another to be herding them about a city. She wanted to cover them with sheets of protective steel. The thought that an accident of man or machine might hurt them filtered into her consciousness and caused brief and irrational pangs of loss, followed by the manic darting of her eyes at each of their stops on the journey from the gate of the Laguna Rancho Estates to the empty platform and the stairways leading to the street and the bus stop and parking structures beyond.

"Hey, here it comes."

A double-decked white commuter train with periwinkle stripes moved toward them as a snake would, the locomotive yawing back and forth on uneven tracks.

"*Atrás*," Araceli commanded. "Back until the train stops."

The boys opened their mouths as the cars rolled slowly before them, their massive weight causing the ground beneath them to shift and rise.

"Tight!"

"Awesome!"

"*¡Cuidado!*"

The train stopped and two sliding doors opened before them, the boys entering ahead of Araceli, rolling their suitcases straight into the car, whose floor was conveniently level with the platform. With a quick turn of their heads the boys found the stairway leading to the upper deck and began to climb, Araceli scrambling after them, muttering "*¡Esperen!*" at the backs of their feet. They found two pairs of empty seats arranged before a table.

"Hey, we're moving."

The train began its advance away from the station, and Brandon and Keenan were briefly mesmerized by the illusion of flight that came from looking through the railcar's large windows and watching their enclosed space move against the low skyline of the transit center's false downtown, a Potemkin village of parking garages masquerading as office buildings. As the train rolled away from the station, past gates with flashing red lights and waiting cars with daydreaming drivers, Araceli threw herself back into her seat and let out a sigh. *Halfway there, more or less.* The train itself was a clean comfort, with its white walls and stainless steel poles and vinyl seats with aerodynamic shaping and the

plaque by the door that proclaimed its provenance: BOMBARDIER, MON-
TREAL. After dropping off the boys and the briefest of stays at the old
man's house, she would set off south again for Marisela's and await news
of Scott and Maureen. She imagined different outcomes for their family
debacle, including a divorce that ended with an empty house and Araceli
vacuuming after the movers had left, or a tearful family reunion and
ample thanks from Scott and Maureen to Araceli for seeing their boys
through the crisis.

Through the window, the boys saw a landscape of shrinking backyards shuffle past: the repetition of laundry lines and old furniture did
not hold Brandon's attention for long, and he finally looked across at
Araceli and asked, "Can you draw me a picture? Here in my notebook?
Like the dragon you drew for Keenan. That was cool."

"Yeah, it was tight," Keenan said.

"I didn't know you could draw," Brandon said.

"*¿Qué quieres?* What do you want I draw for you?"

"How about a soldier?"

"*¿Un soldado? Fácil.*"

She took his lined notebook and pencil and looked for a blank page,
glancing quickly at his crude war scenes, little stick-figure Brueghels in
which one army of stick men set off cannons and laid siege to rectangular forts and pummeled enemies who raised up stick hands and ran
from scribbled explosions. *This boy is very smart but he does not know art.*
Brandon watched, intently, as she traced some initial lines and a man in
uniform with a weapon held across his chest took form on paper. It was
a musket like the ones in his book *American Revolution* and Araceli
drew it from memory, though she gave her soldier a modern uniform,
with a row of medals and a steel helmet. Then she worked on the face,
choosing features that were deeply familiar to her, and made it stare
straight back at the viewer.

"Wow," Brandon said when she finished. "That guy's face—he looks
really tough."

"Really mean," Keenan added.

The face belonged to Araceli's mother.

Her art session was interrupted, suddenly, by the jolt of the train's
arrival in Fullerton, the last station before Los Angeles. Four people waiting on the platform quickly stepped on board and the train lurched

forward anew. Soon the train was entering the industrial districts south-east of Los Angeles, one windowless warehouse followed by another as the train accelerated and began to vibrate slightly. The buildings began to age, the neutered, primary-colored plaster of the late twentieth century giving way to the earth-toned constructions of brick and cement of earlier eons. Suddenly the warehouses had windows, many dark and frosted over with dust and cobwebs so that they resembled thousands of cataract-infested eyes. The train went faster still and vibrated violently, causing Keenan to squeeze Araceli's hand. Brandon held on to the armrest and felt his head strike the window, and wondered if the train might disintegrate, or if the forces of acceleration might transform this rolling steel box into a time machine that would transport them from the archaic era of brick now visible outside the window, to even simpler ages of wood, smoke, and stone.

The train slowed suddenly as it entered a switching yard with at least twenty parallel tracks. They rolled slowly past rusting hopper cars that had made hundreds of journeys from Kansas with wheat and corn, past tank cars oozing black tar, and container cars with German and Chinese names and bar codes stamped incongruously on their sides. The train made a long, sweeping turn under a freeway bridge and Araceli watched the haphazard cables and wires that followed the tracks moving like a black, horizontal rain. She noted too the random dispersal of trash on the embankment, the plastic bags and food containers sprinkled over the track gravel, the rusting iron overpasses, the graffiti-covered switching boxes, and a lone, stubby brick control tower with wooden doors chained shut. There was a spare beauty to all this decay, it was the empty and harsh landscape of an unsettling dream; these were spaces you were not meant to see, like the hidden air ducts and trash chutes of a glittering mansion, where cobwebs and dust and rat droppings collected freely and concerned no one. Her aesthetic lived in barren places like this, and she missed them. *Here the wind, rain, and sun are free to shape and cook the steel and cement into sculptures that celebrate forgetfulness.* She took a small notebook from her backpack and tried to quickly capture the manic, twisted essence of electrical lines, the bounce of the trash in the wind, the fluid shape of the rust patterns, until Keenan proclaimed, "Everything is really dirty here," and her reverie and her concentration were broken.

The train slowed to a walking pace and a valley of smooth concrete walls suddenly opened alongside the tracks, stretching more than
a mile in the distance, with several bridges vaulting over it. "What's that?"
Keenan asked.

"It's the river," Araceli said.

"That's a river?" Brandon said, perplexed, until he noticed the bottom of the chasm held a narrow channel of flowing water with perfectly
straight edges. "What's it called? Why is it made out of cement? It hasn't
rained, so where does the water come from?"

"Too many questions," Araceli said.

"Too many?" No one had ever told Brandon such a thing.

"Yes."

Brandon looked at the river and saw that a giant with a paint can
had covered the top of the valley with a mosaic of sparkling elephant-
sized letters, spelling words in mongrel greens and tainted yellows that
pulsated inside a pool of gray-blue swirls. Or at least it seemed a giant
had painted them. He wondered if he should ask Araceli, then decided
against it. Probably it was a giant.

"Hey, look, there's people down there," Keenan shouted, loud
enough to get the attention of the four or five other adults in the car,
who looked up from their newspapers and laptops just long enough to
glance at and quickly forget the familiar sight of the soiled caste who
lived by this stretch of track.

"*Los* homeless," Araceli said.

Brandon pressed his nose against the glass and looked downward,
spotting a line of shelters between the train tracks and the river, teetering house-tents of oil-stained plywood, sun-bleached blue tarpaulin,
frayed nylon rope, and aluminum foil. They looked like ground-hugging
tree houses, improvised assemblages built by children and taken over
by tubercular adults. A few humans sat on chairs in between their creations in this village as it followed the curve in the tracks, their roofs a
quilt of tarpaulin and wood forming a long crescent dotted with the
occasional column of smoke. Brandon searched for the sources of these
fires, and spotted a gangly man in aviator glasses tending to a kettle on
a grill. The train rolled slowly toward the man, and for a few seconds
Brandon was directly above him. He bore a long scar on his cheek oozing red and black liquids. A battle wound? Brandon wondered. A cut

inflicted by a knife or a sword? A month earlier Brandon had finished the last volume in a four-book series of novels, *The Saga of the Fire-Swallowers*, and as he sat in the train with his nose pressed to the glass, the violent and disturbing denouement of that epic narrative seemed the only plausible explanation for the existence of this village of suffering passing below him. *These people are refugees; they are the defeated soldiers and the displaced citizens of the City of Vardur.* The novels were a fantasy tale for young-adult readers set in a world of preindustrial stone villages. His father had bought the entire set and read them some years earlier, leaving them forgotten on a shelf for his oldest son to discover, Brandon's fascination growing with each chapter he spent in the company of its villains, a cult of rugged men and boys who engaged in the ritual eating of flames before and after battle. There was something about this homeless camp that seemed to belong to the ancient times described in those books, a way of life untroubled by electricity, or modernity in general. In truth, Brandon never should have been allowed to read the Fire-Swallower books, given their graphic descriptions of scorched-earth warfare, including the slaughter of entire villages and their children with blades forged from various metals, real and fanciful, and the antagonists who filled their speeches with fascistic rationalizations about "the weak," "the strong," and "the pure." It was all meant to be an allegory about the cruelty and demagoguery of the modern age, and its imagery drew heavily from the outrages of the twentieth century, so much so, and so realistically, that the sharp-eyed Brandon had long ago concluded that the story was not entirely the product of a writer's imagination. Long before this train journey Brandon had begun to warm to the idea that the Fire-Swallower saga was, in fact, a thinly veiled, detailed account of a real but primitive corner of the actual world. Entire cities emptied of good people, civilians tortured, their homes and their books set to the torch. How could such injustice exist, how could humanity live with it? He knew he should speak of what he read to his mother, who obviously had no idea about the taboos being broken in the works of literature he carried about the house: "You're such a good little reader," was all she said. It was stunning to be confronted with such adult naïveté, though it was undeniably cool to possess knowledge forbidden to eleven-year-olds who were not as precocious readers as he. Still, the stories told in the saga caused him to lose sleep some nights, until he finally convinced himself that what he was reading was indeed fantasy. And now this, a wounded man, an actual victim of the Fire-Swallowers' wrath, driven to seek shelter by the concrete river with his fellow Vardurians.

"Those flame-swallowing bastards!" Brandon cried out, in imitation of the hero of the saga, the noble Prince Goo-han.

"*¿Qué dices?*" Araceli said. "*¿Bastardos?*" Suddenly the eleven-year-old was saying swear words. *He's only been out of the house and into the world a few hours and already he's being corrupted.*

"It's the Fire-Swallowers," Brandon said in a tone of patient explanation, having realized quickly that Araceli had never read those books: they were in English, after all. "The Fire-Swallowers made these people refugees. They destroyed their towns and houses. They fled and they've come to live here by the river. I read about it in *Revenge of the River-walkers.* The Fire-Swallowers burned down their village, Vardur, because they wouldn't swear loyalty to the evil king. So they had to seek shelter on the riverbanks, but I never thought . . ."

"*Estás loco,*" Araceli said. "You read too much."

No one had ever told Brandon such a thing: in the Torres-Thompson home reading was a sacred act; it was the one activity the children were allowed without time limits or parental supervision. Books were powerful and good, they told truths, and Brandon decided he should ignore his temporary caretaker's remarks and study the Vardurian camp and see what secrets it might reveal. Brandon's memory stretched back only a few years beyond the time they moved into the Laguna Rancho Estates, and his idea of what homes looked like was deeply influenced by the repetitive conformity of his neighborhood, with its association-approved paint schemes and standard-sized driveways. Below him, now, was a place where every shelter was entirely different from its neighbor, many with tiny yards fenced in with loops of electrical wire and plastic bags tied together to form a kind of rope. Before the train made one final turn and headed into the station he spotted one last Vardurian: a woman with a fountain of silvery hair who was sweeping out her shelter with a broom.

Maureen stood over the portable crib in her hotel room and studied her daughter as she took an afternoon nap. Samantha slept on her back, clutching the yellow blanket that accompanied her day and night, her closed eyes peaceful hemispheres, with her rusty eyelashes as delicate equators. With her eyes closed Samantha's oval face was nearly identical to her oldest brother when he was the same age, the boy's sleeping face recorded in a photograph framed in mahogany in their living room gallery: Maureen's separation from Brandon for more than seventy-two hours only heightened the sense that she was looking down at her son and not her daughter, and she began to feel the deepening absence of her boys from her life. *When you see your children sleeping you understand the full glory and beauty of being a mother; you stand tall and awake before their silent need, before their purity and vulnerability.* She looked up at where she was, in a hotel room of slightly overdone southwestern décor, with a Navajo rug nailed to the wall opposite the bed and an authentic, desert-baked ram's skull hanging on the door, and could hear the startled voice of her conscience screaming out, *What have I done? My son! My sons!* She picked up the phone and called home.

At that moment, Maureen's boys were walking dutifully behind their Mexican caretaker, taking their first steps off the train at Union Station. They walked along one of several parallel platforms between locomotive behemoths, one of which was ringing a bell as it rolled away, roughly at the pace of a walking man, into open tracks toward the city beyond. Brandon and Keenan saw porters wearing stiff caps, and seniors defeated by the stacks of luggage on steel carts, and heard a speaker pronounce, "Last call for the Sunset Limited . . . all aboard!" and thought that at last they'd arrived at a real train station. The boys wanted to linger out on the open-air platform, in the meaningful presence of all that rolling stock and those travelers, but Araceli was telling them to follow her, with an impatient "*Órale, por aquí,*" and they descended down a long, sloping ramp, going underground.

They entered a long and wide hallway with low ceilings that reminded Keenan of airports he had visited. Araceli had passed through here during her first days in Los Angeles, and the sight of the crowds of people with huge duffel bags and boxes tucked under their arms reminded her of that other, more innocent Araceli. *Sola.* With a hard-shell suitcase the smuggler had mocked for its patent impracticality, dazzled by the city's alien and sleek feel, suffering a kind of weird agoraphobia because she was in a vast plain of unknown things. The reencounter with her recent past only made Araceli more uncomfortable, more anxious to reach her destination. She looked left and then right and decided to go right, beginning to walk very quickly, navigating smartly between the crosscurrents of passengers, like a *chilanga* again, almost losing Brandon and Keenan because she was in such a hurry.

"Hey, Araceli, wait up," Brandon shouted, and Araceli turned back and gave him a mildly exasperated look identical to the one she showed him two or three times a day in his own living room, bedroom, and kitchen.

Walking side by side now, they passed an electronic sign announcing destinations and departure times, LAS VEGAS BUS, TEXAS EAGLE, SURFLINER NORTH, and then suddenly entered a room where the low ceilings disappeared and the space above them opened up, causing Brandon and Keenan to crane their necks skyward. They marveled at the vaulted ceiling, which was covered with tiles of vaguely Mediterranean or Arabic styling, exuding both warmth and largeness. Chandeliers resembling baroque spacecraft hung from the rafters and both boys silently mouthed the word *Whoa* as they walked underneath them. There were rows of high-backed, upholstered benches where boys in baseball uniforms and weary, sunburned Dutch and Italian travelers sat with clusters of nylon backpacks at their feet. A crew that was in the second day of a music-video shoot was packing up in the unused and locked wing of the station where tickets had once been sold, where the oak-paneled ticket windows served as permanent and oft-used sets.

"I've seen this place in the movies," Keenan said. "I thought it was pretend."

They passed through an arch high enough for the tallest troll or giant to fit through, and then walked out the main door of the station, where they were confronted by the summer sunlight, and cars and pedestrians all moving purposefully northward and southward on streets and walkways. Behind this shifting tableau stood the imposing backdrop of the downtown Los Angeles skyline, the glass skyscrapers of the Financial District, and the stubby stone tower of City Hall, which had a ziggurat pyramid on top, so that it resembled a Mesopotamian rocket ready for launch.

"*No, por aquí no es,*" Araceli said, and she circled back into the waiting room again, the boys scrambling behind her.

She walked up to the information booth and the tall, lean, sclerotic man standing there, the name tag on his jacket announcing him to be GUS DIMITRI, VOLUNTEER.

"We are looking for the buses," Araceli said.

Gus Dimitri was a spry octogenarian and a native of South Los Angeles, old enough to remember when that black and brown ghetto of today was a whites-only haven for Greeks, Jews, Italians, Poles. He had seen more L.A. history than any other employee or volunteer at this transit hub, and when he looked at Araceli and her charges he understood, immediately, that this was a servant woman from Mexico hired to care for the two children that accompanied her.

"Well, where are you headed, exactly, ma'am?"

As the woman fumbled in her backpack for an address, Gus Dimitri took time to think that California had really pushed this immigrant-servant fad to the extreme. *Is it really wise,* he'd like to ask the parents of these boys, *to have a Mexican woman guiding your precious children across the metropolis like this? To have them in the care of a woman lost at Union Station?* At about the time Gus Dimitri had retired from the workforce, California had gone mad with immigrant-hiring—from front yards to fast-food joints, these people did everything now. They were good workers, yes, real old-fashioned nose-to-the-grindstone types. But jeez: Didn't Americans want to do anything for themselves anymore? When he was about the age of this older boy here, he'd sold newspapers on the street himself, making a killing hawking extras on Crenshaw Boulevard for the Max Schmeling–Joe Louis fights. But did American kids even have paper routes anymore? His own paper was delivered via pickup truck by a Mexican guy (he assumed) named Roberto Lizardi, according to the Christmas card that arrived with his paper once a year.

"To Thirty-ninth Street," Araceli said. "In Los Angeles."

"That's back, the other way," he said. "Patsaouras Plaza."

"Thank you."

Araceli quickly circled back into the long, low-ceilinged passageway.

"Where are we going?" Keenan asked. "Why are we going underground again?"

"We are going to take the bus," Araceli explained. "*Tenemos que ir a la otra estación*. Another station, not this one." They reached a wide cement staircase and climbed into a sunlit atrium with several exits. This was the transit center where the buses departed, but Araceli could not remember which gate led to the buses serving the neighborhood in Los Angeles where *el viejo* Torres lived. She approached another information booth and the boys' attention was drawn upward again, this time to the mural on the wall behind the desk: an old steam engine rushed toward a village set amid verdant fields, advancing through a series of orchards, leaving a column of black smoke in its wake. To the left, there was a second mural in which the steam engine ran alongside a blue ribbon of river, which itself snaked past a city thick with squat buildings; in a third panel to the right the same city gleamed with skyscrapers and the river had morphed into a concrete channel.

"Is that what was here before?" Brandon asked, before Araceli could get her own question in.

"Yeah," said the man behind the counter, an MTA employee. "And let me tell you something else—this'll really blow your mind. Where we're standing, right now—it used to be Chinatown. There's all sorts of archaeological stuff they found buried underneath here. Chinese stuff."

"So what happened to the Chinese?"

"Ah, they knocked all that down ages ago. Flattened it."

"Well, that's disturbing," Brandon said, parroting a phrase his mother used quite often.

Brandon pondered the revelation about Chinatown as the man explained to Araceli where she could catch the bus they needed to take. The ground he and his brother were standing on was older than the oldest person he knew, and probably older than the oldest Vardurian, which was a horizon-opening realization for an eleven-year-old boy. Probably if you dug down deep you could find not just Chinatown, but also the ruins of many other cities and villages of the past, just like in that picture book on his shelf where you see the Stone Age, the Roman Age, the Middle Ages, and the Modern Age all inhabit the same stretch of earth beside a river, with battles fought and buildings burned and people buried and cities rebuilt and torn down and rebuilt again as you turn from one page to the next.

"*Ya, vámonos*," Araceli called out. "*Es por aquí*."

The boys followed her to one of several parallel sidewalks and within seconds an empty bus had pulled up and Araceli and the boys climbed in. This bus, Brandon noted immediately, was a battle-worn version of the first bus they had taken in the Laguna Rancho Estates earlier in the day. It appeared to have traveled through a few hailstorms, given the scratches on the plastic windows, and as it headed out of the shady transit center and into the sun of the Los Angeles streets and the light shone inside, Brandon noted the worn seats and the assorted scribbling in the interior. "It stinks in here," Keenan declared. A sweaty, vaguely fecal aroma seeped out of the seats, and the sour sweetness of spilled sugar beverages attached itself to the humid air molecules in the aisles, the smells riding the bus up and down and across the city all day for free.

They rolled slowly away from the transit center, to streets that brought them closer to the glass towers of the Financial District. Brandon and Keenan had seen this stretch of the city many times before, in the company of their parents, from the high perch of a car speeding along elevated freeways. That was the Los Angeles they had always known, the city center that was home to the Dodgers and the Lakers. On those trips they had glided over the heart of Los Angeles, traveling near the tops of its palm trees, driving to museums and parks that were somewhere on the other side of a vast grid of stucco buildings and asphalt strips that stretched as far as one could see into the haze. Studying this landscape from the ground level for the first time, Brandon noticed how every object appeared to be built from bare metal, brick, and concrete, arranged into simple geometric forms: the right angles formed by the traffic lights welded to poles, the open rectangular mouths of the storm drains, the strange tower on the roof of one building assembled entirely from triangles. It was all more linear and rough-edged and interesting, to his young eyes, than the curvy contours of Paseo Linda Bonita.

Sitting next to his brother, in an aisle seat, Keenan was closer to the clusters of passengers who began to fill the aisle after a few stops, grabbing the bar above them. Keenan didn't know it was possible to stand up in a moving bus. An older woman towered above him, carrying a plastic bag filled with documents and envelopes, the heavy contents swaying about as the bus lurched forward. Directly across from Keenan, a seated middle-aged man with green eyes held another plastic bag, his weathered hands covered with small cuts, and through the bag's translucent skin Keenan could make out folded clothes, two thick books, and a pair of pliers. The man held the bag close to his body, inside the vessel formed by his legs and the metal back of the seat in front of him, and Keenan sensed that whatever was inside was very important to him. *These people are carrying the things they own inside the plastic bags my mother and Araceli use to bring things from the market.* Keenan was eight years old, but the poignancy of poor people clutching their valuables in plastic bags close to their weary bodies was not lost on him and for the first time in his young life he felt an abstract sense of compassion for the strangers in his midst. "There are a lot of needy, hungry people in this world," his mother would say, usually when he wouldn't finish his dinner, but it was like hearing about Santa Claus, because one saw them only fleetingly. He believed "the poor" and "the hungry" were gnomelike creatures who lived on the fringes of mini-malls and other public places, sorting through the trash. Now he understood what his mother meant, and thought that next time he was presented with a plate of fish sticks, he would eat every last one. Two passengers in front of him were speaking Spanish, and this drew his attention because he thought he might make out what they were saying, since he understood nearly all of what Araceli said to him in that language. But their speech was an indefinable jumble of new nouns, oddly conjugated verbs, and figurative expressions, and he only understood the odd word or phrase: "*es muy grande,*" "*domingo,*" "*fútbol,*" and "*el cuatro de julio.*"

"*Nos bajamos en la próxima,*" Araceli said as she rose to her feet. "Next stop. We get off."

They stepped from the bus to the sidewalk and the door closed behind them with a clank and a hydraulic sigh. Araceli took in the yellow-gray heat and the low sun screaming through the soiled screen of the center-city atmosphere. *Goodbye blue skies and sea breezes of Laguna Rancho,* Araceli thought. This was more like the bowl of machine-baked air of her hometown: she had forgotten the feeling of standing in the still and ugly oxygen of a real city. "We walk. That way," Araceli said, pointing south down a long thoroughfare that ran perpendicular to the street the bus had left them on, the four lanes running straight toward a line of distant palm trees that grew shorter until they were toothpicks swallowed up by the haze.

"This doesn't look like the place my grandfather lives," Brandon said.

"Is it close?" Keenan asked.

"*Sí.* Just a few blocks."

They stood alone, housekeeper and young charges, on a block where only the bus bench and shelter interrupted the empty sweep of the sidewalk. So strange, Araceli observed, a block without people, just as on Paseo Linda Bonita, but this time in the middle of an aging city with buildings from the previous century. All the storefronts were shuttered and locks as big as oranges dangled from their steel doors, while swarthy men struck poses for the passing motorists from rooftop billboards, their fingers enviously wrapped around light-skinned women and bottles of beer and hard liquor. For a moment Araceli thought that Brandon might be right, that *el viejo* Torres could not live near here. Then again, you never knew in Los Angeles what you might find around the next corner. You could be in the quiet, sunny, and gritty desolation of a block like this at one moment, and find yourself on a tree-lined, shady, and glimmering block of apartments the next. Mexico City was like that too.

Once again, the wheels of the boys' suitcases clack-clacked on the sidewalk as they marched southward. "This doesn't look like where he lives," Brandon repeated, annoying Araceli. "In fact, I'm pretty sure this isn't the place."

"It's just a few blocks," she insisted. In a few minutes she would be free of the care of these two boys and the pressure would be lifted from her temples. Their grandfather would emerge from his door, she would tell him the story of the table and the empty house, and he would make them an early dinner and she would be free of them. They advanced southward, witnessed only by the passing motorists, who were all accelerating on this stretch of relatively open roadway, going too fast to take much note of the caravan of pedestrians headed southward in single file, a boy with rock-star-long hair leading the way, his brow wrinkled skeptically, a smaller child behind him, and a big-boned Mexican woman bringing up the rear and studying the street signs. These were the final minutes before the clock struck five, and the drivers were eager to cover as much ground as possible before the skyline to the north began to empty of clerks, analysts, corporate vice presidents, cafeteria workers, public relations specialists, sales wizards, and assorted other salaried slaves. On this midsummer day, most of these automobiles proceeded with windows sealed and artificial alpine breezes blowing inside, but the air-conditioning was not working inside the Toyota Cressida of Judge Robert Adalian, a jurist at the nearby concrete bunker known as Los Angeles Municipal Traffic Court—Central District. Judge Adalian was driving with the windows open when Araceli, Brandon, and Keenan passed before him at the crosswalk on Thirty-seventh Street and South Broadway, thanks to the rare red light on his drive northward along Broadway, his daily detour of choice to avoid the Harbor Freeway. These pedestrians pushed the button to cross and broke the sequence of the lights, the judge thought as he took in the odd spectacle of a woman who was clearly Mexican with two boys who were clearly not. *It's not their skin tone that gives the boys away, it's their hair and the way they're walking and studying everything around them like tourists. Those boys don't belong here.* Through his open window he caught a snippet of their talk.

"I think we're lost," the taller boy said.

"*No seas ridículo, no estamos* lost," the Mexican woman answered, irritated, and the judge chuckled, because he'd grown up in Hollywood with some Guatemalans and Salvadorans, and the Mexican woman's brief use of Spanglish transported him to that time and place, twenty years ago, when Spanish could still be heard in his old neighborhood, before that final exodus from the old Soviet Union had filled up the neighborhood with so many refugees from the old country (including his future wife) that the city had put up signs around it announcing LITTLE ARMENIA. The light turned green and the judge quickly filed away the Mexican woman and the American boys in the back of his memory, alongside the other unusual event of the afternoon: the sentencing of a onetime sitcom actor whose career had been so brief and distant in time, only the judge recalled it. It had depressed the judge to think that, at forty-four, he was older than his bailiff, his clerk, and his stenographer, older also than the defense attorney and the representative from the city attorney's office. Only the accused surpassed him in age, and when Judge Adalian finally realized that no one in the court was aware of the defendant's contribution to television history, the fifty-two-year-old drunk driving defendant had looked at the judge and raised his eyebrows in an expression of shared generational weariness. "Time passes," the defendant said, and this too struck a chord in the judge's memory, because it wasn't often that the alcoholics who passed through his court imparted any wisdom. The light turned green and the judge glided northward, unaware that in a few weeks' time his memory of crossing paths with the faded actor and the Mexican woman with the two "white" boys on the same ordinary day would win him an appearance on cable television.

Araceli reached the curb on the other side of Broadway and turned right, Brandon now bringing up the rear, because he felt the need to protect his younger brother by walking behind him, lest some monster or Fire-Swallower emerge from one of the shuttered storefronts.

"Don't look at anyone in the eye, Keenan," Brandon said.

"What?"

"This is a dangerous place."

"You can't tell me what to do."

"There might be bad guys inside these buildings," Brandon insisted. "Look at the markings. That's a bad number. Thirteen."

"Really?" Keenan said, and for a moment he saw the world as his brother did, thinking that XIII had to be some warrior code.

Logic told Araceli she was just two blocks away from the address on the back of the old photograph, but now she too was beginning to have serious doubts, given the ominous, spray-painted repetitions of the number 13 on the walls and the sidewalk. She sensed, for the first time, that her naïveté about the city might be leading them to the place where graffiti scribblers and gang members were nurtured under the opaque roof of the smoggy sky, a kind of greenhouse nursery of man-nish dysfunction. Now they walked past a large vacant lot, a rectangle filled with knee-high milkweed and trash, which in the glory days of *el abuelo* Torres had been the Lido Broadway movie theater. As a young man *el abuelo* Torres had seen *High School Confidential* screened here, lusted after the curvy starlet Cleo Moore, and been pummeled by a couple of African-American guys who didn't appreciate his comments during a midweek matinee of *Blackboard Jungle*. Juan Torres and his parents were still in the city-to-farm circuit then, forced with a number of other Mexican-American families to live among blacks. Juan fought the black guys over girls too. Living here and tasting blood in his mouth had shaped his sense of racial hierarchy, and his ideas about where he fit in the pigmented pyramid of privilege that he understood the United States to be. *As dark as we are, we ain't at the bottom.* When he had a glass of sangria or a shot of whiskey too many, the brawling, proud, and prejudiced Johnny Torres of Thirty-ninth Street and the Lido Broadway was resurrected: as during Keenan's sixth birthday party, when he remarked very loudly on how fair-skinned and "good looking" his younger grandson was—"a real white boy, that one"—a remark that led his progressive daughter-in-law to banish him from her home.

If Araceli had not been trailing two children, if she had not been anxious to reach the place that would liberate her from her unwanted role as caretaker of two boys, she might have stopped and taken the time to study the rubble of the Lido Broadway, a half dozen pipes rising from a cracking cement floor like raised hands in a classroom. Time worked more aggressively in the heart of an American city than in a Mexican city, where colonial structures breezed through the centuries without much difficulty. Here, cement, steel, and brick began to surrender after just a decade or two of abandonment. *The people who lived and worked here ran away. But from what?* It was best to keep moving, quickly. She spotted a woman pushing a stroller on the next block and a young child walking beside her, two hundred yards away, next to a liquor store with a painted mural of the Virgin of Guadalupe on its side.

Araceli walked toward the store and the Virgin, and soon she and the boys were entering a neighborhood with houses and apartment buildings that were occupied, clapboard structures, mostly, some with iron fences enclosing rosebushes. They saw a woman flinging a carpet against the stairs of a porch that led to a two-story building with four doors. Brandon noted the strange numbers above each entrance—3754¼, 3754½, 3764¾—and was reminded of the fanciful numbered railroad platform from a famous children's book; he wondered if these doors too might be a portal to a secret world. They passed a two-story clapboard bungalow with the rusted steel bars of a prison, and both boys wondered if some bad guy was being held inside, but a few doors down, they saw an identical structure, with no bars and freshly painted coral-colored walls, an organ pipe cactus rising ten feet high in the garden, alongside a small terra-cotta fountain with running water and a cherub on top. "That's a nice house," Keenan said. "*Muy bonito*," he added, and Araceli thought, yes, they must be on the right track, because the houses were suddenly getting prettier. But half a block farther along they encountered a square-shaped rooming house whose doors and windows had been boarded up, the plywood rectangles forming the eyes and mouth of a blindfolded and muzzled creature. "I really don't think my grandfather lives around here," Brandon said again, and this time Araceli didn't bother answering him.

Two blocks later they arrived at a street sign announcing Thirty-ninth Street and the final confirmation of Araceli's folly: on this block, where the photograph and the street name on the back had led her, there was a collection of powder-blue duplex bungalows, apartments in a two-story clapboard building surrounded by snowflakes of white paint, and two windowless stucco industrial cubes. The address corresponded to one of the bungalows, which faced the street, with side doors opening to a narrow courtyard. Araceli reached into Maureen's backpack, retrieved the old photograph, and matched the bungalow behind the young *abuelo* Torres to the structure before her: the windows were covered with steel bars now and the old screen door had given way to a fortress shield of perforated steel, but it was the same building. Together, the two images, past and present, were a commentary on the cruelty of time and its passage, and of Araceli's chronological illiteracy, her ignorance of the forces of local history. After a day of walking and bus and train rides she had arrived at her destination, and it was clear that *el abuelo* Torres did not live here, and could not live here, because everything about the place screamed poverty and Latin America, from the wheeled office chair someone had left in the middle of the courtyard amid a pool of cigarette butts, to the strains of reggaeton music pulsating from inside one of the bungalows.

"*La fregué*," Araceli muttered to herself, which caused both boys to look up at her in confusion.

"Is this it?" Brandon said. "Is this the address?"

"*Sí. Y aquí no vive tu abuelo.*"

"No, he doesn't," Brandon said. "His house is in a big apartment complex, with a big lawn in front. It's yellow. And there aren't any ugly buildings like those over there."

"Now what?" asked Keenan.

Behind the security door of the bungalow directly before them, Araceli could hear a second, inner door opening. "*¿Se le ofrece algo?*" a female voice asked through the perforated steel shield.

Araceli walked to the door and held up the photograph. "*Estoy buscando a este hombre,*" she said. "*Vivía aquí.*"

Seeing no danger in a *mexicana* with two young boys, the woman opened the steel door and reached out to take the picture, revealing herself to Araceli as a world-weary woman of about thirty whose smooth skin and long, swept-back eyes appeared to have been carved from soapstone. Her nails were painted pumpkin and her hair seemed oddly stiff and perky, given the circles under her eyes, but those same eyes quickly brightened as she took in the photograph.

"*¡Pero esta foto tiene años y años!*" the woman declared, and chuckled after recognizing the black-and-white porch and arriving at the realization that the little shotgun house with the sagging floors and peeling faux linoleum in which she lived had been standing so long, and that once it had been possible to live there without metal barriers to keep out predators: she wouldn't live there now without bars on the windows. She returned the photograph and gave Araceli and the boys the same dismissive look she gave the impossibly earnest young men with narrow ties who visited her earlier in the day searching for the family of Salvadoran Mormons that had once occupied this same bungalow. "*Ni idea,*" the woman said.

Araceli stomped on the wooden porch in frustration. A day on foot, in trains, and buses, from station to station, neighborhood to neighborhood: for this? In the time they had walked from the bus stop the sun had dipped below the buildings on the horizon, the western sky had begun its transformation into the colors of a smoldering hearth. She looked down at the boys and wondered if they would be able to make it all the way back to Paseo Linda Bonita and how much trouble they would become once she told them they would have to start walking again.

The woman at the door sensed Araceli's predicament, which was centered on the presence of the two boys behind her, both of whom seemed to be English speakers. "I think someone I know can help you," she said, switching languages for the benefit of the boys. "*El negro.* He lives right here behind me. Apartment B. I think he's the oldest person who lives here. They say he's been here forever."

A minute or so later Araceli was knocking on the steel door with the в next to it.

"Who the hell is it? What are ya knockin' so loud for, goddamnit!" Behind the perforated steel sheet, an inner door of wood opened, and Araceli saw the silhouette of a large man with thick arms and a slightly curvy posture. "Oh, shit. Didn't know you had the kids with you," the voice said. "What? What you need?"

"I am looking for this person," Araceli said.

"Huh?"

"I am looking for the man in this picture. His name is Torres."

The man opened the door, slowly, and stretched out a weather-worn hand to take the picture, examining it behind his screen. "Whoa! This takes me back!" the man shouted. Now the door opened fully and the man looked down the three steps of his porch to examine the woman who had given him this artifact. He was a bald black man, inexplicably wearing a sweater on this late afternoon in July, and when he fully opened his door the sound of a television baseball announcer filtered out, causing Brandon to stand up on his tiptoes and try to look inside. The man from Apartment B was easily in his seventies, and still tall despite the stoop in his back. The spaces under his eyes were covered with small polyps, and his cheeks with white stubble.

"What are you? His relative? His daughter?"

"No. They are his, how do you say . . . ?"

"He's our grandfather," Keenan offered.

"You know, there's been a lot of people in and out of this place since I moved here." James "Sweet Hands" Washington had arrived on Thirty-ninth Street as a single man in the middle of the last century, picking out these bungalows because they reminded him of the old shotgun houses in his native Louisiana. The spot at the end of the block occupied by the garment factory had been the site of a car-repair shop back then, and Sweet Hands had worked there for a number of years, dismantling carburetors with the hands dubbed "sweet" first for his exploits on the football field, and later for his exploits with the ladies. Sweet Hands examined the picture, the way the Mexican subject wore his khaki pants with a distinctive mid-1950s swagger, and then the bungalow in the background, and was momentarily transported to that time, when the Southern California sky was dirtier than it was today, and when Sweet Hands himself was a young man recently liberated from Southern strictures. This young man in the photograph looked like he had been liberated too: or maybe he was just feeling what Los Angeles was back then, in that era of hairspray and starched clothes, when the city had a proper stiffness to it, and also a certain glimmer, like the shine of those freshly waxed V8 cruisers that rolled along Central Avenue at a parade pace of fifteen miles per hour. Sweet Hands held the picture a long time, and finally let out a short grunt that was his bodily summation of all the emotions this unexpected encounter with the distant past had brought him. "Johnny. That's his name. Johnny something."

"Torres."

"Oh, yeah. Johnny. Johnny Torres. I remember the Torres people." They were one of the first Mexican families to move into these bungalows, way back when Mexico was a novelty Sweet Hands associated with sombreros, donkeys, and dark-eyed beauties with braids and long skirts that reached down to white socks and patent leather shoes. After the Torres people had left—four of them, he seemed to remember, including khaki-pants Johnny here—there hadn't been many other Mexicans around until well after the Watts troubles. They started to show up in large numbers in the years before the Rodney King mess, in fact. It was quite a thing to be able to measure the passing of time by the conflagrations one had seen, by the looting crowds and the fire-makers. Bad times chased away his "people" in all the senses of the word: his relatives, his fellow Louisiana exiles, and most of the other sons of Africa who once lived here. His people had gone off to live in the desert, leaving the place to the Mexicans. Sweet Hands understood, from the way they carried themselves and from the singsong cadences he detected in their speech (without understanding precisely what it was that they were saying), that they came from a verdant place like his own Marion, a place of unrelenting greenness and tangled branches where the rain made songs on the tin roofs. The Mexicans brought with them that slow, boisterous, and tropical feel of rural Louisiana, and he liked having them around, especially since all his relatives had moved out to Lancaster. The few times his daughter and grandchildren came back in their clean and ironed clothes and told him "This place stinks" were enough for him to ask that they not come back—and to resist their entreaties that he move out to the desert. Here on Thirty-ninth Street, Sweet Hands could still take a couple of buses and find the last place in South Los Angeles that served Louisiana buffalo fish, and he might find two or three other old-timers there to talk about baseball and Duke Snider and Roy Campanella, and watching the Yankees play the Los Angeles Angels in 1961 at the old Wrigley Field, just a short walk away on Forty-second Place. There wasn't any buffalo fish in Lancaster, it was dry as all hell out there, not a place for a man from Louisiana to live. Whereas on certain moist summer mornings the seagulls came to Thirty-ninth Street and circled over the trash cans behind the garment factory, where the taco trucks tossed the tortillas they didn't sell. When Sweet Hands closed his eyes and listened to the caw-caw of the seagulls, he could see the ocean.

"Yeah, I remember this guy," Sweet Hands said finally. "He used to live right there. Where Isabel and her kids live now. Moved out ages and ages ago. I think he moved to the desert. Or to Huntington Park. Used to be that Huntington Park was all the rage. A lot of people from here moved to HP, especially after they opened up that Ford plant . . ." With that he returned the photograph to Araceli, who looked crestfallen. "Sorry." He gently closed the door and got back to his Dodgers, even as Brandon and Keenan stood up on their tiptoes to get a glimpse of the television inside.

"Now what do we do, Araceli?" Keenan asked as they walked back toward the street. The question echoed in Araceli's mind in Spanish: *¿Y ahora qué hacemos?* Araceli looked down Thirty-ninth Street and the end of the path she had followed to get to this place. It would be dark by the time they reached the bus stop and she sensed that walking through these neighborhoods at dusk could be worse than putting the boys into Foster Care, and that the best course of action might be to simply pick up the nearest pay phone and call 911. "Maybe we should go to this Huntington Park place," Brandon offered. "That sounds like the kind of place my grandfather would live . . . by a park." This absurd suggestion only made Araceli feel more trapped and desperate. *I am the woman who cleans!* She pulled down angrily at her blouse, which had been bunching up on her since they had left the house, then plopped herself down on the edge of the sidewalk. The boys followed, their Velcro-strapped tennis shoes next to her white, scuffed-up nurse's shoes in the gutter.

The unwanted closeness caused the muscles of her legs and back to tense. *Why are you so spoiled and helpless? Why can't you have one nosy aunt or uncle or cousin nearby like all the other children on earth?* She was going to have to make a decision about them. Was $250 stuffed in an envelope every week enough to justify this march across the city? Looking across the street and to her right, she saw a phone booth. If she just picked up the line and called, then maybe she could get the Foster Care people without summoning the police. *And then I would be free.* Down the block to Araceli's left, a group of squat men and women with round faces gathered around a taco truck, in a chatty cluster before the swing shift began at what she guessed was a garment factory. Behind them she could see a loading dock with a large opening to a vast interior space with low ceilings and a bluish glow, engines groaning and puffing metallically. The boys from the Room of a Thousand Wonders did not know that there was a world of dangerous machines and a city of dark alleys all around them. Having been thrown together with these two boys, in the inescapably intimate situation of being their sole care-taker, Araceli suddenly felt the great distance that separated her life from theirs. *I am a member of the tribe of chemical cleansers, of brooms, of machetes and shovels, and they are the people of pens and keyboards. We are people whose skin bakes in the sun, while they labor and live in fluorescent shadows, covering their skins with protective creams when they venture outside.* Deeper and farther away to the south, beyond the mean city, there were rocky landscapes where men dug tunnels under steel fences, and deserts where children begged for water and asked their fathers if the next ridge was the last one, and cried when the answer was no. Brandon and Keenan did not know of such horrors, but Araceli did, and had survived them, and she wondered how many scars the boys might have after a night or two, or perhaps a week or a month, in Foster Care, which she imagined to be an anteroom to that dark and dangerous world. Maybe she couldn't and shouldn't protect them, maybe it was better for them to see and know. *Maybe innocence is a skin you must shed to build layers more resistant to the caustic truths of the world.* She wondered if she was living at the beginning of a new era, when the pale and protected began to live among the dark and the sorrowful, the angry multitudes of the south.

Behind them a door opened and Araceli and the boys turned around to see the woman from the first bungalow heading down the steps and walking toward them, with three giggling children trailing behind her.

# 13

Isabel Aguilar peeled back the curtain and spied on the lost strangers through the window of her small living room, which also doubled as the bedroom of her son and the Other Boy who lived with her. The three strangers sat on the curb, two white boys and a *mexicana* in a foul mood. Encounters with disoriented travelers were not unusual on Thirty-ninth Street, where Isabel's rented bungalow stood at the edge of a district of hurricane fencing and barbed wire, of HELP WANTED signs in Korean, Spanish, and Cantonese, where cloth was transformed into boutique T-shirts and steel was cut and solvents were mixed. When lost pedestrians reached Isabel's front step and contemplated the industrial horizon that began on her street, they realized they were in the wrong place and knocked on her door, twisting their faces into question marks: "¿Y la Main, *dónde está?*" "You know where my homie Ruben lives?" "Have any idea, honey, where I might find the United States Post Office?" Isabel answered the door for all of them, and sometimes opened the outer metal barrier, the better to hear their questions, even though she was a single mother living with her two children and the Other Boy who was not her son. She had been born in a town in the municipality of Sonsonate, El Salvador, a place of rusting railroad tracks where the green mushroom-cloud canopy of a single ceiba tree billowed over the central plaza and where neighbors knocked on your door expecting to be invited in.

The big Mexican woman sitting on the curb stood out among the parade of the lost on Thirty-ninth Street first for the startling photograph she presented as a calling card, an image of Isabel's bungalow before the floors sagged and the doors and windows were encased in steel, and second because the children she had with her were obviously not hers. Isabel detected a faint coloring of Oaxaca or Guatemala in their skin—perhaps she was their aunt or cousin. But there was something decidedly non–Latin American in the air of pampered curiosity with which they sized up Isabel and the bungalow. They reminded Isabel of the children she had cared for in Pasadena when she worked there one summer, boys who knew the abundance of expansive homes with unlocked doors and clutter-free stretches of hardwood floor that were swept and polished by women like her. Why was the Mexican woman dragging them around these parts, where the only white people she saw regularly were the policemen and the old man who collected the rent?

"What are you looking at?" asked the Other Boy behind her. "Why are you on my bed?" His name was Tomás, he was eleven, and he had lived with Isabel and her son and daughter for two years. The Other Boy was an orphan, and under strict orders to be quiet and grateful, and to bother her as little as possible, though he was constantly forgetting that last commandment. Isabel turned and gave him a scowl that involved a slight baring of her pewter-lined teeth.

"¡Callate!" she snapped.

Tomás raised his eyebrows, smiled, and turned away, unfazed, returning to the movie he was watching with Héctor, Isabel's son and Tomás's best friend on earth, and with María Antonieta, Isabel's daughter.

Isabel found her natural provincial generosity once again pulling her toward the front door and down the stairs. These small-town instincts had gotten her into trouble before—the Other Boy being the principal reminder of this. But she sensed that outside on the curb there was a woman in a situation much like her own: alone with two children and the Other Boy and only the twice-monthly visits of the father of her children, Wandering-Eye Man, and his cash stipend to make the situation livable. Her ex had visited the previous weekend, which was why

Isabel had had her nails and hair done, but all she had accomplished with that was to make his eyes fix on her for a heartbeat or two longer than usual.

When Isabel opened the door, Héctor, María Antonieta, and the Other Boy paused the movie they had been watching on their DVD player and the three of them followed her out the door and down the stairs.

Isabel leaned down and asked a question softly of Araceli. "*¿Tienen hambre? Tenemos* hot dogs."

"Hot dogs?" Keenan shouted. Before Araceli could answer, her charges were rising to their feet and following the three children into the bungalow. Araceli mumbled a "*Gracias*" as she scrambled after the children and up the three stairs through a doorway whose wood moldings had been painted and repainted so many times over the course of eight decades they seemed to be made of clay. They entered a room where the floor nearly disappeared in the impossible clutter of furniture: a secondhand sofa of coarse fabric, a dresser, two beds, a television, and assorted shelves squeezed between walls of much-abused plaster that held the memories of the dozens of families that had lived there, including a clan of worn-out farmworkers named Torres.

When Keenan and Brandon stepped into this space, their eyes were drawn to the alabaster face of a motionless woman on the television screen. She was holding a large white scepter and wearing a crown of crystals, while riding a chariot pulled by a panther. "Hey, this is a cool movie," Brandon said as he and his brother dropped themselves to the carpet, to watch the image atop the dresser spring into movement, while the three children in Isabel's care positioned themselves around their guests, all five children craning their necks upward to watch an elaborately staged battle unfold between the stacks of folded clothes and towels that framed the television on either side. Brandon's eyes were momentarily drawn to the tall votive candle burning on one edge of the dresser: the flicking flame illuminated Saint James the vanquisher of the Moors, a sword-wielding man on horseback trampling people underfoot, an image that suggested that the memory of warfare and conquest was alive among the inhabitants of this home.

Araceli followed Isabel to the kitchen, which occupied the transitional space between the room where the children were watching television and a third room in the back where there were two more beds and a dresser covered with cold creams, rouges, eyeliner, and perfume bottles and makeup containers that filled the air with a bouquet of ethanol and coconut oil. From this spot, Araceli could keep an eye on the children, and also watch as Isabel drew water from the tap and filled a pot to boil the hot dogs. *La señora* Maureen would be scandalized: she insisted that all cooking in her home be done with bottled water.

"And the kids?" Isabel asked Araceli in a conspiratorial Spanish half whisper. "What's going on with them?"

"They belong to the family I work for," Araceli said in a matter-of-fact voice. "Their parents disappeared on me. And I came looking for their grandfather. I thought he lived here."

"Maybe he lived here once. But I've been here two years and haven't seen any other *viejos* other than Mr. Washington." Isabel opened a cabinet and removed a small, flat package from a space where boxes, loaves of bread, cans, and plastic bags were packed in as tight as passengers on a Mexico City subway, then threw the package into a microwave, and the room was soon filled with the sound of corn popping. Araceli looked over and saw that Brandon was talking to the children who lived here, their heads leaning forward, Isabel's boy nodding, his eyes narrowed in an expression of serious contemplation. She wondered in which language they were conversing.

**W**hen the movie ended, Brandon and the Other Boy renewed their discussion of the plot and characters, talking in a bilingual mix of English and Spanish that leaned heavily toward the former. "I think the *bruja blanca* has to come back in the next movie," the Other Boy, Tomás, was saying. "There's lots of movies where people come back from the dead."

"Who are they going to do battle with if not the witch?" Héctor offered, and then he and Tomás looked at Brandon, because in the twenty minutes they had been watching the movie together Brandon had, with a few comments and observations, already established himself as an authority on the subject.

Brandon moved his head back and forth in a gesture that meant *Yes and no.* The movie was based on another series of books Brandon had read and finished, over the course of Thanksgiving and Christmas vacations and many school nights in between during his fourth-grade year. More than a year had passed since he had completed the seventh volume in the series, but he remembered all the books in great detail. "The witch is really dead and she's not coming back. But she's in another book that comes before this one."

"Really?"

"Yeah."

Brandon began a patient, detailed recitation of the long, winding series of adventures of the characters portrayed in the movie, an epic narrative that involved an apple core, the tree that blossomed from it, a piece of furniture built from the tree, and various magicians, professors, and animals with visionary powers, all unfolding in the City of London and other places in the real world, and in a magical, parallel realm. Brandon had also read about the historical war that took place in the background of the seven-volume fantasy saga, in a big picture book called *Eyewitness: World War II*, and he wove a few events from that conflict into the story that he told Tomás and Héctor, who were shocked to hear that German planes had bombed British cities and transformed entire neighborhoods into flaming rubble. "How could they do that to the kids down there?" Tomás asked, and Brandon replied, "Don't know. That's just the way war is, I guess."

"It happened to my grandpa in the war, in Chalatenango," Héctor interjected, causing the other boys to stop and look at him and await more details, though he had none. Héctor was a shy boy and not a natural storyteller, and El Salvador was a place that might as well have been a place from a fantasy novel, because he had never been there and he knew the country only from the stories his father told him during his twice-monthly visits.

Returning to the fantasy saga depicted in the movie, Brandon told them how, over the course of seven books, it had become clear that the magical and the real inhabited the same physical space—"not like in the movie, where they have to go into that closet to get to the other world." Brandon shared this revelation with Tomás and Héctor with special relish, because it matched his growing sense of the weird urban districts in which he and his brother were traveling. The train had brought them to this place called Los Angeles, where the magical and the real, the world of fantasy books and history, seemed to coexist on the same extended stage of streets, rivers, and railroad tracks. "Did you know that there are Vardurians living close by?" he told his new friends. "The Fire-Swallowers chased them to the railroad tracks and the river. Did you know that?" Tomás and Héctor looked perplexed: *They haven't read those books either*, Brandon realized.

"There are many things happening in this city, but I haven't heard of any Fire-Swallowers," Tomás said, giving a philosopher's rub to his chin. Tomás knew more about the real Los Angeles and its vagaries than other boys his age, and he had never imagined it to be anything other than a harsh kingdom ruled by adult realism and caprice. He was a semi-orphan (that's what Isabel called him sometimes, "*un semi-huérfano*"), a wily survivor whose parents were slaves to a Colombian drug recipe, and each had dragged him separately through some of the filthiest single-room-occupancy hotels in the city. He had a four-inch-thick file in the Los Angeles County Department of Children and Family Services, a set of folders marked with red tabs in the cabinet of the social worker who had lost track of him at about the time he fell to Isabel. He had ridden on top of trains in southern Mexico, snuck into the backs of buses in Calexico, and had once called the Los Angeles City Fire Department's 911 emergency line when his father's eyes rolled back and he had stopped breathing on a bus bench on Main Street, an act of heroism that had later earned the boy belt lashes from his recovered father: "Don't let me fall asleep like that again! You hear me?" Tomás knew his alphabet and went to school now that he lived with Isabel, and he was lucky enough to have a teacher who could see how bright he was despite the fact that he could not read more than a few words at a time. Tomás had learned to place himself in the path of generous and educated people from outside the calculating and cruel milieu that dominated his life—a patient teacher's aide, an alert produce vendor willing to give a poor boy a banana or an orange or two. The well-read, English-speaking boy before him now struck Tomás as another one of those people, and he concentrated on every word the boy was saying, telling himself that he would one day learn to read books so he could study these stories himself. Tomás did not know books could contain dramatic and violent tales rooted in real life. As Brandon wrapped up the final fate of the characters in the movie, the boys were still dipping their hands into the bowl, and starting to chew at the few unpopped and salty kernels at the bottom of the bowl Isabel had set out for them.

"A train crash? No way!" Tomás shouted in disbelief.

Brandon gave a nod of solemnity. "It was a surprise to me too."

"*¡Tomás!*" Isabel cried from the kitchen. "*¡Venite para acá!*" His exclamation had alerted Isabel to his presence at the moment she and Araceli were discussing what else to feed the children. Isabel was short of milk and other foodstuffs, and now she summoned Tomás for a quick run to the market. She believed that running errands was the one thing the Other Boy was good for, and when she saw him coming back with groceries, or hunched over the sink washing the dishes, or at the table chopping carrots, she felt less stupid for having been tricked into becoming his guardian. "*Andate a la tienda y comprame leche y un poco de ese queso que le gusta a mi hijo,*" she commanded. "*Y pan también. ¡Apurate!*"

Isabel slipped two bills into his palm, money supplied by her Mexican visitor. Tomás was a lithe boy with luminous, summer-burned cherrywood skin, and was an inch or two shorter than Brandon, but when he moved through the house and street it was with the confidence and gracefulness of an adult athlete. He winked one of his smart brown eyes at Brandon as he stepped out the door.

Brandon and Keenan jumped on the bed and watched through the window as Tomás walked away. *He's going down the street by himself! Without any grown-up! And now he's jaywalking across the highway!* Nearby South Broadway resembled a highway to Brandon, and seeing Tomás sprint across its four lanes of asphalt was like watching a diver jump off a rocky cliff into a narrow pool of water. Tomás slipped into a gray stucco prison labeled LIQUOR MARKET and emerged a few minutes later carrying one white plastic bag in his right hand and two in his left. Now he executed a return sprint across South Broadway, running with a scurrying gait thanks to the weight of the bag, and in less than a minute he was climbing up the stairs to the bungalow.

"*Esta vez no aplastaste el pan,*" Isabel said at the top of the stairs in Spanish that was too fast for Brandon to understand, though he judged from the harsh tone that Isabel had given him a reprimand, or perhaps another command. Sure enough, a moment later Tomás was in the kitchen, slipping the jugs of milk into the refrigerator. Isabel snapped at him again in Spanish and the boy climbed up on the counter in the kitchen to retrieve a box from a cabinet near the ceiling. From these interactions Brandon was able to intuit that Tomás was not Isabel's son, and that, in fact, he was a slave.

Slavery was another of those vicious human institutions depicted again and again in the various fantasy and history books Brandon pored through. In the prologue to *Eyewitness: Civil War* there were photographs of chains that wrapped around the necks and ankles of slaves, and etchings that showed slaves being whipped, and these images gave greater weight to the tales of slavery in *Revenge of the Riverwalkers* and other works of fiction he'd read. Clearly, Tomás wasn't that kind of slave, since there were no chains to be seen in the house, but he wasn't a free boy either, free to play and shout and read. Rather, Tomás was at the mercy of the pretty but angry woman who ran this household. Now she was making Tomás do something Brandon would never have imagined another boy their age doing: he was serving everyone dinner.

**W**hat was left of Scott's anger melted away in the early afternoon drive back from South Whittier to the coast, and when he made the final turn onto Paseo Linda Bonita, he realized Maureen had every right to hate him. He had behaved poorly the night of their argument, and aggravated his sins to higher orders of shame by leaving his home and his post as patriarch for seventy-two hours. The absence of his family's voices and faces from his direct orbit had brought him a sense of clarity about his own failings, if not necessarily the courage to face the consequences of his actions. He parked the car in the driveway, not wanting to open the garage and set off the grinding motor and door slam that would announce his arrival to the interior of the house. Instead, he performed a quiet sidle into the living room through the front door, sensing that the element of surprise would work in his favor during the reencounter with his wife. He listened for the sounds that would give away the location of his children and Maureen, but heard nothing.

He peeked into the kitchen and found the basins and marble counters in silent repose: the stainless steel sink was bone-dry, and the science geek in him kicked in and deduced it had not been used for several hours, at least. Now he noticed the stuffy air: the air-conditioning was off. This realization led him to begin moving through the house more aggressively and purposefully. When he opened the door to the garage, he was not surprised to find Maureen's car missing, final confirmation that none of his family members were here, because his children would have to be with their mother. Unless . . .

"Araceli!" he called out from the kitchen. "Araceli!" he called out again in the living room. Finally, he opened the sliding door and stepped into the backyard, walking up to the edge of the new desert garden, looking past the alien form of the ocotillo and into the garden's deeper recesses, which were populated by shorter succulents and sandy paths. He turned away from the cacti and returned to the kitchen, and used the phone there to call his wife, but the call went directly to voice mail. Next he moved to the guesthouse, and gave the door to Araceli's room three blows of his closed fist. "Araceli," he shouted again, and then listened for movement in her room, but heard only the very distant whir of a leaf blower, and the taps of a hammer coming from another corner of the undulating hillside subdivision. "Araceli!" The absence of the Mexican employee in the middle of the week was more disturbing than all the other absences; it was a dramatic break in the routine that signaled, in Scott's mind, that a kind of crisis, a deliberate flight, had played itself out here, as if word had come of an impending tsunami, a landslide, a fire. He stepped in a slow daze back through the interior of the house, wondering if he might discover a clue to his family's whereabouts. In the bathroom he found a soap dragon on the mirror, pouncing. *That's weird.* It suggested boredom, like the scratching a castaway might leave in his cave while waiting to be rescued. In the boys' room the beds were made, there were no toys on the floor, and this orderliness also felt unnatural. He opened the closet doors and noticed a conspicuously empty space on the top shelf, and after a few moments remembered that the boys' suitcases were usually stored there.

*They've gone.*

*They've run away.*

He felt his wife's anger at work in the empty stillness. After twelve years, could this be the long-feared final break, the end of their family project? *This is what happens when you strike and injure your wife. She leaves, of course. What else did I expect?* A bland, numb, and lonely future loomed, the silence and emptiness of this child- and wife-free moment stretched out into a future of carpeted and sparsely furnished bachelor apartments. What is a father without his family? A lonely object of scorn or pity. He would be transported back to the directionless, passionless days of his adolescence and young adulthood, when algorithms were his only progeny. Daydreaming about his children, about the daily routines that would no longer be his pleasure to share, he unconsciously followed the same path his sons and Araceli had taken some hours earlier: out the door, into the cul-de-sac, and downhill toward the front gate, accompanied by the same canine protest. He drew the stares of the Mexican landscaping crew that had failed to take notice of Araceli nine lawns and gardens earlier, his distant eyes suggesting to them the sorrow of a wealthy man. *You see: even a big house in a flawless neighborhood like this one cannot guarantee happiness.* At the front gate, the pregnant attendant watched him approach and asked, "Sir, is there something I can help you . . . ?" but he was soon past her, headed toward the bus stop and then into the meadow behind it, following a ghost trail through the grass that led down toward the Pacific.

*We Californians drift to the sea. I will fall asleep on the beach and the rising tides will pick me up and carry me westward, like those Mexican fishermen who left their village chasing sharks, only to find themselves with cracked lips and sunburns weeks later on an island in the South Pacific.*

After they had finished their meal, the four boys and Isabel's daughter sat on the front stairs of the bungalow, with Araceli and Isabel behind them in the living room, Araceli making sure she didn't allow more than thirty seconds or so to go by without glancing at Brandon and Keenan as she listened to Isabel recount in great detail her romance, pregnancies, and eventual falling-out with Wandering-Eye Man. Isabel had opened the inner door to catch an evening breeze after a day in which the sun had beat down on her little structure, and the children had gravitated to the steel security door, and had been drawn outside by the air molecules that squeezed through the pinholes. In between pauses in Isabel's monologue, Araceli heard the occasional passing car on Broad-

way, a whistling firecracker exploding several blocks away, and a meren-
gue from the building next door that was going on about lips and kisses,
and more kisses, in a chorus of *Bésame, bésame, bésame.*

On the porch just past the open door, Tomás was telling the newly
arrived visitors the story of the neighborhood he, Héctor, and María
Antonieta lived in, as Tomás understood it from two years of observations made from the doorway and his bed, which was under the window that faced out onto the street. Many a night he had crawled out from
under the covers and peeked out the window to investigate the source
of a noise, relaying whispered descriptions to Héctor, who was usually
too frightened to get out from under his covers and look for himself: "It's
the police. They've got a guy, I haven't seen him before. He's sitting on
the curb. They're pulling back his hands." "It's just some drunk guy." "She's
crying and she's hitting him on the chest and now he's hugging her
again . . ."

In Tomás's mind the window and the doorway were like a television
of constantly switching channels, with new actors and dramas arriving
to perform on the Thirty-ninth Street set before departing for new lives
in other neighborhoods offstage. Having himself survived a transient
existence, this did not strike Tomás as an abnormal state of affairs. He
watched people pull up to the neighborhood in Chevy Novas brimming
with boxes and towels pressed against the curving glass of rear windows, or jumping off the backs of pickup trucks, or on foot carrying
their belongings in big duffel bags they dragged forward on the sidewalk like stubborn farm animals. They came chatting and laughing in
large family groups, or quiet and alone with flight bags tucked under
their arms, squinting up at the street names on the sign poles to make
sure they hadn't taken a wrong turn. Tomás secretly took in their stories
with his eyes, and now he tried his best to relate what he had seen, to
show his new friends that he could tell tales too, even though he had
never read a book. Thirty-ninth Street was a book-story, Tomás now
realized, although one with characters more varied and fleeting than
those in Brandon's readings.

Many of the events in the neighborhood book-story took place underneath the four streetlamps visible from the front porch, Tomás said.
They were nocturnal machines that came to life with a snap and a buzz
an hour after sundown, and their yellow glow had the curious property

of subtracting the color from the street, so that the events of the night played out like a black-and-white movie. For many months the neighborhood story was dominated by events that took place at the far edge of what could be seen from Tomás's window, at the corner of Calvino Street, underneath a streetlamp recently repaired by a crew of city workers with a truck that had a stretching bucket that lifted a man into the air. A group of young men used to gather underneath the lamppost on Calvino Street, not for its light (which they repeatedly broke with rocks) but for the markings they had painted on the post's metal skin, a tangle of letters and swirls that made the post resemble a stiff, tattooed arm. The young men gathered for conferences, listening with their hands in their pockets as the members of their group took turns making speeches, and then they would wrestle one another and shadowbox, and sometimes they would pick one boy and pummel him while they counted to thirteen. The lamppost was no longer covered with graffiti, and the cluster of young men no longer gathered there because they had gone off to battle in another neighborhood, Tomás had heard, and afterward their spot under the lamppost was occupied for several weeks by police cruisers staffed by bored officers with leaden eyelids.

With the young men gone, other people spilled out onto the streets, Tomás said. On some nights the male workers from the factories played soccer using the no-longer-tattooed lamppost to mark the goal, and their shouts, whistles, and laughter echoed against the buildings. There was a teenage girl who sat in a doorway of the apartment directly behind the lamppost, and for several months a teenage boy had come to court her. They talked for an hour or two each night at the open door, the girl's awkward silhouette framed by a kaleidoscope television light flickering through the doorway. Once the girl came down and sat on the steps next to the boy, pulling down her skirt and adjusting the straps on her blouse, her leg touching the boy's, until the bulky shadow of the girl's mother appeared in the doorway. Tomás said he watched the couple talk for eight nights until the boy stopped coming, leaving the girl on the front steps with her elbows resting on her knees, waiting. After two nights she slipped inside the room with the television, leaving Tomás with a peculiar and enduring desire to see her again, though he never did.

Over here, to the right, on the sidewalk underneath the lamppost near the corner of Thirty-ninth and Broadway, a street vendor had come one Saturday evening to sell toys, Transformers, at a price that lured buyers from distant places. As the crowd of milling people around his wares grew, the vendor gave both Héctor and Tomás a Transformer. The next week more peddlers appeared, men and women selling toy cars made of steel, balloons, dolls, and other objects made of plastic or wrapped in plastic, and the crowds grew even further, enticing vendors of churros and hot dogs to come and sell also. These vendors laughed and chanted the names of their wares, and drew other strangers, who came to glue posters on the lampposts, and finally the crowds on the narrow street grew so large that people were blocking the Saturday traffic. Then the police cruisers returned, their lights strobe-flashing rosy light against the factory buildings, the apartments, and the bungalows, and the vendors disappeared. Today the only reminders of that noisy marketplace, Tomás said, were the broken Transformers that he and Héctor still had and the two or three layers of posters glued to the lamppost a few feet from the bungalow, the paper slowly bending and peeling with age. Tomás pointed out the old posters to the visitors and Brandon rose to his feet and briefly examined the lamppost from the front steps of the bungalow, seeing words and pictures half exposed by weathering.

"Los Tu-ca-neys de-el Nor-tay," he enunciated slowly, taking delight at the phonetically exotic sounds emanating from his lips, foreign words that appeared to derive a meaning from the black leather vests and tiger-print shirts worn by Los Tucanes, a group of troubadours who traveled, apparently, in the tractor-trailer depicted behind them. He imagined them rolling into this neighborhood, which was clearly a crossroads, an outpost, an oasis of some kind. Brandon's books were filled with accounts of such places, gathering-spots in jungles and deserts, in caves and on mountaintops, market towns where the protagonists rested before important battles and other plot shifts. Some secret force drew people to this place. How else to explain all the comings and goings of travelers, warriors, and traders, and then his own arrival with his brother and Araceli on their long trek from the Laguna Rancho Estates?

Some nights, sitting on these steps, Tomás continued, he would see a man walking down South Broadway and imagined he might be his father, especially if the man advanced with the uneven, slumped-over walk of people whose heads were swimming with what Isabel called *estupefacantes*. Tomás wasn't especially eager to see his father, and the sight of these drugged and drunk men often caused him to retreat back into the bungalow, lest the old man come and claim him and renew their hotel-hopping adventures. But Tomás quickly realized it was silly to think this, because his father and mother were almost certainly dead: if they were alive they would have come looking for him long ago, because they needed him to help feed them, and to call the ambulance when they lost consciousness, even if they said they didn't want to be rescued.

"Maybe our parents are dead too," Brandon said absentmindedly. "Maybe that's why they left us alone with Araceli."

"No, they're not," Keenan said. "I talked to them."

Before Keenan could explain further, Araceli was hovering over them, telling them it was time to go to bed. They changed into their pajamas and giggled a bit with Tomás and Héctor in the darkness, until Araceli stretched out on the floor alongside Brandon and Keenan and told them all to be quiet. The weariness of a day spent walking and traveling soon caught up with the boys, and they slipped effortlessly into a sleep that was black and complete, devoid of dreams, fantasies, and illusions.

"Nah, I wouldn't recommend setting out on those freeways, I really wouldn't at this particular moment." The hotel clerk was a smart, cosmopolitan-looking young Iranian-American man of about twenty-five, and he offered his advice with a relaxed confidence that made it just a bit harder on Maureen to leave and rush home to her children, so that she could solve the mystery of the unanswered fifty rings of the telephone at her home. She was several hours past checkout time, apparently; there was no way around that, which was unfortunate, because after the fight over the new garden Maureen had a newfound appreciation of the buying power of the money she would be throwing down the drain by leaving. But more serious than wasted cash was this new fact about the traffic. "Look, I just came in off the Ten, and it isn't pretty in either direction. It could take you five hours to get into the city. It's the Fourth of July tomorrow." Maureen contemplated five bumper-to-bumper hours with a volatile, well-rested baby girl in the backseat. "But if you leave first thing in the morning, it'll be free and clear. And you can have the breakfast buffet you already paid for. We'll have fresh croissants!"

When she balanced the traffic and the croissants against the unanswered phone, the idea that her boys were probably out with their father on some "boys-only" adventure seemed more plausible. They were out, running away from the shut-in fever that gripped the residents of 107 Paseo Linda Bonita on long weekends. She imagined them camping in a forest, the boys snuggled next to their father after sunset, asleep in their underused nylon sleeping bags on a bed of pine needles, underneath the darkening summer sky.

Araceli awoke to the feel of the stiff floor beneath rising and falling with a wavelike motion, and opened her eyes to see the unilluminated, bare lightbulb above her in a pendulum swing. *¿Un temblor?* Unmistakably, yes. And then it was over. Now she took note of the white summer-morning light streaming through the gaps in the thick rubber skin of the curtains, dust dancing in the shafts. She propped herself up from her position on the floor in the center of the living room, and saw Keenan asleep on Tomás's bed, and Brandon on the floor between her and Tomás, resting upon billowing rafts of polyester comforters imprinted with parrots, Japanese action figures, and the logo of a Mexican soccer team. Brandon lay with an open mouth and craned neck that suggested to Araceli a tortured, uneven sleep, and Keenan with a wet hitchhiker's thumb before his mouth. They had slept through the morning street cacophony that seeped past the iron bars and through the curtains: a motorcycle sans muffler, a truck whose passing weight caused the wooden floor to shift, a wino's squealing call to prayer: "Wooooo ooohhh! Mother-fuuuuuuuckers! Earthquake! Come an' get it! Come on!" Araceli considered the pathos of the well-fed and long-haired Torres-Thompson boys amid the exterior noises of poverty and addiction, asleep inside the cramped nest of the bungalow living room, with its particle-board dressers and walls whose gray paint seemed to be perspiring. The boys' thin hair was moist with sweat and they gave boy-sized puffs of breath that floated upward toward the bare glass bulb, now still again. What would Maureen say and do if she were to suddenly appear and see her two princes sleeping in a room with a Salvadoran and a Mexican boy? Her *jefa* would lower her thin, lightly sculpted eyebrows into an aggressive prow of disapproval, she would make assorted English half-word noises of outrage. *Humph! You brought my children here? To this disgusting little bungalow tenement? To sleep next to an orphan boy?*

*Yes, señora,* Araceli would say. *You were gone.* And that would be the end of the argument.

Araceli stepped carefully over the boys on the floor, opened the front door, and walked out into the street, toward the liquor-grocery and its public telephone.

# 14

Their bus headed eastward, deeper into the modern industrial heart of the metropolis, over the north-south thoroughfares and railroad tracks that carried cargo and commerce, into districts of barbed wire and sidewalks blooming with fist-sized weeds, past stainless-steel salt-water tanks excreting briny crystals, past industrial parking lots with shrubbery baked amber by drought and neglect, past storage lots filled with stacked PVC pipes, past stunted tree saplings and buildings marked CHOY'S IMPORT and VERNON GRAPHIC SERVICES and COMAK TRADING, and through one intersection where a single tractor-trailer loomed and groaned and waited. The setting triggered no new reveries in Brandon's overactive imagination, because he was too sleepy to think, having stayed up late into the night thinking about Tomás and his stories about the crossroads on Thirty-ninth Street, and then being forced to get up early by Araceli for the departure to their next destination. They were headed for a park where it was said his grandfather might live.

"I don't know where," Araceli said. "But I know who to ask." She told them about her friend Marisela, and the uncle of hers by marriage who lived in Huntington Park, *su tío político*, a man said to occupy an orderly American suburban house in a neighborhood that was also the one *el abuelo* had moved to, according to Mr. Washington back on Thirty-ninth Street.

"This uncle of my friend can help us," she said.

"You have a friend?" Keenan asked, and wasn't surprised when Araceli didn't answer.

Already, it seemed to Araceli, things were going more smoothly than she expected, the bus was advancing quickly through streets with little resistance from the usual weekday morning traffic. For a moment Araceli was struck by the emptiness, and the sense that she might be missing a key piece of information that explained this strangely quiet Tuesday.

They switched lines on California Street and headed southward, now inside a bus in which they were the only passengers, alone with the driver's unauthorized personal radio. "That was a four-point-eight, centered in Barstow," the radio declared. "L.A. County Fire Chief Bill Abrams asks that we all use fireworks safely . . . There's a red-flag warning in the canyons of Los Angeles and Orange counties, which means acute fire danger . . . It's clear sailing on the freeways for all you holiday travelers . . ." The bus entered a neighborhood of cream-colored mini-Mission cottages with arched doorways, and unadorned apartment buildings that resembled Monopoly hotels, the skyline behind them dominated by the steel monsters of twin power trunk lines, and a half-dozen parallel strings that drew the boys' gazes upward to watch their arcs descend and rise from one tower to the next.

"We're following the electricity," Keenan said.

"Yeah," Brandon said. "We're like electrons or something."

They reached their final stop and moved to the door at the front of the bus, Araceli taking a moment to ask the mustachioed driver, who looked Mexican, "*¿Qué se hizo toda la gente?*"

"*Es el* Fourth of July. *¿No sabías?*" the driver said, the English coming out as harsh as a native's, the Spanish flat and unused. "Wake up, girl. Haven't you been listening? It's a holiday!"

**M**aureen rolled her car out of the spa at the early but sane hour of eight-fifteen in the morning. She arrived at Paseo Linda Bonita without stopping three hours and twenty-six minutes later, according to the onboard computer in her automobile. By then, the sun was noon-high and July-strong, and for some reason her husband's automobile was baking in the driveway instead of the garage, an incongruity that nevertheless lifted the anxiety that had overtaken Maureen the night before. *Scott is here.* She opened the garage door, parked her car, and took pleasure in the feeling of having returned to take charge of the home she had built. With her daughter on her arm, Maureen walked purposefully to the door that led from the garage to the kitchen, step-ping inside with a shout of "I'm home!" Her eyes settled on the familiar and spotless kitchen, each square of clean tile, each gleaming plane of marble a musical note of order. "I'm home!" Maureen shouted again, putting a little rasp into it this time. The sound echoed through the home without an answer, and for a second or two Maureen concluded this must be a silence of resentment, and that her sons and husband would soon emerge from one of the rooms glowering at her because she had left them for four days.

They debarked from the bus onto a wide avenue that seemed very new to Brandon and very old at the same time. A line of storefronts rose over the street, each edifice a bold, rectangular robot emblazoned with the names of commercial concerns: SOMBREROS EL CHARRO, KID'S LOVE, SPRINT MOBILE. The multitudes that filled this shopping district on most days were absent, and in the soft light of that holiday morning there was only an eight-foot-tall teenage girl with braces and a billowing white dress to greet Araceli and her charges. She was frozen giddily in two dimensions behind a curtain of black steel bars, and when Brandon peeked into her darkened storefront prison at the merchandise that sur-rounded her, he saw glittering, child-sized crowns and pictures of char-iot limousines. This was a place, he concluded, where girls came to be transformed, by dollar and by ritual, into princesses. But Brandon didn't like princess stories and his attention quickly returned to the street and to his brother and Araceli, who were both turning their heads north and south and back again.

"Which way do we go?" Keenan said.

"*Tengo que preguntar,*" Araceli said, but there was no one around to ask, and they began to walk down the sidewalk, past parking meters and empty diagonal parking spaces, underneath the fluted tower of a shuttered Deco movie palace, Keenan craning his head to admire the melting green skin of a nonfunctioning bronze clock affixed to the top. After half a block, they found one store with an open door and lights on behind the display windows.

"Not open," said the Korean woman inside. She was kneeling on the floor with a clipboard, surrounded by boxes and racks of rayon blouses. "*Cerrado.*"

"I am not looking for clothes," Araceli said. "I am looking for a street." She showed the woman a slip of paper with the address Marisela had given her.

Myung Lee rose to her feet, took the address, and then sized up the child-accompanied woman who had given it to her. In the four months since opening her business, every day seemed to bring another oddity, another riddle, like this Mexican woman and her handsome children. Myung Lee was a native of Seoul, single, thirty-eight years old, and fluent in the language of local fashions: rayon with tropical flowers and leopard prints and bold décolletages, free-flowing polyesters to drape over bodies of any shape or size. "Maybe I know this street," she said. Geography was easy: what she didn't understand was the stealthy methodology of the shoplifters, or the pricing logic of the wholesalers in the garment-factory district, or why her uncle would lend her $40,000 to open a business, while expecting her to fail. This Fourth of July morning brought more lonely hours of inventory, and more obsessive daydreaming about her uncle and his haughty California millionaire confidence and his thin teenage daughter with her size-two dresses and their mansion in that Asian Beverly Hills called Bradbury. The longer Myung remembered her debt to her skeptical *samchon*, the more she hated rayon and tropical flowers and leopard patterns. Oddly, however, she still liked being in the presence of American women, or Mexican women, or whatever most of her clients were, and as she moved to the door to show Araceli which way to go, she felt the irritation on her face slipping into the pleasantness that was always good retail practice.

"This is over there," Myung Lee said, pointing to the east. "Not far. Two blocks." She placed a hand on Keenan's shoulder and said, "Your boys are very nice," leaving Araceli too stunned to offer any clarification. *Their father must be very fair*, Myung Lee thought, and she imagined this missing white partner as the strangers walked away down Pacific Boulevard. *I am a single woman, yes, but I haven't allowed a man to leave me with two boys to feed and clothe. No.*

"She thought you were our mother," Keenan said. "That was weird."

"*Estaba muy confundida,*" Araceli said, and they headed away from empty Pacific Boulevard into a neighborhood of houses with sandpaper skins painted blue-violet and carnation-pink, with little patches of stiff crabgrass enclosed behind painted brick pillars and iron bars welded in feather and fan patterns. A canopy of intersecting utility wires drew Brandon's eye upward again, while Keenan looked across the street and saw a man leaning against a fence with his hips thrust out in the style of Latin American *campesinos*, a pose that reminded Keenan of the handful of childhood photographs he'd seen of his grandfather. "Maybe this *is* where Grandpa John lives," Keenan said.

"I guess," Brandon said. "It's not as poor as Los Angeles."

They advanced two blocks more and the street name still did not materialize on any of the signs, and Araceli stopped again, and the rolling wheels of the suitcases ceased their noise, and for a moment she and her charges stood in an unexpectedly deep silence. The thoroughfares and the freeways that surrounded the neighborhood were empty in those first hours of a holiday morning, no trucks or forklifts were at work in the nearby industrial districts, and in the absence of the usual noise there was a natural stillness that seemed somehow unnatural. Every Huntington Park resident who was up and about that morning noticed the quiet too; it hit them first through the windows left open on a summer night, and later when they stepped outside. They heard the calls of the birds for the first time in months, the *keek-keek* of high-flying, black-necked stilts heading for the nearby Los Angeles River, the three-note carols of American robins, and the Morse-code tapping of woodpeckers hunting for acorns stored inside the utility poles. As their ears adjusted to the quiet, they heard fainter sounds still: the whistling of air through the wings of the mourning doves, and the creak and rustle of tree branches moved by the weak flow of the July wind. They were small-town sounds, country sounds, and they had the effect of making those who heard them more aware of the charms of their time and place, and of all that was comforting and homey in the cluttered workingman's paradise that Huntington Park wanted to be.

The quiet caused Victorino Alamillo, the only man awake and out-doors on his block, to pause in the unfurling of his American flag, con-templating for a moment his 1972 Chevy truck and camper shell in repose in the driveway, until his eye was drawn skyward by the sight of a crow bullet-gliding one hundred feet in the air. After climbing to the top of his ladder, he stopped again, flag in hand, because from that perch the spread of the quiet across the neighborhood was all the more apparent. He could scan the roofs of his neighbors' houses, see their satellite dishes and kitchen vents and the nearby district of salvage shops, and hear a few distant but sharp sounds: the *fee-bee? fee-bee?* question posed by a black phoebe, and then, most improbably, the braying of an invisible goat. *¿Un chivo?*

Suddenly, the spell was broken by a clack-clack coming from the sidewalk.

"Excuse me," Araceli said. "Excuse! Me!"

Araceli and her charges had stopped at their first encounter with a person who seemed capable of helping them—a man whose flag seemed to imbue him with authority. They had been watching him for several seconds, beginning with his climb up the ladder, flag in hand, looking to Brandon and Keenan like a man claiming a piece of real estate for his country at the end of a battle.

Victorino Alamillo looked down at Araceli, and hearing her marked accent answered, *"Espérate allí un momentito."* Seeing this lost trio, ob-viously in flight from some familial mash-up, brought him fully back to the real Huntington Park, reminding him of the transient, unsettled place this really was. Suddenly, the flag and the hammer he was hold-ing both fell from his hand.

"I think the star means he has a kid who's in the war," Brandon said, pointing to a rectangle with a single blue star that was affixed mys-teriously to the inside of the home's living room window.

"Correct," Victorino said, as he descended to retrieve the flag. "My son is in Kandahar. *En* Afghanistan. He is a medic." He pronounced this last word in a way that conveyed pacifist fatherly pride.

"That's cool," Keenan said.

*"Estamos buscando esta calle,"* Araceli said. *"La calle* Rugby."

*"Está del otro lado de* Pacific," Victorino said, pointing westward. *"Regrésate por allá."*

"*¿Está seguro?*" Araceli asked, rather impertinently. "*Porque una coreana nos dijo que era por aquí.*"

"*Sí, señorita,*" Victorino said. Switching to the authoritative sound of English, he added, "I've lived here fifteen years. It's that way."

Araceli grave a curt "*Gracias*" and without further ceremony headed west, with Brandon and Keenan trailing after. They had entered a landscape of very old American dreams. Huntington Park was a collection of truck farms subdivided a century ago into a grid of homes, and inhabited ever since by men and women lured in by affordable mortgages, by a shared belief in the value of square footage in a U.S. city, the nearby factories, warehouses, and freight trains be damned. For the first third of its history Huntington Park had been homesteaded by English-speakers with Oklahoma and Iowa and other flat American places in their pasts, and for the next third of its history those proud but paranoid people had fought to keep various dark-skinned others out, until finally evacuating in favor of those who dominated Huntington Park in the most recent third of its history: transplants from South Texas, Jalisco, Zacatecas, and East Los Angeles, and other places filled with Spanish-surnamed people. All these home owners, in all these epochs, came and found comfort in the perpendicular streets, in the surveyor's patient construction of uniformity and efficient use of space, in the stop signals, and in the city workers who cleaned the parks. A red-and-white-striped flag and its blue field with white stars had long been a symbol of that nurturing and protective order, and it remained so for many in Huntington Park, even those who still preferred the colors of other flags and the other kinds of order those banners represented.

With the clack-clack of Keenan's suitcase resuming behind him, Victorino Alamillo took his Stars and Stripes and began to hammer, unaware that the sounds were rousing his neighbor Jack Salazar from his bed, causing him to pull back a curtain. *Alamillo is putting up his flag. Finally! He waits until the actual Fourth!* Jack Salazar also had a blue star in the window, and a son in Ramadi, Iraq, and two American flags that hung from the eaves 365 days a year. He noted that with the addition of Alamillo's flag there were now three houses on the block that were bold enough to show their patriotism on Independence Day—*a whole three!*—though one of those belonged to a Pakistani family, and they almost didn't count in Salazar's right-leaning, fourth-generation

Mexican-American opinion. The Pakistani family's flag was plastic, and Salazar sensed they'd put it up so he would stop looking at them suspiciously, or so that he would come over and chat with them as if they were normal Americans, though the truth was that the Pakistani family put up that flag because their daughter Nadia had purchased it during an immigration-rights march in downtown Los Angeles. Nadia Bashir, a twenty-year-old UCLA biochemistry undergrad, had decided that hanging it over the front door would make for a personal and somewhat ironic statement about her family's ongoing state of cultural evolution. On the day she put up the flag, she remembered her uncle Faisal and his tales of his first, carefree travels through middle Canada and middle America in a Volkswagen Beetle in the 1980s, selling bongs from the trunk. The U.S., he liked to say, was still the feel-good country he had known then.

"There are no clans here," he'd say. "That is why the Americans prosper. They don't have these silly, inbred resentments like we do. We are too clannish. It's always held us back."

To which Nadia very often answered, in the sassy and slightly nasal tones of a Los Angeles accent that sounded charmingly provincial to her Pakistani-born, London-educated uncle, "No clans? Gimme a break! Even in this tiny city, all we have is clans!" In Huntington Park there was a large Spanish-speaking Mexican clan, and the shrinking but still influential Mexican-American clan that never spoke Spanish, and a small clan of people who still called themselves white, and the scattered and reserved Koreans and Chinese, and now a very quickly growing Muslim clan, which was the newest in this part of the metropolis and thus the most feared and misunderstood by all the others. Add to this the warring clans of the street gangs with their baroque entanglements, and the caustic comedy delivered by the two political clans viciously facing off every other Tuesday at the meetings of the City Council, and it all looked as messy as anything on the subcontinent. There was an undercurrent of psychic violence to Huntington Park, Nadia thought, alive underneath a façade of coexistence that was as fragile as the quiet that had miraculously enveloped the neighborhood this morning, interrupted only by the clack-clack of three outsiders walking past her bedroom window.

"Maybe we should show someone the picture of our grandpa, to see if he lives around here," Keenan said.

The same idea had occurred to Araceli, until she remembered how ancient the photograph was—she would only make a fool of herself. This neighborhood they were in now, Araceli noted, was clearly newer than the one that housed the shack where *el abuelo* Torres had lived a half century ago, and most of the people she could see stirring behind screen doors and windows were much younger than he was. They seemed unabashedly Mexican to her, despite the occasional U.S. flag. Araceli sensed they were, like her, relatively recent beneficiaries of the American cash boom, that they were housekeepers and laborers just a decade or so ahead of her in filling their dollar-bill piggy banks. No, they would not know John, Johnny, or Juan Torres, so she wouldn't waste any energy asking. Instead, she would find Marisela's uncle and ask him to tap into those rivers of American information that were still a bit of a mystery to Araceli, the lists of names and numbers that smart fingers could make appear on computer screens, and he would make a phone call, and liberate her from her charges and this journey.

Huntington Park more fully awakened in the half hour it took Araceli and the boys to return to Pacific Avenue and cross to the other side, into a neighborhood where they were greeted by the creaking springs of two sets of garage doors opening. Freshly showered patriarchs began to retrieve oil-barrel grills, lawn chairs, and other Fourth of July accoutrements, while behind kitchen curtains stoves sizzled with cholesterol-spiking breakfasts. Brandon felt an order in these sounds and their growing volume, the power of routines repeated behind fences and inside homes, while Keenan grew more convinced they were closer to his grandfather, because these were noises he made with his clumsy, old-man hands. As the day progressed further the neighborhood noises would grow louder and more varied: they would become electric and gas-powered, amplified and transmitted far beyond property lines, with pirated MP3 melodies and power-tool percussion jams ruining the quiet inside next-door living rooms where old men were trying to read, goddamnit, to bedrooms a block away where adolescents were trying to sleep past noon. The growing holiday din reminded every resident of the existence of their many neighbors and all their irritating habits, of their penchant to shout for Mom and their poorly maintained toilets, their excessive hair-drying, and how they badgered their sons and daughters and disrespected their parents. With each hour the noise grew, and it grated, serving as further proof, if any were needed, of the central, inescapable fact that subtracted from Huntington Park's pleasantness: the existence of too many people, too close to one another, in too little space.

The residents of Huntington Park were going to try to forget these many irritations during a Fourth of July they planned to fill with hamburgers and *carne preparada* with cilantro, and mesquite charcoal and the not-necessarily-patriotic acts of crabgrass-lounging and beer-can-lifting. It was a time of down-market plenty in Huntington Park, thanks to second mortgages and their illusory windfalls, and the extra cash on hand from copious overtime working at ports and railyards and warehouses unloading goods from an Industrial Revolution taking place on the other side of the Pacific. *Les va bien*, Araceli observed, *because the Americans still have plenty of money to spend on the things that people like me and these people can do for them.* Araceli did not know, however, that the flow of containers marked with Asian logograms had begun to slow, imperceptibly, and that the burden of mortgages here had begun to grow, as it had elsewhere, leaving the working people of Huntington Park worried about all the purchased pleasures of second cars and debt incurred when garages were converted to playrooms, and thus a bit relieved, relaxed, and decompressed by the prospect of enjoying a free pleasure this evening. For the Fourth of July there would be no tickets to buy, no parking to pay for, no lines to form, but simply the joy of resting and having the show brought to them when the inky curtain of the post-sunset sky fell over the horizon. At that hour they would turn their lawn chairs and their necks toward Salt Lake Park and the municipal fireworks show, and all the neighborhoods across the city grid would be joined together by the light and the explosions of Chinese powder, louder than any other noise on that noisy day. They were sounds of simulated battle meant to unite the respectfully quiet families of Huntington Park and their dysfunctionally loud neighbors in place and purpose, reminding them all of the name of the sovereign land upon which they were standing: Los Estados Unidos de América, the USA. It was a land held together by paychecks with tax deductions and standardized forms available in just about any language, and police cruisers that sometimes stopped late at night at the homes of the most serious violators of aural tranquillity, to tell them to keep it down, if you would, please. And it was home to a suburb where two boys wandered with their caretaker, scanning the doors and windows for a grandfather who had never lived there.

The rest of the home was as perfect as the kitchen. Maureen found no truant dishes wandering about the house, no bowls filled with cereal and curdling milk in the living room. No dirty clothes marred the hallways, none of the small Danish building blocks were tossed about, the windows were free of smudges. In Araceli's orderliness Maureen sensed an explanation for the emptiness. *They've gone off to do something, it seems, and Scott has taken Araceli with him, which would be the sensible thing to do, and Araceli cleaned before they left, because Araceli is like me and cannot step away from a disorderly home.* But what about Scott's car? Had they left on foot, on an expedition to the park, almost a mile away? Or a picnic in the meadows?

Maureen decided she would wait for them to return, and made lunch for her daughter, leaving the pan and dirty dishes in the sink for Araceli to clean. When they had finished, she said: "Come on, Sam, let's go find your brothers . . . and your father." They were probably walking back from the park. "Let's go rescue them, because that's a long walk uphill. Wonder if poor Araceli can make it."

Five minutes later Maureen and Samantha had pulled up to the same park where she had deposited Araceli and the boys in a fit of pique two weeks earlier, but it was empty, all the maids who usually gathered there absent because it was the Fourth of July. She accelerated away quickly, drove back toward the Estates, and stopped at the bus stop, and from the front seat of the car she looked into the knee-high grass of the meadow, which had been bleached golden-green by the sun, remembering that she actually picnicked there with Scott and the boys a few years back, to take in the unobstructed view of the ocean. They would have returned, but for the cow chips that littered the field and ruined the taste of her sandwiches and of the Pinot Noir. Now she searched the shifting surface of the windblown grass for her husband, or her children, or the tall, thick shape of her Mexican employee.

"Where are they, Samantha?"

*Wherever they are, they have to pass by here. On foot, or in a car, they have to enter through this gate.* She had turned off the engine, wondering how long she would have to wait, when she saw a figure emerge on the horizon, a man walking where the meadow dropped steeply, struggling to keep his footing, as if working against an unseen tide.

Araceli unlatched the front gate, followed a straight path through a crabgrass lawn, climbed up to a porch, and rang the doorbell. Her long journey to reach this address was rewarded, delightfully, by the sudden appearance at the door of a ruggedly handsome man in his forties who greeted her with a chivalrous *"Buenos días"* and the same pencil-thin mustache and jaunty smile that had broken hearts when he left Mexico City two decades earlier. Salomón Luján was expecting Araceli and her charges, because an hour earlier he had half listened to his niece's explanation of the Torres-Thompson family saga, while simultaneously watching two work crews install a canopy tent and trampoline in his backyard for the big Luján family Fourth of July fiesta.

Now Mr. Luján stood at his door and heard Araceli tell the story of the absent parents herself. *"Estás haciendo lo que debes hacer, y tus jefes te lo van a agradecer,"* he said. Once a common laborer, Salomón Luján believed that being loyal to your gringo employers was the secret to *mexicano* success on this side of the border, his barrel-chested exertions on behalf of various warehouse owners and construction contractors having lifted him through many layers of North American achievement, including the purchase of this home, his triumphant entry into the water-heater business, and his oath-taking as an American citizen and his recent election to the Huntington Park City Council. He sized up Araceli and decided she too was destined for something better, and, judging from the free-flowing hair styles and leather-sandaled feet of her charges, she was the one who kept order in the hippie household where she worked.

"Stay with us today and tonight if you like, and tomorrow I will find the grandfather," he said, switching to English for the benefit of the two boys. "Today is impossible, because it's the Fourth of July and all the city offices are closed. But first thing in the morning I'll call the city clerk and check voter registration and we'll find him. For the moment, come to the backyard. Our party is just getting started."

He led Araceli and the boys through his living room, which was decorated in a style Salomón's smart-aleck Ivy League daughter called "Zacatecas Soap Opera Chic," with an oil painting of Don Quixote and Sancho Panza on one wall. The Knight-Errant of La Mancha stood for the idea that the Lujáns were descended from a place of nobility and history, where men stood tall on horses and looked proudly over the dry, yellow hills of their patrimony. Don Quixote shared the living room with assorted horseshoes, mounted vintage revolvers, and a sofa-bench and love seat with fragile, wood-carved legs and cream velvet cushions embroidered with gold swirls, both pieces shipped in from "the best kitschy furniture maker in Durango," as his daughter put it. Scattered among these symbols of his romantic outlook were family pictures, including one portrait of the aforementioned daughter in cap and gown, and another of the family patriarch raising a clasped hand on election night with the mayor of Huntington Park. Brandon and Keenan looked at that picture a second or two without knowing what its precise meaning might be, though Brandon surmised from both the image and the air of steadiness and authority of Mr. Luján that he had recently been named president of Huntington Park.

They moved to the backyard, where six rented white tables had been arranged under the mustard-colored light that seeped through the tarpaulin skin of the tent. Salomón led Araceli and the boys past a cluster of half-awake young people gathered at the tables, to the edge of the backyard, where two men with shovels were standing and conversing around a mound of beige dirt that seemed to have bubbled up from the lawn.

"We're having *carnitas*, the way they do it in the ranchos," Salomón told the boys. "There's a pig buried in there."

"Underground?" Brandon asked.

"Yeah, we got hot rocks down there. And the pig, wrapped in foil, cooking. We let it cook for some hours. When it finish, you have very juicy meat. *Sabrosísima*."

Brandon gave the mound a look of innocent puzzlement, causing Mr. Luján and the two sweaty, stubbly-faced men with the shovels to grin: he was, in fact, deeply troubled by the idea that combustion was taking place in the unseen hollows beneath his feet. "I thought fire needed oxygen to burn," he said, but Mr. Luján had turned his attention elsewhere and did not answer, and his two cousins with the shovels didn't speak English well enough to explain the simple physics of their *carnitas* barbecue. After thinking about it for a few seconds, Brandon came to the disturbing conclusion that he was standing over a pit of buried flames, as in the underworlds often depicted in the books he read: souls trapped in subterranean passages, evildoers building infernal machines in caves. He considered, for a moment, running away, until Mr. Luján returned and put his arm on his shoulder.

"Let me introduce you to the people here," he said to the boys. And then he turned to Araceli and said in collegial Spanish, "*Y tú también.*"

For the moment, the only guests were the four young adults sitting half asleep at the table, seemingly hypnotized by the piano resonating from two transistor-radio-sized speakers. A single piano note repeated inside the swirl of a flute, and then a tenor began to sing, pushing into falsetto, and Araceli found it odd that these people with their obvious Mesoamerican features were listening to a rather effete voice singing words in English.

> History involved itself,
> mysterious shade that took its form.
> Or what it was, incarnation,
> three stars,
> delivering signs and dusting from their eyes.

"*¡Buenos días!*" Councilman Luján said, causing his daughter, Lucía, to startle and sit up straight, and her three friends to emit wake-up groans and coughs.

"This is Araceli," he said to Lucía. "She's a friend of your cousin Marisela. And she's visiting us for Fourth of July with the two boys she takes care of. *¿Cómo se llaman?*"

"Brandon."

"Keenan."

"Look, they just finished with the trampoline," Councilman Luján said. "*Vayan a jugar.* Go play."

The boys ran off, while Araceli joined the four young adults. Lucía Luján was nineteen, and Araceli recognized her immediately as the girl in the cap and gown in the living room, even though the thick braids into which she had woven her hair for summer had the curious effect of making her look younger than in the photograph. Her friends wore jewels and studs in the crooks of their noses, and loops inside their earlobes, and presented Araceli with the realization that she was losing touch with urban fashions. Probably they were already wearing these things in Mexico City, or would soon be, Araceli thought. "*Hola, ¿qué tal?*" Lucía said, after rubbing the sleepiness out of her eyes. "I think my cousin told me about you once."

Lucía was wearing the same clothes she had put on the night before, but even in this wrinkled and weary state, she presented a picture of hip and fashionable *mexicana* femininity. She wore a vintage pin-tucked blouse of caramel silk, its shimmering skin playing an odd light-game with the copper tone of her skin and the half dozen friendship bracelets on her wrist. That blouse looked one hundred years old to Araceli and brand-new at the same time. Lucía was two weeks back from Princeton and still suffering from the cruel cultural whiplash caused by her return to Huntington Park: she had lived nine months among assorted geniuses and trust-fund children from across the United States, none of whom understood the contradictions of being a young expatriate from her own, wire-crossed corner of *mexicano* California. A week before finals she had split up with a young man who hailed from a moneyed Long Island suburb, in part because he had talked about coming to Huntington Park this summer, and the thought of him entering her home in his Tommy Hilfiger summer-wear was too much to bear. She imagined him reciting to her friends those Lorca poems he had memorized—*¡verde que te quiero verde!*—and thought, *No, that won't go over well in HP.* She was still trying to figure out where she stood after a nine-month waking dream of calcified eastern tradition and unadorned American ambition. *I am not the same Lucía.* She was trying to figure out too how to tell her father that she had already dropped the premed classes in favor of Walt Whitman, Jack Kerouac, and James Baldwin. Lucía the Ivy Leaguer did not smile or laugh as easily as before, and sometimes she laughed harder and louder and with a kind of cynical meanness her friends did not recognize. Both Lucía's father and her friends had been giving her strange looks as if to say, *Is it possible you think you are better than us now?* It was, therefore, a pleasure for Lucía to fall into conversation with an educated Latina from outside her

Huntington Park and Princeton orbits. After just a few minutes of casual conversation, she had learned a lot about Araceli, the Instituto Nacional de Bellas Artes, and what it was like to clean houses in Orange County.

Araceli said she wasn't sure if she'd ever go back to school, but that she wasn't going to be doing *"esto"* much longer, gesturing rather coldly in the direction of Brandon and Keenan on the trampoline. She had a little money saved up, and the *"aventura"* with the boys would be her last.

Lucía understood everything Araceli said, although her own *castellano* came out slowly and with the simple vocabulary of a much younger person—she had studied French in high school and never been formally educated in Spanish—and she often fell back to English.

"Go with what your heart tells you," Lucía said, and then repeated the phrase in Spanish, *"Haz lo que te diga tu corazón."* She gave a sidelong glance to her friends, who had drifted into semi-sleep again, their heads resting on the table. "I'm studying history and American literature. I don't know why. Just because I like stories, I guess. My dad's got a good story. Maybe I'll write it someday."

Scott had stayed up late into the night on the beach, watching the march of the constellations along the ecliptic, his dark-adjusted eyes making out the oval smudge of the Andromeda Galaxy. He had watched the flight of low-flying birds along the purple-blue twilight waters, the black featureless forms of two helicopters headed southward to Mexico, and the silent, slow drift of lighted ships, and then he had fallen asleep sometime deep into the night, his head resting near the top of the sloping sand that rose from the water. He had been awakened after dawn by the simultaneous assault of the first rays of morning sun on his face and the first wave splashing the balls of his feet. He stretched out, then took a long, slow walk along the beach, listening to screaming seagulls. When he reached a tide pool he'd once visited with the boys, he held back tears at the not entirely rational thought that he might never enjoy such a life-affirming paternal moment again, until finally his rumbling stomach cured him of such melodrama and he decided to begin the long climb back to his house. He would launch a search for his wife and children, who had likely left for Missouri to spend a week, or perhaps a month or two in recreation and exile from their abusive paterfamilias, and perhaps he would go there to plead his case.

He was surprised to spot, halfway through his quarter-mile trek through the meadow, the familiar high silhouette of his wife's car. For a moment he felt a sense of relief and reprieve—they had not left him after all—and then once again a sense of foreboding when he realized he would have to add an explanation for this night out on the beach to his apology for the fiasco in the living room and his absence over the past four days. *She'll think I've gone totally nuts.* He got closer to the car and imagined his unhappy sons inside, and the daughter who would wrap her arms around him no matter what. When he reached the car, smiling despite himself, the electric-driven window lowered theatrically, revealing Maureen's sunglasses, which she quickly lowered to study him and his surroundings with unshaded eyes.

"Where are the boys?" she asked quickly.

"What?"

Maureen had seen Scott appear on the horizon, and she too felt her apprehensions lifting, a motherly reunion just moments away. She too imagined an embrace, or several, dropping to her knees as one did when children were smaller. But no, Scott was alone.

"Where are the boys?" she insisted.

"You don't have them?"

"I have Samantha! I left with Samantha and left you with Brandon and Keenan."

"No, you didn't. I wasn't home."

"What are you talking about?"

"I don't have any of the kids. I left. I thought they were all with you."

"I left on Friday with Samantha."

"You didn't take the boys?"

"Obviously not!"

"Where are they?"

**B**y dusk the Lujáns' ample backyard was filled with a hundred people chewing pork whose succulent juices pooled at the bottoms of paper plates, and triggered memories of summer barbecues in provincial Mexican cities with gazebos and stone churches. Araceli noted that they were significantly better dressed than the summer partygoers at the Torres-Thompson residence. They were all immigrants linked to Mr. Luján by blood, marriage, and business ties, and several were compadres of Mr. Luján and his wife. Not having lost the sense of formality attached to family gatherings in their native country, the men were dressed in freshly ironed shirts tucked into jeans and polished snakeskin boots, and the women wore big jewelry and ran wet combs through their sons' hair, and teased and pulled their daughters' hair into buns, braids, ponytails, and little black fountains held in place with barrettes that bore butterflies and flowers. The men showed off new brass belt buckles with Mexican flags and the names of towns in Jalisco and Durango, and the women moved about in newly purchased jeans or stiff dresses whose wide linen cones resembled the style worn in U.S. movies during the Eisenhower era.

Alongside this older, largely Mexican-born and Spanish-speaking group, there was a younger circle of partygoers, speakers of English and Spanglish, teenagers and sedate twentysomethings who equated good taste with understated flair and the ironic embrace of fashions past. They wore porkpie hats and baseball caps, jeans with narrow legs, canvas tennis shoes and mauve T-shirts of high-quality cotton, and campy links of faux-gold chains. A couple were dressed in baseball jerseys as wide as capes, and the shorts and knee-high white socks that a goofy midwestern suburban dad might wear, their cottoned feet stuffed into *guarache* sandals, a style Lucía liked to call "retro summer gangster casual." They were all people of understated ambitions too, most having graduated to new jobs at hardware stores and composition-writing classes at community colleges, or to long drives across the metropolis to the waiting lists and crowded parking lots of underfunded state universities.

Both groups of guests, young and old, looked at Mr. Luján and his daughter, Lucía, with varying degrees of respect and envy, because in their own way father and daughter were the most successful people they knew. The compadres entered Mr. Luján's home and found its knight-errant furnishings tasteful and elegant, and they saw in Lucía and the famous university attached to her name a shiny specialness that made them sick to their stomachs with worry about their own progeny and how studious and dedicated those children might or might not be. Among her friends too, Lucía was the subject of awe, esteem, and suspicion, because she had gone farther away from Huntington Park than anyone else they knew, and because she had come back from this distant and wealthy place to stand underneath the power wires and sip beer as if she were an ordinary HP girl, even though she knew she would never be an ordinary HP girl again.

Among all these people, young and old, Mexican-born and California-born, the presence at the party of two Orange County boys went largely unnoticed, with Brandon and Keenan slipping easily into the mostly English-speaking orbit of the children, and only a few parents noticing their long bohemian locks, or the ease with which they glided across the backyard in their bare feet and untrimmed toenails. But after just a few minutes no one failed to notice the *paisana* with Germanic height and bronze freckles, dressed like some explorer in a canvas hat, presenting them all with the mystery of her person. She was too old and not casually stylish enough to be one of Lucía's friends, but too young and not formal enough to be one of the compadres.

"*¿A quién llevas en la camisa?*" Araceli asked one of Lucía Luján's friends, switching to English when he didn't seem to understand her right away. "On your shirt. *Ese hombre.* He looks like Jesus, but he is smoking. *Y tengo entendido que Jesucristo Nuestro Señor no fumaba.* Jesus does not smoke."

Griselda Pulido, Lucía Luján's best-friend-forever, heard Araceli's *chilanga* accent, and began to pepper her with questions about Mexico City. Griselda had long thought of Mexico's capital as a kind of Paris, a destination she would visit one day in solemn pilgrimage, a place where a woman with Mexican roots might escape her fraught American existence and find her true self. She wanted to know where the *chilangos* went out at night, what rock bands they listened to, and at which nightclubs they danced. "What is the Palacio de Bellas Artes like?" Griselda Pulido asked. Switching to Spanglish, she asked, "*Tienen las pinturas de Frida allí,* or do you have to go to her house in Coyoacán?"

To Araceli, this woman Griselda seemed as intelligent and curious as Lucía, but with a tragic air that was only heightened by the velvet eye shadow she wore, and cross-combed hair that ran down her forehead and crashed upon the eyebrows. "I got into Brown, which is in Rhode Island, and I thought I'd hang out over there on the East Coast with Lucía, but I couldn't go," Griselda said, and Araceli looked her straight in the eye to say, *I understand completely.* Going to school for as long as they wanted was one of those things *latinoamericana* girls couldn't do, and hadn't been able to do for centuries, the same inequity having kept at least one of Araceli's grandmothers illiterate her entire life. *Our feminine emancipation is incomplete: maybe our daughters, if we ever have any, will be free.* Araceli tried to answer Griselda's questions about Mexico's capital city as best she could, even though she was a bit thrown by the way Griselda weaved English and Spanish together, so freely and without care.

"Lucía and I are going to go there," Griselda said. "*Un día. Tal vez.*"

Araceli wanted to suggest some museums Griselda might not have heard of, but before she could the small man with the smoking Jesus asked her if she'd been to Huntington Park before.

"No," Araceli said. She twisted her mouth into English so Smoking-Jesus Boy would understand her. "But this is a place you can forget easily. So maybe I was here before and I just don't remember." Hearing this, the two homeboys among Lucía's friends stuck their hands deeper in their pockets and squinted approvingly at Araceli through dilated pupils and gave weak and wicked cannabis grins and wondered briefly if this lady had ever been in The Life, over there in Mexico, because she looked like a girl who could handle herself in a fight. A moment later they forgot about her, and looked up at the sickle moon and the first stars of dusk and listened intently to the pulsating bass of the music and how deeply it inhabited infinite space, and then they smelled the fat-laden air coming from the barbecue pit and their stomachs suddenly ached with hollowness, and they decided it was time to get something to eat again.

Araceli was the deepest mystery to all the parents and older relatives present, some of whom were a bit put off when she entered their circle—they were all standing by the tables and their pyramids of pork and side dishes. She was about to plunge her fork into a serving of *carnitas* when she noticed she had inadvertently brought the conversation between the compadres to a sudden halt. "*Buenas tardes,*" she said, eliciting a round of not-especially-friendly "*Buenas tardes*" in return. These mothers and fathers were put off too by Araceli's failure to pay much attention to the boys she was apparently assigned to look after, even when the older of the two approached and said with a stricken plea, "I think someone should tell all these kids to stop playing with firecrackers because it's so dangerous."

"*¿Qué quieres que haga?*" Araceli asked rhetorically, because there was nothing she could do, and the boy snuck away, leaving all those who observed the exchange to wonder what exactly was going on here with this child-unfriendly woman and those American boys.

"It's true what *el niño* says," one of the moms said in Spanish. "Those things are too dangerous. Someone is going to get burned."

"They see more dangerous things at school, believe me," said another mom dismissively, and with this all the mothers and fathers in the circle nodded. "The other day, I go to pick up my son and the entire school is surrounded by police cars and police officers, and there is what they call a 'lockdown.' My son is in the sixth grade, believe it or not, and one of the kids is running down the hallway with a knife. I think he stabbed a teacher in the leg with it."

"*Qué barbaridad.*"

"The things that go on in those schools."

"My son is in sixth grade too, and he doesn't know his times tables past three," one of the fathers said. "'What's six times eight?' I ask him, and he looks at me all confused. So I tell him, 'What are they teaching you there?' and he says, 'I don't know.' In my pueblo, they taught us that in the second year."

"What are we supposed to do?" one of the mothers said.

"You're supposed to go to the teacher and complain," Lucía Luján interjected in English, having just entered the circle on the hunt for her own plate of food. "You're supposed to get in the face of that teacher and say, '*What's up with the times tables?*'"

"*¿Podemos hacer eso?*"

"Of course you can. That's how this country works. Get a classroom full of white kids, and that's what their parents do all the time. They treat every teacher like a worker."

"*Tiene razón,*" Araceli said. "*La señora Maureen, mi jefa, siempre está peleando con los maestros.*"

"But if we go, they don't take us seriously," one of the mothers said, speaking directly to Lucía. "You go to the office and they tell us, 'What are you doing here? Go away. We're busy.'"

They all paused, middle-aged and young, Mexican-born and U.S.-born, and considered the betrayal of the schools, and the steel mesh that covered every window, the security cameras in the hallways, the posted warnings aimed at student and adult alike, and a few of them very self-consciously allowed their eyes to drift over to those young girls and boys who were their blood and their responsibility, running and bouncing in the backyard, each child gleaming and full of promise, and each poor and stripped of it. Boy and girl screams filled the silence that followed, which was heavy with hurt and powerlessness and a certain unfocused sense of workingman's defiance that found no words in which it could be expressed.

Araceli broke the wordlessness suddenly, to say that the kids she cared for seemed to be getting an excellent education.

"Where are they from?"

"*Los* Laguna Rancho Estates. *Por la playa. En los cerros.*"

"The public schools are good down there, I bet," Lucía Luján said.

"*No van a la escuela pública,*" Araceli said. "Private school. *Todo pagado. Y muy caro.* Very expensive. I see the bills."

"How much?" Lucía Luján asked quickly.

Araceli spoke the figure in slow and deliberate Spanish, allowing its mathematical obscenity, its thousands and thousands, to hover over the assembled hardworking, cash-strapped, taxpaying adults and scholarship-funded college students like a blinding glow of fake sunshine. There were one or two gasps, though Lucía Luján's eyebrows rose with only moderate surprise—the tuition for those two boys, together, was a bit more than her tuition at Princeton, before all the financial aid kicked in.

"*Imposible,*" one of the parents said.

"*Estás loca,*" said another.

"*No sea chismosa. Por favor.*"

It was preposterous, and suddenly everyone in the circle except Lucía was angry at Araceli for revealing a figure that, were they to accept it as truth, would temporarily strip them of some of their own moderately elevated sense of accomplishment, by revealing just how small their achievements were relative to true American success and affluence. The compadres with kids in parochial school imagined they were paying top dollar, but in fact it was a small fraction of the sum Araceli had just divulged, even though those gringo boys didn't look so much different than theirs, not especially special, and certainly not that rich.

"*Es lo que cuesta*," Araceli insisted. She explained that she knew this startling fact not because she'd made any effort to find out, but rather because her employers were exceedingly casual with their paperwork and left letters and bills lying around. And with a dollar figure that big screaming from the kitchen countertop, even a normally circumspect housekeeper like Araceli had to take a look.

"You're pretty sure about that number?" Lucía asked.

"*Claro que sí*," Araceli said.

"*No*," one of the compadres insisted. "*Estás confundida.*"

*I might be just a housekeeper and a* chilanga, Araceli wanted to say, *but I know basic English and math and the meaning of commas and decimal points and dollar signs.* But instead she gave a long glance at her disbelieving audience, then shook her head with a dismissive chuckle that was instantly recognizable to Lucía for its thick layering of intellectual condescension. With that all the compadres and Lucía drifted away, leaving Araceli amused and finally able to take a first real bite of the *carnitas*, which were quite juicy. She searched for the boys and spotted them, and then decided she could forget about them again, because here in this big backyard they would be safe.

Brandon and Keenan were running about the backyard with the children of the extended Luján clan. Having watched the men with the shovels remove their dirt and then the foil-wrapped meat, and a few hot rocks, Brandon had persuaded himself that he was no longer in danger from the fires in the earth, though now there were various firecrackers and flames and explosions going off in the air around him. Salomón's brother Pedro had brought three large boxes' worth of assorted hand-held pyrotechnics from Tijuana, and the children were playing with them, the most popular being small silver balls that burst into sparks when the children flung them against the patio's concrete floor.

"I got you! I got you!" a girl yelled as one of her "fire rocks" exploded at Keenan's feet, and Keenan replied by throwing one back at her, and laughing as she squealed.

"Be careful!" Brandon shouted at his brother and anyone else in earshot, though no one listened. A boy was lighting firecrackers and throwing them into the now-empty pig pit and there were no adults stopping him. Gunpowder tickled Brandon's nose, and bits of paper and cardboard from the firecrackers were littering the patio floor and the lawn, and there were other kids igniting sticks that spit fire and whistled, holding them too close to their eyes, and they wouldn't stop even when Brandon shouted out "*¡Cuidado!*" in Spanish. He looked for Araceli, but she had drifted away into the crowd of people tearing at meat from the buried pig with their teeth, and for the first time since leaving his home on Paseo Linda Bonita, Brandon felt truly alone and afraid. The firecracker explosions pinched his eardrums and the neighborhood dogs were suffering too, filling the air with their wailing and barking on this block and all the others surrounding it, begging the humans to cease fire. It was one thing to play war when all the sounds came from your mouth or your imagination, and quite another to be standing in a cloud of gunpowder. Now he heard a powerful explosion, felt the thumping vibration in his chest, and then the echo of the boom. "An M-80!" a boy shouted, and Brandon wondered why no one in the backyard was ducking for cover when there were bombs exploding out on the street.

A flash of light on the horizon caught his eye, and he turned to see three fire bursts growing in the shape of dandelions against the dark gray sky, followed by the muffled sound a few seconds later of distant cannons.

"*¡Son los* fireworks *de la ciudad!*" someone shouted, just as more burning dandelions emerged, their light shining on the distant transmission lines and the towers. "The city fireworks show!" someone else said, and now everyone was turning and watching as more bursts followed, some in the shape of flying saucers, in green and crimson and yellow, some drooping like jellyfish, others slithering through the sky like serpents, and finally one forming a large orb that loomed over the towers and the neighborhood like a small planet, causing many oohs and ahhs from the people gathered in the Luján backyard.

The planet fell from the sky and the explosions stopped, suddenly. For ten, twenty, thirty seconds the adults and children looked up at the blank sky and waited for the next burst of light. They saw only a large cloud of smoke, drifting slowly eastward like a white Rorschach test across the dark sky. From beginning to end the sixty-third annual Huntington Park Fireworks Extravaganza was the shortest in city history, having lasted just four minutes and thirty-five seconds, the city having failed to take note of the nationwide fireworks shortage caused by a warehouse explosion in China's Guangdong Province some months earlier.

"That's it?" someone said in English.

"*¿Se acabó?*"

"What a rip-off!"

Standing by the table where the *carnitas* were being carved, City Councilman Salomón Luján stood with a large serving fork, took in the empty horizon, and uttered a useful English exclamation that had been one of the first to drift into his vocabulary:

"Oh, shit."

After a harried exchange of shouted questions and answers during their five-minute drive up the hill to Paseo Linda Bonita, Maureen and Scott realized that Brandon and Keenan had been alone with Araceli since Friday morning, and that neither had talked to the boys since calling home on Friday evening. The length of their absence stretched out to unseemly numbers: four days, more than ninety-six hours of blank and unknown chapters in their sons' lives, ninety-six hours in which they had abdicated their parental responsibilities. *When they are small, you are vigilant at the playground, you never allow your eye to stray from them for more than a few seconds*, Maureen thought. *And if you lose sight of them, for twenty seconds, for a minute, you are transported suddenly into an abyss of guilt and panic, and you scan the surroundings against the idea that your loss will endure forever, until you spot them and your heart returns to that calm place where parents most seek to live.* Maureen drove past the guard shack without bothering to acknowledge the pregnant woman on duty, and violated the 25 MPH speed limit signs, flying over speed bumps and making several squealing turns up the sinuous streets of the Laguna Rancho Estates. She pulled into the garage and ran into the house, leaving Samantha still strapped in the car with her father.

Although Maureen had been in the house thirty minutes earlier, and recognized the improbability that her sons might have returned in that short time, she called out their names again: "Brandon! Keenan!

Mommy and Daddy are home! Brandon! Keenan!" This maternal reflex became more of a plea and lament with each repetition, until Scott said, "They're not here," which caused Maureen to turn and snap at him, "I can see that!"

Scott began looking for a note from Araceli, and for clues about her departure and destination. There was nothing in the kitchen, the place where one might have expected her to leave a message. In the living room he was distracted by the great open space where the shattered coffee table had once been, and thus failed to notice that one of the picture frames on the bookshelves was empty. He moved back to the kitchen, where he informed Maureen of the undeniable conclusion that their children had not been home for a while. "If you look closely you can tell the bathrooms haven't been used for at least twenty-four hours, if not longer," he said. "And no one used the kitchen until you got here and made that meal for Samantha. Right?" Before Maureen could answer, Scott headed toward the door that led from the kitchen to the back-yard and the guesthouse, and stepped across the open space to Araceli's door again, and tried turning the handle.

"Do we have a key for this door?"

For the next ten minutes, Maureen and Scott searched their home for a spare guesthouse key, until they found a plastic sandwich bag filled with keys in a drawer in the laundry room. They rushed back to Araceli's room: neither had set foot in this locked corner of their property for the four years Araceli been their employee, respecting the Mexican woman's privacy and trusting her to keep it clean. They opened the door and entered a space of unexpected clutter and mystery. Their eyes were drawn immediately upward, to an object hanging from the ceiling of the small living room. It hovered over a small drafting table and many drawings taped to the walls, along with pictures cut from magazines, a floating sculpture that drifted very slowly in the faint, hot breeze that seeped through the room's lone, partially opened window.

Maureen stepped back to the doorway so that she could focus on the object in its entirety. It was a bird of prey, assembled from one hundred or more blue, white, red, orange, and yellow disposable forks, knives, and spoons that Maureen had purchased for the last few birth-day parties. The utensils had been fused together into a bird about three feet long, its clawed feet made from broken fork prongs, while many serrated knives were layered together to form the teeth, and two layers or more of utensils formed the body and wings, the smooth plastic covered, haphazardly, with ripped-up strips of discarded clothing and dishrags, the various textures creating an especially meaty-looking representation of flesh and feather. The sculpture had the crude quality of an object formed by a series of haphazard and violent collisions, and in a letter to one of her friends Araceli had called it *El Fénix de la Basura*, the Garbage Phoenix. Araceli liked it both for its disturbing, otherworldly quality and as a commentary on her situation in the United States: she dusted it once a month, but had recently considered taking it down, because in the one-woman artistic circle that followed her work, the Garbage Phoenix was becoming passé. Maureen studied this creation and then examined the drawings on the walls. There was a eight-by-eleven-inch self-portrait in which Araceli had enlarged the size of her own nostrils, and rendered the rest of her face in a Picasso-inspired abstract geometry, but without the master's sense of balance and composition. There were several pencil and charcoal sketches of shoes and sandals ascending and descending the steps in the Tacubaya Metro station, their rotting laces and heels melting into concrete steps covered with swampy moss and dripping water. And there was a collage of hands, assembled from magazines that were stacked on the floor: *My magazines, the ones I threw in the recycling bin*. Maureen studied the hanging sculpture and the drawings, and felt she was looking into the mind of a woman upon whom various psyche-smashing torments had been inflicted. *Is this the same woman who has lived in my house for four years and fed my children and cleaned my clothes? No. This is a stranger. She sulks while she cooks for us, and then she sits here in her free time and creates monstrosities with the broken fragments and discarded objects of our home.* The grim aesthetic of the utensil bird, the cavernous nostrils, and the melting shoes suggested, to Maureen, self-hatred and a suppressed desire toward destruction. Understood in the light of her art, Araceli's surly everyday nature took on new meanings, and this sudden, unexpected insight was all the more unsettling in the light of Scott's announcement that "I looked and there's nothing here, no note, no clue." Araceli had taken the two boys someplace without giving word of where she might be.

Still holding Samantha, who had reached up to try to touch the mobile, Maureen returned to the kitchen and wondered what they should do next.

Forty minutes after the fiasco of the fireworks, Brandon and Keenan stood on the front porch of the Luján home on Rugby Avenue, having been drawn there, along with much of the Luján family and their guests, by the shouting and chanting coming from the street. With Araceli at their side, the Torres-Thompson boys cast a disoriented squint at a crowd of about one hundred people, all of Latin American descent, gathered in the middle of the roadway, under the flickering light of a streetlamp. Some carried beer bottles in foam sleeves, and others held folded lawn chairs, but all shared the disheveled, sun-burned, and offended look of Fourth of July recreation interrupted and unfulfilled. They had come from the park, and they had come from their lawns, confused by the empty sky, the missing explosions, and the very ordinary, very unpleasant sounds of car alarms and car stereos and crying children left in the truncated show's wake. The vacuum caused by the sudden lack of explosive noise was filled by their own voices tell-ing them to be angry, telling them to remember where they lived. It was a holiday insult added to all the usual, daily HP insults—the dirty tap water, the aggressive parking cops, and the annual surprise of supple-mental property-tax fees. "Those fucking council incompetents! Again!" "*¡Pinche ciudad de la chingada!*" And when a certain, very *metiche* woman at the park suggested Luján was to blame, they began to head off in a group to his home, gathering more people on the way.

Councilman Luján appeared on the porch, hanging both thumbs on his belt, and even the children in the crowd seemed enraged, their high-pitched voices adding a feminine squeal to the crowd's collective chant.

"*¡Afuera los Tres! ¡Afuera los Tres! ¡Afuera los Tres!*"

"Out with the three?" Brandon asked no one in particular. "What's that about?"

"They mean my dad and Councilwoman María and Councilman Vicente," said Lucía, who was standing behind him. Sensing the boy was smart enough to understand, she quickly explained the political dispute that pitted her father and two allies against a corrupt mayor. "So whenever anything goes wrong, the mayor blames my dad. And his Special Friend, that lady in the back over there, she gets her rabble from *el movimiento* to come out and harass us because we want to reform things." With that, Lucía stepped to the front of the porch and down the steps to the concrete path that ran through the front lawn, and leaned forward into a screaming shout: "Go home, losers!"

"*¡Rateros!*" someone in the crowd shouted back, starting a new chant with the Mexican Spanish idiom meaning "bandit" or "crook." "*¡Ra-te-ros! ¡Ra-te-ros!*"

"You stole the money for the fireworks!"

"Get out here and defend yourself like a man, Salomón. We see how you spent the money for the fireworks on your own party. *¡Ratero!*"

Having heard Lucía's explanations, Araceli scanned the back of the crowd and spotted the mayor's Special Friend, a woman with a black head of hair-sprayed raccoon quills, her temples sporting identical white wings. She was light-skinned and small inside her wide summer paisley dress, and she held at her side a cell phone, which Araceli understood to be the instrument by which the Special Friend rounded up crowds and exerted her will. The Special Friend spotted Mr. Luján on the porch and gave him a long, self-satisfied stare, like a half-deranged chess master sizing up the effect of a game-changing move on her opponent. Finally she raised her eyebrows quickly, as if to summon a reply from her rival—but Mr. Luján seemed unfazed. "*No hay que hacerles caso,*" he said to his daughter and anyone else who would listen. Mr. Luján said this with calm conviction, a deepness of thought that hinted at reserves of belief and self-awareness. Now the Special Friend was back on the phone, summoning additional troops. Araceli could see the Special Friend and Mr. Luján were locked in a familiar struggle, the same one played out in village councils and big-city demonstrations in their native country, at inquests and in courtrooms, between those who understood that wielding power meant being a paternalistic shepherd to the stupid flock and those who dreamed of an Empire of Reason and a literate citizenry. Araceli could see the Special Friend and Councilman Luján were standing on opposite sides of Mexican history, even as they stood in the United States.

A man in the crowd wearing a backward baseball cap and an incipient beard stepped forward to stand on the edge of the lawn and send a glob of spit toward Lucía, causing Councilman Luján to remonstrate with the spitter and then to pull back his daughter to the safety of the porch.

Keenan, who had never seen an adult use his saliva as a weapon, grabbed Brandon's hand for security. "What is this?" he asked his brother.

"I think it's a lynch mob," Brandon said with the amused detachment of an anthropologist describing some primitive rite. He took a weird comfort in the idea that he had stumbled upon another case where life clearly and obviously imitated literature. He had believed lynch mobs were creations of novelists and filmmakers, but here was one before him, with real people showing their canine teeth and twisting their faces into other expressions that suggested incipient revenge. "I've read about them in books. In this lynch mob, no one is carrying torches. But I guess torches are not, like, required for it to be a lynch mob."

"What are they going to do?" Keenan asked. "Are they going to hurt us?"

"Well, I don't see them carrying any rocks, so I guess they can't stone us. I predict they'll start throwing those bottles and cans. Unless the police get here first. In a situation like this, it helps if the police show up. They call that 'restoring order.'"

A minute later two police cruisers slowly wheeled up to the block, each painted white with slanted steel-blue letters proclaiming POLICE, and progressively smaller letters declaring HUNTINGTON PARK, and the department's wordy motto: DEDICATED TO SERVICE THROUGH EXCELLENCE IN PERFORMANCE. Police Chief Mike Mueller emerged from one of the vehicles, standing tall and thick and midwestern in navy wool, and strode into the space between the contending parties, raising his hands like an announcer in a boxing ring. "I'm sorry, but I'm going to have to remind all of you, once again, that we have a whole new city ordinance related to so-called political gatherings on residential streets."

He kept his arms raised and turned his beef-fed torso 360 degrees, his preferred method for ending these "Mexican standoffs." "Okay, all right, everyone go home now." The crowd in the street obeyed, as did the members of the Luján family on the porch, until Lucía stood alone on the front steps and started a chant directed at the retreating lynch mob.

"*¡Re-for-ma! ¡Re-for-ma! ¡Re-for-ma!*"

Brandon soon joined the chant too, his voice squeaking as he tried to match Lucía's. "Ray-for-mah! Ray-for-mah!"

Keenan stood on tiptoe and joined them too, trying to mimic the Spanish sounds, as his brother was. When the last of the lynch mob was gone and the chanting had stopped, Keenan turned to his big brother and asked, "Who's Ray Forma?"

"*No sé*," the boy answered.


Maureen and Scott stood in the kitchen looking at each other, studying the main work area of their servant, the unwashed plastic tumbler and bowl in the sink the only objects out of place: the leopard skin of the marble countertops gleamed, spotless, even the windows suggested they might squeak if you put a cloth to them. The perfect kitchen and the disturbing art were both the work of the same Mexican woman, and Maureen felt blind and ignorant in the face of this newly revealed proof of human complexity: *I took her for granted, allowed her to seep into the white noise around me*. It was not immediately obvious what Maureen and Scott should do next, and they wandered about the house, hoping that the ring of the phone or chime of the front door would liberate them from waiting for something to happen. For the moment, it seemed likely, or at least probable, that their two sons and their employee might appear at the door at any moment. It was Maureen and Scott's experience as parents that all crises eventually ended and their home returned to its placid normality. Fevers dropped, cuts were stitched up, X-rays were taken, and doctors pronounced the children resilient and fated to healthy lives, and when it was all over the home's routine comforts—the hum of television sets, the salty smell of cheese and prepared meats cooking in the kitchen—confirmed their faith that good parenting values and vigilance would protect them.

But very quickly the passing time and the empty home and all its objects and boyless silence became an excruciating judgment on their own actions, a slow ticking punishment. "Where could they be?" Maureen asked as she wandered into the boys' bedroom and studied the modular plastic boxes that contained their toys. "Where did she take them?" Maureen repeated the questions out loud several times as she moved from the boys' room to the media room and the kitchen, carry-ing Samantha through the house on her shoulder, trying to get her baby girl to take the noon nap that was now two hours overdue. *The time is all wrong for her to go to sleep now. She will be awake late into the eve-ning. She can sense something is wrong; she can sense her parents are panicked.*

Maureen ran through her mind what she knew about Araceli, won-dering if she could summon a fact or name that might provide an an-swer or clue to the question of where she had taken the boys. The mother who had given Maureen Araceli's name was in South America as of three years ago, having become an expatriate for a U.S. company in São Paolo, Brazil, and Maureen had no number for her. Araceli was from Mexico City, if Maureen remembered correctly. It took some ef-fort of memory to produce Araceli's last name: Ramírez, a name con-firmed moments later when Scott found, in Araceli's bedroom, a stack of postcards addressed to her and also the bank book for the savings account Scott had set up for her four years ago. The savings book re-vealed the last name Ramírez too, but the address was their own. "We have a full name, but that's it. What else do we know?" Maureen had no idea what Araceli's parents' names might be. How many people lived in Mexico City? Ten million? Twenty? And how many Ramírezes might there be in such a metropolis? Such a common last name offered these Mexican people a kind of anonymity. *They're all Ramírez, or Garcia, or Sanchez.*

"Where does she go on the weekend?" Maureen asked Scott.

"I think she said to Santa Ana. I'm pretty sure I heard her say that once."

Scott decided he would go through the old phone bills and check for any unfamiliar numbers. He returned from the office with a stack of paper, began scanning, and soon realized he would find nothing. "I think I've seen her use a card or something when she calls Mexico," he said. "And Santa Ana is a local call." The toll-free access numbers for the long-distance services left no trace on the bill, which was pre-cisely what Araceli had intended—she didn't want to owe the Torres-Thompsons any money for the phone bill, and felt the details of her Mexican life were hers alone to possess: they were not for others to see, or study, or to be amused by. Araceli was "very private," as Maureen put it to her friends, and until this moment Maureen didn't mind, because she equated Araceli's reserve with an efficient and serious approach to her job. For a year before Araceli joined them the Torres-Thompsons had a Guatemalan housekeeper, Lourdes, who kept a continual lament about the daughter she had left behind in a place called Totonicapán, often weeping as she did so. After one tearful soliloquy set off by the sight of children her daughter's age celebrating Brandon's seventh birthday in the Torres-Thompson backyard, Maureen had decided to let Lourdes go. Madame Weirdness, the childless woman from Mexico City, came to take her place. *I have allowed this person to live in my home for four years without once having a substantial conversation about where she is from, about her brothers and sisters, or about how she got here. I have allowed this foreign mystery to float from one room of my home to the next, leaning into the vacuum cleaner, flexing forearms as she mops with that look that often goes far away. I have allowed this state of affairs to persist, and may have placed my sons in danger, in exchange for her chicken mole, for the light and tart seasoning of her black beans, and for the passion we share for the sanitizing power of chlorine.*

Maureen's ignorance about Araceli's life beyond Paseo Linda Bonita meant she had no information on which to base even an educated guess about where the Mexican woman might have taken Brandon and Keenan. "Where did she go? What is she *doing* with them?" If Scott was right and they hadn't been in this house in two days, at least, then the situation became even more inexplicable: Why would a woman who had shown so little interest in her sons suddenly take an overnight excursion with them? As the light shining through the windows lost its white sheen and aged into a faint yellow, and the shadows in the succulent garden turned longer, and the memory and guilt over her own absence from the home grew fainter, Maureen's thoughts took on a darker and increasingly suspicious hue, leading her to declare, just a few minutes before sunset:

"I think we're going to have to call the police."

# 15

Not long after the lynch mob dispersed, Keenan put his thumb in his mouth and wandered to the backyard and slumped down in a lawn chair. Araceli found him there, and realized her charges needed to go to bed. She approached Lucía, who offered her bedroom, saying, "I'm going to be out late." The boys could sleep on her bed, and Araceli in a sleeping bag on the floor, she said, and soon Brandon and Keenan were dozing off underneath a poster of Frederick Douglass, a photograph of a teenage Spanish matador clipped from a magazine, and the orange and silver tassel from Lucía's high school graduation cap. Araceli dozed off quickly too, studying the image of the bullfighter in the dim light projected by a streetlamp through the sunflowers on Lucía's curtains, and wondering what her *gordito* Felipe would look like in a bullfighter's tights: comical, most likely. She wondered if he had tried to call in her absence.

"My children are missing. My two sons."
"What is your name?"
"Maureen Thompson."

"And you are their mother?"

"Yes."

"Are you calling me from your home?"

"Yes."

Maureen had punched 911 into the kitchen phone, and had reached a female voice that was following the passionless protocol of emergency operators, establishing essential facts in a weirdly detached voice.

"What are their names?"

"Brandon and Keenan. Torres. Torres-Thompson."

"How old are they?"

"Brandon is eleven. Keenan is eight."

"And when did you last see them?"

"Yesterday," Maureen said quickly.

"Yesterday?"

Maureen paused at the operator's tone of surprise, and in the brief silence she could hear a roomful of voices in the background. "No, no, I mean day before yesterday."

"Sunday?"

"Yes, Sunday morning." Maureen could not bring herself to say four days ago. Had she been slightly less panicked she might have felt the need to unburden herself of the full, complicated truth. But it would have taken a very calm, rational frame of mind to untangle for a stranger how a mother and father could abandon their sons for four days, and how it all went back to a dying garden and an argument in their living room. "My husband and I. We went to a spa." She looked up at Scott, who was shaking his head, but this only strengthened her conviction that taking the time to explain their fight in the living room and the events that followed would only slow the search for their sons. *This is not the time to revisit our little episode with the table.* And what did it matter anyway? The important thing was to find the boys, to bring them back to the shelter of this home. "We left them with the maid. Sunday. With their nanny." Two tones sounded, an automated notification that the conversation was being recorded. "We told her we would be back this morning, but we were a little late. And we've been waiting all day for her to come back with the kids. We don't know where she is."

"We?"

"My husband."

"He's there with you?"

"Yes."

"His name?"

"Scott Torres."

At the Orange County Emergency Communications Center, the operator considered the choices on her screen, which required her to classify the urgency of the dozens of dramas, mundane and bloody, that were whispered and screamed at her through her headset each day. Satisfied that the two children in this case were in the presence of an approved guardian (the nanny) and that the usual perpetrator in missing children cases (the father) was present, she reached the correct conclusion that this was probably not an abduction in which the children were in imminent danger, but rather some sort of household miscommunication. The caller was clearly lying about the last time she saw her sons: *Probably she's trying to get us to move quicker*, the operator thought, *probably she saw them just a few hours ago.* Emergency Operator II Melinda Nabor was a Mexican-American single mom with two young boys at home who were being looked after by their grandmother while she worked, and it was her experience that parents and "caregivers" got their signals crossed all the time. The "caller location" flashing on her screen was an address in one of the ritziest neighborhoods in the county, and she imagined herself saying, *Get a grip, lady. I'm sure your expensive Mexican nanny has everything under control.* Sometimes the operators let slip words of wisdom to the confused people on the other line, but Emergency Operator Nabor never did so, she always stuck to the call scripts and protocols, with their comforting sense of logic and professionalism, and their ability to channel events of all kinds into a machinery that translated human folly into codes and correct "unit deployments" from the twenty-eight overlapping law-enforcement jurisdictions in her calling area. In this case, it would be the county sheriff, to a community so rich it collectively preferred to be unincorporated rather than pay for its own city government.

"We're sending a patrol car out there."

"Thank you," Maureen said meekly.

"Orange County sheriffs. They should be out there shortly."

"Thank you."

•

Deputy Ernie Suarez was taken by the incongruity of the setting, a red-eyed mother lost to a mourning lament in her perfectly appointed living room, the father holding the baby girl because the mother was so distraught. "My beautiful boys. I left them and now they're gone," the mother cried. "They're gone!" He had entered the Laguna Rancho Estates only once before, on a domestic violence call that was coincidentally in a home on this very same block, an old sailor beating up on his Vietnamese wife, who didn't cry or scream about pressing charges, but just looked out the window at the ocean, dazed, most likely thinking about the continent on the other side of that curving blue hemisphere. Otherwise this part of his patrol area was a dead zone. He'd drive his Chevy Caprice past the front gate, wave at the guard, and accept a thumbs-up as the signal to execute an accelerating U-turn back down to the real city and the real work.

"We left them with their nanny. With our housekeeper," the husband said, repeating the story the mother had told before she started weeping.

"Araceli is her name, right?" the deputy said, looking at his small notepad.

"Yeah."

"And a last name."

"Ramírez."

"Age?"

"Late twenties. I think."

"Where's she from?"

"Mexico."

"Immigration status?" Deputy Suarez knew he really wasn't supposed to ask that question, but the word "immigration" was out there in the air, in the television news chorus, the talk radio banter: immigration, immigrant, illegal, illegals. You heard "Mexico" and you thought of one of those *i*-words, and you thought of a crime. And when you heard a Spanish surname that ended with a z, like his, you thought of Mexicans and the various federal codes they violated when they jumped over a steel fence into the United States. Other than that z, Deputy Suarez had no connection to Mexico himself, and saw no contradiction between his growing concern about Mexico and *i*-words and his Texas Gulf Coast family history.

"I have no idea whether she's legal or not."

"But you're pretty sure she's from over there? From Mexico."

"Yes."

Deputy Suarez bit his lip with concern. A few weeks back he had traveled down to the Border Patrol station in San Ysidro, to have lunch with an old sheriff's deputy pal and to get a closer look at a potential career move into federal law enforcement. As a result of this conversation Deputy Suarez's vision of Mexico had undergone a rapid devolution. Up to then, he'd thought of the Border Patrol gig as a chasing-chickens kind of job, a human roundup in the desert, and Mexico as a colorful haven of booze and cheap handicrafts. But to hear his old pal tell it, there was a terrorist army growing on the other side of that fence, flush with cash from cocaine and crystal meth. These lawbreakers lorded over Baja with their automatic weapons and their fleet of luxury SUVs stolen from law-abiding Californians, and they had weird nicknames like "Mister Three Letters" and "The Crutches." They controlled the smuggling rings that brought people through the desert and sometimes right through the checkpoints because there were customs agents on the take: "You can smell it," his friend said. It disturbed Deputy Suarez to think that there were places where the waters of corruption ran so deep and wide that even the well-paid agents of the U.S. government could be swept in. The drug gangs ran kidnapping rings that snared doctors and schoolteachers and the children of the Tijuana rich, and they tortured their enemies and tossed their bodies onto highways with notes attached and severed fingers stuffed into their mouths. "There's some scary fucking shit going on down here, bro." Deputy Suarez had gone to TJ as a child, and he remembered holding his mother's hand as she weaved between the teeming market stalls, worrying that he might get lost. Now there were these new, real-life demons set loose in that city behind the fence.

"You think she might have taken them to Mexico?" the deputy asked Scott.

"No. No. I mean, no, I don't think so. But I'm not sure. What? Do *you* think she might have taken them to Mexico? Does that happen?"

"Hey, it's what doesn't happen that surprises me."

Scott led him to Araceli's room, thinking the deputy's professional eyes might see something there he could not. "This is some weird stuff," the deputy said out loud. His eye was drawn to one of the cutout magazine pages stuck to the wall with tape: it showed an oil painting of a woman prone on a bed, her face shrouded by a white sheet, legs spread open. A baby with the face of an adult woman bearing a single eyebrow emerged from the woman's vagina. Deputy Suarez said, "Jeez, that's really sick," and took a subconscious step backward. He had managed to complete four years of high school and two years at Rio Hondo College without studying a single work of modern art, and he was also in the minority of people of Latino descent in Southern California who had never heard of Frida Kahlo. *This is what they call "pathology." I remember that from my criminology class.* He next looked at Araceli's cubist self-portrait and mistook it for a drawing of one of the two missing boys. *What is the word for this? "Dismembered." The face is dismembered.* He started to wonder if perhaps the children were being harmed by this person in some hidden place.

Having seen enough, the deputy left the room and asked the father for photographs of the two boys and the nanny, and the man and his wife disappeared into other rooms deeper in the house to search for them. Once he was alone, the deputy called his station. There were two or three kidnap-to-Mexico cases every year in the county, though they always involved immigrant families and domestic disputes. A cross-border kidnap case in the Estates involving a nonrelative screamed urgency. At any rate, it was the usual procedure in cases of suspected child abuse and missing children to speak directly with the watch commander.

"Hey, Sarge, I'm up in the Estates and I think this is pretty serious. I've got two missing children. Possible kidnapping situation."

"Huh?"

"I said I got a child kidnapping situation. Possible. Up here in the Estates."

"In the Estates?"

"Yeah."

"Aw, fuck."

"Yeah, that's what I'm talking about. I got two missing kids from the Estates. Looks like the nanny took 'em. Mexico, maybe."

"She took 'em to Mexico?"

"Maybe. Don't know. Looks like a line of investigation."

"You got a ransom note?"

"No. But she didn't have permission to take them anywhere either."

"How long they been missing?"

"Since Sunday," the deputy said, but then checked his notes and saw the parents had told him two different times. "Or yesterday, I guess."

"Yesterday? Are you sure they're not just late coming back from Knott's Berry Farm or something?"

"Negative."

There was a long pause on the other end of the phone, and Deputy Suarez understood why: among other things, when a peace officer declared a child missing, a county child-abuse file was opened, and an elaborate system of reports and notifications was triggered. The case entered a federal database, and county social workers were notified. It was a big bureaucratic to-do, and if the nanny suddenly walked up to the door in half an hour, it would all be just jerking off.

"So that's your call, on scene there? Two missing kids in the Estates?"

"Yes."

"How old?"

"Eight. Eleven."

"Possible two-oh-seven kidnap to Mexico?"

"Yep."

"Fuck."

"Yeah, exactly."

Over the course of the next several hours, the story of the Mexican housekeeper and the two missing boys from one of the richest neighborhoods in Orange County gathered mass and momentum in the digital flows of the news stream, pushed along with a flotsam of facts and half facts and speculations. It began with a stilted, bare-bones Sheriff's Department press release: "missing since Sunday . . . ages 11 and 8 . . . in care of Mexican national . . . Border Patrol advised . . ." This information was delivered to various news organizations by the hopelessly archaic method of fax, and first landed in the hands of a reporter at the Sunset Boulevard headquarters of the news-tip agency City News Service. Working without any supervisor present at the cash-strapped company, a twenty-three-year-old scribe at the agency called the South County sheriff's station at 1:45 a.m., eliciting from the half-alert deputy manning the phone that the case might be a kidnapping. "The deputy who rolled out on the first call says it's a possible two-oh-seven to Mexico." The CNS reporter then tagged the item for the agency's 2:00 a.m. news roundup with the keywords "Child Kidnapping—Illegal Immigrant," an act of journalistic carelessness that would take up an entire chapter in a PhD dissertation in the Communications Department at the University of Southern California two years later. "I boiled it down to the most exciting part," said the former reporter, who was by then in law school. The City News Service bulletin appeared on a list of "break-ing stories" dispatched by old-fashioned wire transmission to morning assignment editors at every newspaper and television and radio station in Southern California, and by six in the morning Pacific Daylight Time the story was on the websites of the CBS affiliates in Los Angeles and San Diego, the latter reporting the "enhanced surveillance" at the border. That San Diego television report, accompanied by the first officially is-sued photographs of Brandon and Keenan, caught the attention of the midday editor at a Miami Beach–based news aggregation website, who made the story his lead item, with a headline in the usual all-caps, tabloid-inspired, thirty-six point font. CLOSE THE BORDER! CALIFORNIA BOYS IN ALIEN KIDNAP DRAMA. Perusing this website's unique blend of celebrity gossip, political news, and weird animal and weather stories was a guilty pleasure in office cubicles and on laptops and smart phones across the country, and its fans included millions of American mothers whose children were in the care of women named María, Lupe, and Soledad.

The morning after the Fourth of July, Brandon and Keenan wandered over to the backyard of the Luján home alone and listened to the roof of the tent pop as it caught the occasional breeze. They had left Araceli behind in Lucía's room, snoring as she slept off four consecutive restless nights, next to a nightstand and a bubbling lava lamp that Brandon had turned on in the morning to read. They had moved quietly around their temporary guardian and through the silent house, past the bedroom door that vibrated with an older man's tectonic snore, through the living room, where a pair of empty plastic cups with cigarette butts sat on the coffee table, and finally to the empty backyard. At the pit they used splintering pieces of discarded and weathered lumber they had found nearby to poke at the stones inside, wondering if they might get in trouble for doing so. They discovered scattered pieces of foil and bits of charcoal, and a few scattered bones that had been chewed and tossed inside and basted with ashes and dirt, but failed to discover flames, or melting rocks, or any other sources of combustion.

"It's only rocks," Keenan said, and looked at his older brother, aware of his disappointment.

"Maybe, maybe not. Just because you don't see something doesn't mean it isn't there."

They wandered around the backyard, kicking at the paper cylinders that once held firecrackers and picking up the sticks of bottle rockets. Brandon gathered some scattered beer cans and stacked them into pyramids and arranged them into small forts that he bombarded with the spent firecracker casings, and they collapsed with a realistic clank. Once they finished, they plopped themselves down on the rented picnic benches, resting their elbows and their heads on the tables like students struggling to stay awake in an afternoon class.

"I wanna go to Grandpa's," Keenan said.

"Yeah, me too."

Keenan wondered if crying would help, even if it was not the spontaneous bawling that came from scraping your elbow or being called a nasty name by your brother, but rather the self-conscious, manipulative weeping he sometimes heard from his younger sister, Samantha, who cried for any reason, and who always seemed to get her way. He told himself he would employ this strategy with the next adult that came into view, and then he heard a screen door being pushed open and slamming shut, and saw Lucía Luján run toward him and his brother. Griselda Pulido trailed after her, both women wearing stylish evening clothes that suggested they had been up all night, their faces wide awake with strange expressions that merged surprise, delight, and concern.

"We just saw you guys on TV," Lucía said. "You're missing."

"What?"

"The TV says you're missing children. On the news."

"We're missing?"

"That's what they said."

"But I'm right here," Brandon said. "How can I be missing?"

The boys followed Lucía and Griselda to the Luján family living room and the glowing television screen. They were disappointed to see images of a brush fire racing up a hillside. "Hey, you were on just a second ago," Lucía said, and she picked up the remote control and began switching channels.

"*¿Qué pasó?*" Araceli said behind them, having been awakened by the sound of doors opening and slamming shut.

"We saw the boys on TV," Griselda said.

"*¿Qué?*"

"On the news."

Several images and voices cycled through the screen: a blond starlet on a red carpet, waving to a crowd; the green-clad members of Mexico's national soccer team tackling and embracing a goal-scorer during a game from the night before; a supermarket with empty shelves and a floor covered with boxes and cans, the words BARSTOW EARTHQUAKE underneath; two Spanish news anchors in a studio, engaged in a chatty, light back-and-forth with the pregnant weather woman, who rubbed her belly and stuck out her tongue cartoonishly, causing the two anchors to slap the table, laughing.

"I saw you guys," Lucía said. "I swear."

"You're crazy," Araceli said. "You're just like this boy here. Imagining things."

"They said they were lost," Griselda said in English. "*Perdidos.*"

"There we are!"

"Cool!"

Brandon and Keenan were suddenly grinning broadly on the television screen, the imperfections in their front teeth frozen in the high-definition transmission for several seconds, causing Brandon to subconsciously raise his hand to his mouth and then close it shut and to think, *My mom is right, I am going to need braces soon.* Maureen had retrieved this image from her digital camera some eight hours earlier, as the first of many detectives stood in her living room. It was a cropped close-up from a picture taken at Keenan's eighth birthday party, a late afternoon image that showed the boys standing over the cake in the gathering's final, exhausted hour, because in all the others from earlier in the day they were wearing papier-mâché helmets.

"Police are asking for your help this morning in finding these two young boys, little Brandon and Keenan Torres-Thompson, of the Laguna Rancho Estates," a male voice was saying gravely. "They've been missing two days, Nancy, and their parents are frantic to see them."

"Oh, my God, they're so cute!" The screen cut back momentarily to the news studio, where Nancy, the female co-anchor, had brought her hand to her mouth and twisted her eyebrows into a face that was too theatrically mawkish given the subject matter, and the screen quickly moved to another still image.

"They are believed to be in the custody of their housekeeper, a Mexican immigrant. Araceli Ramírez is her name." Maureen had searched frantically for thirty-five minutes through her boxes of family pictures before finding a photograph in which Araceli appeared. It was a fleeting image, also taken in the dim light of a late afternoon, but at another birthday party a year ago, Brandon's tenth. Araceli stood fuzzily in the background of a larger photograph that had been cropped out, save for the ear of the main subject—Maureen, who was posing in the missing portion with a newborn Samantha in a chest-hugging sling. Out of the range of the flash, Araceli appeared in a blurred gray profile, walking quickly in her *filipina* across the backyard lawn, passing behind her boss with a stack of dirty dishes, following the quail-bangs that popped from her forehead. It was not an image that flattered. Removed of its context, its fuzzy quality suggested something furtive about its subject, as if she were already in flight when it was taken. "The boys' parents apparently left the boys in the care of the housekeeper, and the housekeeper disappeared—with the boys."

"She disappeared with them?"

"That's what the police say."

"God, let's just pray that they're safe."

"Their mom and dad are obviously anxious to see them."

The report ended, leaving Araceli and the boys in the living room with the unsettling sensation that they occupied bodies and faces that had just been transmitted, via airwaves, cables, and satellite dishes, into many more living rooms besides this one across the metropolis. Araceli was confused over the meaning of the phrase "disappeared with the boys," and wondered if "disappear" carried exactly the same mysterious and nefarious definitions as *desaparecer*: and then Lucía spoke the English word out loud and Araceli realized, from her tone of surprise and restrained disgust, that there was no difference at all.

"They say you disappeared with them. That you took them. Didn't you have permission?"

"*¿Permiso?*" Araceli spat back. "*Me dejaron sola con dos niños. Me abandonaron.*"

"But now they're looking for them."

"Yes, I know," Araceli said, switching languages because Lucía didn't seem to fully comprehend. "But they left four days ago and never told me anything. I was all alone."

Griselda retook the remote and waded anew into the selection of channels, until she reached a shot taken from a helicopter, a plugged-up flow of automobiles on one side of a freeway. The words at the bottom of the screen had caused her to stop—MISSING CHILDREN—and now Griselda raised the volume to better hear the repartee between another studio anchor and a man who seemed to be speaking from inside a blender.

"We've got Captain Joe McDonnell in Sky Five over San Ysidro, over the U.S.-Mexico border . . . And whoa, look at that line."

"That's right, Patrick. We've got a two-mile backup, and from what I can see now . . . it stretches far beyond the last San Ysidro off-ramp. And it's all due to the case of those two missing children. They're eleven and eight years old, and they may have been abducted by their Mexican nanny. Apparently the detectives in this case have reason to believe she may be taking them to Mexico."

"That's right, Joe. Brandon and Keenan Thompson of Orange County. Here they are. And here's their nanny, Araceli Ramírez. She is from there, apparently, allegedly, so they're checking all the cars crossing the border. We understand. They haven't closed the border completely, now, have they, Captain?"

"No, Patrick. As you can see, if we zoom in here . . . there is some traffic going past the checkpoint, but it's at a real snail's pace. A snail's pace, because in a case like this, in this kind of Amber Alert involving a suspect, a possible Mexican national as the suspect, they don't want to take any chances."

The camera's eye zoomed back, briefly taking in the U.S. and Mexican flags at opposite ends of a twenty-lane stretch of concrete, and the inspection booths, and then the long, curving, interlocking-puzzle pieces of cars on the southbound roadway in the United States, simmering and stationary between shoulder and center divider, the boxes of tractor-trailers, pickup trucks, and taxis, and a car hauling a boat. The camera then turned back on itself and showed how the parallel lines of vehicles climbed and banked northward, toward the San Diego downtown skyline, a hazy Oz many miles distant. Finally the broadcast switched to a taped shot, taken on the ground, of a U.S. customs agent holding a piece of paper printed with Brandon and Keenan's picture as he peered into a van.

Araceli grabbed the remote from Lucía's hand and turned off the television, hoping to stop the delusional machine's madness, which would spread if she allowed it to keep flashing its images and its lies. *In the news I am a fuzzy criminal. Officers are looking, agents are checking.* They were searching for the boys, to rescue them, and they were looking for Araceli, so that they could arrest her. *Maureen did this. Because she came home and found no boys, because she wants to punish me for acting like their mother, even though I never asked to be their mother. I never wanted that.* Her instinct to keep away from her *jefes'* children had been right after all. She had crossed a boundary by thinking she was their guardian. And they would arrest her, because she dared to save those parentless children from Foster Care.

Now she caught Griselda and Lucía staring at her. *Could it be true?* they seemed to be asking themselves. *Do we have a child abductor among us?*

"*Están locos,*" Araceli said dismissively in Spanish, referring to the newsmen and newswomen, Maureen and Scott, and the two young women in the living room with their doubts all at once. She turned and repeated this in English to the boys, who knew the truth, hoping they might say something in Araceli's defense. "They are crazy. They say I took you."

"I wanna go home," Keenan said. The television news had unsettled him further, because seeing a television report that said you were missing seemed to be a step closer to actually being missing. He didn't want to be "disappeared," a state which he imagined to be something like sitting in a white room in another dimension while you waited to return to the world of the known and definite. "I don't want to be missing. I want to be home."

Brandon was worried about being missing too, but at the sound of Keenan's pleading whine, the older brother in him kicked in. "We should call home and tell them where we are," he said, his voice rising with the discovery of a simple and quick solution to their dilemma. "Then they'll pick us up!"

"Good idea," Lucía said.

"Then I should go," Griselda interjected quickly. "Before the police get here." She gave Lucía a knowing look that turned pained when she realized her friend didn't get her meaning right away. "Because they'll start asking everyone questions."

Lucía's eyes shifted in confusion, then fixed on her friend until she understood. "Oh, yeah, right. Of course. You should go."

"What?" Araceli demanded, suddenly irritated by the mysterious dialogue between friends. "The police are looking for you too?"

Griselda Pulido shook her head and said bluntly, in English, "I don't have papers."

It seemed impossible. Here was a young woman who spoke about music and boyfriends in English, who was obviously educated in the freewheeling, free-girl-thinking of U.S. schools, a privilege imparted to the country's brightest daughters, announcing solemnly that she was an *indocumentada*. This predicament didn't match, somehow, with the thin silver bracelets on her wrist, her slender and confident bearing, her gentle, even voice of the academically inclined. Nor did it match with her puckish party outfit, a billowing spinach-green dress with forest-green leggings and elfin slippers, all of which suggested an actress fresh off the set of *A Midsummer Night's Dream*.

"*Pero eres gringa,*" Araceli said.

"No I'm not. I'm *mexicana.*"

"*¿De veras?*" Araceli insisted. "*Pero ni hablas bien el español.*"

"I could speak Spanish a little better, yes," Griselda said calmly, and suddenly she radiated a youthful, black-haired confidence and inescapable meekness all at once. "But I've never really lived in Mexico, so it's understandable." After a pause to consider the paradox of her status,

Griselda lowered her voice and said, "I came when I was two. And I've never been back, because I can't go back. Brown was going to let me in anyway, but they couldn't give me any financial aid."

This was a shock to Araceli. Griselda had been an *indocumentada* when she was still in diapers; it seemed a country would have to be excessively cruel and cold to place such a label on a baby girl, and keep it on her even as she grew into an English-speaking woman.

Lucía placed a hand on Griselda's shoulder. "You should leave, then. When the boy calls, leave right away." She turned to Araceli, and spoke with a sternness that she would later regret. "And maybe you should go too."

"*¿Qué?*"

"*¿Tienes documentos?*" Griselda asked, and quickly discerned the answer in Araceli's sudden silence and discomfort. Griselda knew that wordlessness too; it came from carrying a secret so long you forgot you were carrying it, until someone or something reminded you of its existence and you felt the pressure of the words against your skin, and you realized the words were always there.

"Hi, Dad," Brandon said into the phone. "We're here." He paused to listen to his father's voice. "Yeah, we just saw ourselves on TV. But I'm not missing. I'm right here." Now an excited shouting could be heard, miniature adults celebrating inside the earpiece, clapping, screaming in joy. "We ate tacos last night," Brandon continued. "They cooked a pig. With a fire in the ground. But I don't think it's burning anymore . . . What? The address?"

"It's 2626 Rugby Street," Lucía said, and looked at Griselda. "In Huntington Park."

Brandon repeated the address to his father. "Yeah, Araceli is here with us. She's been taking care of us. We rode on a train, and on some buses too. We saw a river, but it didn't have water in it." Suddenly he narrowed his eyes to a look of irritation. "And where did *you* go? Is Mommy there?" He listened to the answer, and turned to Keenan. "He says Mommy can't talk right now, but she's okay."

Keenan took the phone and announced flatly to his father that he was okay too. "I love you too," he said, and immediately hung up, because he thought of a phone I-love-you as meaning more or less the same as goodbye.

The clatter of the phone on the receiver was the cue for Griselda to reach over and give Lucía a kiss on the cheek. Without any more drama Griselda moved calmly to the front door, turned, and smiled and waved to the boys and to Araceli, mouthing the Spanish word for luck as she did so. *Suerte.* The screen door closed behind Griselda with a slap and Araceli watched through the living room window as she walked across the lawn, onto the sidewalk, gliding in her slippers and wide dress past parked cars and other lawns, a green fairy *indocumentada* walking without worry, her unhurried air causing her to melt into the surroundings, another Mexican-American, another *mexicana* on these streets with so many other people with stories and faces like hers. That's how you did it. You acted as if the city belonged to you. You walked with the pace of a limber woman taking her daily stroll. *I can do that too, and slip back across the city, and maybe back to Mexico, with a little stop at the bank to get my money.* Araceli liked the idea of thumbing her nose at the police and the immigration authorities with the simple fact of her absence, her unwillingness to answer questions or offer explanations, even though she had no reason to run away, no reason to hide from anything, except for the inconvenient matter of her Mexican citizenship. They would arrest her and sort out the truth later. *But I don't want to be a prisoner, not even for a few hours.* Araceli had digested, over the years, a regular diet of stories from across the U.S., fed to her by Spanish-language radio and television, all offering ample evidence that those who arrived on this side of the border without permission were returned home via a series of humiliating punishments. Meat packers, garment workers, mothers with babies in swaddling clothes: Araceli had seen them on the television, rounded up in vans, into buses with steel mesh over the windows, gathered up in camps behind fences, onto airplanes that landed on the tropical runways of San Salvador and Tegucigalpa and other places, far away from those other places they had learned to call home—Iowa, Chicago, Massachusetts. *Pobrecitos.* When this saga was on television you could dismiss it as the bad luck of others. She was too busy to worry, and too much at peace with the risky life choices she had taken. But now that her name and her face had been fed into that tragic stream of the wanted, the apprehended, and the deported, she felt the need to resist. *My words and my true story will not buy me my freedom, not right away.* Araceli would speak her story in Spanish and *la señora* Maureen would tell hers in English: it was obvious to her that the two languages did not carry equal weight.

"*Me voy*," Araceli announced happily. "Good luck, boys. I'm glad you didn't go into Faster Care. Lucía and her father will take care of you until the police come."

After returning to Lucía's bedroom to retrieve the backpack she had been carrying, Araceli passed through to the living room one last time, patted Keenan on the head, and placed a hand on Brandon's shoulder.

"I leave them with you," she said to Lucía, and to Mr. Luján, who had just entered the living room. "*Cuídenlos, porfis.*"

Araceli took a moment longer to consider the surroundings, the grown-up man and his daughter, giving them the kind of cursory, self-assuring once-over a hurried mother might before leaving her children in a familiar day-care center. Then, remembering the police were on their way, she stepped toward the front door. "*Adiós, niños,*" she said, adding an unnecessary "Stay here," as she stepped into the furnace of July daylight and down the Luján family steps, across the lawn and the patch of street where the lynch mob had gathered the night before, following a path that would lead her back to the bus stop, where she would begin a journey to some new place unknown to her.

Among the tribe of sheriff's deputies, detectives, social workers, and assorted county officials gathered in the Torres-Thompson living room, it was the presence of the representative of Orange County Child Protective Services that Maureen found most threatening. Olivia Garza was 220 pounds of Mexican-American woman on a five-foot ten-inch frame whose labored breathing and loud exhales of exasperation filled the silences in the room. This rotund stranger had spent quite a lot of time inspecting the pictures on the bookshelf, and Maureen sensed that she was looking for clues in the faces she saw there, in the body language of her wedding pictures, the grooming of her boys in their school portraits.

Alone among the assembled members of the Endangered Child Emergency Intervention Team, Olivia Garza did not feel the need to hide her skepticism. She had a unique gift for untangling family dysfunction and had worked her way up from Case Worker I in the Santa Ana office with the files of 127 children whose parents and guardians were raccoon-eyed heroin addicts, pugilistic plumbers, wannabe street-corner kingpins, and shoplifting Chicana versions of Scarlett O'Hara waiting in Fullerton subdivisions for their tattooed heroes to slam the door in their faces. She was especially adept at spotting the custody-fight manipulations, the Halloween-scary fictions mothers and fathers made up about their exes, but had also rescued babies dying from malnutrition, plucking them from their cribs and from the sticky kitchen floors of Santa Ana apartments. She had cornered the thirteen-year-old sons of Newport Beach glitterati in Anaheim crack houses too: *de todo un poco.*

Olivia Garza did not believe a Mexican nanny would take off with her two charges in a kidnapping adventure with two boys the ages of the Torres-Thompson children. Or, rather, she had not yet been presented with any facts that would allow her to believe such an unlikely scenario. What is she going to do? Sell them in Tijuana? Make them her own children, teach them Spanish, and raise them in a tiny village in the mountains? None of this had she expressed to the other members of the intervention team. She didn't need to, because the two sheriff's detectives sent out to the scene had reached the same conclusion, more or less, though they were trying hard to be deferential to the weeping mother and the worried father.

After hearing the basic outline of the story from the father, Olivia Garza had wandered about the house. Too clean, she observed, too perfect. She looked into the Room of a Thousand Wonders and was unimpressed. If you saw too many toys, it implied distance, parents who substituted objects for intimacy, though the presence of so many books, and the variety of their sizes and subjects, was reassuring. Olivia Garza picked up a handful and examined the dog-eared pages of a novel, and then the worn cover of a picture book on medieval armor and decided, *These kids are going to turn up by the end of the day.* The members of Olivia Garza's elite team had been precipitously assembled here simply because the family lived in the zip code with the highest per capita income in their district, and because the photogenic boys had attracted the news crews gathered outside. *Some things are so obvious you just want to force them out like a wad of spit.*

She encountered the two detectives back in the living room, off by the windows that looked out to the succulent garden.

"Is there anything else here I should see?"

"Have you seen the nanny's room? It's a little house in the back."

They entered the guesthouse, which wasn't much smaller, truth be told, than the condominium in Laguna Beach where the childless Olivia Garza lived with her two cats. One of the detectives reached up and tapped at the mobile, watching it spin and bounce.

"Interesting," Olivia Garza said.

"Art," Detective Harkness said.

"Yeah, that's what they call it," Detective Blake said.

"This is what got our responding deputy all worked up," Detective Harkness said, waving his hand at the drawings, the collages, and the mobile, which didn't bother him at all.

The intervention team had been called up just before dawn, roused from their beds, and in the full light of midmorning there was an everyday clarity to the situation that had eluded the first responders the night before.

"My theory: the nanny took them to Disneyland or something and got lost or delayed on the way back," Detective Blake said.

"Yeah, they're probably sleeping in a hotel someplace, dreaming about the apple pie they had for dinner last night," Detective Harkness said.

"I predict, after the all-points," Detective Blake said, "that they turn up around lunchtime."

"Nah, earlier," Detective Harkness said. "Ten, ten forty-five at the latest."

"What do *you* think, Garza?"

She looked about the room, shuffled the papers and envelopes on Araceli's table-desk, and finally said, "These parents have lied to me. And I don't like it when people lie to me."

"And how many years have you been in Child Protective Services?" Detective Harkness said.

"That's what we do, Garza," Detective Blake said. "We go places, and people lie to us. And then we catch them in their big lies, and we make them feel bad, and then they cry and tell us smaller lies."

"I don't like it when people lie and force me out of bed early," Olivia Garza said. "And I don't like it when they make me walk past the TV crews without having had a chance to put my makeup on."

"You mean you can look even more beautiful than you do already?" Both detectives chuckled. "You're funny, Garza."

Olivia Garza brought her bad temper back to the living room, refusing to sit on the couch or at the table in the dining room, and decided to continue her self-consciously insolent pacing instead, as if daring the other members of the team to put up with her. After listening to Scott again recite, without much conviction, the story Maureen had first told the 911 operator, she addressed the parents for the first time.

"How much do you pay this woman?"

"Two hundred and fifty dollars a week," Scott said.

"Under the table. Right?"

There was no answer, but Olivia Garza pressed ahead. "Do you leave your kids alone with her often?"

"No," Maureen said, breaking a long silence. "We never have. Before. We had another person . . ."

"You've never left her alone with them and then you go away for two days and leave two boys with her?"

"That's what they've been telling us," interrupted the representative of the district attorney's office, who was sitting on the sofa seat at a right angle from Maureen.

Olivia allowed the silence to stand there and make her point. The two detectives had been doing the same thing, off and on, for an hour, walking up the story to the parts that were not quite believable, and then stepping back because the representative of the DA's office had placed himself next to Scott and Maureen and was, with his repeated words of support for the alleged victims, preventing the detectives from probing any further. Olivia Garza and the detectives both wondered the same thing: *What are these people hiding?* Something small and insignificant, Olivia Garza concluded, a fact not completely essential to the recovery of their children: some family embarrassment, or petty crime. Probably she and the detectives could pry the truth from this couple, but for the presence of the representative of the district attorney's office, who was leaning forward in his seat, over the space where the coffee table used to stand. He was conspicuously overdressed in glossy Brooks Brothers sharkskin, and looked intently at Maureen and Scott, his clothes and demeanor suggesting a corporate-minded Catholic priest.

Ian Goller was the third-ranking member of the district attorney's office and his official title was Senior Assistant District Attorney for Operations, but unofficially he was the district attorney's fixer and protégé. Goller had mobilized the Endangered Child Emergency Intervention Team at 5:25 a.m., after sitting down to his morning news and coffee ritual, and seeing the faces of the boys flashing next to the words

ORANGE COUNTY MISSING CHILDREN. Ian Goller was thirty-eight years old and, like Olivia Garza, he lived alone, though in a much more spacious condominium with a view of the harbor in Newport Beach. He had turned up the volume and heard the outline of the story, and in two deep breaths and two heartbeats he felt the great swell of popular indignation it might provoke. A nanny who was, more than likely, an illegal immigrant: absconding with two Orange County children with All-American looks. It would make the good people and voters of Orange County angrier than a dozen Mexican gangbanger murders, or twenty homicidal drunk drivers with Spanish surnames and no driver's licenses, and, as such, it was precisely the sort of high-profile case for which the emergency-response team had been created.

Ian Goller was a native of the Orange County suburb of Fullerton who liked to tell people that his otherwise plain and unassuming hometown had once been home to the science fiction writer Philip K. Dick. "You know, *Blade Runner*?" Fullerton had produced no other greatness, as far as he knew, other than a perennially excellent college baseball team, and Goller himself was a graduate of San Diego State University and the middle-of-the-pack Chapman University School of Law. At the DA's office he put in long hours, unlike many of his colleagues, and quickly worked his way up from traffic court and DUIs, his rise aided by a few idiosyncrasies that identified him as an Orange County local, and thus made him a favorite of the OC-born DA. Goller still allowed his blond hair to reach his collar, wore a braided leather Hawaiian surf bracelet over the French cuffs of his dress shirts, and in his youth had flirted with a career as a professional surfer—which had led to a recent profile in *California Lawyer* as "the surfing prosecutor."

Now, sitting with these two parents in their well-appointed living room in the Laguna Rancho Estates, he could see that he was in the presence of an Orange County mother who cared. He could feel it in the dust-free air, the good and life-giving scent of the nearby ocean, in the baby dictionaries and well-worn swing set, and see it in the way she stroked her baby girl's back, as if to comfort the child when she was really comforting herself. As he contemplated the fate of the boys this OC mom had left in the care of a Mexican nanny, Goller saw everything that was at once satisfying and frustrating about being a prosecutor.

Protecting children and prosecuting abuse was the purest thing a lawyer could do: the victims were sinless, and the defendants were invariably transparent scumbags, convicted by juries with great speed and relish. And in the suspect's copper-tinged face and nationality, he saw the math of the multitudes that would one day drive him out of the profession altogether, because naïve Latin American immigrants like her were filling up his courtrooms. This was a painful realization for the son of an old-line Democratic family to make, and one he'd arrived at after years of observation, and despite his steadfastly liberal outlook on most other issues, from abortion rights to preserving the local wetlands. Ian Goller's meta-knowledge of how foreign nationals clogged his superior court flowcharts, matrices, and spreadsheets, along with the victim-centered culture at the DA's office, with its victim's rights manifestos and procedures, tilted his view of the case decisively in favor of Maureen—despite her nervous and not-entirely-consistent recounting of events.

Ian Goller thought of this woman's children, and about other children he had not been able to rescue, and he bowed his head in silent, private prayer.

Seeing the prosecutor lower his head and clasp his hands suddenly and without explanation only filled Maureen with more dread. She did not understand the source of the prosecutor's intense stares, nor of the obvious irritation of the big woman who represented Child Protective Services. *These are the people who take children away from parents.* The arrival of the obese Mexican-American woman, especially, with her large nose and ruddy skin with a strange Indian-ebony mixing, and the plastic ID badge with the county seal, was nearly as frightening to her as the idea that Brandon and Keenan were wandering the city somewhere. Maureen entertained the prospect that the police might find her children, listen to Araceli's true and entirely plausible story, and then decide to take her children away. *Maybe I should tell them now what really happened: that it's been four days, not two, and that Araceli had no idea we were leaving.* How much trouble had she gotten her family into with that small lie? Maureen decided she would reveal the complexity of the situation, how she and Scott had played a part in its unfolding, and perhaps this small truth would bring her children to her quicker, and loosen the surly mask of the representative from Child Protective Services, the only other woman in the room besides Maureen, and the only one of the strangers who seemed to sense the hidden and juvenile chain of events that had brought them all here.

Maureen was about to launch into her confession when the phone rang.

Araceli walked through the neighborhood at a leisurely pace, past aging front-yard cacti and blooming rosebushes, and the unpainted gray skins of newly built cement homes with gabled roofs and dangling wires for light fixtures. She walked past pickup trucks with gold wings painted on their sides, three-toned pickups with mismatching doors and hoods, and pickups with the color schemes of Mexican soccer teams, and then squeezed between two more pickups after jaywalking across California Street. Despite her deliberately unhurried pace, she decided it might be better not to walk in a straight line, but rather to make large zigzags through the grid of streets, especially now that a helicopter had appeared overhead.

The aircraft was chop-chopping like a lawn mower in the airspace above the Luján home, and it did not take much imagination to conclude that the police were at that moment engaged in the "rescue" of Brandon and Keenan. Araceli marveled at the fact that in this country police could emerge from the empty sky in the time it took to walk five blocks. The police would now return Brandon and Keenan to the Room of a Thousand Wonders and the two-dimensional superheroes of their bedsheets. The helicopter was loud enough to bring a scattering of people to their front doors, to look up and wonder who or what the machine was looking for.

Now the helicopter began to move, making circles concentric to the point where it had started, banking and turning in ever larger circles until its spinning blades and green body dipped over Araceli's head, a giant mechanical dragonfly whose beating squeal announced crisis and urgency. Araceli began to walk faster as more people came out of their homes and stood on their lawns, craning their necks upward. An accelerating automobile drew their eyes back to the ground, a Huntington Park police patrol car zooming past with exaggerated masculine purpose. Araceli halted her sidewalk march and watched the flashing lights of the patrol car reach the end of the block, cross the intersection, and then accelerate into the next block with another throttle burst and thought, *They're trying to scare me out into the open. They think that if they zoom through here I will begin to run, and give myself away.*

She began walking again, but was aware that by stopping and starting with the passing of the patrol car she had drawn attention to herself.

"Hey, that's her!" shouted the voice of an adolescent boy standing behind her on the sidewalk. She continued walking without looking back. "That's the lady! From the TV!"

Araceli took a few more steps until a second voice shouted from one of the doorways, "*¡La secuestradora!*" She turned and saw a woman with dimpled cheeks pointing at her from a cement porch, with the glee of a person who has scratched the skin of a lottery card and discovered a twenty-dollar prize. Araceli stumbled away, walking faster, frightened as much by the voyeurism of the people around her as by the idea that they might hand her over to the police. "*¡Es ella! La vi en el canal 52. ¿A dónde vas?*" She began a light jog, thinking that she might be safe as soon as she turned the corner and escaped this block and its Greek chorus of television watchers, people who believed she was the *secuestradora* in the news montages, a villainous taker of children.

"*¡Córrele!*" a man shouted with a gusto usually reserved for horse races and cattle roundups.

"*¿Y los niños?*" a woman's voice pleaded as she turned the corner, and Araceli was tempted to turn and say, *I don't have them, I never took them.* She reached a block where narrow bungalows were lined like railroad boxcars in parallel rows, their square lawns transformed by drought into flat and featureless dust squares. Plastic curls of Christmas lights hung from the eaves, and all the residents were inside, glued to their televisions, she guessed, looking at Araceli's fuzzy picture on their screens. A block later she found herself standing underneath the enormous zinc torso of a power transmission tower, eight lines attached to four arms that stretched out like a woman having herself measured for a dress. The lines loomed above a corridor of vacant land that ran several straight miles through residential neighborhoods, one tower following another until they gradually disappeared into the midday ozone bake of dirty-blue haze and nothingness. Araceli took a second or two to contemplate the hugeness of the tower above her, and the oddity of the notch that had been cut into the grid of homes. She jumped over the short fence that proclaimed NO TRESPASSING and began to walk under the trunk lines, thinking there would be no nosy television watchers to bother her as she walked here, and that she might be able to follow the lines northward to the peopleless heart of the metropolis, and the safety of factory buildings and warehouses. Her legs labored against the uneven, weed-covered ground, because she was entering a kind of urban wilderness, a nursery of odd flora sprouting up through the mustard grass. A cypress tree, its canopy shaped like a large wing. Sickly rosebushes without buds. Strawberry plants clinging to a patch of loam. Bamboo grasses and a stunted palm with thin leaves that sprouted, fountainlike, from its trunk, and the wide, tall bouquet of a nopal cactus. She had stumbled into the back closet of California gardens, the place where seedlings of plants discarded and abandoned came to scratch their roots into the dry native soil. If she hadn't been on the run, she might have stopped to admire this freakish landscape, and she might have noticed too the cluster of cameras and lights in the distance.

Instead, the film crew saw her first, when, about eight hundred yards to the north, an Estonian cinematographer peered into the viewfinder of his camera. Araceli was under the second tower in the distance, a woman stumbling forward in the dancing waves of rising heat, lifting her legs over the weedy land like a woman wading through snowdrifts. "Someone is in my shot," the cinematographer said, his neck bent and face attached to the eyepiece. "They are coming into the shot."

"Again?" the director called out. "Where?"

A dozen or so members of the small film crew began squinting at the horizon. They were shooting the coda of an indie feature with a modest $3.1 million budget, and they had already been bedeviled by the appearance of the helicopters, which were driving the sound guy loopy. At the director's behest the cinematographer had filmed the circling craft for two minutes and forty-five seconds, capturing their lead actor looking up at the machines circling over the wires, the expression of foreboding and curiosity on his tanned face completely in line with the themes of the screenplay. Electrical towers appeared at the end of each of the film's three acts, and the cinematographer had shot other towers and wires in the San Bernardino Mountains, and in the plain of tumbleweeds outside Henderson, Nevada, and the Cimarron Grasslands of southwestern Kansas. The Huntington Park shoot was intended for the epilogue, the towers and the barren channel of weeds at the actor's feet symbols of the protagonist's failed search for self in Las Vegas casinos and a Kansas beef-processing town.

"I told you these Eastside locations were a bitch," the key grip said. "I told you." Most of the local residents had behaved themselves: they were used to being put out by film crews drawn to the grim and epic backdrop, and only the appearance of an A-list actor or Mexican television star really got them very excited. Every few minutes, however, there was the straggling homeless person, or a gangbanger on his bicycle, people who hadn't read the letter: *Sorry for the inconvenience: We're bringing a little bit of Hollywood to your neighborhood!*

"Now I see him," the director said.

"Her. It's a she."

At that instant a helicopter swooped in close to the trunk line and a police car emerged with a squeaky skid on one of the streets that cut through the corridor. Two officers jumped out of the car and the figure of the woman began to run toward the crew.

"Whoa, they're chasing her."

"They've got their sticks out."

"Is this real?"

"Batons. You call them batons, not sticks."

"Are you getting this?" the director yelled to the cinematographer. He called out the name of the lead actor, a bright young prospect whose presence in the film had assured its funding—he was a twenty-four-year-old Australian with a sparse chestnut beard that matched his eyes, and a Gary Cooper everyman quality that screamed out he was destined for big-budget greatness. "In character," the director said. "Stay in character." The actor took a breath and a moment to remember his drama-school improvisation training and stretched his arms down at his sides. He relaxed his facial muscles into a look of genuine puzzlement and muted pleading captured in profile as he watched the foot chase that was now headed in his direction, a Mexican woman towing a cloud of dust and two running men in black, a spectacle now about one hundred yards distant.

"They're going to beat her," a crew member said breathlessly. "They're going to beat her to a pulp."

"Take a step toward them. Just one step."

The actor moved hesitatingly toward the running woman, as if he wanted to help her but was not sure he could.

"Good. Now one more. Just one. Are we still getting this?"

"Yes, I'm on a tiny f-stop," the cinematographer said. "The depth of field is magnificent."

"Beautiful."

Weeks later in the editing room, the director and his editor would incorporate about seventy-five seconds of this footage into the final version of the film. Araceli never saw the camera, or the actor, or the film crew. She was focused on the men trailing behind her and the idea that she might elude them. They had come to grab her and bind her hands in plastic strings, but she still found herself suppressing a laugh as she ran, even with brambles scratching at her ankles, because there was the quality of a schoolyard game to being chased around like this. *There are other, easier ways of returning to Mexico. They will grab me and drag me across the dirt like a calf in the rodeo, and then cage me. We must endure these rituals of humiliation: this is our Mexican glory, to be pursued and apprehended in public places for bystanders to see.*

*If you let me go, señores, I will merely walk to the bus station and buy a ticket back to my country.* No les molesto más. They were far behind her, at first, and for a moment she entertained the thought that if she could reach the next street, or slip into an alleyway or a backyard, she might elude them and find her own route home. But she was not a good runner. The first police officer quickly closed the gap, sprinting with a determined, middle-aged ferocity that surprised and frightened her, his face turning crimson and sweat bursting from his face and chest. When he reached her he was still running much too fast, and stumbled on top of her while trying to apprehend her, his body crushing hers as they both fell to the soil, their mouths filled with dirt and sticky weeds.

BOOK THREE

# Circus Californianus

I would take up wickedness again . . . And
for a starter I would go to work and steal Jim
out of slavery again . . .
—Mark Twain, *Huckleberry Finn*

# 16

Araceli refused to speak for the first two hours she spent in custody. She did not complain after being covered with dust by the police officer's clumsy collision tackle, or offer a retort to the taunt of the second officer, who said, "Back to Meh-hee-coe for you, buh-bye," as he escorted her to the patrol car. She said nothing as they walked past the cluster of residents who repeated in whispers the accusation they had heard on their Spanish-talking televisions: *la secuestradora*. She resisted the temptation to sling back a riposte when one of the more ignorant members of the crowd spat at her in English, "What did you do to those kids, bitch?" She merely squinted up into the midday glare and the fleet of circling television helicopters, which had joined the police helicopters in an aerial hyena prowl, and then at the crowd, recognizing a face or two from the lynch mob that had gathered outside the Luján residence the night before: they were looking at her with the same mixture of morbid fascination and inch-deep pity with which a *chilango* crowd greeted a corpse on the sidewalk, and she thought of all the sarcastic things she might say if she had the nerve. *Look, and look closely, because any one of you might be next.* But of course she said nothing, and she kept to her mute act as another set of officers took her fingerprints and escorted her to a holding cell at the Huntington Park Police Station. Nor did she speak as a third set of officers drove her across many suburbs and freeways and interchanges, through city air heavy and opaque with the gray haze and smoky aroma spewed by a distant and massive brush fire. When she arrived at another holding cell, at the South County Operations station, she told herself she would remain silent until they escorted her across the border, or until she landed at the airport in Mexico City. *Obviously, I would prefer to take the plane back.* She'd watch the route she took to this country pass beneath her feet, backward: the American highways, the desert passes, the Sonoran cities, the toll roads through arid landscapes dotted with oak trees and adobe walls painted with the slogans of presidential candidates, and finally the mouse-maze sprawl of that last metropolis she had once called home and would call home again soon, that city of museums and galleries and monuments that Griselda wanted to visit, but could not.

They brought her to an interrogation room and told her to sit down and she began to think about what she would say to her mother when they saw each other, and how much time would pass before she found herself working in that cramped kitchen next to the old woman again. She wondered if there might still be a way to get to that money she had in the bank in Santa Ana. Saving that money had been a "bad girl" thing to do, but now it might emancipate her from her mother's kitchen and open the path to a new, radical Mexican self. There were rebellious things a woman could do in Mexico if she didn't care what people said, bohemian gathering spots that awaited the free spirit: Huatulco and the hippies on the Oaxacan coast, Palenque and incense-burning shamans of Veracruz.

Now three men entered the room: a police officer in a stiff wool uniform and a brass badge; a green-eyed police detective of about fifty in gray blended slacks, emitting an air of slovenly boredom; and a smartly dressed man of about thirty-five, with a narrow face that sprouted like a tree stump from his stiff collar, and blond hair that swooshed across the top of his head like a golden wave frozen at midcrest. Alone among these three, the last man was not perspiring, and he took a seat at the table where Araceli was sitting, the older police detective squeezing next to him, and after an elbow collision or two it was clear the room was too small to accommodate them all. The room was about the size of the walk-in closet off the master bedroom in Paseo Linda Bonita, and the three men bumped chests and shoulders as they tried to sit down at once on the empty chairs, until the officer in uniform finally stood up and took a place in the open doorway.

"Damn. Couldn't we get something bigger?" the younger man in the suit said.

"Budgets," said the man with the gray slacks. "We asked for more rooms. So they took the ones we had and split 'em in half." Settling into his chair, he now introduced himself as Detective Mike Blake, and said the younger man in the suit was Assistant District Attorney Ian Goller.

"And your name, according to this card we have here, is Araceli N. Ramírez," the police detective said, speaking with a weary congeniality that caught Araceli by surprise. He placed a manila envelope on the table, removed her Mexican election card, and studied it, as if he were trying to discern the meaning of the words Instituto Mexicano Electoral, which circled an eagle clutching a serpent. "Interesting. I guess you need this to vote in Mexico."

Araceli remained silent, remembering the little speech given by the officer who'd put her in the patrol car, reading in Spanish from a card that he drew from his back pocket: *Usted tiene el derecho a guardar silencio. That's another thing I really like about this country,* she thought. *The right to keep your lips pursed together like a chaste nun in a convent is enshrined in their Constitution, and there is no officer or judge who can force you to open your mouth.*

"Had lunch yet?" Detective Blake asked. "Because I can get you something to eat. But I need you to start talking to me."

"Or we can send you back down to that little cell without lunch," Goller said.

"Look, I'm sure it was just some misunderstanding, right?" Detective Blake said. "Explain it to us."

Araceli looked firmly into their English-speaking eyes and wondered if she should trust them.

"Listen, we know you speak English perfectly well," the representative of the district attorney's office said brusquely. Ian Goller had received this essential bit of information from Maureen back at Paseo

Linda Bonita, and he now believed that Araceli was deliberately pretending not to understand, which only added to his frustration. He had seen this behavior many times before: criminal suspects from foreign countries who believed their non-English-speaking tongues gave them additional immunity from speaking the truth. "So why did you run away?"

Araceli almost replied to this question, because of its transparent stupidity. *Why does the rabbit run from the fox?* she wanted to say. *Why does the hen run from the woman with the knife in her hand?* Instead, she narrowed her eyes and glared back in approximate imitation of an irritated Mexican schoolteacher.

"Wanna go back to the cell?" Goller barked. "We'll send you back now. Without lunch. Or you can just tell us what you were up to. Why would you take those two boys on a little jaunt? To what purpose? Where did you go?" It had been ages since Ian Goller found himself sitting across a table from an uncharged criminal suspect—he was, almost exclusively, an administrator now—and he was quickly falling back to a bad habit from his early days as a prosecutor: losing his professional detachment. "Here's what I see. You took these children without permission to a dangerous corner of the city. You left two good parents worried sick inside the house, without a clue to where you might be." The detective sitting next to him was looking irritated, but Goller didn't notice and wouldn't have cared if he did. "You never expressed any interest in the welfare of these boys and suddenly, when you're alone with them, you go off. Why?"

The assistant district attorney did not fully appreciate the bewilderment that had suddenly taken hold of Araceli's face, though the detective did. Detective Blake decided he should try and take back control of the interrogation. But before he could, Goller blurted out, "What did you think? That you were their mother? Or was it money you were after? Because, obviously, you weren't being paid enough for all the work you did. Right? So you wanted more money."

Araceli took a few seconds to digest the insinuations and to study the man making them. She was struck by the embittered outrage with which the assistant district attorney embraced his vision of her. He seemed to believe that she lacked basic human morality and intelligence; at the same time, he thought her capable of great criminal cunning. Certain backward men in Mexico looked at all women this way and Araceli was momentarily reminded of a few ugly encounters in her past. "You just couldn't stand working for this family," Ian Goller continued, and fell back in his chair with a satisfied lean, as if he had figured it all out, striking the flimsy wall of the interrogation room as he did so and causing the tiny room to shake. "They trust you with their kids and you want to make them suffer? I don't get it. Or are you just incredibly irresponsible?" Araceli tried to see the events of the past week as this excellently dressed and coiffed gentleman imagined them. She formed a mental picture of herself taking Brandon and Keenan to a bank, exchanging them for their weight in gold; or to some mustachioed broker of stolen children, for a stack of pesos. In the prosecutor's vision, Araceli was doing those things, while Maureen and Scott were two parents who dutifully entrusted Brandon and Keenan to her, maybe even kissing them goodbye as they left them in her care. These absurd thoughts, and the prosecutor's look of deepening revulsion, caused her mouth to explode suddenly with a loud and sustained guffaw, what Spanish speakers call a *carcajada*, an onomatopoeia that suggests a cackling bird. Araceli's laugh, however, was a deeper mammalian sound, born below the esophagus, a laugh she associated in her youth with certain mean-spirited street vendors in Nezahualcóyotl, and with her own *hidalguense* grandmother. She laughed and felt the lifting of the day's sum of tension, a release that gave her mirth its own momentum, and she leaned forward in her chair with a true burst of joyfulness that showed the three men in the room the grinning teeth that had seduced Sasha "the Big Man" Avakian so long ago. She kept on laughing as her eyes caught those of the detective and the police officer, who were both raising their lips in subtle smiles that suggested they got the joke too. Her laughter pinged off the steel table and the glass of the two-way mirror that dominated the room, for thirty seconds in all, until she finally stopped and let out a satisfied half sigh.

The detective thought, *That's definitely not a perp laugh.*

The police officer lifted the Kevlar shell underneath his uniform and concluded, *Naw, this lady ain't a kidnapper. Too bad we gotta hand her over to the immigration people.*

The assistant district attorney had precisely the opposite reaction: *All but an admission of guilt. With her aggressive laughter she mocks and challenges us.*

"I was taking them to their grandfather!" Araceli said suddenly at the top of her voice in English. "Because those people you put on the TV, that mother and father, *los responsables*, left me with Brandon *y* Keenan for four days! *¡Sola!* Since Saturday morning! I had no more food to give them."

"They told us they were gone for two days," the detective said.

"*¡Mentira!*"

"That means 'lie,' in Spanish," said the police officer in the doorway, whose name tag identified him as CASTILLO.

"By the grandfather, you mean who?"

"*El abuelo* Torres."

"John Torres?"

"Yes."

"Is that who this is?" the police detective asked, producing the black-and-white photograph of *el abuelo* Torres that Araceli had left in her backpack.

"*Sí*. I mean, yes. That is him."

In short order the police detective established Araceli's story, which began with the fight between Maureen and Scott and the broken table, and led to her own, ill-advised journey to the center of Los Angeles, and finally to Huntington Park, and her flight after seeing herself on television. "I see the television say I am a kidnapper. What am I thinking?" she said. "That is why I run. As fast as I can, which is not very fast, I am sorry." Goller remained silent, seemingly disoriented by the detective's sudden burst of questions and Araceli's unhesitating answers.

"I did not wanna see Brandon and Keenan in Faster Care," Araceli said.

"What?" the detective said.

"In Faster Care. *Porque no estaban sus padres.* Because they no had parents! I didn't want them to go."

"To go where?"

"To Faster Care."

"She means Foster Care," Officer Castillo interjected from the doorway. "Not 'Faster Care,'" he added with a roll of his eyes. "Foster Care."

Detective Blake studied the old photograph and the address scrawled on the back and slumped in his chair, feeling exasperated by the small comedy he had been drawn into. After a month in which he had crossed paths with a Taiwanese child-smuggling ring and a methaddict grandmother whose idea of discipline was a lighted cigarette, and after three trips with preschoolers to emergency rooms for examinations and photograph sessions for that grim and perverse task known as evidence collection, he was more annoyed than relieved by the harmless stupidity of this case. There was no crime here to investigate, but there were others awaiting him. *Serious shit follows bullshit—it always works that way.* A few seconds later, he rose to his feet and left the interrogation room, with the assistant district attorney following behind him, and they began an argument that continued during the twenty minutes it took them to drive back to Paseo Linda Bonita.

Deputy Castillo escorted Araceli to the holding cell, where she had three hours alone to study the art on the walls, which consisted of five representations of a unicorn with bulbous legs, three crucifixes tipped with arrowheads, and an exquisite rosebud, all drawn in pencil lines that had faded into ghost images in a fog of glossy, waterproof yellow paint. She thought she might ask one of the guards to lend her a writing instrument, because once they did set her free her time would be her own again, forever, and why not use this time to get started? Perhaps she would add a Picasso bull or an El Greco horse to the gallery.

"Sir, a pencil, please, is it possible?" she asked Deputy Castillo when he returned. Unexpectedly, he unlocked the door and held it open.

The news-aggregator website kept a flashing police-car light on its home page, along with a series of rapidly rewritten headlines, as the news of Brandon and Keenan's alleged kidnapping and rescue unfolded, scoring three-point-four million "hits" over the course of the first three hours, with the traffic doubling for the next two hours, when the site linked to footage obtained by an ABC news affiliate: forty-five seconds of Araceli running and being tackled by a police officer, as captured by the film crew in Huntington Park, and sold by the director for one thousand dollars—worth two days of on-location catering, the director would later tell his friends. Soon the footage began circulating on national cable shows, and by midafternoon assignment editors and managing editors across Southern California were dispatching a battalion of wiseass reporters to stake out the south county sheriff's station and Paseo Linda Bonita.

At the front gate of the Laguna Rancho Estates, the guards let through anyone carrying the Day-Glo-green rectangle of a laminated plastic press card issued by the sheriff's department. Outside the Paseo Linda Bonita home the reporters pestered the sheriff's department patrolmen and lower-level public information officials on the perimeter for details of the boys' "drama," and set up tripods and light reflectors on the lawn. A second media cluster laid siege to the Luján family home in Huntington Park, where the councilman had sealed all the doors and windows, leaving the reporters to hound the neighbors for some throwaway speculation about possible kidnappings and flights to the border.

"Police sources say that Councilman Sal Luján is not a suspect in the case," went the report on KFWB all-news radio, delivered by a baritone-voiced veteran of riots, celebrity trials, and airplane crashes, big and small, a macho reporter-gumshoe who was on a first-name basis with mid- and high-ranking police officials in most of the dozens of jurisdictions in Los Angeles and Orange counties. "Seems he's just a Good Samaritan who got caught up in the drama of the two boys. But authorities say they're still trying to figure out what this lady Araceli No-eh-my Ramírez was up to. But, once again, the children she absconded with are said to be safe . . . Reporting from Huntington Park, this is Pete . . ."

The case was a "troubling mystery," said the NBC television affiliate reporter, a portrait of gray-haired youthfulness well known to Southern Californians for the calm urgency of his reporting on the edge of brush fires, mudslides, and assorted gangland crime scenes. "We really don't know what shape those boys are in or what they went through. We don't know if this Mexican nanny will be charged with anything. We don't know what, exactly, her intentions were," the reporter said, summarizing all he didn't know when his affiliate patched him into the network's national cable feed. For several hours the repeated transmissions of Araceli's blurred backyard photograph were juxtaposed with the footage of the searches and lines at the border, and of Araceli being tackled, and of the gleaming white home in a neighborhood most often described with the adjectives "exclusive," "hillside," and "gated." As interest in the story deepened in the early Eastern Daylight Time evening on national cable news, the class of professional tragedy-pundits chimed in. They were former prosecutors and defense attorneys who specialized in taking small bites of nebulous information and chewing them until they became opinions and insights based on "what my gut tells me" and "what we know and what we don't know." Some opined, why not, on what they believed they knew about Mexican women and the well-off families that could afford to place their children in the care of foreigners. These comments intermingled with those of faceless callers to nationwide toll-free lines, for whom Araceli grew into a figure of menace and dread, while Maureen and Scott became objects of pity splashed with a touch of envy and populist scorn. "There's a good reason to stay at home and be a mom, and not leave your kids with a Mexican girl, even if you can get one for ten bucks a day," a caller opined in Gaithersburg, Maryland, speaking to the woman of the flaring nostrils, who nodded gravely.

In those American homes where Mexican, Guatemalan, and Peruvian women actually worked, mothers and fathers digested the news, and looked across their freshly dusted living rooms and tautly made beds and gave their hired help a closer look. They asked themselves questions that they usually suppressed, because the answers were, in practice, unknowable. *Where is this woman from, and how much do I really know about her?* Many of them were familiar with the superficial details of their employees' lives. The most empathetic among them had studied the photographs that arrived in the mail from places south, little faraway images with KODAK imprinted anachronistically on the back, of wrinkled parents in village gardens of prickly pear cacti and drought-bleached corn, of children in used American clothing celebrating exotic holidays involving the burning of incense and parades with religious icons. The knowledge of that distant poverty provoked feelings of admiration, guilt, and mild revulsion in varying degrees, and also a sense of confusion. *How can we live in such a big world, where hooded sweatshirts and baby ballerina dresses circulate from north to south, from new to old, from those who pay retail to those who pay for their clothes by the pound?* Now toss into this mystery a villain, and the possibility of hidden peccadilloes and secret motives of revenge, and the result was a slight but noticeable uptick in the volume of phone calls in the greater Southern California region, as mothers in cubicles, mothers leaving yoga sessions, mothers leaving staff meetings, mothers at the Getty and the Huntington, at the Beverly Center and the Sherman Oaks Galleria, looked away from their monitors and turned off their car radios, and picked up office phones and cell phones and called home, just to check, just to listen to the accented voices of their hired help, to see if they might hear an intonation suggesting deception, the verbal slip of the schemer. "Everything okay? *¿Todo bien? Sí?* Yes? Okay, then." When they returned home they counted the items in their jewelry boxes and some examined the arms and necks of their children for bruises, and a very few even asked their toddlers, for the first time in weeks, if Lupe and María and Soledad were really "nice" or if they were ever "mean," to which the most common responses were, "What?" and "*¿Qué*, Mommy?"

# 17

Brandon sat with his legs crossed on the floor of the living room, telling the story of the journey he and his brother had taken to a distant land called Los Angeles. For the first time in his young life he had an audience of strangers listening to him with the same expression of urgent concentration that adults put on their faces when they talked and argued among themselves. The grown-ups sat on the edge of the couch and the love seat, and on a chair from the dining room, four adult men and two women in various states of formal dress, and with assorted metal and plastic badges and communication devices attached to their garments, accessories that, in Brandon's eyes, established their membership in officialdom. None of this made Brandon nervous. Rather, he saw in the presence of people introduced to him as "the officers" and "the social workers" a confirmation of the fact that he had survived an adventure tinged with danger. He had gone to a place far from the warm security and predictability of his home, and had returned to tell the tale.

"And then we got on this train that had two levels, and we left for another place. In Los Angeles," he said, his younger brother nodding alongside him. "This other place was made of bricks, mostly."

"And wood," Keenan added.

"Yeah, and wood, I think. And we went by a river," Brandon continued. "Or was it a canyon?"

"Yeah, a really big canyon," Keenan said.

"With bridges over it. And there were these people living there. Refugees from the Fire-Swallowers."

"The Fire-Swallowers?" Olivia Garza asked.

"Yeah, those are the people who came and destroyed the village of Vardur at the end of *Revenge of the Riverwalkers*."

"It's one of his books that he reads," Keenan said. Seeing the adults confused, he felt compelled to inject some explanation. "When Mom and Dad left, and Araceli said she would take care of us, she really didn't take care of us—I mean, she didn't tell us what to do like Mom does. So Brandon started reading more than he usually does. And when he reads—"

"Yeah, but these people I saw were real people," Brandon interrupted. "They had scars on their faces, from their battles with the Fire-Swallowers. Then we went to a big train station. And then we got into a bus, and we were looking for Grandpa's house, because Araceli said we should look for him. But we found this other place instead, where there are houses that are like jails, I guess. And then we found other houses that had half doors and quarter doors, and three-quarter doors, and other things I thought only existed in books. But they were real. And then we found a shack, which was in this place that's kind of like an oasis in the desert, where people come from all over to meet and sell things. We met this boy, who's a slave. I have a book about slavery, and he didn't look like any of the slaves in that book, but he was still a slave. We stayed with him in his shack. And he told us about the warriors who used to live across the street, and the battles they had, which always lasted thirteen seconds. The lady who lived there, she was really mean to this boy, and she made him work."

"That's true," Keenan said. "He really was a slave."

"Right. He was like my age, but he was a slave. So we slept there one night, until we woke up in the morning and heard some guy screaming outside."

"I didn't hear anybody screaming," Keenan said.

"You were still asleep, but I heard it. It was right after the earthquake."

"There was an earthquake?" Keenan said.

"Yeah. So this guy, he was like in pain, or something. He was yelling like he was hurting in his guts. And then everybody got up and we went to another place, which is called a park even though there isn't any park there. We went there because we thought Grandpa lived there, I guess, but he didn't live there either. At this park place they had a fire burning in the ground, to take a pig and turn him into bones. And the fire was burning hot, even though it was buried, because later we touched the rocks that were under the ground and they were still hot. But before that, everything started exploding around us. A bomb exploded in the street. And Keenan was holding some fire in his hand, and I told him to drop it, but he wouldn't listen to me."

"No, I didn't."

"Yes, you did. Don't lie. I saw you. You were holding fire, it was sparking from your palm, and then the bomb went off in the street. That's when I wanted to cry. After that a lynch mob came to the front porch, and they started yelling at us, because they were against the guy who lived there, and we started yelling back the name of Ray Forma, who is against them. Ray Forma is like some sort of hero that protects people against lynch mobs. These people yelling at us, they didn't have torches, but it was a lynch mob, I'm pretty sure, and they were really angry at the guy who lived there, because he's a president. But then the police came and chased away the lynch mob and we went to sleep and when we woke up the next morning we were on television so I got on the phone and called Dad."

The assembled audience of adults stared at Brandon with perplexed mouths agape and brows wrinkled, each mystified by the nonsensical details of Brandon's story and his straightforward and sincere way of recounting them, and the way Keenan sometimes nodded in confirmation of what his brother said. Adults and children had been momentarily transported into a shared state of mystery and innocence, a kind of mental blankness where anything was possible, and the adults allowed themselves to entertain, for the briefest instant of grown-up time, the possibility that these two well-spoken boys had actually returned from a magical land. Even Olivia Garza, who believed she had heard every kind of story a child could tell, did not know precisely what she should make of Brandon's monologue, so she simply looked at her digital recorder and turned it off.

Detective Blake and Assistant District Attorney Goller rose to their feet simultaneously, while a second detective named Harkness patted both Brandon and Keenan on the head and said, "Thanks guys." Detective Blake called back the parents from their temporary exile in the kitchen and left the boys with them, and the committee retired to the backyard for a tête-à-tête. For a few moments, they stood in a circle and looked at one another with now-what expressions.

"I don't know what to make of that," Detective Blake said finally. "That kid's got quite an imagination."

"This is what happens when you leave them alone too much, in my opinion," Olivia Garza said. "Whether it's TV, or books, or computer games. There are drawbacks. They slip into their own world."

"God knows what really happened to them," Assistant District Attorney Goller said. "I'm not a psychologist, but maybe this is some sort of emotional fantasy response to severe trauma."

The eyes of everyone present turned to the staff psychologist from Child Protective Services, a twenty-nine-year-old recently minted PhD from UCLA named Jennifer Gelfand-Peña. This was Dr. Gelfand-Peña's first time with the so-called emergency intervention team and she had overdressed for the occasion in her best, virgin-wool business skirt, and now she thought it strange that they were meeting with a representative of the district attorney's office and two detectives, given the manifest innocuousness of the case.

"What do I think?" she said with a pretty-woman cheerfulness that made everyone else in the group deepen their growing irritation with her. "I think the view up here is spectacular. I'm sort of bummed because I think we're missing the sunset. I also think this desert garden is really beautiful, but it's kind of over the top." Her colleagues shot her stony glances, but she seemed unconcerned. "And in my professional opinion, this kid Brandon is a fascinating case. He's got the verbal and reading skills of an eighteen-year-old. And the socialization of a seven-year-old, which isn't surprising, since he's very sheltered up here, and since he goes to the most expensive, touchy-feely private school in the county. So I think what's probably going on is that he's just read too many books."

"Well, the way I see it, the boy basically confirmed what the maid told our detective here," Olivia Garza said. "She said she was taking them to the grandfather. Right, Detective? And that's what the boy said. He said they were alone in the house with the maid and they left to look for the grandfather."

"But he didn't know since when," Detective Blake offered.

"Yeah, kids are terrible with time," the staff psychologist said.

"No harm, no foul, as far as I'm concerned," Detective Blake said. "I don't see what we can hold this Mexican lady on."

"So we're going to throw the parents' statement out the window?" Goller said. "Shouldn't we be investigating, at least, for child endangerment?"

"Eleven one sixty-five-point-two?" Blake said. "By the parents? Or the maid?"

"No, not the parents, because they left the boys with an adult guardian," Goller said. "But I wasn't thinking about that so much as a two-seventy-three-A."

"Interesting," said Dr. Gelfand-Peña, which was her ironic way of saying a child abuse charge seemed far-fetched.

"Really?" Olivia Garza said.

"Do we have evidence of either of those crimes?" Detective Blake asked.

"Remember that address our victims appear to have visited first?" Goller said. "I called the LAPD. It's smack in the middle of the gang-infested garment-factory district of L.A. If taking two Orange County kids to that hellhole isn't two seventy-three-A, then I don't know what is."

"Felony two seventy-three-A?" Detective Blake said. "I don't see it. Misdemeanor two seventy-three-A? Maybe."

"Do we go back and question the parents again?" Olivia Garza asked.

"We've got their statement," Goller said.

"Can't we just drop the whole thing?" Jennifer Gelfand-Peña asked.

There was a collective silence in which the three senior members of the emergency intervention team—Goller, Blake, and Garza—looked at one another and waited like *pistoleros* in a western for one to blink. The truth was, once you amassed as many resources as they had, it took a bit of courage to simply cry out, *Sorry! False Alarm!* After all, K-9 units had been assembled to search the hills, Explorer deputies had marched through the meadows, and a suspect had been named, with her alleged crime denounced. They had called an Amber Alert and semi-sealed-off the border for a few hours, all in the name of protecting two Orange County children. Some grown-up had to be held responsible for this mess.

"From what I can tell," Goller said finally, "and from what I can see of this family, and from having questioned this woman, I think it's pretty obvious Ms. Ramírez didn't like her employers. So she conspired to dump their kids someplace. Just leave 'em somewhere god-awful. If she 'willfully' placed those boys in a situation where they might be endangered, then that's two seventy-three-A. That's the law."

Detective Blake was unconvinced. He sensed familiar political-theatric motives at work, the usual DA baloney. "Well, you go ahead and make your phone call, Mr. Goller. And I'll make mine."

"You know Goller, sometimes things really *are* what they seem to be," Olivia Garza said. "It's pretty obvious we should just call it a ten-forty and go home."

"No, I don't think that I'll be able to do that," the assistant district attorney said, raising his chin and directing the group to look up at the sky and its spreading wash of ultramarine ink. The beating engines of two television helicopters had slipped into the airspace above them as they were debating the case. "They pulled those choppers away from the fire to cover this," Goller said. "That's huge. My guess is that we're live on national cable right now." The assistant district attorney allowed the members of the emergency intervention team to ponder the meaning of the hovering crafts, and the small globes attached to their undercarriages. "Unfortunately, we're in America's living room now," he said. "Therefore, we must proceed with an abundance of caution."

They were smack in the middle of that great spectacle Goller had foreseen in his condo during the first hours of the morning, when Brandon's and Keenan's faces first flashed on his television. And already he sensed where its pressures might take them.

"So go ahead and release your suspect if you have to, Detective," Goller said. "But in a few days you might have to pick her up again."

After a first kiss of his daughter's forehead, after looking at his two sons, embracing them, and confirming, with a scan of his eyes and a few minutes in their untroubled presence, that they had suffered no harm, Scott found himself stepping back and away. "We missed you, Dad," Keenan said, and the simple statement brought a rush of water to his eyes. He turned to his wife, seeking a glance, a shared moment of understanding and forgiveness, but she was aggressively not looking at him, so he drifted off into a state of shocked silence, in which he listened to his wife repeat, again and again, "Are you okay? Are you okay?" Then, after the police and the social workers and the psychologist had finished their "talk" alone with Brandon and Keenan, and after he and Maureen had a second reunion with their sons that was a shorter and less emotional version of the first, he drifted away from the room entirely, leaving his wife to assuage her guilt by reading to the boys and Samantha from a large picture book, in a kind of forced imitation of domestic bliss that, Scott guessed, was intended for the police and social services officials still huddled in their yard. Scott looked at Brandon rolling his eyes because *Ladybug Girl* was not exactly his idea of compelling literature. *My son is eleven, but he's already a book snob.* Eventually Scott drifted to the television room, to the high-tech masculinity of objects plugged into the wall, and reached for the television's power switch with a Pavlovian purposelessness, flipping through the cable channels. He stopped when he reached an aerial news shot of a structure on a dead-end circle that looked familiar. When he saw the graphic that read MISSING CHILDREN FOUND he knew it was his home, and he considered the size of the crescent-shaped backyard, and how much of it was filled by the desert garden. From the air, and in the fading illumination of dusk, the garden looked like a herd of small spiked animals escorted by tall cacti shepherds. He thought that it all made for an aesthetically pleasing composition of circles and lines when you saw it from the sky, before the little commentator in his head finally woke up and he realized, *Holy shit, there's a helicopter floating above my house.*

Before he could rise to his feet to go to the window to look for the helicopter, the television switched to a video clip shot from the ground, footage that showed Scott himself talking with a sheriff's deputy at his door several hours earlier, a few minutes after Scott had received that phone call from Brandon. The deputy was smiling and patting him on the back, and Scott guessed that this image was supposed to convey the idea that the drama had been resolved happily, and sure enough seconds later there was a shot of his two sons walking up the driveway, escorted very quickly by a deputy to the front door. The television cut to a studio shot, of a woman with flaring nostrils and stiff blond hair that sprayed forth, fountainlike, from her head, and a band of gold coins around her neck, and she was speaking to a camera with a kind of vehemence that Scott found unappealing, until she stopped suddenly and just stared at the camera for several seconds and began nodding. This caused Scott to reach for the volume and turn it up. The woman on the television was listening to a caller with an accent that Scott recognized as upper New England.

". . . and I just look at those two precious little boys, Nancy, and I wonder, what did that Mexican lady want with them? What was she thinking she was gonna do with them? I just wonder."

"That's what we're all thinking," the blond host said, which led Scott to change the channel, inadvertently causing Araceli to appear on the screen. She was being escorted to the police car, earlier in the day, with her wrists clasped together with plastic strings. *Oh, my God*, Scott thought. *What have we done to this poor Mexican woman?* The screen cut to another shot tagged LIVE: ORANGE COUNTY, CALIFORNIA, which showed his $250-per-week housemaid emerging from a police station, winding her way through concrete obstacles meant to fend off terrorist attacks. "Araceli Noemí Ramírez, kidnapping suspect, has now been set free, with investigators saying . . ." Araceli was walking away from the cameras, studying the news-gatherers filming her from a distance with the same quizzical and annoyed look she gave Scott when he asked for catsup to apply to her turkey sandwiches. Now she stopped, to listen to a shouted question, apparently, and the camera zoomed and shook, with his large domestic employee bouncing at the center of the frame as she turned and walked away with long and loping strides, an image that reminded Scott of that footage of Bigfoot supposedly walking through a clearing in a California forest, a video moment halfway between the real and the simulated, like those shots of turban man and binocular lady Elysian Systems sold to the government.

Scott was changing the channel again when Maureen appeared at the door behind him.

"Scott. The police say the reporters outside won't leave," she said, and there was something startling in hearing her address him. "They say they're going to wait until we make a statement." She had not slept

in two days and she was fading quickly, her voice dreamy and faraway.

"I'll go out there and talk to them."

"No, I have to go with you. You can't be out there alone."

"Why?"

"Because they need to see both of us. We both need to be there. To
defend ourselves."

"What?"

"People are talking about our family. All over the city. Didn't you
know? Stephanie Goldman-Arbegast just called. They were driving in
from the airport and heard people talking about us on the radio. About
the boys and Araceli and me and you. For an entire hour. People are saying we're bad parents. We have to show ourselves. Because people are
saying things about us. Didn't you know?"


The news of the "kidnapping" had circulated in Spanish too, in
a flow of words only slightly less robust than in English, beginning in
the morning, when a popular FM radio talk/variety jock interrupted his
usual series of bawdy jokes and barnyard animal noises to reflect on *el
caso*, lowering his voice an octave into what he called, off the air, his
"citizen voice." "Friends," he said in Spanish, "this is a case that might
impact each and every one of us. I don't know what this lady is doing
with these boys, but if you're listening to me, *señora*, or *señorita*, take
them home. Let's remember that our relationship with these people is
built on trust. Because I know there's thousands of *nuestra gente* out
there taking care of these little *mocosos* with blond hair and blue eyes.
And if just one of us messes up like they say this lady is, a big load of you
know what is going to fall on top of all our heads." In kitchens where
meals were being prepared by women named Lupe and María and
Soledad, the anxiety level rose significantly after listening to this lec-
ture, and rose further after Lupe and María and Soledad saw the reports on the city's three Spanish-language television stations, and the
footage of Araceli in flight. So by the end of that fifth of July, the floors
gleamed brighter, the food was prepared with extra care and fewer
spices, until, in the evening when Lupe and María and Soledad arrived
home to the cluttered hominess of their apartments in South-Central

and Compton, or when they settled into their cramped servant quarters in Beverly Hills homes, and they turned on their televisions and their radios to hear the happy news that Araceli Noemí Ramírez had been set free and that she had been *exonerada* of all charges.

On Spanish-language television, the images of Araceli walking free were broadcast with commentary that took on a thinly veiled tone of the celebratory, the rising voices of a soccer victory, or the birth of a celebrity baby. "*Salió una mujer libre, con la cabeza alta, y digna.*" It had all been a misunderstanding, they reported in voices a half breath short of a sigh. The charges against Araceli, now dropped, were a false wrinkle in the freshly starched blanket of responsibility for which *latinoamericana* nannies were famous. *Una mala comunicación.* On the telephone, "*la soltaron*" became the refrain: They let her go, they let her slip away. It was an observation dropped into conversations that soon swung back to the mundane quotidian chatter and melodramatic gossip about school meetings and *comadres* who were pregnant again and jobs opening up in "*casas buenas,*" and the irritating behavior of employers in "*casas malas.*" They let Araceli go and everything was back to normal until the next morning, when the workday began in the early morning darkness, and Lupe and María and Soledad entered kitchens and bedrooms and looked for the faces of the women who paid them, their *jefas*, and saw the upturned corners of pert lips, the flaxen caterpillar eyebrows that rose in recognition and comfort: *Yes, I know you, you are my Lupe, my María, my Soledad. You are here again, on time, and you will wave your chestnut hands and return these sheets and comforters to order, and you will erase the grease from the kitchen surfaces and keep the ants away, and you will change my baby boy's diaper, and I will leave you here alone in my nest, alone with my child and my possessions, because of that moment of faith and calculus when I close my eyes and feel that thing called trust.*

Maureen led Scott back to the living room, where Assistant District Attorney Goller was standing alone by the front door with the attentive look of a best man awaiting the bride and groom at a wedding. When Maureen reached the door, he gave her a comforting smile, put his arm around her shoulder, and lowered his chin to speak sotto voce, even though no one else but Scott was listening.

"There's about a dozen reporters out there. Don't let that scare you." He guided Maureen gently to the picture window and pulled back a corner of the drapes, revealing the spectacle of lights and telescoping microwave antennas outside; they felt to Maureen like an alien force, gathered on her lawn with nefarious cinematic intent, fed by the electricity generated by their humming vans. "The sheriff department's PIO was just out there fifteen minutes ago. The public information officer, I mean. And he gave a statement, saying they were releasing your employee, and not charging her with anything. He said this was all a, quote, 'misunderstanding.'"

"Right," Scott said quickly.

"But when they pressed him for details, he got off his script," Goller continued. "He started saying some things that weren't on the release. He said some things that our friend Detective Blake told him, apparently. He said your employee was trying to, quote, 'rescue' your children because you had, quote, 'abandoned' them."

"Fuck," Scott said, which earned him a pointed look from his wife.

"That's what he said. 'Rescue.' Which, of course, implies that you two placed your children in danger."

"Jesus," Scott said.

"Why would he say that?" Maureen asked. "Why would anyone care? We got our boys back."

"He said that because he needed to explain how it was that a sheriff, an American sheriff, could simply release an illegal immigrant onto the streets, especially one that was just a suspect in a child abduction case."

"Child abduction?" Scott said. "But is that really—"

"The PIO had to give them something," Goller continued. "So he gave them you, in so many words."

"Us?" Maureen said.

"And as soon as he made that suggestion, well, it got the reporters excited. They started throwing around phrases like 'irresponsible' and 'negligence' and asking if we're going to 'press charges.' Being reporters, they don't really understand what those words mean. But when they start asking those kinds of questions, Child Protective Services will eventually get their noses in the case." Goller quickly explained the competing bureaucratic imperatives that would soon envelope Maureen, Scott, and their children, and how it was that two good parents could easily end up before a skeptical judge in family court. It shouldn't be that a mother and father who called the police in search of their boys ended up under the scrutiny of Child Protective Services, that crude, cheaply staffed machinery, as Goller saw it, where parents were studied under a lens of maximum disbelief. But it happened all the time.

"So what do we do?" Maureen asked finally.

"Number one, you go out there and speak very calmly and show these people who you are," Goller said. "You're the very picture of a happy California family. Just you standing up there will do a lot to calm the waters, so to speak. You don't answer any questions. But you do say that you're thankful to the sheriff's department and the Huntington Park police and the media—it's important that you remember the media—that you're thankful to all of them for helping to find your two sons. If they shout any questions, you don't answer. You just say thanks and walk away. Okay?"

Scott digested this information as he walked down the lawn, Maureen following after him with Samantha over her shoulder, having left the boys inside their room with the assistant district attorney. Like a family condemned to the guillotine, they walked with heads bowed toward the spot where the lawn dropped off and sloped downward. A cluster of microphones attached to two poles stood waiting there, their steel silhouettes glinting against a cloud of white light from the television lamps. Scott felt the heat of the lights on his skin, and a kind of nakedness he had not felt since he was an adolescent. *Here we stand before you, my American family and I: have pity on me, their bumbling provider and protector, and on them, because they aren't to blame.* He approached the microphone to speak, though before he could open his mouth someone yelled out, "Is that Torres with an *s* or with a *z*?"

"An *s*," he said, and smiled, because the question calmed him and brought him to the moment.

"I, we, my wife and I . . . we just want to say thank you to everybody," Scott began. "To the sheriff's department, to the Child Protective Services people, to everyone. And to the media too, for getting the word out. Brandon and Keenan are home safe now. They're going to be okay." In ten seconds, he had reached the end of all he could say.

"Were they kidnapped?" a male voice asked in a tone that suggested irony and disbelief. "Was there a note?"

Scott could see the wisdom of Ian Goller's advice: unwrapping the full and complicated truth for this assembled rabble of news-gatherers would be an act of suicide. "And we're glad this is over," he continued, ignoring the question. "Thanks for coming." He sensed, in an instant, that his attempt at expressing finality had fallen flat. In the time-swallowing silence that followed, he became aware that he, Maureen, and Samantha were on live television, because he could see their family portrait, animated and mirrorlike in miniature, on five monitors that rested at the feet of the reporters, each with the words LIVE: LAGUNA RANCHO ESTATES in various fonts. "So good night, everyone. And thank you."

Maureen mouthed the words *Thank you* silently, with perhaps a bit too much wan affectation. They were just turning to leave when a voice boomed from behind the blinding lights.

"I have a police source that says you, quote, 'abandoned' your children. For four days. You just disappeared, apparently. Why?" Scott and Maureen were caught off guard by the questioner's bluntness. The voice belonged to the veteran KFWB reporter, who had arrived at the scene just a few minutes earlier, after a gear-grinding race from the south county sheriff's station, where an off-the-record conversation with the chief of detectives before Araceli's release had tilted his view of the case toward the Mexican woman.

"Why did you leave them alone in this house for four days?" None of his colleagues were surprised by the radio reporter's directness. His gadfly irritability with interview subjects was legendary, and included a live television dress down of the chief spokesman for the United States Army Central Command in Riyadh during the first Gulf War. "It's a simple question. Did you abandon your children to this illegal immigrant?"

Maureen could not see the questioner, a stranger who was standing on her property and slandering her before a live television audience. He was yelling from behind the pack of cameras, beyond the white aura of light bursting behind the reporters' heads. "That's a lie!" she snapped. She had a moment to think, *This is the most desperate thing I've done in my entire life*, but failed to notice the surprised and mildly disgusted expression on the woman in the first row of reporters, which might have given her a clue to the response of her viewing audience. "How dare you!" After thirty-six hours without sleeping, her eyes were amnesiac droopy, but she could not accept a total stranger saying she was a bad mother. Her hair was flat and stringy, and she was wearing the same dress she had put on the morning she left the desert spa, a spaghetti-strap pullover whose patterned sunflowers now hung forlornly from her shoulders. Her fuming shout only made her look more haggard, poor and harried, as if she'd stepped off some trashy tabloid-reality stage. Later, Maureen would see this moment replayed on television and understand what she had done as an act of self defense, more desperate, even, than being nineteen years old and trying to escape from underneath the sweaty grip of a drunken college friend, the only time in her life she'd actually used her fists and teeth to inflict injury. "I did *not* neglect my children. That's a vicious, vicious lie!"

"Yeah, we got it!" the reporter said sarcastically.

"Pete, gather yourself," one of the other reporters said.

"C'mon. Tell us what happened."

Maureen squinted and searched the silhouettes of the reporters one last time, and turned and walked away, Scott mumbling a thank-you at the microphones and then scurrying after her.

Araceli thought the cameras outside the sheriff's station might follow her, but they did not. She walked quickly around the corner, through the station's parking lot and its fleet of patrol cars, and into the empty center of Aliso Viejo, where the streets were free of pedestrians after four-thirty in the afternoon. The police had returned her money, and in her first moments of freedom she was momentarily fixated on that act of honesty. *Transparencia*, they called that in Mexico, an idea symbolized by the clear, large plastic bag in which her belongings had been gathered and catalogued. *Now, that's an example of* el primer mundo *if there ever was one.* In Mexico, you paid cash for your freedom, and the police made sure you left custody with nothing but your wrinkled clothes and all the stains you acquired during a night or two in jail: it had happened to a couple of her alcoholic uncles. A bribe and it was all forgotten. If your car was stolen, you paid the police to get it back for you, which had happened to her father, in the *comisaría* in Nezahual-cóyotl. Here at the sheriff's station, by contrast, Araceli had been set free not by monetary payment, but rather with truth and laughter, and this realization made her chuckle again, all by herself on the street corner, and reminded her of that folk saying: *La que sola ríe, en sus maldades piensa.* She who laughs alone is remembering her sins. "That's dumb: I haven't committed any *maldades*. I'm just a poor *mexicana* trying to find her way." The detective had asked her, simply, for a phone number at which she might be reached—"in case we need some help with the investigation"—and had then handed her the plastic bag. She advanced one block down the street before she realized she didn't know where to go next. Returning to the home of the Torres-Thompsons was out of the question. *No los quiero ver.* She did have the money in the plastic bag, and briefly considered buying a bus ticket to the border: she had enough for a ticket to Tijuana, and for a *torta* and taco once she got there, but not enough to go any farther. And getting her money out of the bank was impossible without returning to Paseo Linda Bonita. So she called Marisela, with a quarter dropped into the last pay phone left in the center of Aliso Viejo, and asked her friend for *posada* for a night.

"You were on TV," Marisela said. "You're still on TV."

"*Estoy cansada.* I think I'll sleep for two days."

"Did they hurt you? When I saw them grabbing you on the news, when you were running, I told Mr. Covarrubias, 'Oh, my God. They're going to break her arm!' And then we saw you walk out and you looked fine."

"They were polite. Once they realized I am not a *secuestradora* . . . So can I stay with you?"

"Let me ask my Mr. Covarrubias and see what he says." Araceli heard the sounds of dishes being moved about the kitchen, and the formless chatter from the television, and then the very clear jingle of a beer commercial, followed by an exchange of voices.

"He says he's going to drive out there to pick you up," Marisela said with a cheer. "He's really angry about what he saw on the TV. He says we have to help you. He's running out the door right now. Expect him there in about twenty-five minutes."

In her home on Calmada Avenue in South Whittier, Janet Bryson was angry too, though for entirely different reasons. She watched television dumbfounded as Araceli Ramírez walked to freedom, perched on the edge of her old but homey and recently reupholstered couch, in a big house with a faulty air conditioner. The heat and the events on the television put her in a foul mood. She'd begun to follow the drama of Brandon and Keenan before dawn, in the final hours of her hospital swing shift, catching the first images of the boys on the television in the empty reception area. Later, at home, she searched for details on the Internet and then sat down in her living room to watch the final, insulting denouement of the day's events live on Channel 9.

"They're letting her go? What is this?"

Janet Bryson did not personally know any of the protagonists, of course, although her home happened to be eight blocks from Scott Torres's old home on Safari Drive. She was a nurse technician, and a divorced single mom raising a teenage boy in a two-story ranchette with a layout identical to the former Torres residence, a home plopped like his on the flat surface of forgotten cow pastures, alongside a concrete drainage channel called Coyote Creek. A small thread of brackish liquid ran in Coyote Creek during the summer, fed mostly by the runoff from storm drains that collected the water wasted by neighbors who babied their lawns, rose gardens, and low riders with twice and thrice-weekly deluges. That thread of brackish water attracted crows and cats and, occasionally, a flock of feral parrots with emerald and saffron plumage, and now, as Janet slumped back into the newly stiff cushions of her couch to fully absorb the release of yet another illegal alien criminal suspect into American freedom, one of the parrots gave a loud, humanoid squawk just beyond her backyard fence.

"Oh, shut up, you stupid bird!"

Janet Bryson felt roughly the same about Araceli Ramírez, the nanny kidnapper, and all the other Mexicans invading her space, as she did about the untamed parrots. Like the Spanish-speaking families in her subdivision, the parrots were intruders from the south. They were the descendants of escaped pets and, in a landscape that was the natural home of gray-brown house sparrows and black crows, they were disturbing for the ostentatious display of their exotic colors. Five years earlier she had written to the SPCA, the Sierra Club, and the Audubon Club about how disturbing it was, what a violation of natural rhythms and habitats, to have these tropical birds gathering on the telephone wires and bathing in the creek. Only the Audubon people had written back, with a polite and oft-circulated letter decrying the "invasive species" but lamenting the expense and impracticality of rounding up all the birds, which were in fact six different species of the genus *Amazona*.

The Mexicans came after the parrots. There had always been a few, but they were English-speaking and generally decent folk back in the day when Janet Bryson was a newlywed and lived in this same home with her former husband. She could talk to those Mexicans because they were Americans, and she could even see a bit of herself in the family comings and goings she witnessed on their driveways and in their garages, the household routines shaped around automobiles, football, and the holidays. Their cousins and grandparents concentrated for Thanksgiving and their lights went up every Christmas. But then came the slow drip of Spanish speakers, the inexorable filling of her block with actual nationals of that other country. She'd knocked on the door of one of the first of these Spanish-speaking families when they moved in next door, offering a plate of brownies because it was the neighborly thing to do. A man of about thirty with a head of black Brillo-pad hair had greeted her, seemingly perplexed by the gesture and also delighted by the appearance of a still-hot white woman on his doorstep. Moments later, this man's wife had joined him at the door and had given Janet Bryson a reluctant "thank you"—or, rather, "tank you"—and then a dismissive up-and-down, as if to say, *No, my husband won't go after this one.* And they still hadn't returned her plate several years later! Janet Bryson didn't forget a slight, which was why she hadn't spoken to her ex-husband for several years, not since an incident at a Super Bowl party involving one of his girlfriends. She remembered the missing plate as more Mexicans arrived, with one family on her block raising a Mexican flag on an actual flagpole they planted on their front lawn, in violation of a building code no one bothered to enforce.

The parrots squawked and waddled in the wash, and thrived and multiplied on a diet of oranges and lemons, and their sudden bursts of noise, their early morning squawk-chorus, often startled Mrs. Bryson awake, as did the Mexicans who revved up their old cars at six or seven to get them going. The parrots flew in groups of about twenty, in large, diamond-shaped formations, and the Mexicans moved in clusters, pairs of men standing over engines, groups of women and girls carrying pots. The Mexicans always seemed to be plotting, with the men putting arms around one another, speaking in lowered voices. Most ominously, she heard, several times a week, one of them make a seven-tone whistle. It was a kind of signal, a summoning, the last note trailing off in plaintive demand. What was the meaning?

Janet Bryson had begun to study the Mexicans in the same way she had studied the parrots, by plugging keywords into Internet search engines, and then by writing letters and emails in which her sense of dislocation found voice. She had come to see herself as part of an under-the-radar network of concerned citizens, isolated voices scattered about suburbs like El Monte and Lancaster, fighting the evils of bilingual education and the bad habits of these people, such as using their front lawns to park their cars and dry their laundry. From her Internet friends, she learned about the conspiracies hatched at the highest levels of government and finance to join together the United States, Canada, and Mexico into a single country, with a single currency called the Amero. She had seen schematic drawings that were said to represent the superhighway that would link the interior of Mexico to Kansas City, and thus accelerate the country's plunge into foreignness. Watching the Mexicans on Calmada Avenue plot, and reading about the much larger scheme to transform her country, was like living in a dream: the events were strange, menacing, and out of her control.

Janet Bryson worked, sacrificed, and kept an eye on the Mexicans for her only son, an ungrateful sixteen-year-old who was beginning to talk English like a Mexican: she could hear it in the way he stretched out the vowels into a long whine in words like "really" and "guy," and the gangster intonations with which he pronounced phrases like "so what." "Why are you talking that way?" she would demand, but he would just shoot back that annoyed sneer that had taken over his face since he turned thirteen. Before he met Mexicans, Carter was a boy who understood they were a mother and son against the world. She had recently given him the keys to his first car and he had rewarded her by working on it in the driveway with one of the Mexicans, and then disappearing every afternoon and most evenings in that old Toyota Celica, leaving her alone in the house to think about her Mexican neighbors and to watch television, where the news was filled with Mexicans. If you looked closely, you saw them everywhere: on the edges of fires, at basketball games, in mug shots. And now in the face of that running woman, the stealer of children who, for mysterious reasons, was now walking free.

On the day that Araceli Ramírez became a national celebrity, Janet Bryson stood on the front porch of her home and called out to her son, "Carter! Where are you going?" He waved but didn't answer. She had been planted in front of her television set for most of the day, and her obsession with the story had caused her to consume, all on her own, a family-size bag of cheese curls. *It's not good to eat that way.* But what else could she do? Those boys looked like her boy, in the old grade school picture with the brown fixer stains in the hallway, Carter before hormones swelled his arms and thickened his neck. Two American boys spirited away southward into Mexico. Unprotected. She found herself actually weeping when word of their rescue had flashed on *Headline News.* "Thank God!" She slipped into the kitchen and made herself a late lunch, and allowed the television to fill the house with noise as she waited for whatever epilogue the news might bring. And then she had heard the announcement of the Mexican woman's release, and the scurrilous insinuations against the American parents.

When Maureen shouted, "That's a lie," Janet Bryson shared her sense of motherly indignation, and felt herself instantly freed from the state of vibrating meaninglessness that seemed to settle over her mind and home during those long hours when her son was away. *We should all shout like that.* Janet Bryson wanted to shout at the next-door neighbor with the string of Christmas lights circling a backyard shrine, whose nighttime glow filled her bedroom 365 days a year, to shout at the unseen young Mexicans who had taught her son to whine at the end of his words. She had to do something; she had to join her shout to the shout of that American mother who had been wronged. She had to rally the troops. She returned to her computer and started writing.

# 18

In thirty minutes, Maureen told Stephanie Goldman-Arbegast the entire story, beginning with the fiasco of the birthday party and the drunken ramblings of Sasha "the Big Man" Avakian and the planting of the desert garden. They were sitting in the kitchen, with Samantha's somewhat plump, pre-toddler body squeezed into a now-stationary hand-crank rocker. Samantha was about three months and fifteen pounds past the appropriate age and size for this contraption, Stephanie Goldman-Arbegast observed, and it disturbed her, mildly, to see her old friend subject her baby to this uncharacteristic and extended moment of in-attention. Stephanie Goldman-Arbegast was used to seeing Maureen in elegant control of just about any situation that presented itself, moving slowly and deliberately and in good cheer in the face of poolside scrapes and wine-glass mishaps. Stephanie admired and in many ways sought to emulate her old playgroup friend, even though, in a few, select en-counters over the past few months, she'd noticed how the old, even-tempered Maureen was being slowly ground down by the demands of two growing boys and a baby girl. But never had Stephanie Goldman-Arbegast seen Maureen in the sleep-deprived and disoriented state in which she found her today, circling aimlessly about the kitchen as she spoke, and finally wiping the tears from her face as she brought the strange and accidental tale forward to the argument that ended with the broken living room coffee table, and her journey with Samantha into the desert, and her return to the spotless and empty rooms of this home.

"And that's how we got into this mess," Maureen said, and as she looked up through her swollen eyes at her old friend the phone rang once more. Peter Goldman picked it up after the second ring in the dining room, where he was drinking wine with Scott.

"The reporters," Maureen said. "We're living this media plague. They've made us into a story."

"It was big on the morning shows," said Stephanie Goldman-Arbegast, who had black hair cut man-short for the summer. She was a lean woman of forty with the no-nonsense air and taste for embroidered blouses of her Wyoming forebears.

"They called here last night, before we took the phone off the hook so we could sleep. The *Today* show. Scott talked to them and told them to leave us alone."

"And then there's the stuff in the papers. And in the blogs."

"The blogs? I can only imagine."

Stephanie removed three printed pages of blog posts from her purse, and held them so that Maureen could see them, a sampling of the 316 postings on the *L.A. Times* website as of late morning. She did this simply so Maureen would know, because that was the job of friends, to be both loyal and alert, and to bring knowledge that might be uncomfortable and unwanted but also necessary. Almost exactly half the postings expressed sympathy with Scott and Maureen: of those, half cited the clip of Maureen shouting back at the reporter in expressing their own outrage at the "liberal" and "immigrant-loving" media for refusing to believe that Brandon and Keenan had been kidnapped. These posters and their paranoid rhetoric held Maureen's attention only momentarily. The other half, however, made various snide observations about the Torres-Thompsons and the Laguna Rancho Estates, about Maureen's "rant" and how "spoiled" she and her husband were, and the obvious "heroism" of the Mexican woman who'd been briefly jailed for "the crime" of trying to save two children who'd been abandoned by their parents.

"Don't take that stuff too seriously," Stephanie said. "I just thought you should know. Maybe I shouldn't have shown you."

"No. I need to see this."

"There was this one guy on the radio. KABC. Some guy from an immigrant association, talking about how Mexican women are the 'salt of the earth,' how they raise our children and do heroic things every day, and how Araceli is, what's the word, 'emblematic' of this big 'font of mothering' these Latina nannies provide. I tried calling in to defend you, to say something, but—"

"A font of mothering? Araceli?"

"Yeah. It was some really overwrought expression like that."

"Unbelievable." Maureen scanned a few of the English postings, then stopped and returned them to her friend. "Araceli is the real mother, I guess," she said with sarcastic resignation. "I'm just the rich parasite."

"Ignore them. You know who you are. You're a great mom. To three kids. And now with Guadalupe gone? All by yourself you're raising them. None of those people know how hard you work. And who cares, frankly?"

Above all, Maureen was offended simply by the idea that distant strangers would offer their glib and automatic opinions about her home and family. They peered into her household and made a wicked sport of her, Scott, and their children, extrapolating conclusions based on a few photographs released to the public, their own prejudices about people "like her," and the recorded moment when she chose to defend herself before the intrusive white light of the television cameras gathered on her front lawn. These faceless strangers could type insults and collectively craft the big falsehood of Araceli's lionization, without knowing that the Mexican woman disliked Maureen's children and frowned at them as she served them dinner, and that she had once had the gall to tell Maureen, "These boys have too many toys to keep in order. They are not organized in their brains to have this many toys." *Araceli questioned my sons' intelligence, she sat for hours in her room playing artist with our trash, she recoiled at the sight of my baby girl's spit-up. But now she is a Mexican Joan of Arc.*

"It's true that I left, that we left her alone in the house," she told Stephanie finally. "But that doesn't give her the right to take our children on some bizarre journey to the city, for God knows what purpose."

"No, it doesn't."

Maureen thought of the daily vigilance necessary to keep domestic order and to stay true to her values and raise children who would be good citizens and thinkers. It was all a private, selfless act, and now she was being mocked as precisely the opposite. Araceli was responsible for this chorus of snarky and misspelled voices against her.

"How could she not believe we were coming back? That doesn't make sense to me. She doesn't even leave a note. That woman was always off. And why take them into Los Angeles, of all places?"

"She was wrong to do that."

"She placed them in danger."

Stephanie Goldman-Arbegast kept silent and gave her friend a weak nod of solidarity. She sensed that Maureen would eventually add her voice to those seeking to punish Araceli, and she did not approve. *I will not hold this against my friend.* Here before her was a good woman in an impossible situation. She lived for her children. Her children were her art. And now the city belittled her as a bad mother. *Would I act any different? If my jaw tightens in anger when my New York in-laws criticize my parenting, how would I act if an entire city were sitting in judgment?* Stephanie watched as her friend bit her lip and turned to look at her sleeping baby girl.

"This rocker is too small for Samantha, isn't it?" Maureen said finally, as if she had stepped out of a fog and found her daughter, unexpectedly. "I can't put her in this thing anymore. She's all squeezed into it. What was I thinking?"

In the space Araceli knew as the Room of a Thousand Wonders, Brandon and Keenan huddled with their friends, Max and Riley Goldman-Arbegast. For once they had not drifted immediately to the pleasures of interlocking plastic blocks arranged as imaginary parapets, forts, and bunkers, or the distractions of handheld electronic games. Instead, they talked about their recent adventures: the Goldman-Arbegasts' trip to Europe, and the train journey that Brandon and Keenan had taken out of their home and into another world in the center of Los Angeles.

"We saw the Parthenon in Athens," Max said.

"Is that where Zeus lived?" Keenan asked.

"No, that's Mount Olympus," Brandon corrected. Both he and Max, the older of the Goldman-Arbegast brothers, were great fans of Greek mythology.

"And then later we went to London and saw the marbles the English took from the Greeks."

"The Greeks played with marbles?" Keenan asked.

"No. They're these big flat pictures carved out of marble," Max said. "And we saw the Rosetta Stone."

"When we went to L.A., everybody spoke in Spanish, mostly," Keenan said. "We saw *el cuatro de julio.*"

"I learned how to say 'thanks' in Italian," Riley countered. "It's '*grazie.*'"

"And we saw you and Keenan on television," Max said.

"Yeah," Brandon said flatly. "We were on lots of TV stations."

"Lots and lots. Like every one, I think," Riley said.

"Were you scared when that lady kidnapped you?" Max asked, rushing in the question, as if he had been waiting to ask.

"Nah, I don't think she kidnapped us," Brandon said. "We were looking for our grandfather. But we got all mixed up. We saw some cool things, though."

"We saw the Colosseum," Riley said.

"Were there gladiators?" Keenan asked.

"Nah," Max said. "It's all ruins now."

"Parts of L.A. are ruins too," Brandon said. He began to share a few more details of his journey to Los Angeles, and his encounters with war refugees and lynch mobs, though this time with less gusto than before. He had already tried telling the story to his parents, only to be interrupted by so many of his mother's questions that the story didn't sound like his anymore. *Why is it*, he wondered later, *that stories begin to turn old the first time you tell them? Why won't a story allow itself to be told over and over?*

"I think L.A. sounds cooler than Europe," Max pronounced once Brandon had finished.

"I guess," Brandon said. "I really wanna go to Greece, though. And Rome too."

The four slumping boys remained sitting in a circle; the older boys felt their bodies slip into an unease, a too-bigness that hinted at their coming adolescence. Finally, Brandon noticed a book sticking out of Max's back pocket.

"Whatcha reading?"

"It's an old book I found on my grandpa's bookshelf when we stopped to visit him in New York," Max said. "He said I probably should be older to read it. Because there's stuff in it I shouldn't read 'cause I'm only twelve. But then he gave it to me anyway when my mom wasn't looking. It's got some bad parts. Some parts that are really bad, actually."

"What? Like murders and stuff?"

"Nah. I can't describe it. There's no dragons or warriors or elves like in all the other books I read before. But it's really, really cool. And bad. There's kids smoking in it."

"Smoking?"

"Yeah. Cigarettes. It's, like, the best book I've ever read."

Max gave a conspiratorial scan, and then took the old paperback from his pocket and handed it to Brandon, who examined its timeworn cover, and a title whose meaning he could not immediately decipher.

"You can keep it," Max said. "I finished it in the car."

Brandon opened the first page and began to read. When the narrator promised to describe "what my lousy childhood was like," Brandon was hooked.


"You know, eventually, they're going to prosecute that poor woman because of me." It was one of the few comments Scott had allowed himself to make about the situation, and Peter Goldman decided he would try and ignore it. "It's either her or me. Or us, I mean. I guess we deserve to be punished more." They were near the bottom of the bottle and had been talking baseball and football, for the most part. Having bared his guilt for a moment, Scott caught himself, took another gulp of wine, and looked up at his old friend, who seemed more amused than outraged by Scott's situation. *Here's one person*, Scott thought, *who won't sit in judgment*. Scott was trying to think of something witty to say to chase away the unwanted pathos of the moment, when the phone on the dining room table before them rang again and Peter Goldman picked it up.

"No, he's not interested," Peter Goldman said. "That's right. Thank you. Bye-bye, now . . . bye."

"Thanks for doing that, buddy," Scott said. "I really owe you."

"Every good quarterback needs a good offensive line. Especially when the pass rush is as murderous as the one surrounding this household, let me tell you." They had a camaraderie forged during five years of school meetings, birthdays, and excursions to amusement parks, a brotherhood born of their marriages to women who dragged them all over the city and erased many hours of potential sports viewing, all in the name of family obligation.

There was a knock on the door. Three evenly spaced and polite taps, followed by a pause, and three more evenly spaced but louder taps. Peter Goldman rose to his feet and said, "I'm on it." A moment later Scott felt a shaft of warm light enter his home through the half-open door and heard the mumble of a voice from outside. After a quick back-and-forth, Peter came walking back to the table.

"It's a guy from the district attorney's office."

"Not again. Fuck."

"Should I tell him to go?"

"No. I have to talk to him."

Scott stood up and walked to the front door and swung it open.

"Mr. Torres, we haven't been able to get through on the phone," said Ian Goller. He wore a light-swallowing charcoal suit and a thin red tie over a starched white shirt, and to Peter Goldman, who had never met him before, he radiated the unrealness of an actor who'd wandered off the soundstage of a Technicolor spy flick. Goller had been shot back to Paseo Linda Bonita, quickly, by the dizzying spin of the news cycle, and the clamor of a vociferous segment of the voting public inside Orange County, and an influential segment of watchers and commentators beyond the county's borders. These voices were demanding, via various forms of digital and analog media, that Ian Goller and his colleagues in the district attorney's office apply the "rule of law" in the case of Araceli Ramírez, alleged childnapper.

Goller had arrived at the district attorney's office, off the beach and with his hair still wet (figuratively speaking and maybe literally too), with certain idealistic notions firmly rooted in his brain—specifically, the belief that criminal law was a scientific pursuit in which American and European traditions of jurisprudence were applied to the dispassionate weighing of facts and the protection of the public. During his ascent to the upper layers of the agency, and with his eventual admission to the walnut-paneled sanctuary of the district attorney himself, this idealism had aged and matured into a more realistic understanding of the job and its responsibilities. Above all, he had come to learn it simply wasn't possible for a public servant to ignore public opinion—completely—when defining right and wrong. The perceptions of the people counted, their collective fears and wants, what outraged them and what did not. In this case, the law-abiding sensibilities of many an Orange County resident had been offended by the suspect's unauthorized arrival in the United States of America. It made them skeptical and suspicious of her actions with the boys, and eager for punishment. In nonlegal terms: they would not cut her any slack. So he couldn't either. Goller found himself more or less obliged, therefore, to dive into the unpredictable waters of a politically necessary but potentially tricky prosecution.

Once he took such a plunge, however, Goller needed to make sure he could reach the other side. In other words, he needed to make sure he didn't lose. And for that, he needed to clean up the image and stiffen the resolve of the victims.

"Have you read the newspaper this morning?" Goller asked Scott.

"This has been a really trying time for my family," Scott said slowly, pinching the space between his eyes, while resisting the temptation to reach across the table and serve himself another glass of wine.

"I understand. But you should see this." Goller placed the local news section of the *Orange County Register* on the dining room table. The headline in question ran on the lower half of the page, incongruously below a photograph of children at a public swimming pool in Santa Ana.

## CHILD PROTECTIVE SERVICES TO INVESTIGATE PARENTS IN MISSING BOYS SAGA

Goller allowed this piece of unpleasant information to settle in as Scott slumped back in his chair, pushing it away from the table as he did so, adopting a pose of aggressive nonchalance in which the sky-blue fade of his jeans stretched out into view. Peter Goldman thought that Scott looked just like his son Brandon when he did this.

"What happened to you and your sons is being twisted by certain people," Goller said, with an expression of fatherly concern. Maybe it was the wine, or maybe just the pressure: whatever it was, Scott was having trouble paying attention.

"Scott. Can I call you Scott?"

"Sure."

"I take it you're a native Californian, Scott. Right?" Goller said, though he already knew the answer.

"Uh-huh."

"Where did you go to school?"

"South Whittier. St. Paul High."

"Ah, I went to Mater Dei, in Santa Ana. And I think we're about the same age."

"Probably. But what does that have—"

"I want you to understand what's happening around you," Goller interrupted. "Let's be blunt: there's a lot of people taking a certain perverse pleasure in what's happening to you."

Scott had no answer to this statement, no observation. He wanted to say he didn't care what people thought, he didn't care about Araceli or the newspapers or the television. But he did.

"So why is it happening?" Scott asked with a teenager's skeptical insolence.

"It's because California's changed. Because it's not the same place it was when we were growing up."

"It's not?"

"No. Think of the way people respected certain things. In the past, no one would have questioned the good intentions of two good American parents like you and your wife."

"Probably not."

"Now they do. And why? Because you're being accused by a woman with thousands of defenders. Fine: it's their right to stand up for her, to say she's being victimized by the system. But these people, they see me, and you, as their enemy. It's totally whacked that they think that way, but that's how it is. And now they see in this case a chance to make all of us look silly."

"I really don't mind looking silly," Scott said, without completely meaning it. He was confused by the direction Goller had taken their conversation.

"Well, it's more than looking silly, isn't it?" Goller continued. "Really, these people want to humiliate you, so that they can make the Mexican woman the hero. And why? For an idea." Goller was going to go abstract, and back in time, because he had learned that Scott was a programmer, and sensed the man needed to see a robust architecture of ideas before he took any action. An outline for this talk had come to Goller as he drove to the Laguna Rancho Estates, through undeveloped marshes and hill country, past towering eucalyptus trees and the bare breasts of yellow hills. In general, being a DA in his hometown was a daily assault on Goller's childhood memories, but this place by the sea, with its open vistas and untainted, orderly neighborhoods, transported him back in time, to his Orange County youth of puka shells and Op summer shirts. Certain things were clearer to him when he came here, and now he would explain these essential truths to Scott, show him the larger picture.

"Think of this moment we're living in, this craziness, from the perspective of history. California history," Goller began. "We grew up in the same kind of places, really. Me in Fullerton, and you in Whittier." Their homes had been parked on the same plain of scattered orchards and cow patches southeast of Los Angeles, and they had gone to schools that were big rivals back when there were "still enough big German and American kids around to make up a good football team." California was a paradise of open land and sea breezes, the sliver of Eden between the desert and the sea. This was the California of Scott's and Ian Goller's birth, a place of quiet, neat settlements separated by the geometry of melons and cabbages growing in fields, by the repetition of citrus groves, the scent of orange trees blooming. "That beautiful place was our playground. It was a place where anything was possible, where the open spaces matched how we felt about ourselves. How we saw the future." This paradise was gone, Goller said; the orchards had been plowed over to make room for new neighborhoods, rows of houses that became more ramshackle, more faded from one decade to the next. In the years since he'd been a DA, Ian Goller had been forced to see the decay of his hometown up close. There were too many people here now, a crush of bodies on the sidewalks and too many cars on the highways, people crowded into houses and apartment buildings in Santa Ana, in Anaheim, cities that used to be *good* places to live. The landmarks of Scott's youth, the burger stands and the diners, were now covered with the grimy stains of time and something else, an alien presence. There was more trash on the streets than ever. Who threw trash on the streets when Scott and Ian were boys? No one. Everything had been corrupted and despoiled. But most people simply didn't care. They allowed these multitudes to fill the state. Outsiders, most of them uneducated, people without prospects in their own country. And when those multitudes produced, with a kind of mathematical inevitability, the inmates that filled the jails and prisons, too many Californians averted their eyes and pretended it wasn't happening. Worse, the defenders of these people twisted everything, and demonized American families like Scott's for having the good sense to live behind the gates that protected them from the criminal anarchy outside. These people were now cheering the idea that his family would be investigated.

Scott had been looking at the oak surface of the table, and at times directly into the eyes of Ian Goller as he spoke, and had failed to notice that at some point in Goller's talk Maureen had entered the room with Stephanie Goldman-Arbegast, who was holding a sleeping Samantha. They had been drawn in by the sound of the stranger's voice, with Maureen at first amused by the incongruity of Goller's black suit on a hot July day, and by the way he slipped into a geeky trance as he spoke. His motives soon became perfectly clear to Maureen, and in another set of circumstances she would have asked him to leave. *I don't like to hear that meanness, that intolerance,* she might have said. But these were not normal times, and she found herself a bit taken in by the emotional pull of his argument. *I don't really understand anything anymore. I am surrounded by mysteries and apparitions: like the presence of this man in black. This man is telling me what to feel as much as he's telling me what to think.* It was not the immigrants she thought of as alien, as much as the L.A. reporters who had parked themselves on her lawn, and who now staked out the front gate to the Estates. They were a disorderly and insistent clan of microphone men and women, of camera-holders and question-shouters, and they reminded her of the City of Los Angeles proper, and her first days in the metropolis. She had come to California expecting something altogether different than what she had first encountered, as a single woman in her twenties in an L.A. neighborhood called Mid-City, an ugly place of wide thoroughfares and gray liquor stores and bunkered apartment buildings with underground garages that were rape traps. She carried Mace in her purse back then, and put a steel lock over the steering wheel of her parked, single-girl Honda Civic with its Show-Me State license plates. Quickly she had found a way to escape southward. *That's why I'm living here, on this hillside overlooking the ocean, instead of in some condo off La Cienega, or in Brentwood. Here I have found a purer version of California.*

"There are people who believe that this change in our hometown is a natural and inevitable thing," Goller continued. He watched as Maureen stepped forward and picked up the newspaper on the table, and saw the indignation that filled her eyes when she saw the headline. "It's in their interest to treat this Mexican woman as the victim, and you as her victimizers. And that's the way everyone will see it, unless you tell them differently."

Maureen looked at him with equal measures of skepticism and curiosity. He was a strange, elegant little man; it was not every day you met someone who could make a harsh and angry line of argument sound gentle and reasonable. "I don't quite get what you're telling us," Maureen said. "We're supposed to start talking about immigration and the undocumented, or the illegals, or whatever, and that's going to get the media off our backs? Isn't that just going to get us deeper in a mess?"

"No. You don't talk about those things. Definitely not. Your part is very simple. You just tell your story to someone with a sympathetic ear. You tell them your story, and you erase the idea that you're just this crazy family." He had them now, Scott especially: he was daydream-listening, processing truths. "There's a reporter I know. He's actually the local guy for one of the cable news networks. He'll guide you through an interview, I believe, without compromising you on anything."

Stephanie Goldman-Arbegast watched Maureen take a piece of paper with two phone numbers from Goller and give the faintest nod of assent. *No, Maureen, don't.* In a short while, Stephanie would politely round up her husband and children and they would leave, and not return. Maureen was going to link her fate to the kidnapping story circulating among the nativists and rightists on talk radio, when instead she should be telling the story of the broken coffee table. That's how Stephanie saw things. People would understand a woman's desire to escape an angry husband. But Maureen had too much pride to do such a thing. Maureen wanted, with the stoic resolve of a British monarch, to protect the family image: she did not want the world to think of her sprawled helpless on her back.

For a moment, Stephanie felt more connected to the Mexican woman who had worked in this house, the hardworking oddball and perfectionist who had been Maureen's shadow since Stephanie had first come for a playdate. *The sad thing is that Araceli and Maureen are really so much alike.*

Goller shook everyone's hand and left. Stephanie followed her husband to the window, where he studied Goller walking down the path and to his car.

"He's got a surfboard on top of his car," Peter Goldman said, laughing at the incongruity as Stephanie looked at his parked BMW and saw it was true. "Look, he's starting to take off his jacket. He's like Batman or something."

About a mile down the coast, there was a surf break called Cotton's that was one of the best-kept secrets on the coast this summer. A little slice of Orange County goodness, known only to the locals, a place where, after a terrain-shifting winter storm, long walls of water now moved left over sand and rocks, large and steady at middle tide. Ian Goller thought that he might, with a little luck, have it to himself late on a quiet weekday afternoon like this one.

# 19

In his small kitchen-dining room in Santa Ana, Octavio Covarrubias made Araceli a breakfast of eggs with chorizo, fresh-squeezed juice from oranges plucked from the tree in the backyard, and a side dish of fried nopals, from the petals of an enormous cactus plant that grew in a vacant lot down the street. With every serving he raised the eyebrow that was hovering between his Jupiter eye and his moles Io and Europa, and asked if she wanted more coffee. Araceli grinned widely at the sight of this unshaven family patriarch of about fifty-five, a semiretired truck driver dressed in faded green work pants, holding a pan and making breakfast for her when, to her knowledge, he never even made breakfast for himself. "*Ay*, Octavio," his wife, Luz, said, after she noted the irony too, "*a mí nunca me haces* breakfast. *Qué bonito sería* if you brought me breakfast in bed one morning." Since Araceli's arrival at his home last night, Octavio Covarrubias had a sudden and strange need to dote over her, a woman whose presence on earth had only faintly registered in his consciousness before.

Octavio Covarrubias was impressed that an ordinary *mexicana* could be put through an arrest and a symbolic flogging by the machinery of the English-language media, survive with her *mexicana* dignity *más o menos* intact, and then enter his living room, of all places. He was an avid reader and a faithful consumer of cable television news in two languages, and almost always this made him nothing more than a passive witness to the way his people were crushed, time and again, in American courtrooms, on desert smuggling trails, and in Arizona detention centers. He read and pontificated so much on these issues to his neighbors on Maple Street that they called him *licenciado* behind his back, because his outrage and verbosity reminded them of a certain kind of annoying politico-bureaucrat back home.

When Araceli was on her last mouthful of eggs, Octavio Covarrubias began to speak. "*Proceso* has a correspondent here in Los Angeles," he said. "Maybe we should call him, because *Proceso* will want to write something about you, I'm sure." Octavio Covarrubias was a *Proceso* subscriber, receiving the Mexican investigative magazine by mail from Tijuana every week. Before Araceli could respond, he began describing a report by this same *Proceso* correspondent about a facility for the detention of immigrant children in San Diego County, and a Televisa report on the same story, and then later more reports on CNN en Español, and finally on CNN in English. Octavio's news appetite was such that he could explain to his wife and neighbors why the U.S. Army was to blame for the flooding of the Mississippi and the conspiracies behind the assassination of the Mexican presidential candidate Luis Donaldo Colosio, and the links between drug cartels and former President Salinas de Gotari. Having been forced to drop out of his final year of high school in Durango, his dream of a degree in political science unrealized, he studied the news instead, in the belief that he might understand the seemingly unpredictable events of the world, which were obviously orchestrated to keep his people poor, ignorant, and enslaved.

Araceli ignored the passing question about the *Proceso* reporter, and helped Octavio and his wife clean up. Her hosts obviously wanted her to fill in the silence with an insider's account of her arrest and the news they had seen on TV. But she couldn't think of where to begin.

"So, it looks like they treated you okay?" Luz Covarrubias said, as Araceli dried a plate with a cloth and handed it to her to put away. "*No te veo traumada. Te veo tranquila.*"

"*No me imaginaba,*" Araceli said suddenly. Octavio and his wife thought she meant she never imagined she'd be pulled into the depths of the machinery of hate, that she never imagined being tackled and having the humiliation broadcast on the airwaves, that she never imagined a million televisions would defame her as a criminal. But no. She meant she never believed she could be pulled so quickly and definitively from her stasis, from her comfortable but boring existence, from the cycles of meals and laundry, into the full mad circus of a life lived without a schedule or rhythm. For this reason, her face brightened with a strange, bemused expression as she said "*No me imaginaba . . .*" a second time. The break had begun with the arrival of that first rabble of barbarian gardeners, the men who took the machetes to Pepe's tropical forest. Those men had ripped her from her roots too and tossed her from a shady jungle into the full California sunlight. Liberated now from jail and from the worry of the fate of Brandon and Keenan, she could appreciate the journey away from Paseo Linda Bonita and into Los Angeles for its carnivalesque qualities. The decaying art of the railroad tracks, the startling dream-sense that came from being in a jail one moment, and then in the silent, spooky glory of the nighttime streets of Aliso Viejo the next. Out here, in the world away from the paradise of the Laguna Rancho Estates, there was the silver skin of taco trucks on Thirty-ninth Street, and the fat tortillas the hungry men and women workers raised to their mouths, and the deep-sea purple of the dying daylight over their heads. Those images belonged in her sketchbook, and then later on a canvas as big as she imagined Picasso's *Guernica* to be. She imagined a composition with orange and red explosions of fireworks in the background, and in the foreground the rabid teeth of a mob that marched and shouted. And why not the horizontal march of the electric transmission towers, and that corridor of feral grasses and palms, a road to unseen American provinces beyond? An artist needs to be out and about: Araceli understood that now. The study of the visual world while on her feet had informed her life in Mexico City, but in the defeat of her creative ambitions she had gone into a kind of retreat, she had accepted the little room the Torres-Thompsons gave her and the bills in the envelope at the end of each week. She felt like Brandon, who saw fantasy and wonderment in everything new. She wanted to find her *gordito*, the dancing painter Felipe, and tell him what she had seen.

"I never imagined," Araceli said after a brief silence, "that I could see things the way a little boy saw them."

"*¿Cómo?*"

"Brandon. He's the older boy. He loves to read. He thought the things he saw in Los Angeles were like the things in his books. He was funny. You see things differently when you open your eyes the way a child does." There were children in this house too, Octavio and Luz's kids, hovering nearby and listening for story details they might share with others.

"Well, it's good to see you calm," Luz said.

"*Sí, me siento calmada,*" Araceli said. Octavio looked a little thrown, a little disappointed by her light mood.

"Next time, Señor Covarrubias," she said, "I am going to make breakfast for you."


The lights came on and Maureen and the television reporter looked at each other through the layers of makeup that covered their faces, and Maureen had one last moment to think, *Ah, this is really show businesses, isn't it?* before listening to the reporter's first question. It had taken forty minutes to transform her living room into a studio. The point of this interview, as she understood it, was to make a public defense of her own motherhood. But as the crew ran black cables as thick as garden snakes along her tiled floor and raised a half dozen lamp stands to varied heights, her stage fright and anxiety had been replaced, momentarily, with a kind of morbid fascination at this glimpse of the inner workings of television news. The crew shielded their portable four-hundred-watt beams with transparent fabric squares until all shadows disappeared and an eerie, even light settled over her living room. They rearranged photographs on the bookcase and produced fresh-cut roses and a vase, and opened the sliding glass doors to the succulent garden and taped L's onto the floor where a high folding chair was later placed, so that Maureen could be photographed with the roses, a family portrait, and a mini-landscape of cacti and the ocotillo plant all looming behind her. The producer, a woman of about twenty-five, had punched a message into one of those handheld devices that required much use of the right thumb, and waited a few minutes for a reply, and had looked up from the screen to announce that Maureen alone would be interviewed, with the boys, Samantha, and Scott making silent cameos in the "B" footage to be shot around the house afterward, in a simulation of their daily living, sans Araceli. Of course, Maureen thought, *I'm the one they want on camera.* Her twelve-second "rant" had been repeated enough in its thirty-six-hour existence for an observer or two on the motherhood blogs to call it "iconic." *Why is it,* Maureen wondered, *that in any walk of life, from corporate CEO, to U.S. senator, to harried flower vendor and distraught Orange County mother, an angry woman provokes such intense feelings? Why is it considered such a remarkable and noteworthy thing for a mother to raise her voice?*

"Maureen Thompson, how are you doing? How is your family?" the reporter asked.

"We're fine. We had a little scare. For two days and one very long night that seemed like an eternity. I mean, to come home to this house and find it empty, to expect to see our boys here, and then, well, to find them missing." She was aware that her voice had begun to tremble, that she sounded tenuous and frail, and as soon as she became aware of this, she realized that this was not necessarily a bad thing. "And then to find out they were all the way on the other side of the city."

"And they're okay?"

"Yes, yes. They've got a story to tell, a wild story, but it appears nothing happened to them."

"A wild story?"

"Yes. It seems our employee, Araceli, took them on a train ride. For what purpose, God knows. They were among the homeless at some point, or so it seems."

"The homeless?"

"Yes. Which is very disturbing, of course."

"But they're okay?"

"Yes."

"Tell us a little about yourself."

"My husband, he's a programmer. I teach art at my sons' school. I'm an art teacher there. Well, a volunteer art teacher, I should say, because they don't pay me anything, but I do get to be close to the boys and their school." Her voice had lost its quaver suddenly. "And we've lived in this beautiful house for five years now."

"Now, explain to us exactly how it was that you found your children missing," the newsman said, and then looked her directly in the eye and added in a markedly more friendly voice, as if he were an actor speaking an aside to the groundlings, "And please, feel relaxed. We can do this more than once if we need to."

"We left on a little trip, my husband and I," Maureen began, and she resisted the temptation to say *separately*, which would have kept her closer to the truth. "You know, when you have three kids, you need a break." *No, I shouldn't have said that. I sound spoiled.* "And our boys are bigger now, and they're easier to take care of, so we thought we could leave them overnight with their nanny and just take Samantha with us. Because Samantha is so little, we thought we should take her with us." She paused, and inhaled fully, because she was stepping closer to blatant untruth than she wanted to go, and she made the mistake of looking down at her floor and away from the camera. Quickly she recovered herself, and felt strangely aware and alert. "Then we came home. And it was so quiet. So incredibly and unnaturally quiet here." Now that she had returned to a full, solid truth she could see its power and how it made the newsman's eyes sharpen their focus with anticipation. "Something didn't seem right. And we went from room to room and didn't see the boys. And I thought, This is so strange. How can Araceli not be here in the house with the boys? I mean, she doesn't have a car, or permission to take the boys anywhere. At first I thought, Oh, maybe she got bored and took them walking to the park or something. It sort of didn't make sense, because she doesn't have a car. But you know how it is: you have in your mind this little voice that tells you not to think the worst. And then it started to sink in that they were gone. And this house started to feel so empty. So horribly empty. And I started to think about where they might be, and what they might be suffering, and how I wasn't there to protect them. And I just couldn't stand it." Yes, this was true: she loved her boys and had lost them for an afternoon, a night, and then a morning, and had spent that time living with the deepest fears a mother can know, an ache she felt in those parts of her body where her boys had once lived and kicked and slithered into the world.

Maureen was burying her subtle falsehoods in a larger truth unknown, until now, to the millions who had followed the story. Their Internet commentary would soon be peppered with sympathetic descriptions: "the screamer" was, in fact, a woman who sounded "quite reasonable." She was an "educated and articulate" mother who "obviously loved her children," had suffered "every parent's nightmare," and who was "clearly telling the truth" about discovering her sons missing.

"Did you ever authorize this woman, your employee, to take your children to East Los Angeles?"

"No. Absolutely not."

"So they were kidnapped?" the interviewer said, making it sound as much suggestion as question.

"Well, they were taken on . . . this bizarre journey. They set off for L.A. And the hills there were on fire that day. So when we got them back, I swear they smelled like smoke."

"Uh-huh," the interviewer said, and Maureen knew she had answered poorly.

"But we did find some strange things in her room."

"What things?"

"Strange art. Trash that she had played with. It's strange. Because this is someone we thought of as part of our family. She lived with us. We trusted her implicitly. And then I realized I didn't even know who she was."

"Now, tell us about this," the interviewer continued. "There's this clip I want to play for you. It's become sort of famous now." On a small monitor at the interviewer's feet, her twelve-second rant played again, and she cringed at the way her nostrils flared and her jaw tightened as she shot back at the reporter, as if she were a suburban mother bear snapping at the camera-toting naturalist threatening her cubs, an effect heightened by the way she searched behind the cameras for the man who had insulted her.

"Really, why were you so angry?"

"I had just been reunited with my sons, and I hadn't slept for two days. I was just incredibly stressed out. I mean, to go through all that: first, the worry of not knowing where the boys were, if they were okay. And then, you know, the joy of having them with us again. I was completely wiped out. Plus, I couldn't even see this guy, because he was standing near the back. And here I am, the mom of these two kids who've been taken away, and he's accusing me. But I shouldn't have yelled like that. Like I said, I was just incredibly exhausted."

"Of course," the interviewer said. "We can only imagine."

They wrapped up and when the four-minute, twenty-five second segment aired later that evening near the top of the 8:00 p.m. cablecast, Janet Bryson turned on her TiVo and watched it three times.

In Santa Ana, Octavio Covarrubias missed the interview because he was preparing and serving a marinated *carne de res* barbecue in Araceli's honor. An hour or so later, with the main course served to the small party of family and neighbors, he slipped into the empty living room for a moment to feed his news fix, and caught a few seconds of Maureen's interview when it was replayed on the cable news station as an intro- duction to the show hosted by a very conservative man who Octavio Covarrubias watched, occasionally, with the same sense of stealthy in- tent that Janet Bryson felt when she studied the Mexicans in her neigh- borhood. Octavio needed to get back to the party, and told himself he shouldn't watch this man tonight, but he allowed himself to listen as the man began to talk about "the illegal who was set free." This tele- vision man was always well dressed, Octavio noted, and tonight he was wearing a black suit with rather bright white stripes, and Octavio thought that, if he ever bought a suit, it would be one like that, because it had a certain big-city, old-time gangster movie look to it, though the way he moved in his chair and talked to his guests suggested to Octavio a po- liceman: a man who runs his small fiefdom with aggressive self-assurance, who intimidates with a crackling diction and an unflagging faith in his right to do so.

"Do we really want to entrust our children to these people from this essentially backward society?" the man was saying. He was in New York, but was talking, via satellite link, to the reporter who had sat down with Maureen Thompson. "Isn't it a sign of weakness in our social fabric that we do this? It's the most important job we have. It's the foundation of our civilization, for chrissakes. Motherhood. Why should we sell it off, to the most desperate and least educated people, as if we were hiring a day laborer to dig a ditch? I'm telling ya, and I know a lot of people aren't going to agree with me, but it just sounds to me like an essentially stupid thing to do."

Luz Covarrubias entered, with Araceli trailing behind her.

"Octavio!" Luz snapped reprovingly. "*¿Por qué estás mirando a ese hom- bre feo, ese hombre que nos odia?*" his wife asked, not for the first time.

"*Porque hay que saber lo que piensa el enemigo,*" he said.

"*Basta,*" his wife said, and she grabbed the remote control from the front table and punched the mute button, because she knew from prior experience that he wouldn't let her turn it off completely.

Octavio Covarrubias turned to Araceli and put his hand on her shoulder. "*Ese hombre te quiere encarcelar.*" On the TV, the man who wanted to send Araceli back to jail peered into the camera without speaking for a few seconds, then gave a dismissive nod, followed by a playful bobbing of his head that, Araceli guessed, was meant to convey incredulity. His hair, she noted, was the color and thickness of a weak mountain stream during a summer drought, and his lips were arranged in a crawling half smile with the geometry of a roller coaster. *Ese hombre*, all by himself, Octavio added, might have the power to lock her up again. Millions watched him. "*No lo entiendo.*"

Octavio drifted away, leaving Araceli with a plate of leftover barbecued beef she had brought in from the backyard, alone before the television. She had seen this commentator flicker past during the nighttime page-turning of channels on her television, but she had never stopped to watch him. Now she saw that his eyebrows and mouth, in close-up, were a theater all to themselves. He played to the camera with his eyebrows, which moved like elaborate stage machinery above the radiant blue crystals of his eyes. His eyebrows rose, fell, twisted, and contorted themselves in ways that appeared to defy the limits of human facial musculature. The camera pulled back as he brought his body into the show by leaning back in his chair, and he puffed his cheeks quickly with a suppressed laugh, and finally shook his head, and gave a forty-five-degree turn to face another camera.

It was frightening to think that the brain behind that face could somehow shape her fate, and Araceli quickly reached over and turned off the television, the image of the man shrinking to a point and going dark with an electric pop. What other eyebrows, mouths, and brains were out there, conspiring to put her behind bars again, and what did they see in her, that they would want to punish her so? The thought made her want to put on running shoes, to see if she could outsprint the men in uniform this time. But no, she was tired of running. *No voy a correr.* She would wait and prepare herself. For starters, she would get another tortilla and make herself a taco out of the beef on this plate, because when a man is as good a cook as Octavio Covarrubias, you really shouldn't let his food go to waste.

# 20

A pretty and tiny Latina woman of about twenty-five arrived at the Covarrubias residence first, with a long, thin notebook in her hand. She had swept-back eyes with chestnut irises and strands of thin coal-black hair; a significantly older and taller man of rugged features who smelled of cigarettes accompanied her. They were an odd, English-speaking couple in a Spanish-speaking neighborhood, and a decidedly bad omen for a Mexican woman who expected to be arrested at any moment. Araceli might have taken the man for a retired cowboy, but for the camera in his hand and the nylon bag on his shoulder. *These people have probably not come to arrest me*, Araceli thought, and after they introduced themselves as journalists, she stepped outside onto the porch, and then onto the lawn, to see if there was a police cruiser lurking nearby. After a few moments of conversation on the grass it became clear that these two *periodistas* had not expected to find Araceli alone. "There's no cops here," the photographer said in a half question and half observation, after glancing inside the living room.

"*¿Cómo que cops? ¿Entonces sí me vienen a arrestar?*"

"Uh, I think that I, that we . . ." the reporter began, and she gave a guilty, girlish smile that was inappropriate to the moment. "*Disculparme, por favor, no sabía,"* the reporter began in Spanish, but stopped, because that language was obviously not her first, and was barely her second. She handed Araceli a business card, a stiff little rectangle with glossy letters that rose from the paper, inviting one's fingers to linger over them, claiming the title *Staff Writer* for its owner, a *Cynthia Villarreal.*

"Well, this is awkward," the photographer said, and he reached inside the pants of his jeans and grabbed a cigarette and put it in his mouth but did not light it. "The captain will not be pleased to see us, I think."

"Well, they told me ten-fifteen."

"It's ten-oh-five, my dear."

"Dang. I thought we were late. But we're early."

The photographer shook his head and, having determined that the young scribe with him was going to take a while to figure out what to do next, he began to shoot, capturing Araceli as she stood on the lawn, looking up at the sky. She searched for prowling helicopters, and then scanned the cars on the block and the distant intersections. The first frame the photographer shot, of Araceli's worried squint searching the street for the authorities, would be on the web in an hour and on the front page of the newspaper the next day, a haunting and lonely close-up of a notorious woman in limbo, waiting for her abductors to arrive.

"Um, Kyle . . . ," the reporter said, but Kyle ignored her and held down his finger, the camera shutter opening and closing six times with the staccato beat of a flamenco song.

*"¡No les tengo miedo!"* Araceli shouted suddenly, turning to face the journalists. "I am not afraid! No. Why I be afraid? For nothing!" The photographer let off another burst of shutter openings as Araceli spoke, and those images too would appear on the web, in an essay of eleven images that his Los Angeles newspaper would headline "Arrest, Anger, and Drama in Santa Ana," accompanied by the breathless audio narration of Cynthia Villarreal: "Araceli Ramírez knew that she would soon be taken into custody, but her response was a defiant one." The second shot in that series featured Araceli looking directly into the camera, her mouth open and index finger pointing skyward at the moment she was repeating, *"¡No les tengo miedo!,"* an image with echoes of Latin American protest marches, as if Araceli were a market woman in a Mexican square, among tens of thousands of other women with open mouths joined in an outraged chorus over the price of onions, or the torture and murder of a comrade.

Now the rising pitch of accelerating engines announced the arrival of four sheriff's cruisers: two parked in front of the Covarrubias home with red and blue lights flashing, the others taking position at either end of the block, sideways, as if to seal off the street. A burly but handsome sheriff's captain emerged from the first cruiser. He was freshly shaved, with three bloody nicks on each cheek and an expression of wounded befuddlement that overcame him as it sank in that his "little reporter friend," as she was known at the station, had tipped off the suspect to his arrival. He gave a plaintive opening of his arms and shouted at the reporter, "What's going on?"

"I'm so sorry, Captain. Sorry!"

"Get that lens off me, jerko!"

"Negative, Captain," the photographer said. "You're on a public street."

"Shit," the captain said, and at that moment he decided that this was the last time he'd try to impress Ms. Villarreal, who was fifteen years younger and almost two feet shorter than him. He turned to Araceli, who now stood before him on the lawn, her arms folded across her chest. "You obviously know what I'm here for."

Araceli said nothing and in the few heartbeats of silent standoff that followed, shouts could be heard coming from the homes and backyards around them. "*¡La migra!*" An invisible but audible panic was unfolding around them, with the percussion of slamming doors and windows opening so that people could stare down at the police cruisers from second-floor windows, followed by more, indecipherable yelling from the next block, and the scratchy and hurried tennis-shoe strides on the cement sidewalk of a young man in a CLUB AMÉRICA *fútbol* jersey. The soccer fan walked with his hands in his pockets across the street, and then glanced once over his shoulder at the officers, and finally broke into a trot as he reached the corner. *Get away, get away.* The residents of Maple Street had been sitting snugly in their homes for two days, watching Araceli's short sprint and capture looping on their televisions, listening to secondhand reports in Spanish detailing the English chorus of *los medios norteamericanos* for her rearrest. Word had spread that the subject of this broadcast frenzy was living among them, but now the arrival of the deputies' brass badges and their dangling batons and the flashing lights of their cruisers transformed this novelty into a threat, and brought to life the goblins that haunted their daily consciousness. *The* paisana *from the television has brought* las autoridades *to our* *neighborhood, and now they will take us all away before we can finish our breakfasts and wash the dishes.* Córrele, córrele.

"For some reason, these people think we've come to enforce the immigration laws," the captain said. "It's because of you, little lady," he said to Araceli. He cupped his hands and gave a halfhearted megaphone shout: "Attention, neighbors! I am not the *migra*. I am not here for any of you."

In a building down at the end of the block, a woman from rural Guanajuato grabbed her infant son and executed a panicked climb into the attic of her two-story duplex, then crawled into a nook of stacked boxes and took her cell phone to call *el licenciado* Octavio Covarrubias. The self-educated, self-appointed conscience of Maple Street often gave out his number to the new arrivals, presenting himself as a levelheaded, semiretired family man who might be able to help people in trouble. The ring tone on his phone sounded as he stood on the porch, and its burst of trumpets and accordions from a song by Los Temerarios broke the trance of the standoff on the front lawn, where the sheriff's captain was trying to think of a way to persuade the woman named in the arrest warrant to get into his patrol car quickly, the better to calm everyone around them.

"*Sí, quédate allí escondida,*" Octavio said into the phone, which caught the attention of all the Spanish-speakers around them, including one of the deputies.

"Hey, Captain," the deputy said. "There's people hiding in these houses."

"Probably in the closets and the attics again," said another deputy.

"God, I hate that."

The captain ignored his underlings and turned to Araceli. "The quicker you come with us, young lady, the sooner the good people of this neighborhood will be able to come out of their closets." Araceli was standing ten feet away from him on the lawn, but he didn't want to step toward her and simply grab her, because if she tried to run away she might spread the panic to other blocks, and if she resisted and his deputies had to restrain her, they could have a minor disturbance on their hands, in full view of the press.

"*¿Y para qué me vienes a piscar?*" she asked.

"For child abuse," said the captain, whose encounters with Orange

County suspects had familiarized him with some of the basic Spanish idioms used in such cases, though he had no idea of the full range of uses of the verb *"piscar,"* a California-Spanish mongrel of the English "pick" that had managed to sneak into Araceli's speech through the daily drip of Los Angeles television and radio. He looked down at the warrant and repeated three words he saw there: *"Felony* child abuse. Child endangerment, to be precise."

"I don't understand," Araceli said.

"It means you put the children in danger. *Peligro, los niños.*"

Araceli shook her head and gave the captain a murderous look. He was trying to be gracious, but he was an extension of the eyebrows on the television, and now it was clear that the eyebrows and the other faces on the news had persuaded the authorities to invent any reason to detain her. What's more, the *norteamericanos* were at war with themselves over whether they should throw her in jail or allow her to live free, with the sheriff's captain standing before her obviously in the latter camp, even as duty forced him to arrest her.

*This is like living with* el señor *Scott and* la señora *Maureen: they cannot decide what they want for dinner, or if they want dessert, so they have me going two ways at once.*

"That's a good girl," the captain said, and did not notice as Araceli gave him another penetrating stare for that unnecessary bit of condescension.

Janet Bryson's contribution to the campaign to return Araceli Ramírez to jail, and eventually back to Mexico, began at the southernmost point on her big fold-out map of Orange County, in the community formerly known as Leisure World. She was out collecting handwritten and signed letters, having been rallied to do so by the One California activist organization, and her first stop placed her underneath the hanging ferns inside a Leisure World veranda of breeze blocks, where a woman held a dog in her purse, and stroked its long hair and compliant head. "God bless you for doing this," the woman told Janet, recounting how her Shih Tzu had been frightened by the firecrackers on the Fourth of July, set off a mile away in the uncontrolled neighborhoods where "those people" lived. "It was so unfair, because Ginger had just had surgery, the poor thing." They were united, Janet Bryson and the woman with the dog, by their sympathy for Maureen Thompson and their contempt for illegal immigrants and lawbreakers of all stripes, but when she drove away Janet Bryson could only think about how lonely the woman seemed, and how unnatural it was to carry a dog that way. Next she drove her son's Toyota Celica northward into the suburbs of central Orange County—her own Chevy Caprice having again failed to start this morning—and wondered about the meaning of the pink dice hanging from the rearview mirror. Was that a gang thing? This worrying possibility stayed with her as she advanced along Main Streets and First Streets lined with the rusting steel and broken glass tubes of the neon signs of their heyday. Once people drove their rumbling Ramblers and El Caminos down and across these overlapping grids, along Beach Boulevard and Katella Avenue, the thoroughfares that carried people of her father's generation past malt shops and burger joints, to the tower marquees announcing double features at drive-in theaters. The drive-ins were all Swap Meets now frequented by the illegals and the Vietnamese. She remembered sitting in the backseat of her father's Ford Falcon, unbuckled and unworried, behind his parted and moist hair, and feeling her bare legs sticking to the vinyl seats. Janet Bryson knew she could never make those old days come back. Instead, in this work of letter-gathering, this volunteer activism, she felt like a woman weather-stripping her windows and basement in September: it was something she did not so much with the hope of making things better, as much as to keep them from getting worse.

The letters Janet Bryson carried were filled with warnings of the impending criminal and budgetary doom wrought by the legions of illegal crossers; she was retrieving these missives personally for afternoon delivery to the Orange County Board of Supervisors. The One California group had emailed and faxed its members talking points to be included in the letters, and a separate list of individual crimes and crime-types attributable to illegals, including: the "epidemic" of identity theft; the murder of a sixteen-year-old boy outside a beach park the previous August by members of a Los Angeles street gang; a sudden spike in DUIs in Anaheim; and the rape and murder of a twelve-year-old girl in Fullerton. Each writer chose from this felonious buffet and plopped phrases into one of five different form letters written by One California. They wrote in the creaky cursive of a septuagenarian, or squeezed five hundred words of all capitals onto a single page of notebook paper, or typed on old IBMs and Olivettis. The writers had been encouraged to fill their letters with their own observations about the larger problems of illegal immigration, and at red lights Janet stopped to peruse these sections.

> Araceli N. Ramírez should be arrested and deported no matter what the outcome of the criminal proceedings the County undertakes against her. Illegal Mexican labor lowers wages while demanding entitlements. Examples: Title One schools, WIC, Medical Care, Bilingual education. Not to mention they breed like there's no tomorrow, regardless of whether they can support their children because they know the state will subsidize them.

> The Latino movement backing this woman is AGGRESSIVE. The pressure and the outright numbers of people moving into this country, the outright force of the Spanish language is a clear statement of revolution. I am shocked by this Latino movement which is now supporting this woman despite her obvious crimes against two innocent American children.

> To those who want to point out how much these illegal immigrants like Araceli N. Ramírez contribute to their society because they <u>like</u> their housekeeper and their gardener, and because they <u>like</u> paying less for tomatoes, spend some time looking at the <u>real</u> California around us. Look at our full prisons, our higher insurance rates, our lowering education standards, the new diseases spreading in our cities. For me, I'll pay <u>more</u> for my tomatoes.

Janet Bryson's journey took her next to a Garden Grove apartment block the color of overripe avocado flesh, where a too-thin woman of about forty with bony, sunburned shoulders handed her a letter through a security gate and said, "Don't go yet, hon. Want some iced tea?" Janet climbed up briefly to the woman's apartment and living room and sipped and listened to the woman describe "the unraveling of my life." Her husband had succumbed to liver problems three years earlier, "and my mom died a year ago this week in Kenosha." She too complained about the Fourth of July noise and smoke, but also about the disability bureaucrats and her glaucoma, and the neighbors who stole her newspaper, and how she heard her dead husband speaking in the hallways on certain warm summer nights, until Janet finally said, "I'm so, so sorry. But I really have to go." It pained Janet Bryson that she could not listen more. She picked up the last letter at 3:45 p.m. on Citrus Avenue in Yorba Linda, four blocks from the Richard Nixon Library and Museum, and made her away southward on the State Highway 57 freeway to Santa Ana. By 4:55 p.m., she had managed to deliver one copy of each letter by hand to the five offices of the members of the Orange County Board of Supervisors.

At 5:30 p.m. she was back on Interstate 5, heading north toward South Whittier in heavy traffic, but feeling light and free of the congestion of red lights braking and cars inching forward. She touched the passenger seat, where the letters had lain, and gave a sigh of satisfaction, thinking how she would type *Mission Accomplished* in the subject line of the email she would send to the One California office when she got home. And then she remembered the woman with the dog, and the woman who heard ghosts, and thought she had helped them that day simply by listening. *Owe no man anything, but to love one another, for he that loveth another hath fulfilled the law.* She felt attached to something larger than herself. Not just the story of the wronged American family, but also to other homes and automobiles where women looked out their windows and into the city and tried to make sense of what they saw. She turned on the radio and found it tuned, by her son, to some Spanish hip-hop monstrosity: so she changed the station, finding some rock-and-roll songs from her father's era. Those joyous anthems with their ascendant guitars and big soul choruses matched the way she felt. Her reverie lasted through forty more minutes of bumper-to-bumper, until she reached her exit at Carmenita Road and she turned northward home.

John Torres was well inside the house on Paseo Linda Bonita before Maureen became aware of his presence. He had talked his way past the useless guards at the front gate easily enough: they were quickly persuaded that a seventy-year-old man was harmless, and Maureen was sweeping in the kitchen when he opened and stepped through the un-

locked front door. He quickly found his grandsons in their bedroom—
"You guys are reading? In the middle of a summer day?"—and was hugging
them and bribing them with twenty-dollar bills by the time Maureen
could rush into their room. She glared at the old man with a *how dare
you!* affixed to her lips that died, undelivered, when she saw Brandon
and Keenan waving greenbacks ecstatically before her.

"Look! Grandpa gave us money!"

"Hello, daughter," John Torres said with a stiff cheerfulness, and
Maureen wondered if he knew how much she hated hearing him call
her that. He was dressed like an angry workingman forced to play a
round of golf against his will, copper jowls resting over the collar of his
polo shirt, khaki pants affixed to his bony frame by a belt that was
about six inches too long. Now he grabbed at its flapping leather tongue
as he waited for her to reply, because he sensed that she was studying it
and judging him and his simplicity. She was, in fact, looking at his fingers and hands, and thought that the contrast of the wounded digits at
the end of arms stuffed into a teal shirt summed up all his contradictions, and for that reason she resisted the temptation to say, *Hello, Juan*,
which was his birth name, after all. Scott had discovered this a few
years back, when helping the old man with some Social Security paperwork, and Maureen had rather spitefully called him that on that last
time he had come to this home, two years ago. It was during Keenan's
sixth birthday, in a moment of high dudgeon following his outrageous,
bigoted, and incorrect observation that Keenan was "the white boy" and
Brandon was "the Mexican." It was the sort of thing he said when he
had too much alcohol, which was nearly every time he arrived for a
family gathering, and she had resolved at that moment to banish him
from Paseo Linda Bonita for at least a dozen birthdays.

"Hello, Grandfather Torres. To what do we owe the pleasure?"

He seemed a bit taken aback by the polite greeting, having failed to
notice the sarcasm in it. "Well, I have a television," he began. "And I've
been watching my grandsons on it for a couple of days now, and the one
time I called here I got some stranger who hung up on me when he
heard me say, 'What's going on over there?' So I figured I'd have to come
over here and see for myself."

"As you can see, everything is under control."

"Is it?" He looked around the room, at his grandsons, who were now busy putting away the two twenties he had given each of them in little plastic safes with numbered combinations. "The newspaper said they were going to investigate you."

"No, Scott just . . ." Maureen stopped and gestured with her palms in the direction of the boys. "Should we be having this discussion here?" But John Torres was looking straight into her eyes, demanding an answer to soothe a kind of skeptical parental concern she recognized. "Scott just called," she lied. "He went to talk to those people at the county. And they dropped it."

"Because they arrested that Mexican girl you had here. Right?"

"What, they arrested Araceli?" Brandon shouted. "They're going to put her in jail?"

"No, no, they're just asking her questions," Maureen said, and would think later that it had been a long time since she had deceived her children.

"Someone needs to cut the grass," the elder Torres said abruptly.

"Scott will do it."

"No. I will." The old man touched each of his grandsons on the head, and left the room with the air of a man eager to get started on a new job. Ten minutes later she heard a grinding roar from the front yard, and she looked out to see a septuagenarian in a polo shirt digging his leather Top-Sider shoes into the overgrown, spongy grass. The old man pushed the machine over the sloped lawn with surprising efficiency, though after less than thirty seconds he was already covered with beads of sweat, and she wondered if he might have a stroke. *He tackles this physical task with the same gusto Scott attacks a programming problem.* After an hour of grinding, whizzing, and sweeping with various implements, motorized and muscle-driven, he was done. When Samantha woke up from her nap Maureen wandered out with her daughter to inspect his work. He had cut the lawn with a perfection that made the living thing look plastic, or painted, an evenness that was unnatural but also pleasing to the eye.

"Your grandfather knows how to cut a lawn," Maureen said.

# 21

First came the excitement of rushing through the jail, after being told she would face the judge, and then finding there was an anteroom before you got to the court. The guards guided Araceli into a cube-shaped room and directed her to wait alongside two other women on a bench bolted to the floor, one a Latina with eyebrows that looked like they were drawn with a 0.5-millimeter drafting pencil; the other an African-American woman with a head covered with parallel rows of hair and skin, as if plowed by a miniature farmer. The old cement walls of the cube-cell were freshly painted, and in their bone-colored blankness Araceli sensed hundreds of existential agonies, endured by people in much worse situations than hers. Araceli knew that her fate ended in Mexico, that at the end of her current visit to purgatory she would step into the disorderly but familiar sunshine of a Mexican border town, and that afterward she would walk to a bus station or a telephone booth and decide what to do next. It might happen in a year, or two, or maybe even in a few days, but eventually that would be her fate, and it calmed her to know this with certainty. The Latina woman to Araceli's right apparently did not have such knowledge to settle her nerves, because she was repeatedly folding and unfolding a piece of paper. Finally she looked up at Araceli and showed her a row of crooked teeth, as if to say hello. She was gaunt and sallow-faced, with the nervous energy of a twenty-year-old, though she seemed a decade older than that, at least. She also seemed battered and confused, but not especially worried about being that way.

"I'm going to make a run for it," the woman whispered into Araceli's ear. Seeing Araceli's confusion, she switched to thickly accented Spanish: "*Voy a correr. Para ser libre.*"

"*¿Qué?*"

"When we get into the court, there's just a little fence. *Chiquito.*" The woman glanced at the other inmate on the bench, who seemed to be nodding off, and then raised her voice well above a whisper. "It's a tiny fence about as high as your waist. I'm going to jump over. And I'm gonna book it for the back, and into the hallway, and down the stairs if I'm lucky. If I'm lucky I'll get to the front steps and out the door. Now I can do it, because I'm still in my own clothes. Later, they'll have me in jail blues, and I won't make it. I have to do it now, because if I don't, I'll be locked away forever."

Araceli gave the woman a glance that said, *Please stop bothering me with your lunacies.*

"I ain't lying. Because this is my *tercer* strike. *Uno, dos, tres* strikes. *¿Entiendes?* I got my first two strikes with my crazy *novios.* Armed robbery and ADW. Assault with a deadly weapon. Now they got me because I was making eyes at an undercover cop over on Pico. They got me good. And for looking at that cop, and asking him for fifty bucks, I'm looking at twenty-five to life, believe it or not. I said, 'Okay, honey, if you ain't got fifty, forty'll do,' and that's when he showed me his badge, the tiny, ugly little fuck. So I told him, 'Don't do me that way, Officer. I'm begging you. I got two strikes. I'll do you for free, just let me go.' But he was a real tight-ass, and that's why I'm here, and that's why I gotta run." She gave Araceli a wild-eyed look of desperation and mischief. "You're not understanding me, are you?"

"You're going to run?"

"Yes."

"Don't tell me," Araceli said. "I don't want trouble for me."

The door opened and the paper-folder left, giving Araceli one last ugly smile. Araceli listened to the closed door for a minute or so, in anticipation of the noises of anarchy the inmate's attempted escape would set off, but heard only mumbling vibrations of calmly spoken words. Five minutes later, the paper-folder returned with her head bowed, and a palm filled with paper shreds. She averted her eyes from Araceli, sniffled, and began weeping loudly. Before Araceli could ask what had happened, the bailiff called out, "Ramírez and Jones," and Araceli stood up with the other inmate and followed her braided head into the courtroom.

Unlike Araceli, Jones wore a thin chain around her arms and legs, and a blue jumpsuit. The bailiff directed Jones to a chair in front of the judge, and Araceli to a steel folding chair next to the door they had just passed through. "You're next," the bailiff said to her. Forms were shuffled before Jones, an attorney sat next to her and whispered in her ear, and she was asked over and over again if she understood a statement about rights and procedures. Jones nodded several times, and looked impassively at forms that were placed before her, and at the finger of a man who was either a clerk or an attorney and who indicated places she should look. Then he gave her a pen, and whispered into her ear, and she began to sign her name. Araceli had never been in an American court before and wondered if most legal business was conducted this way, with gestures, mumbles, and whispers. Nearly everyone drifted through the proceedings with heavy, tired eyes, even the bailiff, who spent most of his time at his desk. What could be producing this drowsiness? Was it the early hour, the long banks of fluorescent lights, was it something in the air-conditioning? Was it all the paperwork, the forms in triplicate, the stacking of so many manila files? Araceli sensed that the bad-teeth, *tres*-strikes girl had entered this room determined to run, but had been anesthetized by the lights and the drone of bored voices. Now the judge began to speak. He looked like a schoolteacher, and sounded as if he was reading to the defendant from a prepared text, but he wasn't looking at any papers before him and for a second it seemed as if he was reading words that were suspended in the air. *What a strange trick!* When the inmate stood up to leave, Araceli saw that her wrists and ankles were still shackled and linked together, even though she looked too lethargic to be a threat.

Finally, the judge said, "We're ready for Ramírez, Araceli."

She walked to the bench, and a skinny, older man with thick glasses stood next to her. "We're ready, Your Honor," the older man said, and Araceli was puzzled by his use of the first-person plural, which seemed to join him to her for some purpose. "I'm your public defender," the man whispered into her ear suddenly. "But just for today. For your arraignment. Later, you get someone else."

She nodded and looked back over her shoulder at the courtroom: there was, indeed, just a very short barrier separating the place where Araceli sat from the public gallery and the doors at the back of the courtroom. The only guard present, the bailiff, stood near the judge, and in the gallery there was a single witness, a man in business attire with a Mexican flag pin on his lapel. He gave her a twinkling-finger wave, and Araceli wondered if he was there to take her back to Mexico.

"Are they going to deport me?" she asked the public defender in a whisper. Resigned as she was to returning to Mexico, she did not like the idea of having other people decide for her what she should do. A woman should be able to pick the road on which she traveled, and it riled her to think the men gathered in this room—because there were no other women present now, besides her—would decide for her. She looked up at the judge, a kind of anti-angel in his black robes and white hair, holding the keys to the gates of freedom.

"I asked you a question," she repeated to the public defender in full voice, loud enough to cause the other attorney, standing above a table next to hers, to look across. "Are they going to deport me?"

"No, not for the moment," the public defender whispered back from the corner of his mouth, and before Araceli could ask him to elaborate, he, the judge, and other people in the court began to speak in another language she only vaguely recognized as English, a torrent of numbers and terms that she did not understand, with roots that seemed to be in Latin, except for some of the very last words the judge spoke before she was directed back into the cube and the jail beyond.

"Ten thousand dollars."

Assistant District Attorney Ian Goller monitored the routine arraignment of Araceli N. Ramírez from his fourteenth-floor office, in a room adjacent to the office rarely occupied these days by the district attorney, because the boss was on the road, testing the political waters in preparation for a long-shot run for the Republican nomination to the

U.S. Senate. Ian Goller was, at that moment, a worried man, though not for the reasons that should have preoccupied him. The matrices and spreadsheets that mapped and tallied the flow of cases through the courtrooms in the lower floors of his building, and in five satellite courthouses across the county, were arranged on his antiquated, smudged computer screen, and they pointed to a rising flood of drug trials that would eventually lead to a breakdown in the ability of the district attorney's office to meet its legal mandates. But the slow drip toward judicial chaos did not concern him this morning, as much as the simple contents of a clear plastic bag, and a single piece of paper in a manila folder. Through the skin of plastic he could see the train and bus tickets retrieved from Araceli's backpack, while the manila folder contained a copy of a hotel sign-in sheet retrieved by a sheriff's detective who had just returned from a trip to the desert. The tickets confirmed, with those stamped digital codes that juries loved, the truth of the time frame of the defendant's version of events, and the document from the hotel-spa, along with a statement from one of the clerks, offered a disturbing contradiction to the statement of his primary witness.

*One day and it's already falling apart.* He hadn't handled a case himself in a while, and it had been a long time since he'd been confronted with the elemental messiness of a criminal prosecution seen in its prosaic details, with prospective arguments and "facts" tainted by the poor memory and moral fallibility of human beings. *This is why I'll never go back to litigating. Because people are idiots and they lie even when, no, especially when you put your faith in them.*

If his boss were there, Ian Goller would walk into his office, past the door with the seal of the district attorney and its scales of justice. The Sage of Santa Ana, with his undeniable trial and political skills would then tell him how to handle this conundrum casually and effortlessly, but there were only pictures of his boss's children in that office, and diplomas, and various photo-trophies of the district attorney's encounters with national politicians and conservative celebrities, including a snapshot with a distracted and now-deceased President of the United States. Ian Goller could look at those pictures and the district attorney's confident grin, and intuit what he should do next, and he could even hear the district attorney saying it: *Just kick the can down the road and see what happens. Fifty-fifty, it'll go our way.*

The trial attorney he eventually assigned to the case would likely protest his inability to lift *The People v. Araceli N. Ramírez* over the low bar of proof required for a successful preliminary hearing. But a natural outcome already suggested itself, an obvious deal resting like a jewel box inside the charges the district attorney's office had just filed. Simply negotiate the charges down from felony to misdemeanor in exchange for a guilty plea, give the defendant credit for time served and hand her ass forthwith to the Immigration and Customs Enforcement representatives at the county jail. She would then be swiftly deported, as were the legions of other foreign nationals without papers who landed there. News of the defendant's erasure from the American justice system and media orbit would satisfy the constituents clamoring for punishment, and the defendant, in turn, would receive her freedom—in Mexico. Basic fairness to the people of California dictated such a result. After all, the defendant was one of two million residents of the state living every day in violation of Section 8, Title 1325 of the U.S. Code. It fell to county prosecutors to enforce this statute, indirectly, by waiting for each of those two million people to run afoul of some state law, be it a homicide or a DUI. Goller still saw in Araceli N. Ramírez's actions a basic ignorance of American ways, and the recklessness and bad choices that characterized the existence of so many other, unambiguously guilty defendants. He believed the public defender would find the plea offer appealing, as long as the public defender did not see these train and bus receipts, and the hotel clerk's statement, and realize just how weak the prosecution's case really was. Thankfully, the rules and practices of discovery were such that the DA could plausibly delay releasing this information to the defense until after an expedited preliminary hearing. Given the nonviolent nature of the charges, the administrator at the public defender's office would likely assign the case to a Deputy Public Defender II who would see the plea down to a misdemeanor as an easy and fair resolution, a quick deal that would allow him or her to bank a little extra time to work on the thirty or forty other cases on his or her plate. Deportation was, at any rate, a federal matter beyond the purview of mere county officials: every attorney in the two concrete buildings on the opposite sides of Civic Center Drive accepted such outcomes as a matter of course. There was a door at the end of the maze of jail cells and courtrooms into which a fifth of all the defendants in the county disappeared; the door opened to a vortex of weeping Spanish souls that drained into Tijuana and Mexicali and other forsaken places. Goller told his lawyers that each case that ended in deportation was, in its way, a victory for the rule of law. Even the most liberal member of the public defender's office long ago accepted this state of affairs without effective complaint, and it fell to the PDs in courtrooms to explain to defendants again and again that they were about to be deported. Very often this information was relayed at ostensibly happy hearings during which sentences were reduced and probation granted, the news given by twenty-five-year-old PDs in quick murmurs relayed by whispering interpreters, which caused the oft-repeated paradox of defendants weeping inconsolably even as the judge was telling them to behave themselves after being "released." They cried because they knew their American lives were coming to an end, and in the galleries their sons and daughters and wives wept too, once the truth set in. It was a cruel thing to watch, but it was as it should be, Goller thought. Soon, inevitably, his defendant and her problems would pass through the door that led to Mexico.

As he contemplated the quarter-inch-thin newborn baby of paperwork called *The People of the State of California v. Araceli N. Ramírez*, Ian Goller could already see its final fate on that day when, as an inch-thick folder, it would be rolled away into that mausoleum called Archives.

For the first few days without Araceli, the disorder at the home on Paseo Linda Bonita began to gather momentum at first light with the unmade beds, whose comforters and sheets endured in the shape of lumpy cotton corpses until late in the afternoon. Only Maureen tackled that essential household task, until she finally scolded Scott into action: "If you could make *our* bed, at least, before you leave in the morning." He grumbled and complied, but left it all uneven. Was it that he didn't care that the comforter was drooping on her side of the bed, or was it some kind of eye condition that prevented him from seeing it? She was going to have to teach the boys to make their own beds, and give them some incentive to do so, perhaps an allowance. *They're old enough to do chores now. I swept floors and folded clothes when I was a girl.* Then there was the kitchen, whose crowded sink soon evoked the dishwashing station of a cheap diner, with sticky pots and pans beginning to climb upward and over the edge of the sink by 10:00 a.m., their leftover contents becoming encrusted as noon approached. All three bedrooms, the hallways, and the living room were littered with the sweaty fabric of shirts, socks, and underwear of every size but her own. She found Samantha's soiled socks hiding under the couch, and pajama tops in the backyard, and children's picture books on the floor underneath the dining room table. And then there was Samantha herself. Though the smallest member of the family, she tossed more objects into the splatter of disarray than everyone else put together. No one could tell her to pick up her hand puppets, her dolls, her stuffed lions, her rubber blocks, her Tinker Bell wand. Apparently, Araceli had spent a good amount of her day picking up after Samantha, who required a pair of eyes on her at all times and thus subtracted from Maureen's ability to be in all the corners of the home where she needed to be. *Samantha, you came to this world to make your mother's life more beautiful, and feminine, but you've also made it infinitely more complicated.*

The only solution was to spur gadget-man into action.

"Scott. The dishes. Could you, please?"

He studied the spread of steel bowls and plastic plates across the kitchen's marble counters, three complete sets associated with the preparation and serving of breakfast, lunch, and dinner. "Why didn't you use the dishwasher?"

Maureen didn't answer this question, and allowed the aggression in her silence to linger until she heard the water start to run in the sink.

When the school year began and Maureen started volunteering three days a week at the boys' school it was going to be very difficult. She was going to have to find day care for Samantha because they could never again hire a stranger to work in their home.

The consequences of their years of comfort, their pampering by Mexican hands, were there to live with. Voices of judgment continued to occupy the space beyond the pine, glass, and tile cocoon of Paseo Linda Bonita, and she sensed they were growing in volume and meanness. The need to escape that noise gave a greater focus and purpose to her cooking, scrubbing, folding, and other domestic pursuits, as if each muscle exercised in domesticity were building walls that sealed her off from those profane outsiders. But how long could you transform your home into a monastery, with all the televisions and radios permanently off, and the phone off the hook, before you went crazy? She tried calling Stephanie Goldman-Arbegast, but the awkward silence and transparent excuses that followed her invitation for Max and Riley to come and play in the backyard and swim in the pool dissuaded her from calling again. *What have I done for my friend to treat my family with the frigid distance the uninfected have for the diseased?* For the rest of that day, Maureen understood that she had lost a part of herself when she stepped out the door with Samantha that fateful morning. *Goodbye, happy innocence.* She suppressed the recurring thought that she should call her mother. *No, that would be much worse.* Instead, she turned on NPR because she knew she would find dispassionate, adult voices, and for forty-five minutes she allowed the reasoned cadences of its afternoon news report to fill the living room and kitchen. She listened to a Prague coffee machine, the musical speaking-voice of a Louisiana shrimp fisherman. It was all very eclectic and relaxing, until she heard the sudden teaser: "Next, from California, a story that many people say defines the social divide in that sunny place. It's a case involving two children, their parents, and a Mexican woman . . ." Maureen took three leaping strides across the room and hit the OFF button. *Social divide? My home is a social divide?*

Her "social divide" was, at any rate, erased now because Araceli was gone and in jail again. This knowledge caused Maureen to feel a pang of guilt every time she did something in the house that Araceli would have done. When she picked up a sponge at the kitchen sink, or emptied out the dishwasher, or took out the trash, she felt she was standing in Araceli's footsteps. *Is there a special place of torment, down there in the circles of hell, for those women who betray their sisters? I can speak the words that will set her free: but if I do, will I lose my children?* The anger that she felt toward Araceli in the first days of her sons' disappearance had dissipated. *It's a natural, motherly thing, to seethe at the person who took your sons.* Now her guilt was assuaged only by the information provided by the assistant district attorney at her front door this morning—he had come to "warn" her that the "alleged abductor" of her children would likely go free in a plea bargain. He seemed to think this would make her bitter, that she would spew motherly recrimination, and she pursed her lips in a kind of simulated grimace, but in fact she was re-lieved. *We worked on this house together, Araceli and I, it was our joint project. The orbit of men, of news and jurisprudence, has driven a wedge between us.* Then the prosecutor had added that Araceli would be likely deported, and this had caused Maureen to ask her only question: "De-ported? For a misdemeanor?" Araceli probably would have been deported anyway; it was inevitable once the police descended on her home. *I am responsible for the exile of the woman who worked in my home. Or rather, Scott is. And me. We are.* She thought these things as she prepared and poured her daughter's milk, and in her distraction the white liquid spilled over the top of the bottle and onto the table where Samantha was sitting.

"Milk!" the baby screamed.

"Oh, my God, Sam, you talked! Your first word!"

"Milk!" her baby girl repeated.

Maureen gave her daughter a kiss on the forehead and reached for a rag to clean the spill. When she knelt down to wipe the white drops on the floor, a small moving object at the foot of the table caught her eye. It was an ant, and she watched it join the flow of one of two serpen-tine threads that converged on the tile underneath her daughter's high chair. The ants were bumping, circling, and shifting around a spot of spilled and dried Cream of Wheat. Maureen followed their highway across the dining room to the kitchen, and found it led out into the backyard, passing underneath the door that Araceli once opened every morning to begin work.

**W**hile Maureen studied the ants and remembered Araceli, the story of the seemingly soon-to-be-deported *doméstica* caused the mayor of Los Angeles to daydream while ostensibly perusing the menu at his favorite downtown eatery. "The filet mignon here is so tender," the may-or's political consultant said, "you can cut it with a spoon." The mayor of Los Angeles glanced across the white cloth of the table and the sweat-ing goblets of water and gave the consultant a listless and distracted shake of the head.

"I'm thinking the Asian tuna salad," the mayor mumbled. "Lost my appetite."

The mayor had slipped into a brooding funk, a rare twenty minutes of reflective silence, causing his consultant and even the regular customers at the Pacific Dining Car to take notice. He was a man who spent most of his waking day in conversation and monologue—on the phone, in his City Hall office, in parking lots and passageways, in elementary school auditoriums, at doughnut shops, in Westside receptions, in his official Lincoln Town Car. The mayor was a self-described pathological talker who liked to brag that he'd been talking nonstop since the age of four; he knew his consultant had two small children and that he could call and find him awake at dawn. Six hours earlier, he had done just that, after catching the appearance of an up-and-coming state senator from Fremont, California, on Univision's *¡Despierta América!* talk show. "Hey, I just saw Escalante talking about that Mexican nanny again," the mayor had said, without preamble. "He's going to town on this. He was on Telemundo yesterday. And someone told me they heard him on the radio a couple of times."

"Really," the consultant had said wearily into his kitchen phone, while watching his eight-year-old son and six-year-old daughter eat Cream of Wheat and simultaneously twirl their chestnut ringlets. The consultant was a New Jersey transplant of Italian heritage with a wild shock of gray Beethoven curls, a lefty pamphleteer who had risen from 1980s rent-control battles to become the master tactician of the progressive wing of the state Democratic Party, helping a variety of principled and competent leaders win election to office. "I think it's obvious why Escalante's doing this," the consultant began. "He's not on anyone's radar, because he's never done anything. A Latino politician who has to wave his arms like crazy to get the attention of *Latino* voters isn't going anywhere. He's got no shot at winning any statewide primary. None."

Araceli Ramírez was a cause célèbre and a deepening obsession among the mayor's core Latino supporters, but the consultant's position on what the mayor's position should be in her case had not changed. It was the same at 6:45 a.m. in the kitchen of his Northeast L.A. bungalow as it had been in two previous conversations on the subject: keep closed lips and fight the temptation to opine. "You're the mayor of Los Angeles—this is in Orange County. Leave it alone. Because if you don't, this crazy family and their nanny could blow up in your face."

At 6:45 in the morning, the mayor had accepted this counsel as wise and obviously true. He had forgotten about Escalante and the proto-martyr languishing in a Santa Ana jail cell. Then, in the waning moments of his third and final public appearance of the morning, at the Bonaventure Hotel, he had been given another rude reminder of Araceli's existence. The mayor was paying a courtesy call to a group of striking hotel workers, and had just finished up with a few words in his thick-accented but steadily improving Spanish, when one of the striking maids reached over and squeezed his wrist. She was a short woman with the angular face and short hair of a female prize-fighter, and she had pulled the mayor close to her. "*No tengas miedo,*" she said, in a tone that recalled the mayor's late mother. "*Ponte los pantalones. Di algo para apoyar a Araceli. Me enoja que no hayas dicho nada sobre esa pobre mujer.*" The mayor gave a grimace-smile and pulled away, startled a bit by the strength of the woman's grip.

"She told me to put my pants on," the mayor said suddenly to his consultant as his salad arrived. "That last woman in the hotel. The short one. Did you see her? I actually recognized her once I was forced to take a look. Die-hard shop steward. Walked precincts in each of my campaigns. She told me she was angry I hadn't said anything about the Mexican maid. 'Put your pants on,' she said. 'And say something to support Araceli.'"

"What is that, some sort of Mexican thing? Not having pants?"

"Yeah. Precisely."

"Well, that's emasculating. Is that why you ordered a salad?"

"Very funny," the mayor said, and with that he gave his famous, world-conquering grin—it was the flash of erect porcelain that had gotten him elected mayor, and that got him into trouble, sometimes, when he directed it in private at petite, single young women in their thirties. He dug into his salad, took a few bites, and began to talk. "But she has a point."

"She does?"

"The way she sees it, she didn't vote for me just to run the City of L.A."

"Right. The whole icon thing. The long-oppressed people thing."

Legions of people expected the mayor of Los Angeles to opine on the case of a wronged Orange County nanny simply because they shared an ethnic heritage. They saw in his election the fulfillment of his people's long-held aspirations for power and respect. Never mind that most of the voters who had elected the mayor to office were white: he was expected to speak out in favor of immigration reform and amnesty and other subjects far beyond the influence of his actual, quite meager powers, as outlined in the city charter. When he spoke out for immigrant legalization, like these people expected him to, it caused another kind of voter to focus on the seeming threat of his Mexicanness, and a few to harden their belief that he was the leader of a Chicano conspiracy to enslave white people. His Mexican heritage was, at once, his greatest political asset and his heaviest albatross.

"Not saying anything at all makes me look weak," the mayor said. He did not use that word often in referring to himself, it was a sort of taboo in the mayor's circle, and hearing the mayor say it caused the consultant to sit forward in his seat. "People are starting to think I'm running away from it." The mayor's career, from a rough-and-tumble Eastside childhood, to UC Berkeley and a quixotic minor crusade or two as a civil-rights lawyer, to the state legislature, and finally to election as the mayor of the second largest city in the United States, was a dance between affability and toughness, charm and ruthlessness. He understood that "weak" was poison in politics, just like it was on the streets of his youth. The early chapters of his biography were set in a preppy Chicano Catholic school, where the mayor-to-be wore cardigan sweaters and played Black Panther dress-up games, and finally got into the fistfights that led to his expulsion. When the mayor heard the word "weak" and its many synonyms he felt a twinge of the old aggression, and his silence for the past twenty minutes had come from having suppressed a powerful desire to tell that hotel maid to go fuck herself.

It was a rare moment of self-doubt from a politician on an incredible winning streak, a man who spent his day subjecting his consultant and everyone in his circle to his constantly shifting enthusiasms, his volatile self-belief. He was going to plant a hundred thousand trees, hire a thousand police officers, and lay a cute TV reporter or two—all by Christmas. Now the imprisoned nanny was mucking it all up, and threatening to detract from his brilliance, and she was doing it all the way from Orange County. The mayor sensed that the pro-Araceli grumbling would eventually spread to his old civil-libertarian circles and to the unofficial club of well-to-do Westside liberals who funded his campaigns. A few of these people had already written letters to the editor, emails, op-ed pieces, and Internet postings that commented on Araceli's "railroading" as emblematic of the "marginalization" of immigrants in the justice system and the workforce, and the "power relations of narrative and belief" in the city between immigrants and nonimmigrants, and other nonsense like that. The mayor understood that these people measured his silence in such matters, it was a running tally they kept in their heads. They kept expecting him to break out in a rash of cowardice.

"I'm going to have to say something," the mayor said.

The consultant brought his hands together in concentration. He was a wordsmith, an avid reader of history, and a dedicated student of marketing and message. Quickly he arrived at a broad outline of what the mayor might say—the trick, as always, was to make an essentially moderate and cautious position sound bold, principled, and eloquent, a skill all great American politicians possessed going back to Lincoln. He shared his ideas with the mayor and once he was done the mayor smiled at him and said, "Brilliant."

"The key thing is the tone," the consultant said. "You want to sound measured. Like an adult. Above the fray."

Several hours later the mayor was in East Hollywood, at a memorial service for one of the last remaining survivors in Southern California of the Armenian genocide. When the event was over he addressed the four television reporters outside, who were expecting a few innocuous Armenian-centered remarks. "I'm going to take pity on you guys today, and make a little bit of news," the mayor whispered into the ear of a female reporter. "I'm going to say something about that Mexican nanny. Get ready." There was a brief scramble, a hooking up of microphones, a positioning of cables and cameras, and when it had settled, the mayor began:

"Like a lot of people, I've been following the arrest, and now the prosecution, of Araceli Ramírez. It's a case that has a lot of people concerned. And while it isn't appropriate for me to comment on the facts of an ongoing criminal case, I'd like to make just one observation. One of the beautiful things about this country is that everyone, no matter if rich or poor, immigrant or citizen, is entitled to a fair trial. To be judged on the facts, and not on passions or prejudice. I'm concerned about the passions surrounding this case. I think everyone needs to take a step back, and allow the facts, and only the facts, to determine the outcome. We grant our prosecutors a lot of power to protect us—and that's good. But we also trust them to use their power with discretion. I am confident that that will be the case here."

Two hours later, Ian Goller sent a transcript of this statement via BlackBerry to his boss, who was traveling in Bakersfield that afternoon. The district attorney of Orange County sent back a one-word answer: "Surprising." Goller's feelings were stronger. *It's outrageous. This isn't even in his jurisdiction.* The assistant district attorney felt a few pangs of wounded local pride, until he stepped back to think about what would lead such an ambitious and savvy politico to comment on *The People v. Araceli N. Ramírez.* Clearly, the mayor believed that Los Angeles and the Laguna Rancho Estates rested atop the same shifting tectonic plates, and he spoke cautiously to keep his footing as the ground beneath him rumbled. Goller's own Republican boss might soon feel the same political tremors and decide that pursuing a weak *Ramírez* case wasn't worth the risk. In "serious" California political circles both the right and left feared ethnic earthquakes, which was one reason why the immigration problem lingered and deepened.

The longer Araceli Ramírez stuck around Orange County's courtrooms and jail cells, Goller concluded, the bigger the political problems she presented. The mayor of Los Angeles had spoken, ostensibly, to temper a rush toward final judgment. But his brief remarks only strengthened Goller's resolve to shuffle her off U.S. soil and on her way to Mexico as soon as possible.

# 22

Araceli's back ached because she spent much of the waking day turning and twisting on a thin mattress, feeling it slide back and forth over the steel sheet her jailers called a bed frame. She waited for night to fall and day to come back again. When the thin rectangle of her cell window briefly glowed orange in the morning, she could imagine she was somewhere else. Back in colonia San Cosme in Mexico City, where her last *chilango* boyfriend lived, the sun warming their faces, rows of fault-shaken buildings leaning over the sidewalks; or on the subway train when it climbed up out of the ground and ran in the open air, the passengers squinting in the sudden pulses of light. What a mistake it had been to leave Mexico City. Her step north had brought her to a cell in Santa Ana, to become familiar with the angles in the walls, the sounds of the corridors, among inmates hypnotized by the collective need to sleep. The ritual dispensing of pills caused a powerful drift of inmate will toward the recreation room at the end of the corridor, where a television set filled the jail with a perpetual stream of canned laughter and commercial jingles and their tin echoes. Her fellow inmates stayed in this neutral, half-conscious state even at three in the afternoon, when the natural sun was bearing down on people in the world. They were all in a kind of frozen storage, these women in their blue jumpsuits, sitting on their beds, some with charcoal blankets thrown over them, a hundred grungy little dolls in their cells stacked up like toy blocks, reminding her of a Diego Rivera piece from his red-star Marxist didactic days, a painting depicting bodies filling a bank vault. *Frozen Assets.*

On his first day back at work, Scott was chased away from his office by too many "Are you okays?" and too many hugs, and by not getting a single IM from Charlotte, who turned her head away with a snap when he caught her studying him through the glass. At home it was Maureen who averted her eyes, even as she handed him a shopping list for the grocery store. But at the market, with the list in hand, it was all stares. First, the Latino guy at the end of the line of carts, who gave Scott a good long look that passed quickly from initial surprise to irritated aggression. This guy was, what, thirty, thirty-five? His bald-headed look transported Scott back to South Whittier and to the first recruits to a lifestyle his father told him was "for losers who don't want to learn good English." He had a goatee and the unanchored expression of a man about to enter middle age unawares and unprepared. Five, ten seconds passed, and Scott gave him a what's-up? raising of his chin, but the guy didn't blink. Scott pushed forward into the grocery store and began to fill his cart dutifully, but when he reached the checkstand he endured another, shorter glare of recognition from the Latina cashier, followed by a frown and then a look of deliberate indifference. He had seen this cashier perhaps a half dozen times but never engaged in conversation with her, and he now sensed she was disappointed with him somehow, and that his surname had something to do with her reaction. *I'm supposed to be one of them.* This explained too the stare from the shopping-cart *vato.* Scott Torres was being judged by a set of rules of tribal loyalty, simply because he possessed a Mexican surname. *So strange, the clannishness of these people.* Scott, with his one Mexican name, was responsible for the jailing of a woman with three: Araceli Noemí Ramírez. She was just a face and a name on the television, and he their customer, a familiar face—and yet they scorned him. Scott's presence here at the checkstand, his basket filled with jars of baby food and diapers for his daughter, and juice boxes for his sons, meant less to this cashier than the abstract construction of Araceli, a Latina martyr in a jail cell.

"Is there something wrong?" Scott asked the cashier, whose name tag announced EVANGELINE.

"Is there?" Evangeline asked cryptically, and he was left to think about the question as he wheeled out from the store with his purchases in the cart, grasping a receipt between his fingers that was nearly a yard long.

The representative of the public defender's office was a tall, elegant woman with a low-key demeanor, a Filipino surname, and a button nose that suggested a heritage that owed as much to the *Mayflower* as to Manila. Ruth "Ruthy" Bacalan-Howland was about thirty years old, and she paused to think for a second or two whenever it was her turn to speak, looking down at her hands and then using them to pull idiosyncratically at the batik fabric of her long skirt. "Of course, you should not plead guilty to a crime you did not commit, no matter how good a deal it seems," she said to Araceli. "*Mucha gente lo hace, supongo*, but really that's not the way the system is supposed to work."

They were in the attorney conference room, which they had all to themselves. Ruthy Bacalan, a deputy public defender, had listened to Araceli explain the series of events that had landed her in "a very strange North American circus," as Araceli put it in her accented but clear English. The attorney had then laid out the government's offer, speaking the occasional confident if somewhat accented Spanish. She translated "misdemeanor" into the closest Spanish equivalent she knew: "*delito menor*," a phrase that didn't quite carry the innocuous shadings of the English original. "So if you plead guilty to this *delito menor* they will release you from jail—but directly into the hands of *migración*. To the American legal system, it's considered a crime as serious as going through a red traffic light. But it does mean that you will never be able to return here again—legally—since they will hand you over to the immigration people that work inside the county jail even when they are, technically, 'releasing' you from jail. Of course, even if you fought the case and won, you still might get deported." Ruthy Bacalan sat perpendicular to Araceli at a square table, with her long legs crossed one over the other, exposing her leather hiking boots, which had pink trim and pink shoelaces. The deputy public defender wore these shoes because she was seven months pregnant, with swollen feet that kept her perpetually off balance. "If you fight it, you get a chance to call witnesses. I would be your attorney, and the government would pay for everything. Gratis. But, once again, if you lost," the public defender continued, "you could go to a prison for five years. Then you would certainly be deported." Araceli forgot, momentarily, what the attorney was saying, and remained fixated on her footwear. *These are shoes for an active outdoor woman,* Araceli thought. *Girlie-pink and rugged leather. With those, you can climb a mountain in feminine style. I'm pretty sure I've never seen shoes like that in Mexico City, not even at the Santa Fe Mall.*

"Can I ask you, señorita, where did you buy those boots?"

Ruthy Bacalan was momentarily taken aback—apparently, people whose futures hung in the balance did not often interrupt the conversation to ask about her shoes.

"Oh, these. At the Sport Chalet."

"If I am ever released from this place and allowed to live in the United States," Araceli said, "I will go to this chalet and buy a pair of those shoes. In fact, I will tell you that I want to stay here, and not accept the very generous offer to be deported directly to Mexico, because Los Estados Unidos de América is a country where women can wear boots like that."

"So you're not going to accept the government's offer?"

"No. ¿Para qué?"

"*Fantástico*," Ruthy Bacalan said, her face erupting into youthful brightness, as if an undergraduate had suddenly arrived to chase the gloomy attorney away. Ruthy Bacalan had been preparing to resign from the public defender's office, and not because she was pregnant and carrying forty-seven cases as a Deputy Public Defender II. Her recent conversion to Buddhism helped her with the stress, and she felt quite prepared to be a working mother. No, what was causing Ruthy Bacalan to doubt her commitment to the public defender's office was the lack of fight and purpose in the work, her servitude to the assembly line of advancing manila folders, and the flow charts that established all the hearings and procedures through which a soul had to be squeezed before emerging either guilty, exonerated, or in various legal limbos on the other side. She had come to this job out of a sense of civic duty and compassion, a belief that she might be able to reduce the suffering of the defendants who passed before her and imbue them with at least some constitutional dignity. In the cramped office she shared with two other deputy public defenders, she had sat down to meditate for ten minutes before leaving for this interview, and realized immediately afterward that she needed to place herself in a job where she might more directly confront the inequities of her time. Maybe as a teacher in an "inner city" school, or as a union organizer, or perhaps simply as a stay-at-home mom raising future citizens with good Buddhist values. And now this defendant had appeared before her, prepared to take a defiant stance in a case that might attract some media notoriety and send a small message to the city and the nation beyond.

"I think you can win this case," Ruthy Bacalan said quickly and eagerly. "Everyone in the office was expecting you to take the guilty plea."

"Why would anyone plead guilty if they did not commit the crime?" Araceli asked. "That makes no sense."

"A lot of people do it. There are a lot of things about the law and the courts that don't make any sense."

"What you were saying before, *licenciada*? Let me make sure I understand correctly," Araceli said. "You were saying I might be punished for trying to tell the truth. I mean, if I lose the case. Because I would be telling the truth—that I am not guilty—but they could send me to prison for a longer time because I tried to tell the truth."

"Yes." Any layperson could see it, Ruthy Bacalan thought. The shock of seeing principles of the law sullied and mocked—it was the expression on the face of every idealistic attorney after a week or two inhabiting a deputy public defender's skin. "There is this beautiful idea. A word with Latin roots: 'justice.' Of course, it's the same word in both our languages. *Justicia*." These were the opening words to a little speech Ruthy Bacalan sometimes gave to undergraduate classes in the law, but never before to a client. "The justice system is like plumbing. In cases like yours, the basic problem is that there are too many defendants to fit in the system—so we lawyers use tricks to squeeze you through. Against this there is a tradition in the law that says everyone should be treated fairly. My job exists, for example, because a poor man from Florida sat down and wrote a letter to the Supreme Court, with paper and pencil.

From his jail cell. Thanks to him the laws were changed so now everyone gets a public defender, gratis. A fighter like that can change the law. United States history is filled with people like that."

"Mexican history is the same," Araceli said.

"I imagine it is."

"But I am not a fighter."

"Neither am I. Not truly."

"But I think I want to be respected. *Merezco respeto.* And I want to respect the rules too. The rules say you should not lie."

Above all, the thought of pleading guilty to a *delito menor* and accepting the convenience of a "deal" offended Araceli's sense of order and decorum. It only added to the sense of unraveling about her: that she was living in a metropolis where all the objects, once arranged in order, had been shuffled out of place. *When you live far away, you never associate California with clutter.* When Araceli was in a messy home, when the beds were not made and the dishes were left unscrubbed, she invariably felt pangs of disappointment and loss. She had been this way as a girl in Nezahualcóyotl, when her mother slipped into those seasonal depressions that kept her from working for several days at a time, once or twice a year. And she was that way as a woman living in the guesthouse on Paseo Linda Bonita. Now Araceli could see that this place called California was like a home that had fallen into a state of obsolescence and neglect, a conclusion confirmed by the fact that this idealistic woman with the pink-trimmed boots had been forced to make an absurd offer: tell a lie and you can go free. The truth had been building for a long time now—it had been there for her to see intimately in the Paseo Linda Bonita home, in the increasingly frayed interactions between Scott and Maureen, the sense that she was living with two people confused and angry with the familial roles assigned to them. She felt this same unsettled sense when she first entered the center of Los Angeles with Brandon and Keenan, when the mob confronted the councilman in Huntington Park, and when the woman of *los tres* strikes plotted her escape and then surrendered and wept. She wanted to take all the exhausted American people she'd seen and give them freshly starched clothes to wear, and she wanted to take all the misplaced objects and polish them and put them back where they belonged.

"These laws you have. In some ways they are pretty," Araceli said. "But in other ways they are ugly."

The American police would politely release you if they knew the truth of your innocence; they would not accept bribes, apparently, and they placed the property they took from the people they arrested in transparent bags for later return. And yet their courts would blackmail an innocent woman into a devil's bargain, just so they could keep the flow of the accused moving swiftly through their concrete buildings.

"*Entonces, a pelear*," Araceli said.

Ruthy Bacalan beamed. "Yes, we fight." She explained what would happen next: the court would schedule a "mini-trial" called a preliminary hearing. "I'll push for that quickly. If we lose that, and we likely will, we go for a full trial."

The two women shook hands and gave each other a half embrace before leaving the room via separate doors. Araceli took a slip of paper from the guard and followed a yellow line on the concrete floor that led away from the room and twisted and turned down a labyrinth of corridors. On those few occasions when she ventured out of her cell, the expanse and openness of the county jail surprised Araceli: the prisoners shuffled back and forth without escorts, up and down the hallways and escalators, women walking with leisurely strides in groups to the cafeteria, carrying trays of food and boxes and envelopes, guided by a greasy rainbow of painted floor lines. The jail had the structured bustle of a huge office building, a weird corporation where the secretaries wore their hair in dirty strings, or shaved at the sides, and every employee dressed in a blue or a yellow jumpsuit.

She walked back to her cell block, ten minutes through a corridor maze, and remembered what she had told the deputy public defender: "I am not a fighter." But perhaps she was. She could be a Mexican super-hero wrestler, the Masked Inmate, springing into the air in her yellow jail overalls, with ankle-high pink leather boots and a purple cape trailing behind her. She gave another solitary chuckle and thought that it was nice to be able to get out of her cell and talk to Ruthy for an hour, and then to jostle through the rushing crowds of secretaries in the yellow jumpsuits who crowded the passageways.

Halfway back, just past the point where the orange line turned off toward the cafeteria, Araceli felt a jolt to the head and stumbled, tumbling through an instant of blindness. She landed facedown on the floor and regained her sight, touching yellow and blue and green lines on the cement, trying to remember which one she was supposed to follow.

"Baby stealer!" someone shouted above her. "*Kidnapper!*" Someone kicked her in the spine as she tried to rise to her knees, sending her back to the hard coolness of the floor. *Someone is trying to kill me.* The inmates formed a circle around her, she could see their feet sticking out through the rubber sandals everyone had to wear, toenails freshly painted ruby and tangerine. *Where do they get nail polish in here? How did I miss the dispensing of the nail polish?* A whistle sounded and all the painted toenails ran away, replaced by the heavy black shoes of a guard. Araceli looked up and saw a tall uniformed and muscular Scandinavian giant with a ponytail. The guard pulled her up, but Araceli's head wanted to stay on the ground. "Gotta get you outta here, girl," the guard said. "Get up. Or the crowd will re-form." Araceli's legs wanted to give up, but the guard wouldn't let her fall, and they started to walk back toward the cell, Araceli taking three good steps for every bad one that couldn't support her weight, being held up by this woman with the torso of a weight lifter. "You gonna make it?" the guard asked.

"*Creo que sí*," Araceli said.

They started to move forward again, the guard's arm around Araceli's waist. Suddenly the guard lifted her into the air with a grunt, and all of Araceli's thoughts were erased by the unexpected sensation of being embraced by the stout construction of the guard's arms as she carried Araceli over the lines on the floor. Araceli wanted to coo, it felt so good, all the tension in her spine and face and the pain of the blows suddenly slipping away.

Maureen opened the front door at 4:50 in the afternoon, thinking that it was Scott, but found instead an older, heavier, and slightly darker version of her husband. John Torres carried a suitcase and wore the expression of a man forced to rescue a drowning woman too stupid to know she couldn't swim. "It has come to my attention that you guys are kind of falling apart here," he announced. "That's why I'm back. And that's why I'm gonna move in. I'm going to take that little house in the back your maid had, since I'm assuming she ain't coming back. I'll stay four nights a week, which is probably as much as I can take."

Maureen opened her mouth to speak, but could not find words to resist the affront.

"I can cook. I can clean as well as anyone," he said, with a kind of wounded determination. "And I sure as hell know how to make a bed, which is more than my son knows. I won't do the dishes, but I can cook a pretty mean pot of beans and just about anything these kids will eat for breakfast. You can leave your boys with me here and I can babysit, and you can take a break with my granddaughter, which I take it was what led to this mess anyway. And I'd say you probably need a break too, because, to be frank, you're looking kinda worn down, daughter-in-law." He took in her frazzled appearance with a quick up-and-down. "I know you're not supposed to say something like that to a woman, but let's get down to brass tacks here. You need the help. You're wearing out like some of the guys I used to pick lettuce with. I'll work for free. Just let me eat my own arroz con pollo is all I ask."

*El abuelo* Torres disappeared into the kitchen and then into the backyard and the guesthouse. Scott found him thirty minutes later, with his head in the refrigerator.

"Dad? What's going on?"

"I'm looking for a decent cheese to make these kids a quesadilla. That's something I know they'll eat for dinner."

Scott walked away, feeling he had entered a nightmare in which he sleepwalked through scenes from his childhood, the past returning with an eerie and familiar sense of doomed domesticity.

"My father is cooking dinner?" Scott asked Maureen in the living room.

"And living with us."

"In this house?"

"In the guesthouse, yes."

"Why?"

"Not my idea."

"Can we make him leave?"

"I suppose we could," Maureen said. She took in the smell of melting cheese wafting in from the kitchen. "But can we afford to?"

After serving his grandsons and granddaughter a dinner of quesadillas and sliced apples, with the boys grinning at him and calling out, "Can we have another one, Grandpa?" the elder Torres returned to the silver range. He prepared baked potatoes and chicken thighs spiced with tarragon, the kind of simple but hearty meal you might get at a diner, and slid it across the kitchen table to his son and daughter-in-law.

"Enjoy," he said flatly.

"Thank you," Maureen answered weakly.

When they were finished he left the dishes in the sink for Maureen and went out in the backyard and grabbed one of the footballs and yelled out to Brandon, "Go long." After a few tosses Keenan joined them and they played catch for thirty minutes, until the elder Torres began to cough and he plopped down on the grass and said, "Let's sit down and take a rest and look at this pretty desert we've got growing here."

Grandfather and grandsons admired the stiff petals of the prickly pear cactus, the spiny yuccas, and held very still when they saw a crow perch itself on top of the ocotillo. It turned its head side to side to examine the humans below with each of its eyes.

"Damn, that's pretty," the elder Torres said. "It's been a long time since I seen the desert like this. Grew up in the desert, you know."

Brandon sensed his grandfather was drawn to the cactus in some profoundly adult and emotional way, and he half heard and half imagined a cowboy twang in his speech. Perhaps he was a south-of-the-border cowboy like the venal gunslinger with a Mexican accent in that spaghetti western Brandon watched with his father once, until the cowboys started cussing and his father told him he had to leave.

"Is this what Mexico looks like?" Brandon asked.

"Wouldn't know. I'm from Yuma, in Arizona." The elder Torres looked at his grandchildren, saw their expression of innocent confusion, and allowed his natural defensiveness to slip away. "My father was from Chihuahua. I was born there, but it's been a long time. I suppose it probably still looks like this."

"Are we Mexican?"

"Just a quarter. By me, I guess."

"Only a quarter?" Keenan said. He thought about the math lessons at the end of second grade, and did not understand how a human being could be divided into fractions. One-quarter, two-thirds, three-eighths. Were his bones and muscles split into Mexican parts and American parts? Could his greenish-brown pupils have a quarter Mexican pie slice, two American pie slices, and an Irish pie slice, and if he looked in the mirror with a magnifying glass, could he see the slices and tell them apart?

"Yeah," their grandfather said. "Just a quarter."

"Is less Mexican better than more?"

"Don't know. Some people think it is. These days, though, I ain't so sure."

At 8:45 p.m. the elder Torres retired to the guesthouse, and by 9:15, when Maureen entered the kitchen to make herself some tea, she could hear him snoring, a faint animal rumbling of stubborn helplessness squeezing through the two walls that separated them.

The next morning he awoke at 6:00 a.m., entered the kitchen, and made his son a ham, tomato, and cheese omelet for breakfast. When Scott had finished eating, his father gave him an order.

"Do me a favor and scrub out a couple of toilets before you leave for the day."

"What?"

"Listen. Your wife is allergic to the toilet bowls, and I'm gonna have a lot on my plate today."

"But I'm going to work. I'll be late."

"I thought you were the boss there."

Twenty minutes later the elder Torres found his son on his hands and knees in one of the home's four bathrooms, attacking the porcelain with a scrubber.

"Man, this is gross," Scott said.

"You've got two boys. What did you expect?"

Scott rose to his feet, lowered the toilet cover to sit, and took a break, studying the sink and the tub, both of which were awaiting his attentions.

"Did Araceli really do all of this? By herself?" Scott asked. He looked at his hands, which smelled of bleach. "You made breakfast, and dinner last night. Maureen's doing the baby's laundry. I'm cleaning the fucking toilets. I can't believe that one woman did all of these things."

"Yeah," the elder Torres said. "And she did them well." He examined his son's work on the toilet, and added, "Don't forget to scrub down on the sides. You need to get back down on your hands and knees to do it right."

For the next few days Scott and Maureen remembered Araceli in their muscles, and in their wrinkled and bleached hands, until the tasks became familiar and routine and her prominent place in their memories began to fade, very slightly.

# 23

"Somebody paid your bail." The guard named Nansen, who had carried Araceli to safety just yesterday, looked a little disappointed. "Ten grand, paid in full." Araceli walked through the jail corridors for what she hoped was the last time, trying to imagine who her benefactor might be—a man, a tall man, a gringo? Would his act of kindness present additional complications? After her clothes were returned to her at the Inmate Reception Center, she walked through one last set of doors into a room where the guards didn't care about her anymore, a waiting area with plastic chairs and the feel of a seedy bus station. Standing in the middle of the room, with the lost look of a passenger who had missed his connection, was a thin, white-haired, and pale man of about fifty with ruddy, cratered skin, in a brown tweed jacket and a white cotton dress shirt that dangled over the top of his jeans.

The attorney opened his arms in greeting. "Araceli! I've been here for over an hour. I'm Mitchell Glass. From the South Coast Immigrant Coalition," he said. "We paid your bail."

"Why?" Araceli realized, of course, that she should say thank you, but her need to understand what was happening outweighed any pretense. There was a moment of awkward silence while Glass considered the question.

He explained, in slow and condescending English that sped up and was less condescending after Araceli frowned at him, that the coalition had received the funds to free Araceli from a group called the Immigrant Daylight Project, a large circle of benevolent and open-minded people from Manhattan, Austin, Santa Monica, Cambridge, and many other places. "Usually they pay bail for people who are in immigration detention. So they can get out and live among free people while they appeal the verdict. Out of the shadows and into the daylight. Get it? The directors thought that, given the attention to your case, they would pay your bail too. Plus, it wasn't a huge amount."

"*¿Y qué tengo que hacer?*" she asked.

"Nothing," Glass said. "These people just want you to be free while you fight your case."

Araceli did not know it, but not long after her second arrest the Daylight Project had sent off a flurry of emails and posted letters calling on its members to "help throw a wrench in the prison-industrial complex" by "emancipating Araceli N. Ramírez, the latest member of the fastest growing sector of the incarcerated population"—undocumented immigrants. The group's fund-raising literature was a bit heavy-handed with its use of slavery metaphors, and included broken chains on its logo and references to the Underground Railroad in its brochures. But they dealt almost exclusively with those in federal detention and their decision to pay Araceli's bail caught Ian Goller and his office completely by surprise. It had been ages since the Orange County District Attorney's Office had a defendant whose fate worried faraway liberal crusaders. Generally speaking, alien inmates without family members on the outside stayed inside the big house, there was no habeas corpus for them, no writs, no appeals, no purchased freedom.

For the moment, however, Araceli was a happy and unlikely beneficiary of the Bill of Rights, as free of overbearing authorities as the New Englanders who stood up to King George, a startling fact which she confirmed by scanning the street and the parked cars as she walked toward the jail's parking lot. *No one is following me.* Qué milagro. *The sun is shining on my face. Daylight.* She wanted to ask about her public defender, but instead Glass told her something about a "rally."

"What?"

"We're going to a little meeting," he said as they entered his car. "Your case inspired us to organize this."

They arrived at the campus of a Catholic church and its affiliated school and parked on its basketball court, then marched briskly around the chapel, Glass leading the way to a collection of nearby bungalows and square buildings painted industrial-tan. *Is this a political meeting?* she wanted to ask. *I am not a fan of politics.* Araceli began to feel annoyed with this Glass, even though he had liberated her from jail. He was a step ahead of her, but she reached out to grab him by the dusty sleeve of his jacket.

"Wait," she said. "*Necesito saber.*"

"What?" He stopped his forward march and gave her a mildly flustered look.

"What do I have to do for the money?" Araceli demanded. "For the bail? What do they want?"

"Nothing. All you have to do is go to court on the day they tell you."

"*¿De veras?*"

"Yes. Let's go now," Glass said. "Please. People are waiting for us." They resumed their frantic scurry across the school's black asphalt playground, with Araceli wondering why the playgrounds and classrooms were empty of children, until she remembered it was the middle of summer and school was out.

They entered a long room with high ceilings that was filled with people sitting in rows of folding chairs. A speaker was addressing the audience in Spanish from a small stage, a very short, light-skinned woman who spoke in an amplified, high-pitched whisper. "*Es que son unos abusivos,*" she said in a Central American accent. "*A mí no me gusta que me hablen así.*" Most of the audience turned toward Araceli and Glass as the door opened, and several people smiled at Araceli when they saw her, though none beamed broader than a wool-pelted, bureaucratic-looking, and unmistakably Mexican man and his equally well-dressed acolytes sitting in the front row. These men now rose from their chairs as one, rudely ignoring the speech that was still in progress onstage, and moved toward Araceli with outstretched hands.

"No, Consul, not now," Glass said brusquely as he moved his body forcefully between Araceli and the Mexican diplomat.

"That's the consul of Mexico in Santa Ana," Glass whispered into Araceli's ear as they climbed up the little steps to the stage. "A real publicity hound. Don't talk to him. He's useless."

Now Araceli stood on a platform, above an audience of about one hundred people, nearly all of whom were gazing at her with the delight of unexpected recognition. They knew her face from the television reports. She was a celebrity, a realization that brought a sardonic grin to Araceli's lips which, in turn, only seemed to make everyone around her happier. *The liberated inmate is grateful because our movement has set her free.* Araceli had a moment to marvel at the power of television and newspapers to make her face known to strangers. There were younger people, most of them Latino college students, it seemed, and older people of European stock in distressed cotton. One of the college students, a young woman with hair worked up into a kind of half beehive, raised a phone to take Araceli's picture.

Glass stepped up to the microphone. "Just a few minutes ago, we posted bail for our friend here, Araceli Ramírez," he began. At this the audience broke into a hearty applause. Was that big guy in the back Felipe? *Could it be? No.* Now everyone was beaming, except for three severe-looking young men with identical close-cropped haircuts and earrings that opened weird, hollow spaces in their lobes. They were members of a club with rules Araceli did not recognize, and their jaws were locked in grim defiance, as if they had been the ones put in jail, not her, and they seemed to be making a point of cupping their hands and clapping harder than anyone else.

"We're going to ask Araceli here to say a few words, but first . . ."

*Say a few words?* She looked at Glass and wanted to tap his shoulder to ask if she had heard him correctly, but he was still addressing the audience. "You and I, we all know what this case is about," he said, his bass voice finding a Brooklyn rasp or two as it rose in volume. "This is about racism; it's about the powerful imposing their law on the weak." Several people in the audience nodded in assent because Glass had spoken a truth that Araceli could see too, even through her stage fright. "Well, we're here, all of us are here to say that we're tired of the police raids, we're tired of our young Latino men and women being harassed, we're tired of the *migra*." His voice rose even more to match the ascending volume of the audience, the people calling out, "Yes!" as if this were some sort of evangelical service.

"And this case, this case our friend Araceli has against her, this is the worst. She has done absolutely nothing wrong. Nothing!" He was spitting into the microphone now. "And if they can lock up Araceli

Ramírez and take away her freedom for nothing, then they can do it to any of us. Now we're saying we're not going to tolerate this. We're not going to allow our Latino men and women to be railroaded!" Nearly everyone rose to their feet, a few were shouting words Araceli couldn't make out, they wanted to hear more, but Glass seemed to have run out of steam. He turned to Araceli, who was standing at his shoulder, and looked at her: it was her turn.

She whispered into his ear, "*No sé qué decir.*" Out in the audience, a hundred people were standing before their folding chairs, their eyes locked on her.

"Just tell them you hope there is justice," he said.

Glass put his hand at her back and nudged her toward the microphone. She brought her lips close to it and spoke softly. "*Quiero justicia.*" The sound of her voice, turned to metal, bounced off the walls. "*No hice nada.*" She stopped, wondering what to say next, suddenly at a loss for words, as if she'd picked up a text of her speech and found all the pages blank. *Is that all I have to say?* "*No hice nada,*" she repeated, feeling parrotlike. "*Soy inocente.*" They expected a waterfall of words, and suddenly she didn't want to disappoint them, but her sense of urgency only muzzled her more. "*No sé qué más decir,*" she said, and the words came out with a nervous near-giggle that she would remember as the sound of her failure. One of the shaved heads in the back started clapping, all alone. And then it was as if he'd opened a faucet, because everyone joined in and the applause became a wave of sound, growing denser as it approached the stage and crashed at her feet. Now she thought of what more she could say: she would thank the people who paid her bail, and Glass for coming to get her out of jail, she would say that she agreed with everything Glass had said. But now that she had the words, she couldn't speak them, because the applause kept on going, it had a momentum of its own, people were making a point of keeping it going, to show it would not die. All the clappers looked at her with what seemed to her an overwrought pride, as if she'd just had a medal pinned to her chest. There was a young, thin man in the first row, wearing a loose-fitting leather belt of chrome pyramid studs, and jeans fashionably ripped at the knees, and she had time to think that she liked his style. When she studied him closer, she saw he was crying. *He would fit in in Mexico City, except for the fact that he's clapping and crying at the same time—in my city, we are either happy or morose but rarely both at the same time.* Maybe if she started clapping too, they would stop. Glass put his hand on her back again and she understood: she stepped away from the microphone and followed him down from the stage, where everyone reached out to shake her hand.

If Giovanni Lozano hadn't been crying and laughing when Araceli spotted him, she would have taken more time to admire his outfit, and the familiar, punk-inspiring stylings whose fashionability endured in Mexico City as much as Los Angeles. On his black denim blazer he wore a NO HUMAN IS ILLEGAL button next to another of Joey Ramone, and he walked to his car in his ripped jeans with a studded leather belt and the leaning, I-don't-give-a-shit gait of an oversexed musician. He tossed his raven bangs back before stepping in and listening to the engine of his old Dodge turn over with a clank and shuffle that sounded like the prologue to a folk song. As the engine revved and warmed up, he resisted the temptation to fire off some text messages to his friends, because the event he had just witnessed was too big, too monumental, he decided, to be reduced to the usual texting acronyms and abbreviations. Giovanni Lozano, a twenty-six-year-old Chicano Studies maven and perpetual Cal State Fullerton undergrad, had been following Araceli's case on television for days. He was the most active and most read poster on the La Bloga Latina page dedicated to Araceli's case, where he had a large following among the small but growing segment of Spanish-surnamed population that Giovanni called "the Latino intelligentsia, such as it is." His readers were a largely college-educated and over-qualified bunch, their ranks including underpaid municipal employees, unpublished novelists, untenured professors, underappreciated midlevel executives, unheralded poets, and the directors of underfunded nonprofits seeking to house, feed, and teach a tragically undereducated people. These readers appreciated his Spanglish wit, his Orange County Chicano, *Y-Qué* attitude—thanks to them, he was winning the war on Google, outpacing the One California nativist website on "Araceli Ramírez" searches by nearly two to one. As he drove he began to craft, in his head, a succinct summary of the events that had just unfolded: *Araceli Noemí Ramírez is free on bail! La Bloga's campaign—successful! We just saw her at a church in San Clemente.* ¡Qué mujer! *Her speech: short and to the point. Her attitude: arty and defiant, como siempre. A tall, big mexicana, she waltzed past our local, do-nothing consul as if he wasn't there! Ha!* From his very first glimpse of her running in that footage shot under the electric transmission lines in Huntington Park, Giovanni saw in Araceli a symbol of *mexicana* hipsterhood victimized. This vision of her was only strengthened by the details he found buried in the news accounts of her two arrests and double jailing, including the revelation, reported near the end of a story by Cynthia Villarreal in the *Times*, that police had found "disturbing art" in Araceli's room. Giovanni had understood, instinctively, that Araceli was being victimized not only for being a *mexicana*, but also for being an individualist and a rebel. He had studied the photo essay on the web that accompanied the *Times* story on the rearrest, and drew his readers' attention to the tiny silver studs Araceli wore on her earlobes, the too-tight leggings, and the wide blouse with the wide-open neck and small embroidered fringe that was tastefully Oaxacan without being too folksy.

Araceli's presence was an antidote, somehow, to all those sad stories of workplace raids and deportations; she stood for the sophisticated place he and his mostly American-born readers imagined deeper, urban Mexico to be. She was an event of history that had been dropped into Giovanni Lozano's provincial corner of the planet, a force with the potential to separate the Spanish-surnamed masses from their complacency and denial. People like his immigrant mother, who tended to her roses in their home in Garden Grove, telling Giovanni that she felt the Holy Spirit in the faint breeze that blew between the flowers. His mother pretended not to care when he told her how she and her people were being belittled on the radio and on television, in the courts and in the supermarkets, by the racists who attached that slur "illegal" to anyone and everyone with Mesoamerican blood in their veins. *Don't you see, Mother?* he wanted to say. *They want to destroy us! Deport us all! It's a war against our culture!*

*No, my people don't understand shouting. They understand victims and heroes,* he thought. So he would give them an icon. He would take one of those photographs of Araceli from the newspaper website, and he would make a work of art, a portrait-poster. He would take Araceli's face and multiply it, so that many Aracelis floated above the marching crowd at the next rally, in a Warholian statement about the power of her ordinariness and her celebrity. He would paste her to the walls, and put some text underneath her. Perhaps Araceli's own statement from the newspaper. "¡*No les tengo miedo!*" And why not in English too? A Mexican woman with her mouth open to the words: "I am not afraid!"

"I don't know what I know anymore," Maureen said fifteen minutes into the interview with Deputy District Attorney Arnold Chang. Maureen and Scott were confused and evasive about time and their own actions during the disappearance of the children, and they were unwilling or unable to say anything about the defendant that would bolster a felony child endangerment conviction. They were freshly showered and scented, appropriately polite, but also distant to the man who was there to be their champion in court against the woman charged with endangering their children.

"She never did anything you found strange?" Chang asked.

"Strange? Oh, yes, lots of things," Maureen said. "We called her Madame Weirdness."

"You'd say hello and she wouldn't answer," Scott said.

"I got kind of used to that after a while. Who needs to hear 'hello' all the time in their own house?" Maureen said. "But she did seem unhappy a lot of the time."

"Almost all the time," Scott said. "But that's not a crime, I guess. Unhappiness is not against the law."

"What was she unhappy about?"

Maureen and Scott thought about this question for a few moments, reviewing their memories of the four years they had lived with Araceli for some insight into their employee's inner life. They looked at each other blankly, then separately gave the prosecutor a startled and embarrassed shrug.

"We have no idea," Scott said.

"I'm guessing that she was lonely," Maureen said. "That she expected more from life—because, you know, she's obviously very smart. But she worked hard. We have to give her that."

"She did everything," Scott said. "Everything. And never complained."

"She grumbled," Maureen corrected. "She was rude. But did we ever hear a real complaint? No."

The "victims" wanted the case to go away, the deputy district attorney concluded, and that was a common enough reaction. They wanted to return to their normal, untroubled lives. But then the husband took it a step further.

"I'm not sure Araceli needs to be prosecuted," Scott said suddenly, bluntly. "I really don't think she did anything wrong."

Maureen lowered her eyes, feeling suddenly exposed and naked, but not entirely surprised. She allowed Scott's statement to fill the space above their dining room table unchallenged, knowing that her silence was a loud proclamation of assent. *If Araceli didn't do anything wrong, then what about me?* She had contributed to Araceli's jailing with that small lie to the 911 operator, and then she had all but denounced her former maid in a television interview, with insinuations that caused the Mexican woman to be jailed again. A simple statement by her husband had forced her to confront these truths. And it was all happening here in the living room, before yet another stranger.

"But she took them, or placed them, rather, in a situation of peril," the deputy district attorney said.

"Because of us," Scott said. "It was our fault."

"Stop," the deputy district attorney snapped, raising his palm like a traffic policeman, and both Maureen and Scott understood why.

"Can't you just let this go?" Scott said, with frustrated insistence. "Because the longer it goes on, the deeper you're digging us into a big mess. I mean, the media, everything. It's going to swallow up our family."

"There's something you need to understand," Deputy District Attorney Chang said after a few moments. "It's not your decision to make. This case doesn't belong to you. It belongs to the People now."


"Well, that went smoothly," Scott said once the deputy district attorney had left.

"We spent the last twenty minutes talking about the desert garden and about his kids," Maureen observed, and with that she turned away from Scott and walked over to the portable playpen in the middle of the living room and took out Samantha.

"She's spending a lot of time in there," Scott observed, but his wife ignored him and gave him the baby, and in a few moments she had disappeared into the kitchen and then emerged again with an apron.

"There's some things we need to talk about," Scott said. Before the arrival of the representative of the district attorney's office, Scott had spent the morning on the phone, speaking to a representative of Child Protective Services. He had to sit down with his wife and sort through how they were going to work their way out of this mess, but now she walked away from him again, tying the apron around her back and disappearing into the kitchen. *How is it that women are so good with their fingers behind their backs and we men are not?* The image of motherly dexterity and purpose stuck with him as he took the baby and headed for the backyard. He took Samantha outside and rolled a ball around the grass with her, and enjoyed the crazy, baby-tooth giggle she gave when it slipped away from her. "Ball," his daughter said, her voice mostly a big, squeaky vowel. When they had finished playing he looked for his wife, thinking that he might grab and hold her attention with the momentous news that their daughter had just uttered her first word. He found her in the boys' room, on her knees, examining the contents of the boys' bookcase.

"Hey, Samantha is talking now."

"I know. She said 'milk' a few days ago. Didn't I tell you?"

"No." He studied his wife, who was taking books and dropping them into a box with harried relish. "What are you doing?"

"I had an epiphany," Maureen said, giving a scan of the room Araceli called El Cuarto de las Mil Maravillas. "We have too much stuff."

"What?"

"The kids have toys they haven't played with in two or three years. And books like these that they'll never read again." She held up two slim volumes from a series of detective mysteries written for young readers, one for each letter of the alphabet. Their precocious younger son had finished whipping through all twenty-six more than a year earlier. "Why have we kept these? It's all this stuff gathering dust that's just making it that much harder to keep this place clean."

"Okay," Scott said in the tone with which one addressed children and madmen.

"Of course, the real solution is to move to a smaller house," Maureen continued. "That's what we should have done a while ago." It pained her to think she'd soon have to leave this home built with so much time and care. But there was no other way out. Not any she could see. "We can't have your dad staying with us forever. And if we're not going to have any live-in help, then we can't be in a place that's this big. If we can get rid of about half the stuff we own, we can fit into a smaller place. Maybe a place with a public school district that's half-way decent."

Scott could see his wife would now approach the task of divesting herself and her home of these superfluous objects with the same vigor she had applied to their accumulation. The household was her domain, and he and all the children would live according to whatever principles she embraced: baroque beauty and excess, or simplicity and moderation. *What do they call it when women run everything? Matriarchy? Feminocracy?* He imagined a leaner household, smaller credit-card bills, and a less imposing flat-screen television. Or perhaps no television at all. Hadn't it been that way once, in some other time, in the prehistory of his American family, a time his Mainer great-grandfather would remember? He allowed himself to imagine living in that emptier household with children, perhaps with a vegetable garden in the back instead of cacti or semitropical plants—and then he remembered the nagging matters of the present.

"We need to talk about some things."

Maureen heard him but chose not to respond, because if she did she would lose the momentum that was carrying her through the domestic juggling act of her day. If she stopped she would curl up like a ball on the bed with a bowl of ice cream and the television turned on to faux courtrooms and talk-show hosts who filled the day with common sense and scolding rants delivered to knucklehead moms. Better to sort through this bookcase, separating out the old Dr. Seuss and other very early reader books Samantha might still enjoy. If she could leave the boys' room looking less cluttered, the sense of minor accomplishment would stay with her and lift her through the preparation of lunch. Afterward, she would strap up Samantha for a walk through the neighborhood to see if she might fall asleep, because the baby was starting to skip her naps, which transformed her into a moody afternoon screamer. The visit of the representative of the district attorney's office had thrown Maureen off, set her back, but now the sight of these books had her back on track again. Each book had a little of their past and their hope attached to it, and it would be hard to part with the brightly colored pages of trucks, trains, and spaceships, many with dates of purchase and a name written inside: *Brandon's favorite, Age 3.* There was a poetic order, she could now see, in the seemingly haphazard collection of topics and images in these books. *Here a slice of ancient Egypt brought to life with meticulous drawings, there a child's primer on human evolution. Australopithecus, Homo habilis.* They had purchased these books to transform their children into little cosmopolitan princes. But all this was too much. She considered a collection of art-history primers, which her sons never cracked open. Michelangelo and his Sistine Chapel were gathering dust, because her sons were unmoved by the hand of God touching Man.

"The child services people called this morning," Scott said behind her.

"Uh-huh."

Scott lowered Samantha to the floor and allowed her to begin walking through the room, thinking perhaps that would get his wife's attention away from the books she was sorting. There was something remarkable, and also very predictable, Scott thought, about this moment: he and his wife had been thrust into a public crisis, suffered embarrassment on television, in the newspapers, and on the Internet, and yet the essential dynamic in their marriage remained unchanged. *I'm trying to help us avoid disaster and she is still not listening.*

"Maureen, we need to focus," he insisted. "Child Protective Services got set off by the stuff about the spa. About you being at the spa alone. Apparently there's another, quote, unquote, 'wave of anger' building against us. The media found out about MindWare, and me being a software millionaire, supposedly, and how much our house is worth. Peter Goldman said they're calling us 'symbols of excess.'"

"Peter told you that?" Maureen asked, finally turning to face him. "You talked to him?"

"Yes. This morning. I called him after I talked to the child services people and that nut Ian Goller. Goller called just before his guy came out here. He said we should go to the courthouse when Araceli's hearing starts. And this time we should take the boys."

"But he said last week we didn't have to."

"Not to the trial. To a rally outside. On the same day."

"A rally? A rally against the immigrants? What for?"

"Because of the kids. Goller says it'll keep pressure on child services to leave us alone. That's why I told that guy I wanted to drop the case. Because this whole thing is getting too crazy and weird. But now I don't know. What happens if I tell the child services people the same thing I told the DA guy? That it was our fault. What do we say?"

Instead of responding, Maureen took a deep breath to gather herself, then walked over to the room's large closet and opened it. She allowed the quiet to linger, and then focused her eyes and attention on the next challenge before her: a half dozen plastic containers filled with toys. The only solution here was to order the boys to go through everything and decide what they wanted to keep and send the rest to Goodwill. *Responsibility: they are just the right age to learn a lesson about managing their living space.*

"Maureen," Scott insisted. "Please! We have to talk about this."

She turned to face him and spoke in a calm but determined voice. "Don't you understand? I'm trying to take control of our lives too." She stretched out her arms and held her palms upward and gestured around the room filled with the artifacts of their frenetic overcollecting, the stuffed shelves of make-believe objects, and the overflowing plastic, paper, and fabric inside the closet. "What we need to focus on to keep our family in one piece is in here. In these rooms. Not out there."


"I saw this woman and those two boys crossing the street on Broadway. And it was two days before they show up on the TV 'kidnapped.' I'm certain of it," Judge Adalian told the cable host from the network's Burbank studios. "I told this to the district attorney's office in very clear terms. First on the phone, and then in writing. So what do they do? They ignore me. There is no follow-up. So I insist. I'm a judge and I'm used to getting my way, I guess. They still haven't called back. I find this a bit irritating. So I called up the public defender's office and told the very nice young deputy they have working on this case. And she was very happy to hear that a municipal judge is making a statement that corroborates the defendant's version of events."

Ian Goller listened to the news in his quiet office on a Sunday afternoon and rubbed his temples and tried not to think about the Angels' pitching rotation instead, or the endangered state park at San Onofre, or any other of his usual topics of procrastination. He kept his focus on the news host as she went on to point out other tidbits of information that appeared to "tilt the scales of believability" in favor of the Mexican defendant: "the sighting of Mrs. Thompson, without her husband, at a desert spa during the alleged kidnapping," and "numerous statements by a city council member of Huntington Park, who we choose to believe," the host said sardonically, "even though he has a Mexican last name." The case against Araceli was falling apart very publicly and very quickly—or so it seemed on one cable network. Against this latest and predictably skeptical report, there was the steady flow of letters, emails, and television commentary for his office to continue its aggressive prosecution of Araceli N. Ramírez, especially now that she had been unexpectedly set free on bail. Ian Goller had countered the flow of opinion favorable to the defense with a series of incriminating leaks, including selected passages from the transcript of Brandon's description of his days in the mystery-land of Los Angeles. Ian Goller had fed these bits of info to three different reporters at a Santa Ana Denny's, and had felt oddly spent and empty afterward. Media warfare was tedious and base, but he was forced to wage it: the alternative was to allow the district attorney's office to look ridiculous, and to permit the idea that the DA was pursuing a "racially motivated prosecution" to taint the institution. The subsequent news accounts of Brandon's tales of "war," "slavery," and "bombs" had done the trick, fostering the expected reactions of suspicion and revulsion—one talk radio host asked, "Where did that animal take those boys?" The clamor would not yet die, in some venues it was growing stronger, and for this reason Goller was optimistic. His own view of the case was that a misdemeanor child-endangerment conviction was entirely fair, because of the mental suffering, albeit of a passing nature, that Araceli's actions had inflicted on the two children. He would almost certainly get a misdemeanor plea if he won at the preliminary hearing and the judge ordered her to stand trial on the felony charge—and there were several recent reforms to criminal procedures in California that aided him in that goal. Most important was an initiative recently approved by crime-weary voters that allowed police officers to give hearsay evidence at preliminary hearings, sparing the alleged victims the trauma of doing so. This new law would keep Scott Torres and Maureen Thompson and their sons out of the courtroom, which was especially fortuitous because it was clear that, despite her strong performance in her television interview, Maureen would likely fold on the stand. His lead deputy on the case, Arnold Chang, had returned from his one and only session at the couple's home shaking his head.

"Our witnesses are a bit mixed up."

"They often are," Goller said. "Such is the nature of human memory."

"No, this is worse."

"I figured it might be."

"It's bad."

"They're traumatized parents."

"No, this is worse. They don't want to go forward. They don't want us to charge this woman with anything."

"Did you tell them that the case belongs to the People now?"

"Yes."

Goller nodded that he understood. "Well, it doesn't matter really."

"Boss," his deputy said, "I'm not sure this will fly."

Assistant District Attorney Goller considered this assessment for a few moments and said, "Lucky for us, our case involves a deportable alien. So it only has to fly a little."

"How little?"

"If you toss a chicken in the air and it flaps its wings for two seconds or so, you can call that flying. Right?"


"At least, Señor Octavio, allow me the pleasure of making a salad." Araceli was cutting lettuce, slicing tomatoes in the living room, while in the kitchen Octavio Covarrubias toiled at another meal in her honor, this one to celebrate her rerelease from jail. In a bid to top his previous efforts on her behalf, and to communicate his ever-elevated respect for her immigrant martyrdom, Octavio had decided to prepare the most difficult dish he and his wife could make, the jewel of Mexican cuisine, a sauce so elaborate that he had called in his elderly aunt from the San Fernando Valley to help him prepare it. *Mole*, the chocolate nectar the Aztecs served their emperor and his court, spread over tender chicken breasts. "We spent four hours tracking down the Oaxaqueño with the best *mole* in Orange County," Octavio said. "These people are harder to find than drug dealers."

They sat for the meal, with Octavio looking expectantly at Araceli as she ate the first bite very slowly. Finally, she pronounced, "*Espectacular*. Like honey." Octavio smiled broadly, as did his wife, though the aunt did not—she seemed confused as to why her nephew and his wife were infatuated with a tall *indocumentada* who lorded over the table and spoke as if everyone were obliged to listen.

"They are probably going to deport me, one way or the other," Araceli said casually in Spanish, between bites. "That's how my lawyer explained it to me, *más o menos*. They will probably offer me a deal, where they forget about the more serious and ridiculous accusation against me and just give me a traffic ticket—like when you go through a red light. A traffic ticket for taking the boys to a dangerous place. But if I sign the paper accepting this ticket, then they will take me away. *Para el otro lado*. If I don't take the deal, I might go to *el bote* here in California for a couple of years before they send me to Mexico—that's if we lose the case. And if I win, they might still come and get me. Probably here at this house, or wherever they find me." She looked around the table to judge their reactions—Octavio lowered his thick eyebrows and gave a defiant squint, while his wife opened her eyes theatrically wide with worry.

"Can't you just run away? Just leave right now?"

"No. Because I made a promise to the people who paid my bail. That I would go to court."

"So what are you going to do?" Octavio asked.

"It seems that getting the ticket is the best deal," his wife said.

"Well, a lot of people want to see me fight it," Araceli said.

"Just to show them that our people won't be intimidated," Octavio said.

"*A fin de cuentas, se trata de la dignidad de uno*," she said, and had time to think that it been a very long time since she had used that abstract word—*dignidad*—in reference to her person. "But sometimes you have to be practical. Why suffer in those cells, where any *loca* can hit you on the head, just to prove a point? There isn't much *dignidad* in those American jails."

After the meal, Araceli was sitting alone on the porch steps, thinking about the choices she had made and how quiet the block seemed. Perhaps the neighbors had gone into hiding at the news of her return. She took in the summer stillness, the heat that was dissolving into the fiery twilight sky, the sparrows that were flittering about the jacaranda and maple trees. Just a few days earlier she had stood on the narrow cement walkway that cut through this lawn, facing the police sergeant who had come to arrest her. She was free again, at this same spot, but there was no one to photograph and memorialize her moment of liberated boredom. An ice cream vendor pushed past on the sidewalk, glancing up at Araceli and waving. A moment later, a big red pickup truck turned and pulled onto the street and parked in front of the Covarrubias home. The driver inside looked vaguely familiar.

"*¡Gordito!*" she called out, but quickly realized she didn't know him well enough to address him that way. "Felipe!"

Felipe looked both taller and wider than she remembered, and his black curls longer. He waddled up the path in white pants splattered with yellow and peach paint stains, and gave her the expectant and nervous look of an autograph seeker. *He thinks I'm a celebrity too. How funny!* He reached the porch and stood before her with his hands tucked deep into his pockets. "They told me you stayed here, on this block, but I didn't know which house. So I was going to park my truck and knock on the doors and ask around. But then I saw you sitting here."

"*¿Qué pasó?* I was waiting for you to call me. And then everything happened with the boys."

"I was going to call you, and then my uncle got us a job up in San Francisco for a week. When I got back, you were all over the television. *No lo podía creer.* I called that number you gave me three times, but they hung up."

He sat on the porch steps next to her, putting a pair of large hands on his knees and releasing a big man's exhale. An hour passed by as they talked about her arrest, and all the different television and radio shows in which her case had been covered and discussed, and what Mexico was like and how it would be for Araceli to go back there if she were forced to do so. Not having lived in Mexico since he was eight years old, Felipe had a benign vision of the place as a land where uncles and grandparents lived on *ranchos* amid cows, horses, and poultry, though he knew Mexico City was another world. "I've never been to El De Efe, but I remember Sonora as a beautiful place in the desert." Felipe had gone to school in the United States for the most part, Araceli now learned, and he spoke both English and Spanish impeccably. She prodded him to say something in English, and when he did she gave a mock shiver and said, "*¡Ay! Qué* sexy *eres* when you speak English." He was one of those people who moved easily back and forth between English- and Spanish-speaking orbits without being fully appreciated in either. With each minute they talked, Araceli heard more she liked. The sky began to surrender its glow, the lights turned on in the houses around them, and still they talked, stopping only when Luz Covarrubias stepped outside and gave them two glasses of *agua de tamarindo* and said, "*Qué bonito* to see a young man and a young woman talking so much on my porch."

Out of the awkward quiet that followed, the noise of an engine emerged, and soon Araceli and Felipe were watching as a blue van with a satellite dish turned the corner and parked behind Felipe's pickup.

"Oooh. *La prensa*," Araceli said. "*Vámonos.*"

They rose to their feet, turned, and headed for the safety of the front door, but before they could escape Araceli heard a strangely familiar voice call out with the brio and accent of Mexico City's upper classes: "*¡Araceli! ¡No te me vas a escapar! ¡No te lo permito!*"

They turned simultaneously to face a man in a midnight-blue suit and yellow tie who was sitting in the van's passenger seat, with one leg hanging outside the open door. "Where have I seen that guy before?" Felipe said, though he was instantly recognizable to Araceli. He had a Mediterranean complexion and black-brown hair that was lightly moussed, and presented a sartorial package of male refinement so striking that Araceli could already imagine the cloud of sweet musk enveloping him, even though he was still on the other side of the lawn. Then his name came to her, and she spoke it out loud, the last of the nine Spanish and French syllables coming with the rising inflection of a question.

"*¿Carlos Francisco Batres Goulet?*"

"*¡El mismo!*" he said.

He was the second-most-famous man on Mexican television, the host of a morning news-talk show produced by a network with a near-monopoly on the Mexican airwaves. He walked up the path with an outstretched hand, and Araceli straightened her spine as if to greet royalty, remembering the television set her mother had had going in the kitchen every workday, this man on the screen sitting on a studio couch engaging in casual repartee with rock stars, rebel leaders, and cabinet ministers, or in the field with the weeping families outside a mine disaster in Sonora, or wearing a yellow parka while awaiting a hurricane before the turquoise waters of the Yucatán. Carlos Francisco Batres Goulet was only a few years past thirty, but he was already a kind of walking history book, and as he reached over to shake Araceli's hand in greeting it was with the bearing of a benevolent, outgoing prince of the people.

"*Qué gusto conocerte*," he said.

"*El gusto es mío*," she mumbled back.

Carlos Francisco Batres Goulet had been in Malibu in the morning, having flown out from Mexico City to interview a Mexican actress who was a big crossover success in the United States. He had traveled to her recently purchased home, which cantilevered over a rocky stretch of the beach and the Pacific, and afterward he had phoned the network's headquarters in the San Ángel district of Mexico City to suggest an interview with the famous *paisana* who had been falsely accused of kidnapping. Now he entered the Covarrubias home with a greeting of "*¡Hola!*" and raised a palm in greeting to Octavio, who had stepped out of the bathroom with wet hands, and who now stood dumbstruck in his own living room.

"Carlos Francisco Batres Goulet?"

In a few moments, the newsman's crew began to fill the Covarrubias living room with lights and cables. Batres Goulet and his field producer had quickly decided Araceli would sit on the couch with the newsman facing her from a director's chair. With its faded purple cushions, and with the velvet painting behind it, the couch was an evocative symbol of Mexican working-class humility and bad taste, and both Batres Goulet and his producer knew the setting would resonate with their demographically diverse audience in many different ways. "You will sit here," he told Araceli in Spanish, making it sound more like an artistic inspiration than a command.

After the application of a few daubs of powder and makeup to both their faces, and a sound check, Batres Goulet began the interview. He smiled at her and addressed her with a gentle nod: "*Araceli Noemí*

*Ramírez Hinojosa,*" he said, pronouncing her two given names and paternal and maternal surnames slowly and with the formality appropriate to the reading of an encyclopedia entry, as if recognizing her admission into Mexican celebritydom. Araceli heard the four names and thought about all the places in Mexico they would be broadcast: from her mother's kitchen, to the television next to the stacks of cigarettes in the *abarrote* sundry store on the corner in Nezahualcóyotl, to her father's village in Hidalgo and the little stands with small black-and-white televisions where children and men with machetes stopped to drink *atole* and watch the news, to the breakfast restaurants of Polanco in Mexico City, where businessmen would see her as they ate their *chilaquiles.*

". . . *es usted una criminal, tal como nos dicen las autoridades del estado de California?*"

"No," she answered, her face brightening with amusement, she was not a criminal, no matter what the California authorities said. "I am just a woman who came to this country to work and to do my job," she said in Spanish. "And I ended up getting in trouble for trying to do it."

Guided by Batres Goulet's gentle but skillful questioning, she explained the circumstances that had led her to leave the house with Brandon and Keenan, including the fight between her *patrones* and the broken coffee table, details that now became public for the first time.

"It sounds like chaos, this house you worked in."

"It was only that night and that weekend. For a long time they were good people to work for. *Exigente*, yes. Everything had to be a certain way, but I didn't mind that. You can imagine what it's like to work for a *norteamericano* family with as much money as these people have, and with good taste. The food was excellent. This woman I worked for, *la señora* Maureen, she has a great eye for a tomato. And in this country, it's harder to get a good tomato than back home. That I don't understand."

The newsman laughed out loud and brought a winning smile to Araceli's face, and for a moment she had the jolly look of a Mexican everywoman. He let her go on a bit more and then brought her back to the subject at hand.

"So the moment came when you decided to leave with these boys."

Araceli now explained, because she assumed most people in Mexico would not know, how it was that the American authorities took children from parents and put them in an institution called Foster Care.

"I had to decide. Between taking care of them or calling the police. Obviously, looking back, I should have called the police. Then the parents would be in trouble instead of me. I wish I had called the police!" She said this with a volume and vehemence that was unbecoming, and that bespoke her anger at being chased by the police, tackled on film, and tossed into jail—twice—and finally beaten, all for an act of selflessness. She mentioned all these indignities to Batres Goulet, though much of her harangue was never seen by the Mexican viewing public, because Batres Goulet and his field producer would later edit the three-minute segment to make Araceli look as sympathetic as possible. Her desire to protect Brandon and Keenan had only brought her trouble, she continued, and Araceli could see now that you survived in this country with a certain kind of coldness and distance from others. This was what people said back home about the United States, and it was a cruel thing to have seen that pearl of wisdom confirmed. "I don't even really like taking care of children," Araceli said. "But what was I going to do? *Los niños no tienen la culpa.* I couldn't let them go to the place where the *norteamericanos* take lost children. No."

"Is there a message you would like to send to your family back in Ciudad Neza?" Batres Goulet asked.

"I'm sorry I haven't called," she said with a casualness that suggested she was not sorry at all. That remark too would be cut from the broadcast.

Batres Goulet left the Covarrubias home, navigating through a crowd of about one hundred people that had gathered on the lawn, spilling over onto the sidewalk and around the van. News of his presence had spread quickly through the neighborhood, causing a sort of reverse effect of the appearance of the police on the day Araceli was rearrested. As long as Carlos Francisco Batres Goulet was among them, they sensed, his perfect skin and aura of Mexican television power would protect them, and they repeated the newsman's name with the reverent tones in which one spoke of holy places and holy people. "Carlos Francisco Batres Goulet . . . Carlos Francisco Batres Goulet." When he opened the front door and stood on the porch, there was a girl scream or two, and he waved at the crowd and shook some hands, and in two minutes he was gone and in his wake people still repeated his name.

"Carlos Francisco was here! Carlos Francisco Batres Goulet!"

Thirty minutes after the crowd and their chants had dispersed, Araceli was back on the porch with Felipe. They talked and joked in the restored evening quiet about the newsman and his visit, until the moment when a sport-utility vehicle rolled up and a semi-familiar face emerged at the head of a squad of suited men. The oldest of the men pulled at his lapels as he approached the steps, then gave a distracted *"Buenas noches"* as he peeked inside the Covarrubias home. *"¿Qué se hizo Batres Goulet?"* he asked.

*"Se fue,"* Araceli answered curtly. *"¿Y quién es usted?"*

*"Soy Emilio Ordaz Rivera,"* the man said with the odd, faraway grin of someone accustomed to having his greetings rejected. *"Soy el cónsul de México en Santa Ana."*

Behind him stood three men who mimicked his general appearance, with dark sunglasses in their shirt pockets and cuff links and thin chains on their wrists, filling their tailored gray and black suits with the self-important bearing of men groomed from an early age for glory in Mexico's federal bureaucracy. They were pelted animals that had been baking all day in the California sun at a pointless community function, and judging from the ennui painted thickly on their faces, they thought these surroundings too were somehow beneath them.

"I was hoping he was still here. So I could contribute a little to the story."

"You wanted to be on television? With me?"

"Yes."

"Why?"

The consul lowered his voice and spoke in her ear, with a deliberate frankness that he thought of as a kind of intimacy. "Why does anyone want to be on Televisa? Because it's Televisa, of course."

The consul was in midcareer mire, looking for something more glamorous than Santa Ana, because he was thirty-eight years old and was losing the battle with time and the byzantine hierarchies of the Foreign Relations Ministry. A year earlier, they had offered him the number two position in the embassy in Tegucigalpa, Honduras, and like an idiot he had turned it down, because it seemed that being inside the Southern California media market would be better, but he could see now that the consul in Los Angeles got all the press, all the photo ops with the starlets and the meetings with the visiting ministers. He'd even take the number two spot in Lagos now, if they offered him that, anywhere but Santa Ana, with its long lines of desperate and poor people, where the most important thing he did was ship home the bodies of *paisanos* killed in car accidents, roofing mishaps.

Araceli did not know about the longings and insecurities of the overeducated, frustrated, poetically inclined career diplomats of the Secretaría de Relaciones Exteriores, but she could feel this man's desperation to please his superiors and to be noticed, even as she and Felipe retreated to the living room, closing the door as the consul squeezed in one last plea.

"Call me if Batres Goulet comes back!"

# 24

Araceli had told herself she wouldn't look at the crowds, and as she ascended the courthouse stairs with Ruthy Bacalan, she kept her gaze fixed downward, using a hand to shield her eyes from the sun. When she raised her head for an instant, a flash of black-and-white caught her eye, a poster of an enlarged X-ray of a skull with a rod running through the middle. There was a caption that meant to explain the image, but did not: KILLED BY ILLEGALS. She looked at the protesters grouped behind and around the X-ray and saw a tired-looking woman in a nurse's uniform holding it up, and alongside her stood a group of men and women clutching at various pieces of red-white-and-blue fabric, shouting at Araceli and shaking their fists, raising the volume because she had deigned to look at them. They carried other signs that were just words: MEXICO = DISEASE + DEATH + DESTRUCTION. They screamed "Go home!" to Araceli and also to the group of counterprotesters standing to her left, and now Araceli followed their shouts to study this other group too. Araceli recognized a few people from the gathering at the church where she had failed to give a speech, and they were all holding posters composed of a ridiculous photograph taken when she was about to be arrested for the second time. There were ten two-dimensional

Aracelis bouncing on the staircase, and she thought that she should turn and raise her finger and open her mouth in silent imitation of her pose in that impromptu portrait—that would be a good joke—but she stopped herself when she remembered she was standing on the steps of a courthouse and should respect its solemn function even though the competing bands of protesters were not. A policeman took a step toward the flag people, walking down and across the wide staircase, his arms outstretched, saying, "Keep back!" She had a moment to think how unusual that was, to have a policeman protecting her, and looked to her left when she heard someone yelling her name: a young woman was swinging a Mexican flag back and forth, and Araceli caught the eagle in the coat of arms and thought her *bandera* seemed awfully medieval next to the Stars and Stripes on the other side. As for the United States flag, she didn't understand why so many stripes and stars were crowded into such a small space. *That flag is written in English.* Both sides seemed to be held back by some invisible boundary, allowing Araceli and her attorney to advance in the wide path between them, and Araceli wondered if there was a line drawn on the steps to keep them back, like the Chinese chalk she scratched on the floor underneath the cabinets and inside the closets to keep away the ants on Paseo Linda Bonita. There were a few more students in the group of people who had come to support her, people in their twenties it seemed, their lithe frames inside bright and seductive cottons. Their expressions were wounded and aggrieved, like children who've been betrayed by alcoholic parents. Araceli thought they looked handsome and dignified next to the older and less lithe red-white-and-blue crowd, who all seemed to share the outrage and embittered superiority of good people who've been victimized by slum-born criminals.

Suddenly, the woman in the light green nurse's uniform crossed the invisible line and rushed toward her, causing Ruthy Bacalan to scream, "Hey!"

"Tell the truth!" Janet Bryson screamed a few inches from Araceli's face, and then she uttered the first complete sentence she had ever spoken in Spanish, a four-word phrase she had manufactured herself with the aid of an Internet translation program: "¡*Diga la verdad, usted!* ¡*Diga la verdad, usted!*"

Standing on the other side of the steps, Giovanni Lozano watched in outrage as the woman in green verbally assaulted his martyr-hero, and now he too crossed the invisible line and rushed toward Araceli, reaching out to push Janet Bryson away. A man of about forty in a bus driver's uniform shirt rushed forward to grab Giovanni, and in seconds the two groups had merged into a single mass of vocal cords and flexing muscles on the staircase behind Araceli and her lawyer. Ruthy Bacalan grabbed Araceli by the elbow and said, "Almost there," as they reached the top of the stairs and stepped between a grunting squad of sheriff's deputies heading down into the crowd with batons drawn, and a moment later Araceli and Ruthy entered the still quiet of the new Laguna Niguel satellite courthouse and its concrete plaza.

Surrounded by palms and a crowd of briefcases and the men and women who carried them, the building's faux-Mission architecture and terra-cotta tile roof suggested a resort where lawyers came to unwind. Araceli and Ruthy joined the line of barristers and passed through the center of three tall arches and headed toward a glass door, where a group of men and women with cameras formed a phalanx. *They've come to photograph me again*, Araceli thought, and she raised her head and gave them a good look at her *mestiza* face. But only one of the photographers stepped forward to snap her picture, with all the others looking behind her, causing her to turn to see what had caught their attention, but there was only the empty concrete plaza she had just walked through. She was vaguely disappointed and felt a brief and absurd sense of rejection. *What? There's another celebrity* mexicana *bigger than me? Who is she? A serial killer? She must have done something very, very bad.*

Araceli swung open the last set of glass doors, and she and Ruthy Bacalan stepped into the courthouse and its icy air.

**W**hen Olivia Garza was twelve, a Kern County social worker visited her home. Young Olivia was impressed by the ability of a woman armed with mere plastic credentials to put the fear of God and the law in her father, who never again got quite as drunk or angry. In the years that followed, her mother was never again forced to visit an emergency room on a Saturday night with her children in tow, leading Olivia the young woman to conclude that she wanted to become that person—a stranger who could wield the power of reason and the law over a family in their own living room. After she went to college and joined Orange County Child Protective Services, she came to realize that there were certain mothers who had seen her in their dreams long before they had met her, because they too had been girls who watched a stranger with a clipboard step into their living room. As Olivia Garza entered Paseo Linda Bonita alone for the first time, she sensed that Maureen was one of these people—it was the peculiar air of recognition and fear about her, the sense that she was being forced to repeat a very old and demeaning family ritual.

"Is it just you?" Maureen asked as she guided Olivia toward a large, long dining room table with a platter in the center. "We made you some cupcakes. The kids decorated them."

Maureen had been preparing for the scheduled arrival of the representative of Child Protective Services for two days, drafting everyone in the family but Samantha into the cleaning of the home, and then including Samantha in the final spreading of cupcake frosting and sprinkles, which allowed Maureen to announce to the social worker that "even our little girl helped with these." *El abuelo* Torres had cut the front lawn—again—Brandon swept the path, Keenan helped clean his sister's room, Scott finished the bathrooms, and Maureen had wandered into the succulent garden to pick the tiny explosions of milkweed and sow thistles. It was like the preparation for another birthday party, except that Araceli wasn't around to help this time, which left Maureen more frazzled than she would have been otherwise, and the boys sulking, because they didn't like the idea of "working," since that was something grown-ups did. "Are we slaves now?" Brandon asked his mother, who did not hear him. *If the social worker knew my mom had me sweeping,* Brandon wondered, *and that my hands will soon have blisters from holding that broom and that rake, would it get us all in trouble?*

When Olivia Garza arrived, Brandon and Keenan greeted her in the living room with freshly combed and moist hair, and their hands in their pockets, in a loose approximation of soldiers standing at attention, until their mother told them they could go to their room to read while the adults talked in the dining room. Maureen brought coffee and sat at the table next to her husband, and Olivia felt compelled to reach over and take a cupcake. "Thank you," she said. Looking at the couple and at the baby who was sitting on her mother's lap with frosting on her worm-sized fingers, Olivia Garza asked, "So, how have you been doing?"

Maureen kneaded her lips and looked down at the oak table and the Guatemalan embroidered place mats that covered the freshly polished surface, and said nothing because she was trying very hard to convey her mastery over the situation, and saying just one word about how she was "feeling" would unleash her emotions and set them off to entertain this stranger. As she blinked against the tears welling in her eyes, she did not know, or intuit, that Olivia Garza had arrived at the conclusion that this family's essential normality posed no threat to its children, and that she would soon make the final entry in the case file before formally closing it. It was a decision she'd arrived at moments earlier, in a burst of insight triggered by seeing this living room without police detectives or district attorneys for the first time. She could now *feel* this home and see it properly. And what she saw was a mother whose only crime was trying too hard.

"We're okay," Scott said finally. "Just trying to get back to normal."

There was just one topic to cover, the most recent entry in the file, and Olivia Garza jumped straight to it. It was an allegation of domestic violence related to an open case, and she had to ask.

"So, tell me a little about what happened that night with the table. With the argument you had. The argument that set all this off."

"How did you know about that?" Scott asked quickly.

"The woman who used to work here mentioned it last night on Spanish-language television." Maureen's forehead and cheeks suddenly matched the color of her daughter's blouse. "No one told you? It was on Channel 34, but I'm pretty sure it was mentioned later on cable in English."

"We've been screening calls," Maureen said.

"I imagine it's the table that used to occupy that spot right there," Olivia Garza said, pointing to an empty rectangle of tiles framed by two couches.

"I fell backwards," Maureen said.

"Because I pushed her." Scott sensed he could not lie to this woman who carried a clipboard but wrote nothing down, and who seemed to study everything with a neutral expression. If he lied, she would know, and this would send them into new and ever more tortuous predicaments.

"We were arguing," Maureen said. "It got out of hand."

"Yes."

"It's never happened before," Maureen continued. "We never had a fight like that before. He's not a violent person. It's not the way he handles things."

"I'm a programmer."

"He's a gentle person. I said things. We were just stressed out over money."

"It's not a good situation, the money."

In the course of fifteen minutes all the truth fell into the room. Scott began by laying out the details of their finances: how much they had purchased their home for, the cost of their two sons' private school, how they had spent more because of certain complications in Maureen's pregnancy, and the loss of expected income from investments that "didn't pan out." Maureen was struck by the blunt math of it all; Scott had told her these things in parts, but she had never understood it altogether, how complex and rooted their financial follies were. Together, she saw now, they suffered from a disease of outlook in a chronic and advanced stage, a bloated and myopic way of life.

Scott arrived, finally, at the argument over the garden and the moment he laid hands on his wife. "I just lost it. It was an instant. She was on the floor. The next morning we both left. Separately. I guess Araceli cleaned everything up."

"I went to the desert," Maureen said. "Alone. With my daughter." The sound of her own contrition surprised her. *No, I am conceding too much.* "But Araceli shouldn't have taken them into the city. If she had just waited a day longer."

The social worker nodded, and for the first time scribbled something on her notepad: a sentence, a phrase, a conclusion, an "assessment."

"You mind if I go talk to your boys, alone, for just a minute or two?"

Scott led Olivia Garza to the space Araceli had called the Room of a Thousand Wonders, where Keenan was on his bed reading a graphic novel modeled after a fictitious boy's diary, while Brandon read a little paperback, his stomach on the floor, though he sat up straight at the sight of the social worker.

"I'll leave you, then," Scott said.

"Thank you."

Olivia Garza greeted the boys and pointed at their bookcase. "So many books. You guys read all these?"

"Most of 'em," Brandon said.

"We had more, but Mom threw them away," Keenan said.

"No," Brandon said, giving his brother a hard look. "She gave them to the poor kids' library."

"We read a lot," Keenan said.

"Me too," Olivia Garza said. "When I went to college, I took some classes in reading, though they don't call it that there. They call it literature." The social worker mentioned some of her favorite books, including a thirteen-volume series about the fantastic misadventures of three siblings who retain their innocent spirits and optimistic outlook even as they are orphaned and wander through a cruel adult world.

"I read all those twice," Brandon said. "They're really funny."

Talking to children was the hardest thing in the world to do, and the aim in these "interviews," Olivia Garza had learned long ago, was not the soliciting of information, but rather a sounding of the waters of the subjects' moods and fears, a passive probing of their dispositions. To her practiced eye these boys communicated both intellectual curiosity and a touch of the loneliness that was entirely common in well-off families. And perhaps a little preadolescent ennui from the older one. If they had been traumatized by the flight of their parents, and their journey into Los Angeles, it was not immediately apparent.

"What are you reading now?" she asked Brandon. He showed her the cover of the paperback and then handed it to her in the same way a teenager surrenders a pack of cigarettes to a school principal. "Wow, a classic. This is an advanced book for your age."

"I'm a pretty good reader."

"But do you understand everything that's in it?"

"About eighty percent. No, ninety. When I get to a part I don't get, I just pretend the words don't exist."

"Interesting."

"That way I keep going."

"I should learn to do that."

"It's like the best book I've ever read. It's really real. Next to that, everything else I've read sounds kind of phony."

Olivia was holding the book and leafing through it when Maureen appeared at the doorway, holding Samantha and trying too hard to project an air of motherly nonchalance.

"Is everything okay?" she said with a smile.

"Yes, yes. We were just talking about the book Brandon was reading. What page did you say you were on, Brandon?"

"Ninety-three."

"Do you mind if I borrow this for a second? I'll give it right back, I promise."

Olivia Garza said goodbye to the boys and left the Room of a Thousand Wonders with Maureen.

"Is everything okay?" Maureen repeated when they reached the living room, because she sensed they were not.

The social worker held open the book to page ninety-three and gave it to her. "I'm not sure he's quite old enough for this. And especially passages like this one."

Maureen took the copy of *The Catcher in the Rye*, a book she had never read, though she knew the name of its protagonist. The social worker's thick index finger had been resting on a page where Holden Caulfield was using the cool slang of the middle of the last century, smoking cigarettes and preparing to talk to a prostitute: "She was sort of a blonde, but you could tell she dyed her hair. She wasn't any old bag, though." Just a few pages later the protagonist was talking to her pimp, arguing with the man, the narrator's voice suggesting the casualness and loose morality of an ancient American era.

"Oh, my God. Why is he even reading this? Where did he get this?"

Maureen held the book and looked at the representative of Child Protective Services, and felt the weight of a judgment that was at once holy and official. Her shame deepened when she realized that the social worker had discovered this transgression after just fifteen minutes of conversation with her son. COUNTY OF ORANGE, said the official seal on the social worker's plastic badge: three pieces of the eponymous fruit rested in a green field that itself was nestled inside the center of a sun ablaze with a corona of dancing yellow arms, and for an instant that seal was as disturbing as those dusty old icons of Saint Patrick in her Missouri home, the ones with the snakes at his feet and flames around his head. Her eleven-year-old was consorting with pimps and prostitutes, having been transported to a seamy corner of Manhattan via the art of fiction, and he was doing so in Maureen's very house, in her very presence. *Because I am not really looking at him. I am not here in the room with him.* Now the saints that looked after the Irish and the County of Orange both knew this secret.

"I'm so sorry. I'm so sorry," Maureen said, directing her words not just to the social worker but to everyone she knew. "I thought I was in control of everything. I thought I had it all under control."

*Underneath all the order and beauty around me, things are not as they should be. I've glossed it all over so it doesn't look like Pike County, but underneath everything is just as frayed as that old couch in our living room, as those unpolished and splintering floors.* She felt foolish for expending so much effort uselessly, and when she thought of herself puttering around this living room amid its leather, oak, and wool, she felt an empty sorrow, as if she were standing at the beginning of a dirt path that led back to the places she had run away from. "I'm so sorry." She plopped herself down on the sofa, still carrying Samantha on her hip. She wanted to cry, but could not. Instead she sat there, defeated, and thought about how Brandon had betrayed her, and that she shouldn't be surprised, because he was a man, after all: and then she stopped herself from thinking that, because he was eleven years old and that was absurd. *This is why women go crazy. We live with men who act like boys and boys who want to be men, and we're trapped between what we know is right and what little we can do, between what we can see and what's invisible to us. It's all impossible.* She shook her head and mumbled the word out loud. "Impossible."

"It's not really that big of a deal," Olivia Garza said, reaching into her purse and handing Maureen a tissue from the large supply she carried.

Maureen realized now that there were tears in her eyes. She wiped her face and began to speak, in a voice that was eerily steady. "We are going to change."

"Excuse me?" Olivia Garza said.

"We're moving. To a smaller house."

"Maureen," Scott said. He wanted to stop his wife before she went too far, because she always took things too far.

"We're going to put our kids in public school. In another city." It was a necessary sacrifice, Maureen thought. A surrender. A defeat. They would leave their Eden, and that would be a fair punishment. "If they go to public school, if we live in a smaller house, how much will we save? Twenty, thirty thousand a year? No, more. Right?"

"Yes," Scott said. He felt defeated seeing his wife like this—fighting off tears one moment, and then telling a stranger about a new beginning the next. *I am responsible for this.* In a few weeks or months, when they were living at another house, she would come to the same conclusion, regret all the things she had said, and find a way to blame him for it.

"Well, that sounds all very positive to me," Olivia Garza said. "But don't worry. We don't take away kids because their parents let them read Salinger." She allowed herself a hearty, big woman's laugh. "I really just thought you should know what he's reading. I think it's just the tone—that's what he likes about it. He told me he just skips over the parts he doesn't understand. The rebellious tone. Get ready. Puberty hits earlier these days."

Scott led her to the door, and after what he hoped was a final handshake, the social worker pulled him close and spoke in a low, furtive voice.

"You have nothing to worry about," she said.

"What?"

"I'm not supposed to say this, but I will: my office won't bother you anymore. And no one else can or will. Not the sheriff or the DA. No one."

"Really?"

She took a moment to size up Scott with her large eyes, wondering if he could be trusted with the information. "Go about your lives. But I never said it. You didn't hear it from me."

"We're free and clear? Why are you are telling me?"

"You're a smart guy, Torres," she said, rolling the *r* in his surname suggestively. "I'm sure you'll figure it out."

It was another mystery, like how to cut a lawn cleanly, or the rules of the stock market, and Scott wondered if he'd ever understand. For the moment, he decided he'd keep it a secret, even from Maureen.

The following morning Child Protective Services issued a two-sentence press release concerning "the events surrounding two children at a home on Paseo Linda Bonita in the Laguna Rancho Estates." "CPS has investigated this matter," the release said, "and has closed the case without further action." The memo was transmitted to news agencies via the press office at the Board of Supervisors, falling into the reporters' mail slots along with releases from other agencies announcing the

unemployment figures, the number of county residents receiving public assistance, and the upcoming celebration of Orange County Weights
and Measures Day. By then only a few dedicated scribes noticed or cared,
and just one penned a news brief that appeared alongside the summa-
ries of traffic accidents and robberies in the Orange County daily newspaper. The minds and eyes of the reporters on the county beat had been
spirited away by another drama, playing out on four channels of the
county press room's cable television hookup. This new story involved a
single missing child and had begun to unfold the previous afternoon in
Stanton at about the same time Olivia Garza was leaving the Torres-
Thompson home and Araceli Noemí Ramírez Hinojosa was sitting before
a judge inside the Laguna Niguel satellite courthouse. The protagonists
were a missing eight-year-old girl in a Hello Kitty blouse and her stepmother, an elementary school teacher, and the supporting cast included
crews of divers searching the bottom of a lake. It was a case whose
cruelty and gruesomeness would invite no ambiguity, uniting a city in a
sense of tragedy and revulsion once the child's body was found.

The dead girl had four siblings whose custody would soon become
Olivia Garza's concern, along with the fate of the level one caseworker
who had visited the trailer park where the girl lived twice the year before to investigate several anonymous complaints. Olivia Garza fired the
caseworker herself, and visited the siblings in their Foster Care homes
several times. Many weeks later, after her role in that horrific case had
ended, Olivia Garza remembered her pleasant visit with the Torres-
Thompson boys on Paseo Linda Bonita and how she had reencountered
*The Catcher in the Rye* again, after twenty years. She read the book on
her first Saturday afternoon off and decided, belatedly, that it was probably okay for a bright eleven-year-old to read.

# 25

The ants marched in from their hidden nests in the soil outside and every day they conquered new territories of tile, particleboard, and porcelain. They gathered in pulsating masses around pieces of chicken underneath the dining room table, over the toilet paper in the bathroom trash cans, and inside the kitchen sink, carrying away whatever it was that settled at the bottom of the garbage disposal. As the number of days without Araceli in their home grew, Maureen came upon more fresh swarms each morning, when Scott was still snoring in the last few minutes of post-dawn coolness, with Samantha awake and in her mother's arms, drinking her first bottle of the day. At first Maureen assaulted the insects with water and soap, simply smothering them with wet sponges and paper towels, reclaiming the kitchen and other spaces a square foot at a time, washing both their corpses and their still-slithering bodies down the drain. Within a day the effectiveness of this fight back diminished and the swarms returned in their original ferocity. The ants appeared next in the bedrooms and garage, and in the kitchen there were always two or three ant scouts on the counter where she prepared meals, probing in every direction in an odd shuffle, until she killed them with a squeeze of her fingers. *How did Araceli keep the ants away?*

The ants triggered memories of the time before Araceli worked for

them, in that first year in the Paseo Linda Bonita home, when the trails
the insects forged into the kitchen during a summer-long siege led
Maureen to briefly consider moving out. It was her helplessness before the ants that had finally convinced Maureen she should hire a
housekeeper, and she had gone through various women who struggled
with the insects as much as Maureen did, until she found Araceli. Now
Maureen suspected that Araceli had secretly applied some potent and
probably illegal Third World insecticide to defeat the ants, deciding on
her own to disobey Maureen's admonition not to use chemical poisons.
For a day or two Maureen searched cabinets and shelves in the kitchen,
laundry room, and garage for the bottle or can that contained this magic
potion, but she could not find it. Araceli had defeated the ants, Maureen finally concluded, merely by being extremely vigilant, by never flag-
ging in the disciplined daily upkeep of all the ant-prone surfaces of
the home, by never allowing garbage to accumulate, or spills to linger.
Maureen did not have the energy to imitate this behavior, nor did her
new domestic helper, her father-in-law. The old man cooked, he looked
after the children—sort of—and made the beds, but he would not clean
the floors, no matter how many hints Maureen dropped. *Probably he
thinks mopping a floor is women's work.*

Maureen finally mopped the kitchen, bathroom, and living room
floors herself one night, with Samantha asleep and Scott reading stories
to the boys in their bedroom, and for a moment she felt renewed by the
fake-lemon scent of disinfectant and the wet gleam of clean tile. As she
leaned into the mop Maureen noted the presence of fading chalk lines
along the base of several walls and wondered if Araceli had placed them
there for some reason, and what those lines could mean. They were like
crop circles, an apparition with mysterious and alien meanings, and another example of Araceli's many minor imprints on the household landscape, like her decision to save instant-coffee powder in the refrigerator,
or to leave basil leaves in a bowl of water by the kitchen window. *Basil?
Is that some sort of cure? But for what?* Maureen wiped out the chalk lines
with the same desperate insistence that a student uses in erasing an
incorrect math equation on a chalkboard.

When Maureen awoke the morning after her first assault with the
mop, it was with the anticipation of ant-free surfaces. Instead she found
a new trail entering the kitchen through one of the light fixtures and
splitting into two branches, one crossing the room to the pantry, where

the ants were devouring a loaf of stale French bread. Yet another trail entered from the backyard underneath one of the sliding glass doors, across the former path of one of Araceli's chalk lines, and Maureen followed it to the remains of a dead grasshopper that had somehow been trapped behind one of the bookcases. *This is more than I can take.* She could not look at the sickening nodes of their dirt-colored bodies a moment longer. Several times a day, she felt one or two crawling on her legs and arms, racing for her neck and breasts, and she fantasized about finding their colony's nest, and bringing some cataclysmic destruction upon it that would end ant culture and ant history on this hillside. Finally, that afternoon, she stood in a supermarket aisle she always tried to avoid, and purchased two different cans of poison. When she got home she was so desperate to see the chemicals work that she didn't bother to get the children out of the house before she began spraying.

In the evening Maureen had rearmed herself with the spray can, determined to find any ant scouts or trails that had escaped her initial offensive, and was wandering the various rooms of the house when the phone rang.

Scott answered in the kitchen. "Hello, Mr. Goller," he said, and Maureen listened, watching as he spoke in profile, either unaware or unconcerned that she was eavesdropping.

"No. We're not going to do that . . . We really don't want to be there. No. We've made our statements . . . You go ahead and do that, and we'll be there if you force us to. And you know what: we're pretty clear on exactly what happened . . . Meaning that we left separately and didn't . . . If you'd just let me finish . . . Well, I guess you could say that, but I'm past being embarrassed now . . . No, neither will my wife . . . Right . . . Child Protective Services was already here . . . It was a very nice visit . . . Well, I got the distinct impression we don't have anything to worry about . . . I'm sorry, Mr. Goller . . . I think that would be an injustice, Mr. Goller. Supremely unfair, for reasons that should be clear without me having to say why . . . I understand what the laws are, yes . . . I have to go, Mr. Goller . . . Kids, you know, and dinner . . . Goodbye, Mr. Goller . . . Goodbye."

For the first time since that night he'd pushed her, Maureen allowed her eyes to settle and linger upon her husband. He was as exhausted as she was, but also completely in the present, his eyes pale brown embers giving off the same serene and low-burning glow of a woman in the days after childbirth. *Men don't often look like that.* Scott had somehow understood, from one moment to the next, that they were no longer at the mercy of the melodramatic machinery of the media and the criminal justice system. It had hit him, Maureen sensed, with a eureka suddenness and intensity, like the solution to a programming conundrum. *These prosecutors and bureaucrats have no power over us. None. Because we haven't done anything wrong. We're just as innocent as Araceli. Aren't we?* Every so often her husband did something brilliant like this, shifting his thinking as easily as he might shift his posture or his feet, finding a solution suddenly falling into his arms, simply because he'd stepped out of the box of a problem and examined it in an entirely different light. *That's something he can do that I cannot.*

Looking at him, she began to see the possibility that the original, simple, and indefinable feelings that drew her to him might return.

"Is it over now?" she asked.

"I think it is."

"Really?"

"I don't think he'll be calling us again."

"Thank God."

She was still holding the yellow can whose steel skin was emblazoned with drawings of bugs and a thousand words of warning in minuscule fonts.

After several visits to courtrooms, police stations, and jailhouses, Araceli now understood that Americans associated justice with two dominant architectural styles: the austere cement cubes where walls, floors, ceilings, and passageways blended into a single smooth surface; or the woody hominess of dark paneling that suggested shadowy forests of mystery. This new Laguna Niguel satellite courthouse had a bit of both, and the mood was as somber as those other places, despite the presence of large Latino families with children sitting on some of the benches in the hallways and playing with toy cars and dolls. The look on the faces of the mothers and wives said, *This is where I come to say goodbye to my viejo. Adiós, pendejo, and yeah, I'll look after the kids, because what the fuck else can I do?* This was a place, Araceli understood, where the damned were released temporarily from their dungeons to intermingle with the undamned. The presence of the inmate fathers and brothers in their shackles and jumpsuits sent everyone around them into a funk. The gloom was there to see in the faces of the mothers and the daughters, the judges and the lawyers, including Deputy District Attorney Arnold Chang and Ruthy Bacalan, who had lost the sheen of pregnancy on her cheeks and looked older somehow as she took a seat with Araceli at a table before the judge. There was sadness too in the look of pained exertion on the face of the first witness of Araceli's preliminary hearing, a police officer she had never met before.

Deputy Ernie Suarez was not dressed in police clothing as he sat in the witness box, but rather in jeans and a collared short-sleeve cotton shirt that revealed his rather excessive musculature. He wore a small loop earring that was meant to convey masculinity, but whose effect, Araceli decided, was completely the opposite. Only the badge on his belt identified him as a member of the tribe of law enforcement.

"You are, at the moment, working?" the prosecutor asked by way of explanation.

"Yes."

"Are you working as what they call an 'undercover' officer at the moment?"

"Yes, sir."

"What is this, 'undercover'?" Araceli whispered to Ruthy. It didn't sound good.

"I'll tell you later."

"At the time of the incident involving the Torres-Thompson children, you were a patrol officer assigned to the Laguna Rancho area, correct?"

"Yes."

Guided by the prosecutor's questions, Deputy Suarez proceeded to tell the story of his arrival at Paseo Linda Bonita, of the "distraught" state in which he found Maureen and Scott, and his search of their home for clues of the boys' whereabouts, and how Maureen paced and held the baby.

"Had the defendant left any communication of any kind with the parents?"

"We didn't find any note or message of any kind, sir, no."

"So the parents had no idea where their children were?"

"That's correct, sir. And they were pretty shaken up about it."

Listening to the deputy, Araceli saw the events inside the home on Paseo Linda Bonita that day through the eyes of Maureen and Scott for the first time. Her employers were adrift and afraid in that orderly house Araceli had left behind for them. *I cleaned the sinks before I left, but I didn't think of the most obvious thing: to leave behind a note. I made a mess of things as much as they did.*

As the court session moved on, Araceli could see the prosecutor was building a tale of foreboding around her acts of naïveté and stupidity. The deputy district attorney was a short man in boxy, scuffed black shoes, and a tie that was knotted too loosely. Now he began to fiddle with a computer and a projector, and raised a screen inside the empty jury box. An image appeared on the screen, a video from a Union Station surveillance camera that showed Araceli, Brandon, and Keenan, seen from an eye high above the waiting area, the shiny floors reflecting the atrium daylight into an odd glare, so that Araceli and the boys stood in a menacing glow. The prosecutor had a sheriff's detective state the video's provenance and act as narrator. "The defendant enters the frame at one forty-five p.m. . . . You can see the victims walked in after her . . ."

"Were you able to determine if the two boys have any relatives in the vicinity of that station?"

"To the best of our knowledge, they have no relative within thirty miles of the station."

The video representation of Araceli turned her head in several directions, mulling which direction to take as the boys studied the high ceilings above them. Video Araceli walked away and out of the range of the camera without saying anything to them and they followed after her. Araceli looked at that footage and saw what everyone else did: an impatient woman who never wanted to take care of children, who rushed out of the home without leaving a note because she was too anxious to be rid of them. The video doomed her. *Am I really that selfish and mean?* But how had she allowed herself to be placed in such a predicament in the first place? *You are going the wrong way, woman! Go back to the house and wait!* Why was she always at the mercy of other people? Seeing this stupid woman projected on the screen, Araceli felt an impotent rage that made her want to stand up and shout in Spanglish, *I am a pendeja! Looking for the grandfather? ¡Pendeja!* But she said nothing, and slumped back in her chair suddenly and folded her arms, and shook her head with silent violence. "What's wrong?" Ruthy Bacalan asked. *They are going to put that woman in the video back in jail and then send her home with plastic ties around her wrists because she is a callous sim-pleton.* Araceli fought to hold back the water welling behind her eyes; she couldn't let these people see her cry. *Now I understand why there are all these boxes of tissues in the courtroom.* There was one box on the table before her, another perched on the railing where the witnesses stood, two more in the empty seats of the jury box. *People come to cry here. To see their follies projected on a screen, and then to weep.*

The prosecutor turned off the video, the deputy left the courtroom, and the next witness entered the courtroom.

Detective Blake marched down the gallery aisle like a middle-aged man in a hurry, rose to the stand, said "Yeah, I do" in response to the oath, and plopped down into the witness chair. He was soon asked to relate Brandon's tale of his journey with Araceli.

"The neighborhood this boy described to you," the prosecutor began. "Would you say it bore a general resemblance to the neighborhood near the intersection of Thirty-ninth and South Broadway?"

"Very general. Yes."

"What did Brandon tell you about that place?"

"That it was dirty and grimy. That a lot of people came and went there. That he heard a man screaming. That he slept on the floor, next to a child who was a slave, or an orphan, or something like that."

"On the floor, next to an orphan?"

"Yes."

"Did he say anything about seeing people with scars on their faces?"

"Yes."

When the prosecutor had finished, Ruthy Bacalan rose to begin her cross-examination. She was dressed in her own idiosyncratic version of summer courtroom dress: a white jacket with gold-braided epaulets on the shoulders, and wide white pants and white sandals, an outfit that suggested she had come to represent a defendant being brought on trial before the captain of a luxury cruise liner.

"Generally speaking, during the hour or so you spent with Brandon, did he seem frightened to you?" she asked the detective.

"No."

"Did he appear intimidated by his experience with the defendant?"

"No. Probably the opposite."

"The opposite?"

"Yeah, he seemed like he was having fun telling his story. It was all sort of, uh, fantastical to him. 'Magical' is the word, I guess."

"And how much of that story were you able to verify?"

"Excuse me?"

"Did you make any effort to find out how much of Brandon's story was true? For example, did you find anyone who looked like they had been through a war, like the, quote, 'refugees' Brandon mentioned?"

"You mean, did we find the war refugees Brandon told us about?"

"Yes."

"No." For the first time, the detective dropped his guard and grinned. "Didn't know where to start looking for them."

"Brandon also mentioned something about time travel. In a train."

"Yes."

"Able to verify that?"

"We punted on the time travel, ma'am."

From her chair, Araceli felt the mood in the courtroom turning light, inconsequential. The judge rolled his eyes—twice! *My Ruthy is winning!* The prosecutor was starting to look ill, he was grabbing the table before him with two hands, as if the building were shifting, very slowly, and the floor of the courtroom were suddenly afloat and tossed about by rough seas. "Brandon said his brother had been, quote, 'holding fire,' unquote. Did you find any burns on Keenan Torres-Thompson's hands?"

"No, ma'am."

"Did you find any fires burning underneath the surface of the earth?"

"Excuse me."

"It's in the statement. Brandon says he saw a fire burning in the ground."

"There was a pig cooked, apparently. At the home in Huntington Park."

"And what about the, quote, superhero? Mr. Ray Forma?"

"We were able to ascertain, to a high degree of certainty, that there have been no sightings of any such man."

On the bench, the judge gave a bemused smirk that matched the one on the face of the detective.

"No further questions, Your Honor."

Ray Forma sounded like a stage name to Araceli. There was a student she knew in art school who worked as a clown for children's parties and called himself Re-Gacho. "Really Uncool" was a typical Mexico

City clown who amused and annoyed in equal measures, harassing the moms with double entendres that their kids didn't understand. Yes, Re-Gacho would fit perfectly in this courtroom, where even the bailiff looked grateful for the brief levity of superheroes and time machines at the end of a day of slogging through the calendar. Cover the oak with red and yellow streamers, bring out the balloons, and put a big top hat on the judge. *Qué divertido.*

"The People rest, Your Honor," the prosecutor said, causing the judge's face to come alive again with a sparkle of astonishment. The judge was a balding man with a sallow complexion and a fringe of white hair: up until that moment, he had maintained a temperament of studied even-ness and congeniality. The judge considered the seated prosecutor for an instant, and then his face collapsed into a mask of disapproval, as if the exit doors had been thrown open inside a darkened theater, inter-rupting a bad movie and revealing the sticky, trash-strewn aisles.

"That's it?"

"Yes, Your Honor."

"Ms. Bacalan. I see you have one witness," the judge said after a pause. "Is he here, by any chance?"

"No, Your Honor. I didn't anticipate the prosecutor cutting short his witness list."

"Right. So, tomorrow at nine a.m.?"

"Yes, Your Honor," Ruthy and the prosecutor said in unison.

Sitting in the last row of the gallery with his legs crossed, Assistant District Attorney Ian Goller fixed a dagger stare at Madame Weirdness, the Mexican woman who could make his life easier by making the ra-tional choice and taking the plea bargain. In his desire to avoid defeat he had assembled a squad of attorneys and investigators dedicated to keeping alive the machinery of case AB5387516, in the hope that he would eventually pressure this stubborn woman to accept the inevita-ble. But as he watched the defendant leaving the courtroom behind her attorney, Ian Goller realized she would not give up. Araceli Ramírez was a Mexican national with nothing going for her but a strong work ethic, apparently, and lived unaware of her powerlessness relative to your average American-born resident of Orange County. She owned no prop-erty and had no social security number or credit rating, but walked past him like an exiled empress in denim and sneakers because she inhab-ited another, Spanish-speaking reality where those things didn't matter, a world of people happy with the plebeian pleasures of hurdy-gurdy music and pickup trucks. The assistant district attorney knew, in fact, that there was a pickup with a driver waiting for the defendant in the parking lot. Goller had that information thanks to the investigator he'd assigned to track her movements—an egregious misuse of scarce resources—but the assistant district attorney only now realized how unhealthy his obsession with this case had become. Could it ever be a bad thing to want to win, Goller wondered, when the side you were on was called *the People*? He wanted this woman to make the rational calculation of a defeated American criminal, but of course she would not. His experience with the Mexicans that crossed his path was that they expected the worst and were immovable once they latched on to the idea that the DA's plea offers were the ploy of English-speaking grifters. Thinking of all of this, Ian Goller slipped into a depression, because Araceli's surrender was the only path to victory in the case.

Maybe he should just go hit the waves and cuddle with the moving water and its shifting shapes, with its power to lift a man and make him fly.

Assistant District Attorney Goller was in the parking lot, opening the trunk of his car and confirming the presence of his wet suit and mini board in the back when his phone beeped with another text message: his investigator was following the defendant from the parking lot and was wondering whether to continue surveillance.

*No*, the assistant district attorney wrote back.

He saw *The People v. Araceli N. Ramírez* more clearly now. It was unusual to be burdened at this relatively late stage with so many bad facts: the parents caught in contradictions, the paper trail of their lies, and the older boy and his elaborate fantasies. In the name of efficiency they usually tossed unwinnables like this one out the door. And yet there was still the march of institutional logic, the overwhelming likelihood the judge would order the defendant to stand trial, adding the passage of time to the equation. It would be four months, at least, until the trial: that kind of time often worked wonders, since it brought into play the predilection of defendants to muck up their lives. The defendant might run afoul of the law while free on bail, allowing her to be arrested on another, unrelated charge. Or they might get their deal. If none of those things happened, there would always be another illegal immigrant to arrest and try in another high-profile case, eventually, inevitably. The math suggested it would happen again soon, though it was hard to imagine a case as perfect and full of possibility as two handsome boys spirited away by their humorless Mexican nanny.

Ian Goller had closed the trunk of his car and was contemplating the best route to the sea when his phone chattered again with the announcement of another text message.

Araceli did not notice the assistant district attorney as she left the courtroom and entered a hallway filled with people in sagging, end-of-the-summer day clothes. She walked a step behind Ruthy Bacalan, who was talking into a cell phone, and then into a long corridor where a man and a woman were walking toward them, backs and heels first—after a moment, Araceli saw they were two photographers aiming lenses at a subject, walking backward as the subject walked toward them, as if walking backward were the most natural thing in the world.

The smart-stepping photographers tangoed in reverse past Araceli and Ruthy and suddenly the two women were alone with the subject, a sapphire-eyed man with a light, sun-kissed complexion and a wheatfield of hair that looked as if it had been born on van Gogh's palette on one of the painter's sunnier mornings. He was an A-list movie star, internationally recognized and swooned over, and he was in the courthouse to testify at and savor the trial of an annoying paparazzo. The sight of the A-list star caused both Ruthy Bacalan and Araceli to stop in the center of the hallway to admire him. Suddenly he spotted Araceli and stopped his advance down the hallway.

"Hey, I know you," he said to Araceli. He reached out, shook her hand, and said, "I've been following your case."

"¿De veras?"

"I have." He smiled, spectacularly, and then added, "And I just want to say, good luck to you, señorita," in a voice that seemed a conscious imitation of Jimmy Stewart or Cary Grant or some other star of a bygone age, and in a moment he was bygone too, headed down the hallway to Department 186B to witness the sentencing of a man who would hound the beautiful people of Laguna Beach, Brentwood, and Bel Air no longer.

"Wow," Ruthy said, with a hand at her chest.

"Sí, wow," Araceli agreed.

He left them in a trance as they followed the hallway to the door and the concrete plaza outside and its long-shadowed brightness. None of the distracted newspeople standing in the center of the plaza had noticed that Araceli was walking among them. Five of them were gathered in a semicircle, talking to one another and contemplating the black slabs they held in their raised palms, as Hamlet had the skull of his poor friend Yorick, summoning news of a tragedy with their thumbs. A girl's body was being pulled out of a suitcase in the lake, her stepmother had been arrested, and Ian Goller was speeding toward the scene. The newspeople were all wondering where they would be deployed next, because it was an all-hands-on-deck moment, but Araceli did not know this and assumed that they had simply grown bored with her, and she gave herself a moment to think about how fickle they were, how short their attention spans. None of them had been present to see Ruthy in her white nautical outfit destroy the prosecution in Department 181.

Araceli parted company with Ruthy and made her way to the parking lot, where Felipe was waiting for her. He'd been there for four hours, waiting, sitting in the cab of his truck with a pad of paper and a pencil, drawing, and he tossed the pad into the back of the cab as soon as she approached. They drove back to Santa Ana, and she told him about how Ruthy had taken apart the prosecution, and when they reached the Covarrubias home he walked her to the front door and said goodbye in a very chaste way, as if he were holding back other, deeper things he wanted to express but was too afraid to say. There was something that was supposed to happen next between them, and Araceli wondered if he would allow that thing to be.

"¿Mañana? At the same hour?" he asked.

"Yes. But only if you want to."

"I do. I really do. I don't have any work now—things are slowing down. But even if I did have to work, I would be here, *porque es importante.*"

"*Hasta mañana entonces.*"

"*Hasta mañana.*"

*This is a formal, too-polite parting, filled with unspoken yearnings, like in the villages back home,* Araceli thought, and she reached out for his hand. Their fingers lingered together long enough for her to inhale and exhale once, very slowly, and in that moment Araceli felt infinitely more electricity pass through her skin than when the A-list movie star had touched the same hand.

# 26

On the morning of Araceli's second day in court the large crowds of protesters had disappeared from the front steps of the courthouse. In their place there was Janet Bryson, alone, scanning the street and the parking lot for the friends she had made yesterday, at first perplexed by their absence and then, finally, disappointed by their lack of resolve. "They said they would be here," she said to herself aloud, and when the defendant in *The People v. Araceli N. Ramírez* appeared at the bottom of the steps with another Mexican, Janet Bryson barely noticed, because she was so upset with the unpunctuality and flakiness of her fellow Californians. *What are they doing that's so important that they can't be here? What's on their televisions that's so captivating; what excuses about traffic will they concoct?* Araceli walked up the steps with Felipe and didn't see Janet Bryson. The shouting woman of the day before had dissolved into the background for Araceli, because at the bottom of the stairs Felipe had reached over to take her hand.

Felipe had wrapped his fingers around Araceli's suddenly, instinctively, because he was swept up by the emotion of leading his new friend into a courthouse, which he thought of as a place where people went to disappear and never come back. They could take Araceli away and send her to one of those prisons in the desert, in faraway valleys where people trekked to visit incarcerated fathers and brothers on pathetic road trips where an ice cream for the kids at Burger King on the way back was supposed to make it all better. Felipe had suffered such trips to see his older brother—who was still in that prison, thirteen years later—and when he reached over to take Araceli's hand, it was to comfort himself as much as her. He knew she was someone special and brilliant whose freedom and future were under threat. They walked up the stairs with palms joined for twenty-four steps and thirty-eight paces to the door with the metal detector, until he let go and allowed her to enter the court building alone, and said, "*Te espero en el* parking lot, just like yesterday."

Inside the paneled courthouse, the proceedings resumed with Ruthy Bacalan rising to her feet and announcing, "We call Salomón Luján, Your Honor." The Huntington Park city councilman entered the courtroom, in black denim jeans and a thick leather belt whose bronze buckle bore the initials SL. His nod to the formality of the courtroom was a freshly ironed plaid shirt with mother-of-pearl buttons, and boots polished so that they resembled the skin of the oak table on Paseo Linda Bonita. Once on the stand he recounted the phone call that brought Araceli Ramírez to his home, and the arrival of the defendant and her two charges at her front door. "She told me she was looking for their grandfather," he said in moderately accented English, "because the mother and father had abandoned her in the house, alone, with two *gringuitos*," he said.

"With two what?" the judge interrupted.

"Sorry. I mean with two little American children."

"And did these children you saw," Ruthy asked quickly, "did they seem to be well taken care of?"

"Yes. They look a little tired. But this lady, Araceli, she was in charge. Their hair was long, but she made them comb it. She was taking care of them, yes." After asking Luján to recount how Brandon, Keenan, and Araceli had all slept in his daughter's room—"She's the one going to Princeton, correct?"—and having Luján confirm that he was a member of the Huntington Park City Council, Ruthy moved to the moment at which Araceli fled his home, alone.

"Did she tell you why she was leaving?"

"Yes. Because of the immigration."

"She was afraid because she felt she might be detained for her immigration status?"

"Yes."

"And when she left, did she leave the children in your care?"

"Yes. She could see, on the television, that their mother and father were back home. So she didn't need to take care of them anymore."

"And you had them until the police arrived?"

"Yes."

"Nothing further, Your Honor."

Arnold Chang said he didn't have any questions for the councilman—the prosecutor seemed as eager as Araceli to be out of the courtroom.

"The defense rests, Your Honor," Ruthy said.

"Any affirmative defense or motions?" the judge asked.

"Motion to dismiss based on insufficiency of the evidence," Ruthy said. "I would like to be heard, Your Honor."

"Go ahead."

Araceli watched and listened as Ruthy rose to her feet again and launched into a spirited monologue directed at the judge and, with the occasional sidelong glance, at the prosecutor. "It strikes us as a misuse of prosecutorial power to file charges against the only adult in the household who acted responsibly," Ruthy said. She sometimes held her belly in her palm as she spoke, and she leaned on the lectern once or twice as she described Araceli's attempts to find a safe place for the children first with their grandfather, and then in a "traditional home with a respectable family" in Huntington Park. "Clearly," she concluded, "these are the actions of an adult who's taken the responsibility of caring for two children seriously." When she finished she plopped back down into her chair, and all the men in the courtroom seemed relieved that she did, because it seemed she might go into labor if she kept on talking.

"And the People?" the judge asked.

Now Arnold Chang stood up and began using the same legalisms Ruthy had pronounced, but with a dismissive tone, as if firing tennis balls back across the net. "The facts in evidence establish the vulnerability that is at the essence of the endangerment statute," he said, and

Araceli wrinkled her brow at him because despite his at times abstract and difficult English, the meaning of what he was saying was clear in his flustered, strained brow, and the way he stretched out his arm in Araceli's direction to make a point. "The vulnerability need not be an actual physical threat, but may also include a looming emotional threat over the psyche of the victims. The People argue that the disturbing nature of the journey undertaken by the defendant with the two minor children, into an area of persistent physical dangers, all thanks to the poor decisions of the defendant, falls within the definitions of the statute."

After the prosecutor had stopped and returned to his seat, the judge leaned back into the cushions of his swivel chair and said, "Well, then." Araceli understood that it was now his turn to decide the next stop on her journey through these buildings and their rooms of concrete and wood paneling. He rubbed his bald head vigorously with both hands, in what felt like some odd judicial ritual, then looked at a clock on the wall. He allowed the second hand to advance in its circular motion and kept on looking as it reached the six at the bottom and swung back and began climbing again toward the twelve, leading Araceli to wonder if he was peering into the clock's face and studying it for a message only he could discern. Finally, he turned to the lawyers.

"I'm going to grant your motion, Ms. Bacalan."

This short statement was followed by a long silence whose contours Araceli did not fully appreciate, because she did not know what "motion" meant, precisely, in this context. *Motion.* Moción. *Something is moving. The judge will allow something to move. Me? Do I move? But to where?* The prosecutor sat up straight, as if preparing to launch into new arguments, while Ruthy leaned back in her chair and gave her pen a jaunty twirl between her fingers.

Addressing the prosecutor, the judge said, "You're not even anywhere near a preponderance of evidence."

"I respectfully disagree, Your Honor."

"Well, you can make a trip to the Court of Appeals if you like, counselor. If you feel it's worth it. This court has rendered its decision."

"Your Honor, before you adjourn," Arnold Chang interjected, "there's also the matter of the defendant's immigration status."

"Excuse me?" the judge snapped. He leaned forward and glared at the prosecutor.

"Objection," Ruthy said, almost spitting the word out as she rose quickly to her feet.

The judge motioned for her to sit down, then leaned back in his tall padded chair and brought his hands together before his face as if in prayer. "Counselor, there's a couple of things," he began. "First, I've got a pretty full docket here. Unfortunately, I don't have the luxury of an hour, or even fifteen minutes discussing facts not related to the charges before this court. And second, and most germane, is that big bronze seal that's floating over and behind my head. See that?"

"Yes, Your Honor."

"It's got the San Francisco Bay and a lady with a spear, and it says 'State of California.' Is there an immigration law in the California code that you'd like me to enforce, counselor?"

"No, Your Honor."

"Case dismissed," the judge said. "Ms. Ramírez, you're free to go." He pounded the gavel, which sounded with an odd clack-clack, and rose to his feet and retired to his chambers, carrying an empty coffee cup he intended to fill before returning to the bench for the next case.

They walked up a wide staircase of weathered granite into the open house, a family of five, Maureen holding Samantha's hand as the little girl raised her legs high to navigate each step, Brandon and Keenan and their father following after. Maureen stopped in her climb to look longingly at the Prairie style, Frank Lloyd Wright–inspired windows, each an eye-pleasing geometry of nine glass rectangles separated by thin strips of wood. The windows were authentically old and American, as were the pillars of river stones that held up the rafters of the front porch, and the polished floors in the living room whose brown mirror greeted the Torres-Thompson family as they walked through the front door.

"This is nice," Scott said.

Of all the Craftsman homes they had seen in South Pasadena, this was the purest gem. It wasn't as big as some of the others, but it was the best preserved, and it seduced Maureen with the triangles of its eaves, the sturdiness of its exposed rafters, the long beams that loomed over the living room and jutted out over the porch outside. It was a squat story and a half, perched halfway up a gentle rise above the concrete wash of the Arroyo Seco.

The boys ran through the living room to the stairs and climbed up to the two rooms of a second story that was tucked underneath the sloping ceilings of a pitched roof. The floors creaked and moaned with each of their steps. "It's like an eagle's nest up here," Brandon said, and he lay on his stomach and looked out a window frame that was only six inches off the floor. He scanned the neighborhood, the billowing canopies of the sycamores and oaks, the spotted green fruit of a black walnut tree, and the shadows and shafts of light that cut through leaves and branches to dapple the sidewalk below, and he remembered the tiny talking forest creatures of a novel he'd read a long time ago.

Down in the living room, Maureen paced the echoing floors and thought about how she liked the simplicity and directness of the Craftsman design, with its embrace of early twentieth century American values of openness and restraint. Sunlight and breezes raced through its spaces, which seemed familiar and somehow midwestern. This house embodied the new person she wanted to become, and she felt it was a good sign that at this property, unlike all the others, the Realtor had not done a double-take when he saw the notorious Orange County family from the television news walk up to the door.

"It's from 1919," Scott said, reading the brochure as he climbed the stairs behind them. "The plumbing is probably not great."

"Who cares about the plumbing?" Maureen said. *We're looking for a new beginning,* she thought, *and some old pipes aren't going to stop us.*

She returned to the porch and admired the street, with its wide oaks and denuded jacarandas, each standing in a pool of purple flowers. It was a version of an America that was, a Main Street USA, a *Music Man.* She thought, *Only the streetcars are missing. This is the kind of street where the boys can ride their bikes.* There were no walls separating this neighborhood from the rest of the city, and yet there were no bars on the windows either, no suggestion that the residents lived in fear. *This is as it should be.* Yes, the air was still and dirty here; she would miss the sea breezes living inland. She was losing the California home of her dreams—she had been chased away from it, really, but perhaps it was for the best. *I paid for my ocean view with that horrendous isolation, up on that hill, in that gated and insular place.*

"It's just nineteen hundred square feet," Scott said. "Can we squeeze in?"

"That's the point," Maureen said. "To make do with less."

Scott examined the asking price, a nose more than seven figures, and more than he had paid for the house on Paseo Linda Bonita five years earlier. *Now I might be paying more for less house and no ocean view.* It made sense only for the supposedly excellent local public schools, and for having a home small enough to take care of without a Mexican living with them.

"What if we offer a little less than that?" Scott said to the Realtor, a man with slippery hair and ruddy skin who was just reaching the top of the stairs.

"They may take it. You're lucky; it's a good time to buy. The prices have sort of stabilized the last month or so."

"Do you think the prices will start to drop?"

"No. Not a chance."

Up on the second floor Brandon was still on his stomach, still looking out the window, a bit disappointed by the failure of this new landscape to trigger any vision or hint of adventure. And then a girl of twelve or thirteen appeared below. From his perch he watched her pass before the house, hands folded over her chest holding a book, a long black braid bouncing on the back of her neck, advancing with a slow, feminine glide over the sidewalk squares. The sight of her brought forth an unfamiliar sensation deep in his stomach. *That's a pretty girl.* He quickly forgot about forest creatures and everything else on the street until the girl disappeared from his field of vision, and for the next hour he didn't think about any of the books he was reading, about Holden Caulfield or the dragon in Eragon, and instead he secretly wished they would move to this house so that he might see that girl again and maybe even talk to her.

Maureen walked out the back door and climbed down the stairs with Samantha, and allowed her little girl to roam the fescue lawn in the backyard. There was neither a pool nor room for one. Good. Better that way. The yard was separated from the neighbors not by the high walls of the Laguna Rancho Estates, but by a picket fence not much taller than Samantha herself. Standing at the door that led from the kitchen to the backyard, Maureen could look directly into the property of another Craftsman next door. She saw a woman there in a large straw hat leaning over a row of plants with a hoe. A garden occupied much of the woman's yard, and it was filled with emerald globes and sunflowers reaching skyward, and corn plants that would soon be man-high, each looking as stiff and sturdy as a tree.

"Hi, there," the woman said.

"Hi," Maureen said.

"That's a great house."

"Yes, it's lovely."

"Gonna buy it?"

"We're thinking about it."

The woman smiled and rose to her feet and grabbed a box. She walked to the picket fence and lifted the box to show off the contents, a collection of a dozen red spheres, each the size of a tangerine. Maureen walked across the lawn to take a look and the woman used her gloved hand to shake off some bits of loam and handed a tomato to Maureen.

"They're beautiful."

"I've got too many, believe it or not. I'm taking these to a friend of mine."

"You grew all these?"

"My summer crop. Black cherry tomatoes, planted in April. They're heirlooms, organically grown."

"Organic," Maureen repeated, and thought that the word carried lovely sounds to match its meaning—proximity to nature, purity, simplicity.

"Do you garden?" the woman asked.

Maureen opened her mouth to say no, then yes, but sputtered and said neither.

Finally she asked, "Is it hard to learn?"


"That hardly ever happens, you know that," Ruthy said. "Every once in a while, we get these tiny miracles. I guess that's why I haven't quit yet."

"¿Se acabó todo?" Araceli asked. They were standing alone, outside the courtroom, and she was still confused. At one moment, she was a woman with the ligatures of United States jurisprudence affixed to her skin, at another she was free to leave the courtroom and travel about the continent again. The judge had decided the government was wrong, but was a judge allowed to do that?

"Yes, it's over," Ruthy said. "The case was dismissed. There are no longer any charges against you. Like the judge said, you are free to go. *Se puede ir.* In fact, you should go now, and not hang around here at all. Because the DA's office has gone totally nuts. The deputy DA wanted the judge to hold you for the immigration people, which is totally inappropriate. It's sort of amazing to hear a county prosecutor say such a thing in open court. Did you see how angry the judge got? So don't even go back to that address in Santa Ana. That'll be the first place they'll look for you—because he's probably calling the ICE people right now."

"Thank you, thank you so much for everything," Araceli said, placing her hands on Ruthy's shoulders, as if to hold her steady. She gave her a Mexico City kiss on the cheek goodbye, and as Araceli made her way down the hallway alone, she took one last glance at Ruthy's turning, round silhouette and the hand that rested atop the cotton hillside of her belly. She walked briskly toward the parking lot, to give Felipe the good news and to think about what she should do next. Just outside the courthouse's glass entryway, behind the nylon cordons that blocked a patch of concrete now empty of photographers, Araceli passed Janet Bryson, who was standing alone with a rolled-up sign she had only briefly displayed on the courthouse steps.

"They're letting her go?" Janet Bryson said, having heard the news seconds earlier from the departing deputy district attorney. "Where is the media? Where is the outrage?"

Next Araceli walked past Giovanni Lozano, who had his poster-portrait of her dangling upside down in his grip. "They're letting you go?"

"*Sí,*" Araceli said breathlessly. "*¡Me voy!*" She hustled as fast as she could without breaking into a jog, the memory of her failed sprint from the Huntington Park police alive in her thighs and the panicked tom-tom beat inside her chest. *Don't run, because that will get you in trouble, but move quickly,* mujer, *because they might grab you at any moment.* The ICE agents wore either stiff forest-green uniforms or navy-blue windbreakers, and she scanned the path to the parking lot for them. There was a man following them back from the courthouse yesterday, in a car, driving slowly—perhaps he was with the ICE. Now she turned and saw a swarthy, middle-aged man in a suit, running after her with long strides of his tailored wool pants—could it be? Yes, it was the Mexican consul. "*¡Araceli!*" he called out. "*¡Ramírez!*" She was about to break into a run when she felt a hand land decisively on her shoulder and heard his Mexico City accent call out her name: "*¡Araceli Noemí Ramírez Hinojosa!*"

With his full arm over her shoulder, the consul now guided a still-surprised Araceli back down to the courthouse plaza and a waiting cluster of suited men.

"We're here to help you," the diplomat said, and Araceli detected that sly sprinkling of irony with which Mexican officials flavored their pronouncements. "And, more important, we have something to give you."

One of his suited assistants produced an envelope and gave it to the consul, while another stepped back and aimed a camera.

"We received a request from some people in Santa Ana," the consul said. "We took the account number they provided us. And with the very kind cooperation and signature of your former *patrón*, *el señor* Torres, we secured the money from your account. As you requested."

"I never requested that. From you."

"Well, someone contacted me. And you should thank them. And thank me. Pedro here works in the consulate and is also a freelance writer and photographer for *Reforma*. He'll do a little article for us. Right, Pedro?"

"*Por supuesto, licenciado.*"

Araceli peered into the envelope. "This is a check."

"A cashier's check. Safer than cash. And, if I may be permitted to say, for an amount that is surprisingly large. It's so good to see one of our *paisanas* doing so well for herself. It's made out to the name on your voting card. And if you lost that one, here's another I had made for you and sent from the Distrito Federal. And also a passport, which I think you never obtained."

She examined the new documents, with their seals and hologram squares, and remembered how people suffered a *via crucis* of lines, forms, waiting rooms, and belligerent officials to get these in Mexico City. Now they gave them to Araceli without her even asking: it was a bureaucrat's idea of a Christmas present.

"If you don't mind, we'd like to take a photograph or two to illustrate the story."

"You want to take a picture of yourself giving me my own money?"

"It will just be a second. And it will help us here at the consulate tremendously."

Araceli could not say whether the consul was a good man or a bad man. Clearly, he was at the mercy of that clubby Mexico City culture that took bureaucrats, professors, and even painters and poets and transformed them into obsequious babblers. Araceli had escaped from all that, and she thought she should tell the consul to go to hell and leave her alone, because, after all, what had her government done for her? *They said they would give me classes in drawing and professors who could teach me to master oils, but it was all a trick, because they don't give you brushes or a canvas, or a studio, or the time to become what you dream. Instead our government gives us the roads we take in our northward escapes, and the policemen picking at their teeth and sizing us up to see if we can pay a bribe. It gives us the cartoon pictures of Juarez in our textbooks, and the lessons about the agrarian reform and the Constitution of 1917.*

Araceli wanted to be angry, but in the end she felt pity, and she turned and posed, foot forward and leg extended, like a beauty contestant, because in the end it was all a joke, and because if the police or the ICE caught her again, she might actually need this bureaucrat's assistance. Click. Click-click. Click.

"*¡Gracias, paisana!*"

He offered his business card and she took it, mumbling "*Gracias*" and slipping away, and thinking that a paper rectangle printed in Mexico City was a poor defense against the ICE. *They can grab me at any minute and send me back into tiny, locked cubes, because the eyebrows on the television and the screaming woman on the staircase demand it.*

Araceli found Felipe asleep in the cab of his truck, a baseball cap pulled down tight over his eyes, his largeness barely contained by the weather-scarred red skin of his pickup. His mouth gave little wet puffs, but even in this unflattering state, she found him attractive: above all, because she sensed an innocent, incipient devotion in him. He would wait for her an entire day, without eating, if he had to. Finally she woke him up.

"You're back," he said, startled.

"*Ganamos,*" she said.

"You won?"

"I am free. *Se acabó todo.*"

"*¿Estás libre?*"

"Yes, except that now I have to run away."

"Right."

"How much gas do you have in this truck? Because I need to get far away."

**F**elipe maneuvered his pickup through the streets of Laguna Niguel with an aggression she had not seen before, squealing through a couple of turns, accelerating with controlled desperation, and after a few minutes they were on the freeway, headed north, his truck settled into a fast cruise. "We need to get out of the city," Araceli said. Towers covered with razorlike antennas loomed over the highway, and danger seemed to lurk in every off-ramp, in every Denny's and every Taco Bell, in every parking lot: a reporter, police officer, or immigration agent might ambush her from any of these urban hollows at any moment.

"So we go to the desert, to the east," Felipe said. "That's the fastest way out."

"And after the desert?"

"The desert is big. If we keep going, we get to Arizona. To Phoenix."

"Will you go with me, that far?" Araceli asked.

"Anywhere you want to go. For as long as you want. After Phoenix is New Mexico. After that, Texas, I think. And then, *no sé.* Tennessee, maybe? It's a big country. All the way on the other side is Carolina. *Carolina del Norte y Carolina del Sur.*"

Felipe looked out over the asphalt, the white lines, the traffic drifting toward him and away, and turned and gave Araceli a gentle, mischievous smile. They were beginning a journey without a destination, without limits, on the spur of the moment, with only the clothes on their backs. Araceli guessed he was not normally a rule-breaker or risk-taker. Probably he owed money on this truck. He took no chances with his wardrobe either; he was a man of steady and unchanging habits. And yet, he kept driving. Soon they were on another freeway, headed east toward a place called Indio, according to the green signs that floated over their heads. Felipe said the hard part of the drive started after Indio, when you passed into the Mojave Desert, which you had to cross to get to Arizona. But before they got to the desert there was more city to contend with, the serpentine flow of trucks and campers and convertibles and station wagons all moving very slowly, as if each bumper were attached to the next, a conga line of blinking red lights following the curves of the freeway around office complexes, up into hills of dry grass and their crowns of nectarine-colored condominiums. Felipe's air-conditioning didn't work, so he lowered the windows, the roar of the traffic and the wind joining the grind of the engine, and when they spoke they had to shout. "I think we should buy some water!" she said. "So that we can drink when we cross the desert!" They pulled off the freeway and stopped at a gas station and jumped back on again. Araceli expected to see cactus at any minute, but the traffic was slow and the metropolis went on, exit after exit announcing a new district of the city unknown to her—Covina, Claremont, Redlands—more malls and parking lots extending from the freeway's edge like crops growing along a riverbank. Los Angeles did not want to let her go; it kept its hold on her with its sprawl.

"It's a long drive!" she shouted. "When do we get to Indio?"

"*Una hora más.* I do this drive once or twice a year. To see my family in Imuris and Cananea. Sometimes I go with my father. We go to Phoenix, then Tucson, and from there we drive south, into Mexico. I was born in Cananea, did I ever tell you that? You know, we could go there. I wouldn't mind that. It would be a good place to get a new start. Mexico isn't that bad. You're poor there, but it's *más calmado.*"

She thought about Mexico and the check in her pocket. The amount was a small fortune on the other side of the border. She could start a small business, or buy a house and build a barbecue in the back and cover the patio with bricks. Or she could rent a studio with big windows to let in the light and a concrete floor that she could spill paint on.

On the other hand, there was still the United States, and the promise of even greater riches, and the smooth satisfaction of being a woman who stood her ground. She could find an apartment in this Phoenix place if she wanted to. It was a city in a desert valley where people couldn't survive without air-conditioning, and Araceli wondered if she could live in such a place, without rain, clouds, and seasons, especially now that the traffic had sped up and they had finally reached the outskirts of Indio, the landscape turning dry and chalky. They drove past trailer parks rising from dirt lots, the wind spraying brown dust devils along the ground. A tumbleweed bounced along the strip of dirt in the middle of the freeway, and she sat up and pointed it out to Felipe. "*Mira, Felipe, es una de esas malas hierbas. ¿Cómo se les llama?* Tumbleweed!" She felt proud of herself for remembering the name, wondering how and why she would have learned such an obscure Americanism. Tumbleweed, the plant that rolls like a wheel, which is what the specimen she had just seen was doing, headed toward Arizona like Araceli and Felipe.

A hot wind blew in through the window, the heat of the desert and the black highway rising into the pickup truck, making Felipe sweat, the perspiration dripping down his neck and covering his T-shirt. She reached down between her feet and pulled up another bottle of water and opened it, handing it to him, and you would have thought she'd given him a bouquet of roses. *Even the smallest kindness from me makes him happy—he must be in love. But when will he kiss me?*

"How far is Carolina?" she asked.

"Very far. Maybe four or five days."

"Would you drive five days with me?"

"Yes. Of course."

"Aren't you worried?"

"About what?"

"Getting caught. By the immigration."

"No. I'm a citizen."

"Of the United States?"

"Yes. I got my papers last year. Through my uncle. It took ten years."

"But I don't have papers, and you could get in trouble for helping me. You're breaking the law."

"So?"

"And you still want to drive with me. And help me escape?"

"Yeah."

It took a moment for this small miracle to sink in and feel true. Yes, it was there to see in his serene and satisfied study of the road ahead of them. It was the look of a housepainter after a day of flawless work. He was a big man with big sexy hair, and he was hers. He would even break the law for her.

"*¡Qué romántico!*" she shouted, and laughed, and he laughed too, in a muted and nervous way.

"After we get to Phoenix, we have to decide," he said. "There's two ways we can go. We can keep going east, and go to Texas or Carolina. Or we can go south, to Sonora and to Nogales and Imuris—to my *tierra*. If we go south, we can't come back north, because there are checkpoints with *la migra.*" He turned to look at her and asked, "Where do you want to go?"

"*A mí me da igual,*" she said, because she could see herself following either path.

Soon the last human settlement was behind them and they sped across a vast, open plain of sand the color and texture of flour, covered with skeletal shrubs, maroon mountains rising in the distance, rocky and lifeless. "We reached the desert," Araceli shouted. The road had become a straight line, dipping over the horizon in a watery mirage.

"It's the Mojave," Felipe shouted back.

They were in an eastward flow with sports cars in bright primary colors that zipped past their truck like low-slung missiles, and big sedans with people inside reading books and looking at tiny screens, passengers and drivers cool and comfortable behind shields of tinted glass. They were people of all the American colors, and carried an air of affluent confidence and anticipation: *The road belongs to them and they know it,* Araceli thought, *and they even appreciate it.* There were great big vehicles the size of small homes too, with license plates of many different colors that announced that their owners resided in the LAND OF ENCHANTMENT and VACATIONLAND, or that they were headed to a SPORTSMAN'S PARADISE.

The plain of shrubs and sand undulated as if it were a vast pool of liquid, or an ocean, with mountain ranges standing like islands in the distance. An hour went by wordlessly as they crossed this sea, and Araceli would think later the time swam by, it slid along so smooth and quiet and lovely. She imagined gliding across this desert ocean, with Felipe at her side, until they reached Carolina del Norte, or maybe even Veracruz, and the real sea at the end of their journey, to begin life anew.

Now several tall plants were growing alongside the highway, the long succulent fingers of the ocotillo, their barbed, candy-cane digits reaching for the white sun. Suddenly there were dozens of them, and now hundreds, covering a mountain slope. Araceli was going to comment on the beauty of the ocotillos when another pickup truck identical to theirs began to roll alongside them, the two vehicles cruising together long enough for Araceli to stare through the open windows and examine the face of the driver. He was a *mexicano,* like her, though perhaps ten years older, with a freeway of worry lines carved into his forehead, and a muddy

complexion that suggested Michoacán or Guerrero, or some other corner of her country where the people raised corn. He was looking at the
straight highway with faraway eyes, as if remembering other journeys on
other highways like this one, and suddenly she realized this man was the
person she might become if she stayed in the United States. She imagined a biography for him, a story of crossings, arrivals, money, and dis-
appointments. *There are so many of us on these roads. So many of us from
adobe villages and cinder-block colonias. We are scattered on this highway
between the motor homes and the sports cars, we scrubbers and builders,
we planters and cooks, searching for the next place, the next hope.*

"A lot of people are going to Arizona," Felipe said. "I have a cousin
who lives there. He says no matter where you go, you can find a job in a
day. We'll be there in an hour. The border is the Colorado River. When
we go over the river, we're in Arizona."

Araceli had never been in another state besides California. *It's
called the United States because there are many, fifty altogether.* She wondered if there would be authorities at the border, an official checkpoint
where they would demand to see her documents. If so, they would discover she lacked the necessary stamps of U.S. eagles—she had a passport now, but a passport without a visa was just another reminder of her
Mexicanness. The anxiety about crossing the river and the coming
frontier distracted her until they reached a place called Blythe and the
signs said Arizona was just five miles away.

"What happens when we cross the border?" she finally blurted out.

"What?"

"In Arizona. Do they ask for my papers?"

"No. You just cross."

"They don't check anything?"

"No. Just the trucks carrying fruits and vegetables."

They rattled down the highway, toward an oasis of tree canopies
and green bushes. Soon they were on a wide bridge, rolling across to the
other side. LEAVING CALIFORNIA said the sign as they passed over a muddy
river.

"*¡Adiós, California!*" she yelled with her arms raised in the air, as if
on the last drop of a roller coaster.

"'Bye!" Felipe shouted in English, and they laughed and shouted
together.

On the other side they were greeted by a sign that said WELCOME TO ARIZONA, decorated with what she assumed was the flag of that state, red and yellow rays rising from a patch of blue, a copper star in the middle. Araceli admired its simple abstract expressiveness and thought, *That's what a flag should look like.*

They drove past the checkpoint for trucks Felipe had mentioned, and started to climb away from the river and into a rocky landscape. *This is Arizona, these red stones, already the landscape looks different. I have seen these fire-colored rocks in the movies and thought it was in California, but I was wrong.* She had arrived in a new place, and suddenly days and weeks of worry and fear lifted, and she lay her head against the door, feeling she would fall asleep any minute in this peaceful, rust-colored place, where a dozen tall saguaros had raised their arms to greet her.

Araceli fell into a soothing darkness and dreamed, for the first time, of Brandon and Keenan, that she was guiding them by the hand along the red Arizona rocks, away from a pool of water. Then the sun caught her full in the face and her dreams turned yellow and while these golden dreams lived they wiped out the memories of many years, of all her highway travels, her border crossings, her goodbyes and hellos.

She awoke to the taste of humid air and looked around to see that they were still in the desert. The forest of saguaros had grown thicker and a bank of percolating thunderclouds with bright white roofs and dark gray bellies was looming over the horizon with cathedral-like majesty. For a moment, Araceli wondered if the clouds were an apparition, or an extension of her dream, because the sky had been empty and blue when they crossed the river.

"Look at those clouds," she said.

"*Es un* monsoon," Felipe said. "You see them in the desert in the summer. Looks like we're driving right into it."

The air cooled and thickened and soon the sun disappeared behind the storm, shooting out rays in the patches of blue between the clouds, lines that spread out like a fan, the image in the Arizona flag she'd seen when they crossed the border, yellow streaks radiating from the star. She tasted the humid air again and understood that this storm came from the south, from somewhere deep in the tropical heart of the earth, from Mexico or some other wet and needy land.

Soon they were underneath the cloud bank and it began to rain.

First a few drops, each one large and heavy on the windshield, then thick sheets that covered the road with swirling streams, so that Felipe had to pull over to the shoulder and wait for the storm to pass. Araceli opened the window and let the warm water fall on her face, a rain stronger than any she could remember, a downpour that washed away all the dust of the desert and turned it to mud.

She turned and saw Felipe's face was wet too, and at that moment she leaned across the cab to kiss him. Their lips met in a moist caress. And then another one. And one more, until they stopped and looked at each other and Araceli suddenly felt lighter and younger, and she kissed him again and their arms and hands reached for one another too, until she gently pushed him back and said, "Slow."

The rain stopped and the sound of cars splashing by on the wet road brought them back to where they were—on the shoulder of a highway in Arizona, in flight.

"We have to keep going," she said.

They rejoined the road and in a few minutes they were entering a metropolis, Phoenix, with its low-slung warehouses, and neighborhoods with homes of rocky front yards and cactus landscaping. The sun returned, the clouds retreated, and the highway grew wider, spreading out from two eastbound lanes to three, until they reached the city center and the glass towers pulsated in the returning heat. The highway sank below the level of the street and spread out into four and then five lanes. Several green and white rectangles loomed on the overpasses above them, with odd-numbered highways and new destinations. 17. FLAGSTAFF. 225. TUCSON.

"So we have to decide," Felipe said. "Which way are we going? To Flagstaff if we stay in the United States. To Tucson if we go to Mexico."

Araceli looked up at the signs and thought, *Yes, it's my choice*.

She raised her hand, stretched it out until it almost touched the windshield, and pointed with her index finger.

"*Para allá*," she shouted above the roar of wind and engines, and then she said it in English too, just because she could.

"That way."

# Afterword
## to the 10th Anniversary Edition

When *The Barbarian Nurseries* was published a decade ago, I thought it might soon become a relic, an artifact from the intolerance of a bygone era. No immigrant, real or imagined, would ever again suffer a misadventure like the one Araceli Ramírez endures in this book. I expected Congress to pass a long-delayed immigration reform, allowing the undocumented to emerge from the "shadows," and that tired metaphor would disappear from American speech forever. Then, as now, opinion polls in the United States routinely showed a strong majority of support for giving millions of immigrants a path to legalization. The Aracelis of the United States would become naturalized citizens. And with the settled space of legal status secured, they would build beautiful homes with cactus gardens of their own; or they would create works of art, and all their brilliance and their eccentricities would be fully and officially incorporated into our national life.

Instead, new factions of hyperconservative Republicans blocked one immigration reform plan after another. The hatred directed at undocumented immigrants and people of Mexican descent increased and deepened, and eventually it gave birth to the political career of the most notorious demagogue in U.S. history. Small men and women, infinitely more toxic in their discourse and Machiavellian in their ambitions than any of the characters in *The Barbarian Nurseries*, spread the hateful idea of the criminality and backwardness of Mexican immigrants, until finally, this hatred became a corrosive ooze at the center of American public discourse. The demagogue's anti-Latino-immigrant campaign schtick led to mean-spirited chants of "Build the Wall!" at U.S. high schools, and helped fuel the growth of the "patriot" right, with its torch-light march on a Virginia college town and the storming of the U.S. Capitol. We were horrified by images of new detention centers filled with children separated from their parents. The craziness of *The Barbarian Nurseries* swept up the whole country, and the great, wild "Circus Californianus" I imagined in the final section of the novel, became a "Circus Americanus."

As a child growing up in Los Angeles, I was taught to believe California was a gleaming beacon of modernity and equality, the apex of U.S. history's long march toward equality and justice. When I became a newspaper reporter, I started looking at my hometown and its history with a sharper eye for its bigotries and absurdities. With an LAPD press pass dangling from my neck, I crossed the invisible social boundaries of the metropolis. I entered homeless camps, took a tour of the Los Angeles County Jail and its trails of painted lines, and I watched a man weep at Superior Court when he learned he was about to be deported. I interviewed the ambitious Mexican-American politico who would become the city's mayor, and I stood among the reporters at press conferences, waiting to hear what the police had to tell us about the salacious crime of the day. At about the same time, a new anti-immigrant movement was beginning to take hold of the city's denizens. Long before certain U.S. cable news commentators became obsessed with "illegals," and before xenophobia against Muslim refugees began to dominate European politics, nativism took over talk radio in California, giving birth to a new kind of rage and paranoia. In 1994, California voters approved the anti-immigrant ballot initiative called Proposition 187, which aimed to ban the undocumented from receiving any and all public services, including most hospital services and admission into public elementary schools. In that same year, California's governor won reelection by employing a media campaign that included grainy black-and-white images of immigrants running past the checkpoint where Interstate 5 meets the Mexican border. My home state and its voters had endorsed ethnic intolerance, and made Latino people the scapegoats for the state's economic and social ills. I felt betrayed.

A few months after that fateful election, I witnessed two or three hundred young Latino people (the term "Latinx" was still two decades in the future) marching in a spontaneous protest on a suburban Orange County street. I lived just a few blocks away, and when I returned home I saw teams of immigrant gardeners cutting the lawns on my block, working their way from property to property, like workers in a factory. Suddenly, I imagined the opening scene of the novel: a suburban man struggling to cut his front lawn after losing his Mexican gardener. My first attempt to write this book produced a work that was too angry to be art; my agent then, the legendary and late Virginia "Ginger" Barber, called it "a polemic." I had written a novel about a family with children before becoming a parent myself. So I put the manuscript aside for several years. Like the family in this novel, my wife and I had two boys and a girl, and I learned to change diapers for the first time. I took my children to the park, and read books to them, and I learned the life lessons that only parenting can teach you. I started to wonder if I could bring some of this newfound wisdom to the unpublished manuscript I'd left on an old laptop, and on some obsolete 3.5-inch floppy disks.

Araceli Ramírez wants to be an artist. And today, looking at the pages in which she finally came alive as a literary character and human being, I see my own longing to become an artist too. I am the son of Guatemalan immigrants, and I never knew an artist, or a published writer, growing up. It seemed a pretentious thing to aspire to, and yet it was what I wanted to be. A creator, an intellectual, a thinker. Araceli's artistic aspirations are frustrated; she suffers a common fate in Latin America, where many working families see the education of young women as a luxury they cannot afford. But she has the soul of an artist, and her inability to fully realize this goal helps fuel her dark, sarcasm-tinged view of California. She is an intellectual trapped in the body of a servant; in other words, she's my alter ego. When searching for the words to describe her complexion, I stood before a mirror and studied my own visage, and the phrase came to me immediately: "the light copper skin of a newly minted penny." No one sees the artist in Araceli;

they see a housekeeper, a babysitter. In the years before, during, and after I wrote *The Barbarian Nurseries*, various Angelenos mistook me for a gardener and a parking-lot valet (a woman actually handed me her car keys in front of a Hollywood restaurant). Each time I wanted to scream: "I'm a writer!"

My native country has created, in my lifetime, a new caste of Latino laborers; the acceptance of this inequality has caused the moral compass of the United States of America to spin in all sorts of unexpected directions. "Don't cry in front of the Mexicans," Brad Pitt's character tells Leonardo DiCaprio's in a Quentin Tarantino film as two parking-lot valets stand nearby, and the entire theater laughs. In *The Barbarian Nurseries*, liberal-minded and compassionate Maureen is transformed into an angry "Karen" when confronted with the truth about her family's reliance on an undocumented worker. As I wrote those pages, I was learning about the private, unseen scandal of caste unfolding in thousands of Latino homes. I met two Latina immigrant women (one a single mother of three, the other a grandmother) whose illiteracy kept them subservient and poor for the decades they lived in Los Angeles. When these moms learned to read and write for the first time, they began to decode street signs and letters from their children's schoolteachers. And then they hungered to read more, devouring newspapers and prayer books because each new piece of written information they digested made them feel stronger, and earned them a kind of citizenship. I've seen that kind of longing for as long as I can remember: my mother and father have it, and it shaped the good and bad choices I saw them make during my childhood. *The Barbarian Nurseries* is a tribute to the drive of immigrants to express the full measure of their humanity. Every man and woman who comes to this country has an inner voice that says, "I am more than the limited horizons into which I was born; I am not just a mule to guide the plow, or an automaton in a garment factory." Like Araceli, they have epicurean dreams of escaping the limited and austere horizons into which they were born, and eating well and learning well, and surrounding themselves with objects of beauty.

This is still the central tension in Latinx life. Between the idea that we might one day be full members in the club called the United States of America, with all the privileges that entails, and the reality of a society with deep class divisions that grow wider every year. Ten years on from *The Barbarian Nurseries*, I've met so many more people who carry the label "undocumented" with them. Women in their thirties with doctorates and Harvard educations; and smart young people who work in service jobs but go to school to study filmmaking, or who own their own businesses, large and small. If she chose to live in the United States, Araceli today would still be undocumented. Like so many people, she'd be able to see her middle-aged years approaching and know that she had little prospect of becoming a permanent resident, much less a U.S. citizen. Of course, Araceli might not care one way or the other. She never internalized the stigmas associated with her immigration status. Probably she'd allow all the MAGA insults to roll off her brown skin like the monsoon raindrops do in the novel's final chapter. Like so many of her compatriots, she is a survivor, an idiosyncratic and unpredictable force pushing through the great messy piles of world history.

One of the great pleasures of having written this book is to have readers ask me: Which road does Araceli choose at the end? Does she head deeper into the inner United States, or does she return to Mexico? I answer, honestly, that I have no idea. When I typed the final period on the end of the final sentence of *The Barbarian Nurseries*, Araceli Noemí Ramírez Hinojosa (did you notice she kept gaining more names as the novel progressed?) became her own person, with a free will inside the pearly light of the realm where fictional characters live. She resides there still, in that bright and open territory, where there are no borders, and where everything is possible.

*Los Angeles, California, 2021*

# Discussion Questions

1. What were your initial impressions of the Torres-Thompson family and Araceli? How did your understanding of them change throughout the novel?

2. Maureen and Scott, along with their friends, consider themselves to be progressive. How would they need to change if they were to bring about true progress in their community? Are the newly rich of this century very different from wealthy entrepreneurs from other generations?

3. Do Araceli and the other servants in the neighborhood have any leverage, or are they entirely powerless with their employers?

4. Discuss Los Angeles as if it were a character in the novel. What personalities and history are captured in the neighborhoods Araceli travels to, with and without Brandon and Keenan? How do the extremes of rich and poor affect the city as a whole? Do Brandon and Keenan see the world the same way as other characters in the novel, even though neither one of them has traveled far before (except through fiction)?

5. In Maureen's and Scott's minds, what does good parenting look like? How is this different from Araceli's parenting standards? How does Brandon and Keenan's childhood compare to their parents' childhood?

6. Does Maureen treat her baby daughter, Samantha, differently from her sons? What does it mean for her to have a little girl in a household of

males? When Maureen and Scott have power struggles, does gender come into play?

7. In the scenes depicting Araceli's time off, what is most striking to you about her true self and her lost dreams of being an artist with a college education?

8. What would America look like—economically, socially, and otherwise—if Janet Bryson had her way? Were you surprised when the author revealed how much Araceli earns per week ($250 cash, on top of room and board), as well as Pepe's annual salary range (in the four figures)?

9. At every turn, Tobar finds a place for humor while keeping the story line tremendously realistic. What makes satire the best way to understand the issues of class and immigration raised in the novel? How did it affect your reading to know that the author is a Los Angeles native whose parents emigrated from Guatemala?

10. Discuss the translation and language issues that arise in *The Barbarian Nurseries*, including the moments when non-native speakers try to use Spanish. Is Araceli in some ways protected by the fact that her English is limited?

11. Ultimately, whose fault is it that the Torres-Thompson children were briefly without parents? Could something similar have happened in your household? If so, would you have been grateful to Araceli or suspicious of her?

12. Why is Scott so different from his father? How has Grandfather Torres evolved since the time the photograph was taken?

13. The title is referenced in chapter eight, when Maureen looks at the landscapers and thinks to herself, *"What am I doing, allowing these sweaty barbarians into my home?"* In chapter ten, Araceli uses the expression *qué barbaridad* when she thinks about Maureen's not telling her where she's gone. Who are the barbarians in this novel? What is being nurtured in the "nurseries"?

14. In the closing scenes, many of the characters experience newfound freedom. What did they have to sacrifice in order to gain that freedom? How did their definition of freedom change?

15. How would you have answered Felipe's question—"Which way are we going?"—in the novel's final lines?